The yellowbacks... classics of popular fiction

The yellowjackets or yellowbacks were a great series of bestselling adventure and crime thrillers that had its origins in the mid to late 19th century following on from the 'penny dreadfuls'. They virtually began the mass market revolution of the early 20th century with a clear standard format and imprint/series livery (what would today be called branding). Hodder & Stoughton published the yellowjackets in two main series with series run dates of: 1923-1939 and later 1949-1957.

As the tagline ('where thrillers really began') on the back cover implies, the imprint and series focused on thrillers that were the bestsellers of their time. This current reissue or retro revival if you will, brings back many of these masterpieces, now classics in their own way and extends it further by including key titles from that period that were either great crime or thriller or even general commercial fiction (including sub-genres of noir, horror, gothic, romance, westerns, etc.) influences of their time. There are some perennial favourites and many rarities either lost or not easily available being revived in the current series. Writers and characters ranged from adventure heroes like Bulldog Drummond, Allan Quatermain, Richard Hannay or the Saint through thriller grandmasters Edgar Wallace and E. Phillips Oppenheim, crime and mystery maestros like Patricia Wentworth, GK Chesterton, Agatha Christie and the Detection club, to western and swashbucklers like Zane Grey, Max Brand, Captain Blood and even romance or general fiction classics like Hermina Black, Denise Robins, Marie Corelli or Stella Morton. These were books that had storytelling at their heart and always entertained.

The yellowbacks had both hardback (with varying design elements) and paperback (which built the series look) versions with the latter still carrying the imprint 'yellowjacket'. The current reissues pay tribute to both and use an amalgam of elements from both editions while retaining the complete yellow (or 'mustard-plaster') livery with the author's name in blue beveled type with a 'simulated emboss' effect and a white outer 'outline', and the book title in black. These reissues retain the distinctive size of the original mass market paperback and follow the three main category variations—the thrillers (crime, westerns, mystery, adventure) had blue lettering for the author's name, while Romance and softer general fiction had red; and other categories like humour had green.

For more detail and a full list of titles visit https://www.hachetteindia.com/home/yellowbacks

ARSÈNE LUPIN
THE SECRET OF SAREK
(aka Island of Thirty Coffins)

ARSÈNE LUPIN
THE SECRET OF SAREK (aka Island of Thirty Coffins)

Maurice Marie Émile Leblanc was a French novelist and writer of short stories, known primarily as the creator of the gentleman burglar, adventurer and detective Arsène Lupin, often described as a French counterpart to Arthur Conan Doyle's Sherlock Holmes and E.W. Hornung's Raffles.

Refusing the career that his father had set up for him at a card factory, Leblanc instead went to Paris in 1888, to pursue writing as a journalist. But he soon turned novelist and storyteller. His first novel, *Une femme (A Woman)*, published in 1893 was a success and was followed by other works, such as *Des couples (The Couples)*, *Voici des ailes (Here are Wings)* and a play *La pitié*, released in 1902, which was a flop. In 1905, Pierre Lafitte, the director of the monthly *Je sais tout*, commissioned a short story from Leblanc, with the brief that he was to combine the appeal of A.J Raffles by Ernest William Hornung and Sherlock Holmes. The result was 'L'Arrestation d'Arsène Lupin' ('The Arrest of Arsène Lupin') which was a huge success. Two years later, *Arsène Lupin, Gentleman Burglar* was released, and the rest was history – with one of the most successful series being born.

ARSÈNE LUPIN
THE SECRET OF SAREK
(aka Island of Thirty Coffins)

Maurice Leblanc

Arsène Lupin, The Secret of Sarek (aka Island of Thirty Coffins)
First published in 1919.

This Hodder Yellowback edition © Hachette India 2023
(Registered Name: Hachette Book Publishing India Pvt. Ltd.)
An Hachette UK Company www.hachetteindia.com

1

All rights reserved. No part of the publication may be reproduced, stored in a retrieval system (including but not limited to computers, disks, external drives, electronic or digital devices, e-readers, websites), or transmitted in any form or by any means (including but not limited to cyclostyling, photocopying, docutech or other reprographic reproductions, mechanical, recording, electronic, digital versions) without the prior written permission of the publisher, nor be otherwise circulated in any form of binding or cover other than that in which it is published and without a similar condition being imposed on the subsequent purchaser.

The texts in these editions in most cases have been reprinted as is, with minimal editorial changes and by and large no bowdlerizing for political correctness; though in some editions, a few words and phrases considered archaic, or those considered offensive now, along with archaic punctuation may have been modified in places to make the text more accessible to today's readers. The narratives, language, beliefs, social mores and/or cultural depictions, in these volumes are a reflection of their times and must be viewed as such. They may also contain certain cultural, racial and gender prejudices and stereotypes that may be outdated or clearly wrong then and wrong today; but their removal would be tantamount to claiming these prejudices never existed. The Publisher does not endorse or support those depictions or stereotypes; and these books have been made available for a discerning audience that will read it for entertainment value and a chronicle/record of popular fiction of past times.

Cover design by Priya Singh adapted from the original classic yellowjacket by Hodder & Stoughton.

Cover illustration by Ishan Trivedi.

Series note: Some of the books in the series (unless otherwise credited) may have cover or inside illustrations from the original yellowbacks or early editions, and while full restoration has been attempted, some images may be grainy or faded due to the condition of the original material. The end notes or bonus material or blurb details may have been sourced from the public domain or free use publications such as Wikipedia and attribution is hereby made also allowing similar free use reproduction from here. Sources requiring further specific attribution may write in and further detailing and/or corrections shall be made in subsequent printings/editions.

Reprint specifications may be subject to change including but not limited to finishes, paper, colour sections.

ISBN: 978-93-5731-221-9

Hachette Book Publishing India Pvt. Ltd.
4th & 5th Floors, Corporate Centre,
Plot No. 94, Sector 44, Gurugram - 122 003, India

Typeset in Electra LT STD 10/12.5 pt by Manipal Technologies Limited, Manipal

Printed and bound in India by Manipal Technologies Limited, Manipal

CONTENTS

1. The Deserted Cabin ... 1
2. On the Edge of the Atlantic ... 14
3. Vorski's Son ... 29
4. The Poor People of Sarek ... 49
5. "Four Women Crucified" ... 65
6. All's Well ... 86
7. François and Stéphane ... 103
8. Anguish ... 116
9. The Death-Chamber ... 131
10. The Escape ... 143
11. The Scourge of God ... 159
12. The Ascent of Golgotha ... 176
13. "Eloi, Eloi, Lama Sabachthani!" ... 195
14. The Ancient Druid ... 211
15. The Hall of the Underground Sacrifices ... 228
16. The Hall of the Kings of Bohemia ... 250
17. "Cruel Prince, Obeying Destiny" ... 266
18. The God-Stone ... 284

1

THE DESERTED CABIN

Into the picturesque village of Le Faouet, situated in the very heart of Brittany, there drove one morning in the month of May a lady whose spreading grey cloak and the thick veil that covered her face failed to hide her remarkable beauty and perfect grace of figure.

The lady took a hurried lunch at the principal inn. Then, at about half-past eleven, she begged the proprietor to look after her bag for her, asked for a few particulars about the neighbourhood and walked through the village into the open country.

The road almost immediately branched into two, of which one led to Quimper and the other to Quimperle. Selecting the latter, she went down into the hollow of a valley, climbed up again and saw on her right, at the corner of another road, a sign-post bearing the inscription, "Locriff, 3 kilometres."

"This is the place," she said to herself.

Nevertheless, after casting a glance around her, she was surprised not to find what she was looking for and wondered whether she had misunderstood her instructions.

There was no one near her nor anyone within sight, as far as the eye could reach over the Breton country-side, with its tree-lined meadows and undulating hills. Not far from the village, rising amid the budding greenery of spring, a small country house lifted its grey front, with the shutters to all the windows closed. At twelve o'clock, the angelus-bells pealed through the air and were followed by complete peace and silence.

Véronique sat down on the short grass of a bank, took a letter from her pocket and smoothed out the many sheets, one by one.

The first page was headed:

"DUTREILLIS' AGENCY.
"*Consulting Rooms.*
"*Private Enquiries.*
"*Absolute Discretion Guaranteed.* "

Next came an address:

"*Madame Véronique,*
"*Dressmaker,*
"*BESANÇON.* "

And the letter ran:

"MADAM,

"You will hardly believe the pleasure which it gave me to fulfil the two commissions which you were good enough to entrust to me in your last favour. I have never forgotten the conditions under which I was able, fourteen years ago, to give you my practical assistance at a time when your life was saddened by painful events. It was I who succeeded in obtaining all the facts relating to the death of your honoured father, M. Antoine d'Hergemont, and of your beloved son François. This was my first triumph in a career which was to afford so many other brilliant victories.

"It was I also, you will remember, who, at your request and seeing how essential it was to save you from your husband's hatred and, if I may add, his love, took the necessary steps to secure your admission to the Carmelite convent. Lastly, it was I who, when your retreat to the convent had shown you that a life of religion did not agree with your temperament, arranged for you a modest occupation as a dressmaker at Besançon, far from the towns where the years of your childhood and the months of your marriage had been spent. You had the inclination and the need to work in order to live and to escape your thoughts. You were bound to succeed; and you succeeded.

"And now let me come to the fact, to the two facts in hand.

"To begin with your first question: what has become, amid the whirlwind of war, of your husband, Alexis Vorski, a Pole by birth, according to his papers, and the son of a king, according to his own statement? I will be brief. After being suspected at the commencement of the war and imprisoned in an internment-camp near Carpentras, Vorski managed to escape, went to Switzerland, returned to France and was re-arrested, accused of spying and convicted of being a German. At the moment when it seemed inevitable that he would be sentenced to death, he escaped for the second time, disappeared in the Forest of Fontainebleau and in the end was stabbed by some person unknown.

"I am telling you the story quite crudely, Madam, well knowing your contempt for this person, who had deceived you abominably, and knowing also that you have learnt most of these facts from the newspapers, though you have not been able to verify their absolute genuineness.

"Well, the proofs exist. I have seen them. There is no doubt left. Alexis Vorski lies buried at Fontainebleau.

"Permit me, in passing, Madam, to remark upon the strangeness of this death. You will remember the curious prophecy about Vorski which you mentioned to me. Vorski, whose undoubted intelligence and exceptional energy were spoilt by an insincere and superstitious mind, readily preyed upon by hallucinations and terrors, had been greatly impressed by the prediction which overhung his life and which he had heard from the lips of several people who specialize in the occult sciences:

"'Vorski, son of a king, you will die by the hand of a friend and your wife will be crucified!'

"I smile, Madam, as I write the last word. Crucified! Crucifixion is a torture which is pretty well out of fashion; and I am easy as regards yourself. But what do you think of the daggerstroke which Vorski received in accordance with the mysterious orders of destiny?

"But enough of reflections. I now come..."

Véronique dropped the letter for a moment into her lap. M. Dutreillis' pretentious phrasing and familiar pleasantries wounded her fastidious reserve. Also she was obsessed by the tragic image of Alexis Vorski. A shiver of anguish passed through her at the hideous memory of that man. She mastered herself, however, and read on:

"I now come to my other commission, Madam, in your eyes the more important of the two, because all the rest belongs to the past.

"Let us state the facts precisely. Three weeks ago, on one of those rare occasions when you consented to break through the praiseworthy monotony of your existence, on a Thursday evening when you took your assistants to a cinema-theatre, you were struck by a really incomprehensible detail. The principal film, entitled 'A Breton Legend,' represented a scene which occurred, in the course of a pilgrimage, outside a little deserted road-side hut which had nothing to do with the action. The hut was obviously there by accident. But something really extraordinary attracted your attention. On the tarred boards of the old door were three letters, drawn by hand: 'V. d'H.,' and those three letters were precisely your signature before you were married, the initials with which you used to sign your intimate letters and which you have not used once during the last fourteen years! Véronique d'Hergemont! There was no mistake possible. Two capitals separated by the small 'd' and the apostrophe. And, what is more, the bar of the letter 'H.', carried back under the three letters, served as a flourish, exactly as it used to do with you!

"It was the stupefaction due to this surprising coincidence that decided you, Madam, to invoke my assistance. It was yours without the asking. And you knew, without any telling, that it would be effective.

"As you anticipated, Madam, I have succeeded. And here again I will be brief.

"What you must do, Madam, is to take the night express from Paris which brings you the next morning to Quimperle. From there, drive to Le Faouet. If you have time, before or after your luncheon, pay a visit to the very interesting Chapel of St. Barbe, which stands perched on the most fantastic site and which gave rise to the 'Breton Legend' film. Then go along the Quimper road on foot. At the end of the first ascent, a little way short of the parish-road which leads to Locriff, you will find, in a semicircle surrounded by trees, the deserted hut with the inscription. It has nothing remarkable about it. The inside is empty. It has not even a floor. A rotten plank serves as a bench. The roof consists of a worm-eaten framework, which admits the rain. Once more, there is no doubt that it was sheer accident that placed it within the range of the cinematograph. I will end by adding that the 'Breton Legend' film was taken in September last, which means that the inscription is at least eight months old.

"That is all, Madam. My two commissions are completed. I am too modest to describe to you the efforts and the ingenious means which I employed in order to accomplish them in so short a time, but for which you will certainly think the sum of five hundred francs, which is all that I propose to charge you for the work done, almost ridiculous.

"I beg to remain,

"Madam, &c."

Véronique folded up the letter and sat for a few minutes turning over the impressions which it aroused in her, painful impressions, like all those revived by the horrible days of her marriage. One in particular had survived and was still as powerful as at the time when she tried to escape it by taking refuge in the gloom of a convent. It was the impression, in fact the certainty, that all her misfortunes, the death of her father and the death of her son, were due to the fault which she had committed in loving Vorski. True, she had fought against the man's love and had not decided to marry him until she was obliged to, in despair and to save M. d'Hergemont from Vorski's vengeance. Nevertheless, she had loved that man. Nevertheless, at first, she had turned pale under his glance: and this, which now seemed to her an unpardonable example of weakness, had left her with a remorse which time had failed to weaken.

"There," she said, "enough of dreaming. I have not come here to shed tears."

The craving for information which had brought her from her retreat at Besançon restored her vigour; and she rose resolved to act.

"A little way short of the parish-road which leads to Locriff... a semicircle surrounded by trees," said Dutreillis' letter. She had therefore passed the place. She quickly retraced her steps and at once perceived, on the right, the clump of trees which had hidden the cabin from her eyes. She went nearer and saw it.

It was a sort of shepherd's or road-labourer's hut, which was crumbling and falling to pieces under the action of the weather. Véronique went up to it and perceived that the inscription, worn by the rain and sun, was much less clear than on the film. But the three letters were visible, as was the flourish; and she even distinguished, underneath, something which M. Dutreillis had not observed, a drawing of an arrow and a number, the number 9.

Her emotion increased. Though no attempt had been made to imitate the actual form of her signature, it certainly was her signature as a girl. And who could have affixed it there, on a deserted cabin, in this Brittany where she had never been before?

Véronique no longer had a friend in the world. Thanks to a succession of circumstances, the whole of her past girlhood had, so to speak, disappeared with the death of those whom she had known and loved. Then how was it possible for the recollection of her signature to survive apart from her and those who were dead and gone? And, above all, why was the inscription here, at this spot? What did it mean?

Véronique walked round the cabin. There was no other mark visible there or on the surrounding trees. She remembered that M. Dutreillis had opened the door and had seen nothing inside. Nevertheless she determined to make certain that he was not mistaken.

The door was closed with a mere wooden latch, which moved on a screw. She lifted it; and, strange to say, she had to make an effort, not a physical so much as a moral effort, an effort of will, to pull the door towards her. It seemed to her that this little act was about to usher her into a world of facts and events which she unconsciously dreaded.

"Well," she said, "what's preventing me?"

She gave a sharp pull.

A cry of horror escaped her. There was a man's dead body in the cabin. And, at the moment, at the exact second when she saw the body, she became aware of a peculiar characteristic: one of the dead man's hands was missing.

It was an old man, with a long, grey, fan-shaped beard and long white hair falling about his neck. The blackened lips and a certain colour of the swollen skin suggested to Véronique that he might have been poisoned, for no trace of an injury showed on his body, except the arm, which had been severed clean above the wrist, apparently some days before. His clothes were those of a Breton peasant, clean, but very threadbare. The corpse was seated on the ground, with the head resting against the bench and the legs drawn up.

These were all things which Véronique noted in a sort of unconsciousness and which were rather to reappear in her memory at a later date, for, at the moment, she stood there all trembling, with her eyes staring before her, and stammering:

"A dead body!... A dead body!..."

Suddenly she reflected that she was perhaps mistaken and that the man was not dead. But, on touching his forehead, she shuddered at the contact of his icy skin.

Nevertheless this movement roused her from her torpor. She resolved to act and, since there was no one in the immediate neighbourhood, to go back to Le Faouet and inform the authorities. She first examined the corpse for any clue which could tell her its identity.

The pockets were empty. There were no marks on the clothes or linen. But, when she shifted the body a little in order to make her search, it came about that the head drooped forward, dragging with it the trunk, which fell over the legs, thus uncovering the lower side of the bench.

Under this bench, she perceived a roll consisting of a sheet of very thin drawing-paper, crumpled, buckled and almost wrung into a twist. She picked up the roll and unfolded it. But she had not finished doing so before her hands began to tremble and she stammered:

"Oh, God!... Oh, my God!..."

She summoned all her energies to try and enforce upon herself the calm needed to look with eyes that could see and a brain that could understand.

The most that she could do was to stand there for a few seconds. And during those few seconds, through an ever-thickening mist that seemed to shroud her eyes, she was able to make out a drawing in red, representing four women crucified on four tree-trunks.

And, in the foreground, the first woman, the central figure, with the body stark under its clothing and the features distorted with the most dreadful pain, but still recognizable, the crucified woman was herself! Beyond the least doubt, it was she herself, Véronique d'Hergemont!

Besides, above the head, the top of the post bore, after the ancient custom, a scroll with a plainly legible inscription. And this was the three initials, underlined with the flourish, of Véronique's maiden name, "V. d'H.", Véronique d'Hergemont.

A spasm ran through her from head to foot. She drew herself up, turned on her heel and, reeling out of the cabin, fell on the grass in a dead faint.

Véronique was a tall, energetic, healthy woman, with a wonderfully balanced mind; and hitherto no trial had been able to affect her fine moral sanity or her splendid physical harmony. It needed exceptional and unforeseen circumstances such as these, added to the fatigue of two nights spent in railway-travelling, to produce this disorder in her nerves and will.

It did not last more than two or three minutes, at the end of which her mind once more became lucid and courageous. She stood up, went back to the cabin, picked up the sheet of drawingpaper and, certainly with unspeakable anguish, but this time with eyes that saw and a brain that understood, looked at it.

She first examined the details, those which seemed insignificant, or whose significance at least escaped her. On the left was a narrow column of fifteen lines, not written, but composed of letters of no definite formation, the downstrokes of which were all of the same length, the object being evidently merely to fill up. However, in various places, a few words were visible. And Véronique read:

"Four women crucified."

Lower down:

"Thirty coffins."

And the bottom line of all ran:

"The God-Stone which gives life or death."

The whole of this column was surrounded by a frame consisting of two perfectly straight lines, one ruled in black, the other in red ink; and there was also, likewise in red, above it, a sketch of two sickles fastened together with a sprig of mistletoe under the outline of a coffin.

The right-hand side, by far the more important, was filled with the drawing, a drawing in red chalk, which gave the whole sheet, with its adjacent column of explanations, the appearance of a page, or rather of a copy of a page, from some large, ancient illuminated book, in which the subjects were treated rather in the primitive style, with a complete ignorance of the rules of drawing.

And it represented four crucified women. Three of them showed in diminishing perspective against the horizon. They wore Breton costumes and their heads were surmounted by caps which were likewise Breton but of a special fashion that pointed to local usage and consisted chiefly of a large black bow, the two wings of which stood out as in the bows of the Alsatian women. And in the middle of the page was the dreadful thing from which Véronique could not take her terrified eyes. It was the principal cross, the trunk of a tree stripped of its lower branches, with the woman's two arms stretched to right and left of it.

The hands and feet were not nailed but were fastened by cords which were wound as far as the shoulders and the upper part of the tied legs. Instead of the Breton costume, the woman wore a sort of winding-sheet which fell to the ground and lengthened the slender outline of a body emaciated by suffering.

The expression on the face was harrowing, an expression of resigned martyrdom and melancholy grace. And it was certainly Véronique's face, especially as it looked when she was twenty years of age and as Véronique remembered seeing it at those gloomy hours when a woman gazes in a mirror at her hopeless eyes and her overflowing tears.

And about the head was the very same wave of her thick hair, flowing to the waist in symmetrical curves:

And above it the inscription, "V. d'H."

Véronique long stayed thinking, questioning the past and gazing into the darkness in order to link the actual facts with the memory of her youth. But her mind remained without a glimmer of light. Of the words which she had read, of the drawing which she had seen, nothing whatever assumed the least meaning for her or seemed susceptible of the least explanation.

She examined the sheet of paper again and again. Then, slowly, still pondering on it, she tore it into tiny pieces and threw them to the wind. When the last scrap had been carried away, her decision was taken. She pushed back the man's body, closed the door and walked quickly towards the village, in order to ensure that the incident should have the legal conclusion which was fitting for the moment.

But, when she returned an hour later with the mayor of Le Faouet, the rural constable and a whole group of sightseers attracted by her statements, the cabin was empty. The corpse had disappeared.

And all this was so strange, Véronique felt so plainly that, in the disordered condition of her ideas, it was impossible for her to answer the questions put to her, or to dispel the suspicions and doubts which these people might and must entertain of the truth of her evidence, the cause of her presence and even her very sanity, that she forthwith ceased to make any effort or struggle. The innkeeper was there. She asked him which was the nearest village that she would reach by following the road and if, by so doing, she would come to a railway-station which would enable her to return to Paris. She retained the names of Scaer and Rosporden, ordered a carriage to bring her bag and overtake her on the road and set off, protected against any ill feeling by her great air of elegance and by her grave beauty.

She set off, so to speak, at random. The road was long, miles and miles long. But such was her haste to have done with these incomprehensible events and to recover her tranquillity and to forget what had happened that she walked with great strides, quite oblivious of the fact that this wearisome exertion was superfluous, since she had a carriage following her.

She went up hill and down dale and hardly thought at all, refusing to seek the solution of all the riddles that were put to her. It was the past which was reascending to the surface of her life; and she was horribly afraid of that past, which extended from her abduction by Vorski to the death of her father and her child. She wanted to think of nothing but the simple, humble life which she had contrived to lead at Besançon. There were no sorrows there, no dreams, no memories; and she did not doubt but that, amid the little daily habits which enfolded her in the modest house of her choice, she would forget the deserted cabin, the mutilated body of the man and the dreadful drawing with its mysterious inscription.

But, a little while before she came to the big market-town of Scaër, as she heard the bell of a horse trotting behind her, she saw, at the junction of the road that led to Rosporden, a broken wall, one of the remnants of a half-ruined house.

And on this broken wall, above an arrow and the number 10, she again read the fateful inscription, "V. d'H."

2

ON THE EDGE OF THE ATLANTIC

Véronique's state of mind underwent a sudden alteration. Even as she had fled resolutely from the threat of danger that seemed to loom up before her from the evil past, so she was now determined to pursue to the end the dread road which was opening before her.

This change was due to a tiny gleam which flashed abruptly through the darkness. She suddenly realized the fact, a simple matter enough, that the arrow denoted a direction and that the number 10 must be the tenth of a series of numbers which marked a course leading from one fixed point to another.

Was it a sign set up by one person with the object of guiding the steps of another? It mattered little. The main thing was that there was here a clue capable of leading Véronique to the discovery of the problem which interested her: by what prodigy did the initials of her maiden name reappear amid this tangle of tragic circumstances?

The carriage sent from Le Faouet overtook her. She stepped in and told the driver to go very slowly to Rosporden.

She arrived in time for dinner; and her anticipations had not misled her. Twice she saw her signature, each time before a division in the road, accompanied by the numbers 11 and 12.

Véronique slept at Rosporden and resumed her investigations on the following morning.

The number 12, which she found on the wall of a church-yard, sent her along the road to Concameau, which she had almost reached before she saw any further inscriptions. She fancied that she must have been mistaken, retraced her steps and wasted a whole day in useless searching.

It was not until the next day that the number 13, very nearly obliterated, directed her towards Fouesnant. Then she abandoned this direction, to follow, still in obedience to the signs, some country-roads in which she once more lost her way.

At last, four days after leaving Le Faouet, she found herself facing the Atlantic, on the great beach of Beg-Meil.

She spent two nights in the village without gathering the least reply to the discreet questions which she put to the inhabitants. At last, one morning, after wandering among the half-buried groups of rocks which intersect the beach and upon the low cliffs, covered with trees and copses, which hem it in, she discovered, between two oaks stripped of their bark, a shelter built of earth and branches which must at one time have been used by customhouse officers. A small menhir stood at the entrance. The menhir bore the inscription, followed by the number 17. No arrow. A full stop underneath; and that was all.

In the shelter were three broken bottles and some empty meat-tins.

"This was the goal," thought Véronique. "Someone has been having a meal here. Food stored in advance, perhaps."

Just then she noticed that, at no great distance, by the edge of a little bay which curved like a shell amid the neighbouring rocks, a boat was swinging to and fro, a motor-boat. And she heard voices coming from the village, a man's voice and a woman's.

From the place where she stood, all that she could see at first was an elderly man carrying in his arms half-a-dozen bags of provisions, potted meats and dried vegetables. He put them on the ground and said:

"Well, had a pleasant journey, M'ame Honorine?"

"Fine!"

"And where have you been?"

"Why, Paris... a week of it... running errands for my master."

"Glad to be back?"

"Of course I am."

"And you see, M'ame Honorine, you find your boat just where she was. I came to have a look at her every day. This morning I took away her tarpaulin. Does she run as well as ever?"

"First-rate."

"Besides, you're a master pilot, you are. Who'd have thought, M'ame Honorine, that you'd be doing a job like this?"

"It's the war. All the young men in our island are gone and the old ones are fishing. Besides, there's no longer a fortnightly steamboat service, as there used to be. So I go the errands."

"What about petrol?"

"We've plenty to go on with. No fear of that."

"Well, goodbye for the present, M'ame Honorine. Shall I help you put the things on board?"

"Don't you trouble; you're in a hurry."

"Well, goodbye for the present," the old fellow repeated. "Till next time, M'ame Honorine. I'll have the parcels ready for you."

He went away, but, when he had gone a little distance, called out:

"All the same, mind the jagged reefs round that blessed island of yours! I tell you, it's got a nasty name! It's not called Coffin Island, the island of the thirty coffins, for nothing! Good luck to you, M'ame Honorine!"

He disappeared behind a rock.

Véronique had shuddered. The thirty coffins! The very words which she had read in the margin of that horrible drawing!

She leant forward. The woman had come a few steps nearer the boat and, after putting down some more provisions which she had been carrying, turned round.

Véronique now saw her full-face. She wore a Breton costume; and her head-dress was crowned by two black wings.

"Oh," stammered Véronique, "that head-dress in the drawing… the head-dress of the three crucified women!"

The Breton woman looked about forty. Her strong face, tanned by the sun and the cold, was bony and rough-hewn but lit up by a pair of large, dark, intelligent, gentle eyes. A heavy gold chain hung down upon her breast. Her velvet bodice fitted her closely.

She was humming in a very low voice as she took up her parcels and loaded the boat, which made her kneel on a big stone against which the boat was moored. When she had done, she looked at the horizon, which was covered with black clouds. She did not seem anxious about them, however, and, losing the painter, continued her song, but in a louder voice, which enabled Véronique to hear the words. It was a slow melody, a children's lullaby; and she sang it with a smile which revealed a set of fine, white teeth.

"And the mother said,
Rocking her child a-bed:

'Weep not. If you do,
The Virgin Mary weeps with you.

Babes that laugh and sing
Smiles to the Blessed Virgin bring.

Fold your hands this way
And to sweet Mary pray.'"

She did not complete the song. Véronique was standing before her, with her face drawn and very pale.

Taken aback, the other asked:

"What's the matter?"

Véronique, in a trembling voice, replied:

"That song! Who taught it you? Where do you get it from?... It's a song my mother used to sing, a song of her own country, Savoy... And I have never heard it since... since she died... So I want... I should like..."

She stopped. The Breton woman looked at her in silence, with an air of stupefaction, as though she too were on the point of asking questions. But Véronique repeated:

"Who taught it you?"

"Someone over there," the woman called Honorine answered, at last.

"Over there?"

"Yes, someone on my island."

Véronique said, with a sort of dread:

"Coffin Island?"

"That's just a name they call it by. It's really the Isle of Sarek."

They still stood looking at each other, with a look in which a certain doubt was mingled with a great need of speech and understanding. And at the same time they both felt that they were not enemies.

Véronique was the first to continue:

"Excuse me, but, you see, there are things which are so puzzling..."

The Breton woman nodded her head in approval and Véronique continued:

"So puzzling and so disconcerting!... For instance, do you know why I'm here? I must tell you. Perhaps you alone can explain... It's like this: an accident—quite a small accident, but really it all began with that—brought me to Brittany for the first time and showed me, on the door of an old, deserted, roadside cabin, the initials which I used to sign when I was a girl, a signature which I have not used for fourteen or fifteen years. As I went on, I discovered the same inscription many times repeated, with each time a different consecutive number. That was how I came here, to the beach at Beg-Meil and to this part of the beach, which appeared to be the end of a journey foreseen and arranged by... I don't know whom."

"Is your signature here?" asked Honorine, eagerly. "Where?"

"On that stone, above us, at the entrance to the shelter."

"I can't see from here. What are the letters?"

"V. d'H."

The Breton woman suppressed a movement. Her bony face betrayed profound emotion, and, hardly opening her lips, she murmured:

"Véronique... Véronique d'Hergemont."

"Ah," exclaimed the younger woman, "so you know my name, you know my name!"

Honorine took Véronique's two hands and held them in her own. Her weather-beaten face lit up with a smile. And her eyes grew moist with tears as she repeated:

"Mademoiselle Véronique!... Madame Véronique!... So it's you, Véronique!... O Heaven, is it possible! The Blessed Virgin Mary be praised!"

Véronique felt utterly confounded and kept on saying:

"You know my name... you know who I am... Then you can explain all this riddle to me?"

After a long pause, Honorine replied:

"I can explain nothing. I don't understand either. But we can try to find out together... Tell me, what was the name of that Breton village?"

"Le Faouet."

"Le Faouet. I know. And where was the deserted cabin?"

"A mile and a quarter away."

"Did you look in?"

"Yes; and that was the most terrible thing of all. Inside the cabin was..."

"What was in the cabin?"

"First of all, the dead body of a man, an old man, dressed in the local costume, with long white hair and a grey beard... Oh, I shall never forget that dead man!... He must have been murdered, poisoned, I don't know what..."

Honorine listened greedily, but the murder seemed to give her no clue and she merely asked:

"Who was it? Did they have an inquest?"

"When I came back with the people from Le Faouet, the corpse had disappeared."

"Disappeared? But who had removed it?"

"I don't know."

"So that you know nothing?"

"Nothing. Except that, the first time, I found in the cabin a drawing... a drawing which I tore up; but its memory haunts me like a nightmare that keeps on recurring. I can't get it out of my mind... Listen, it was a roll of paper on which someone had evidently copied an old picture and it represented... Oh, a dreadful, dreadful thing, four women crucified! And one of the women was myself, with my name... And the others wore a head-dress like yours."

Honorine had squeezed her hands with incredible violence:

"What's that you say?" she cried. "What's that you say? Four women crucified?"

"Yes; and there was something about thirty coffins, consequently about your island."

The Breton woman put her hands over Véronique's lips to silence them:

"Hush! Hush! Oh, you mustn't speak of all that! No, no, you mustn't... You see, there are devilish things... which it's a sacrilege to talk about... We must be silent about that... Later on, we'll see... another year, perhaps... Later on... Later on..."

She seemed shaken by terror, as by a gale which scourges the trees and overwhelms all living things. And suddenly she fell on her knees upon the rock and muttered a long prayer, bent in two, with her hands before her face, so completely absorbed that Véronique asked her no more questions.

At last she rose and, presently, said:

"Yes, this is all terrifying, but I don't see that it makes our duty any different or that we can hesitate at all."

And, addressing Véronique, she said, gravely:

"You must come over there with me."

"Over there, to your island?" replied Véronique, without concealing her reluctance.

Honorine again took her hands and continued, still in that same, rather solemn tone which appeared to Véronique to be full of secret and unspoken thoughts:

"Your name is truly Véronique d'Hergemont?"

"Yes."

"Who was your father?"

"Antoine d'Hergemont."

"You married a man called Vorski, who said he was a Pole?"

"Yes, Alexis Vorski."

"You married him after there was a scandal about his running off with you and after a quarrel between you and your father?"

"Yes."

"You had a child by him?"

"Yes, a son, François."

"A son that you never knew, in a manner of speaking, because he was kidnapped by your father?"

"Yes."

"And you lost sight of the two after a shipwreck?"

"Yes, they are both dead."

"How do you know?"

It did not occur to Véronique to be astonished at this question, and she replied:

"My personal enquiries and the police enquiries were both based upon the same indisputable evidence, that of the four sailors."

"Who's to say they weren't telling lies?"

"Why should they tell lies?" asked Véronique, in surprise.

"Their evidence may have been bought; they may have been told what to say."

"By whom?"

"By your father."

"But what an idea!... Besides, my father was dead!"

"I say once more: how do you know that?"

This time Véronique appeared stupefied:

"What are you hinting?" she whispered.

"One minute. Do you know the names of those four sailors?"

"I did know them, but I don't remember them."

"You don't remember that they were Breton names?"

"Yes, I do. But I don't see that..."

"If you never came to Brittany, your father often did, because of the books he used to write. He used to stay in Brittany during your mother's lifetime. That being so, he must have had relations with the men of the country. Suppose that he had known the four sailors a long time, that these men were devoted to him or bribed by him and that he engaged them specially for that adventure. Suppose that they began by landing your father and your son at some little Italian port and that then, being four good swimmers, they scuttled and sank their yacht in view of the coast. Just suppose it."

"But the men are living!" cried Véronique, in growing excitement. "They can be questioned."

"Two of them are dead; they died a natural death a few years ago. The third is an old man called Maguennoc; you will find him at Sarek. As for the fourth, you may have seen him just now. He used the money which he made out of that business to buy a grocer's shop at Beg-Meil."

"Ah, we can speak to him at once!" cried Véronique, eagerly. "Let's go and fetch him."

"Why should we? I know more than he does."

"You know? You know?"

"I know everything that you don't. I can answer all your questions. Ask me what you like."

But Véronique dared not put the great question to her, the one which was beginning to quiver in the darkness of her consciousness. She was afraid of a truth which was perhaps not inconceivable, a truth of which she seemed to catch a faint glimpse; and she stammered, in mournful accents:

"I don't understand, I don't understand... Why should my father have behaved like that? Why should he wish himself and my poor child to be thought dead?"

"Your father had sworn to have his revenge."

"On Vorski, yes; but surely not on me, his daughter?.... And such a revenge!"

"You loved your husband. Once you were in his power, instead of running away from him, you consented to marry him. Besides, the insult was a public one. And you know what your father was, with his violent, vindictive temperament and his rather... his rather unbalanced nature, to use his own expression."

"But since then?"

"Since then! Since then! He felt remorseful as he grew older, what with his affection for the child... and he tried everywhere to find you. The journeys I have taken, beginning with my journey to the Carmelites at Chartres! But you had left long ago... and where for? Where were you to be found?"

"You could have advertised in the newspapers."

"He did try advertising, once, very cautiously, because of the scandal. There was a reply. Someone made an appointment and he kept it. Do you know who came to meet him? Vorski, Vorski, who was looking for you too, who still loved you... and hated you. Your father became frightened and did not dare act openly."

Véronique did not speak. She felt very faint and sat down on the stone, with her head bowed.

Then she murmured:

"You speak of my father as though he were still alive today."

"He is."

"And as though you saw him often."

"Daily."

"And on the other hand"—Véronique lowered her voice—"on the other hand you do not say a word of my son. And that suggests a horrible thought: perhaps he did not live? Perhaps he is dead since? Is that why you do not mention him?"

She raised her head with an effort. Honorine was smiling.

"Oh, please, please," Véronique entreated, "tell me the truth! It is terrible to hope more than one has a right to. Do tell me."

Honorine put her arm round Véronique's neck:

"Why, my poor, dear lady, would I have told you all this if my handsome François had been dead?"

"He is alive, he is alive?" cried Véronique, wildly.

"Why, of course he is and in the best of health! Oh, he's a fine, sturdy little chap, never fear, and so steady on his legs! And I have every right to be proud of him, because it's I who brought him up, your little François."

She felt Véronique, who was leaning on her shoulder, give way to emotions which were too much for her and which certainly contained as much suffering as joy; and she said:

"Cry, my dear lady, cry; it will do you good. It's a better sort of crying than it was, eh? Cry, until you've forgotten all your old troubles. I'm going back to the village. Have you a bag of any kind at the inn? They know me there. I'll bring it back with me and we'll be off."

When the Breton woman returned, half an hour later, she saw Véronique standing and beckoning to her to hurry and heard her calling:

"Quick, quick! Heavens, what a time you've been! We have not a minute to lose."

Honorine, however, did not hasten her pace and did not reply. Her rugged face was without a smile.

"Well, are we going to start?" asked Véronique, running up to her. "There's nothing to delay us, is there, no obstacle? What's the matter? You seem quite changed."

"No, no."

"Then let's be quick."

Honorine, with her assistance, put the bag and the provisions on board. Then, suddenly standing in front of Véronique, she said:

"You're quite sure, are you, that the woman on the cross, as she was shown in the drawing, was yourself?"

"Absolutely. Besides, there were my initials above the head."

"That's a strange thing," muttered Honorine, "and it's enough to frighten anybody."

"Why should it be? It must have been someone who used to know me and who amused himself by... It's merely a coincidence, a chance fancy reviving the past."

"Oh, it's not the past that's worrying me! It's the future."

"The future?"

"Remember the prophecy."

"I don't understand."

"Yes, yes, the prophecy made about you to Vorski."

"Ah, you know?"

"I know. And it is so horrible to think of that drawing and of other much more dreadful things which you don't know of."

Véronique burst out laughing:

"What! Is that why you hesitate to take me with you, for, after all, that's what we're concerned with?"

"Don't laugh. People don't laugh when they see the flames of hell before them."

Honorine crossed herself, closing her eyes as she spoke. Then she continued:

"Of course... you scoff at me... you think I'm a superstitious Breton woman, who believes in ghosts and jack-o'-lanterns. I don't say you're altogether wrong. But there, there! There are some truths that blind one. You can talk it over with Maguennoc, if you get on the right side of him."

"Maguennoc?"

"One of the four sailors. He's an old friend of your boy's. He too helped to bring him up. Maguennoc knows more about it than the most learned men, more than your father. And yet..."

"What?"

"And yet Maguennoc tried to tempt fate and to get past what men are allowed to know."

"What did he do?"

"He tried to touch with his hand—you understand, with his own hand: he confessed it to me himself—the very heart of the mystery."

"Well?" said Véronique, impressed in spite of herself.

"Well, his hand was burnt by the flames. He showed me a hideous sore: I saw it with my eyes, something like the sore of a cancer; and he suffered to that degree..."

"Yes?"

"That it forced him to take a hatchet in his left hand and cut off his right hand himself."

Véronique was dumbfounded. She remembered the corpse at Le Faouet and she stammered:

"His right hand? You say that Maguennoc cut off his right-hand?"

"With a hatchet, ten days ago, two days before I left... I dressed the wound myself... Why do you ask?"

"Because," said Véronique, in a husky voice, "because the dead man, the old man whom I found in the deserted cabin and who afterwards disappeared, had lately lost his right hand."

Honorine gave a start. She still wore the sort of scared expression and betrayed the emotional disturbance which contrasted with her usually calm attitude. And she rapped out:

"Are you sure? Yes, yes, you're right, it was he, Maguennoc... He had long white hair, hadn't he? And a spreading beard?... Oh, how abominable!"

She restrained herself and looked around her, frightened at having spoken so loud. She once more made the sign of the cross and said, slowly, almost under her breath:

"He was the first of those who have got to die... he told me so himself... and old Maguennoc had eyes that read the book of the future as easily as the book of the past. He could see clearly where another saw nothing at all. 'The first victim will be myself, Ma'me Honorine. And, when the servant has gone, in a few days it will be the master's turn.'"

"And the master was...?" asked Véronique, in a whisper.

Honorine drew herself up and clenched her fists violently:

"I'll defend him! I will!" she declared. "I'll save him! Your father shall not be the second victim. No, no, I shall arrive in time! Let me go!"

"We are going together," said Véronique, firmly.

"Please," said Honorine, in a voice of entreaty, "please don't be persistent. Let me have my way. I'll bring your father and your son to you this very evening, before dinner."

"But why?"

"The danger is too great, over there, for your father... and especially for you. Remember the four crosses! It's over there that they are waiting... Oh, you mustn't go there!... The island is under a curse."

"And my son?"

"You shall see him today, in a few hours."

Véronique gave a short laugh:

"In a few hours! Woman, you must be mad! Here am I, after mourning my son for fourteen years, suddenly hearing that he's alive; and you ask me to wait before I take him in my arms! Not one hour! I would rather risk death a thousand times than put off that moment."

Honorine looked at her and seemed to realize that Véronique's was one of those resolves against which it is useless to fight, for she did not insist. She crossed herself for the third time and said, simply:

"God's will be done."

They both took their seats among the parcels which encumbered the narrow space. Honorine switched on the current, seized the tiller and skilfully steered the boat through the rocks and sandbanks which rose level with the water.

3

VORSKI'S SON

Véronique smiled as she sat to starboard on a packing-case, with her face turned towards Honorine. Her smile was anxious still and undefined, full of reticence and flickering as a sunbeam that tries to pierce the last clouds of the storm; but it was nevertheless a happy smile.

And happiness seemed the right expression for that wonderful face, stamped with dignity and with that particular modesty which gives to some women, whether stricken by excessive misfortune or preserved by love, the habit of gravity, combined with an absence of all feminine affectation.

Her black hair, touched with grey at the temples, was knotted very low down on the neck. She had the dead-white complexion of a southerner and very light blue eyes, of which the white seemed almost of the same colour, pale as a winter sky. She was tall, with broad shoulders and a well-shaped bust.

Her musical and somewhat masculine voice became light and cheerful when she spoke of the son whom she had found again. And Véronique could speak of nothing else. In vain the Breton woman tried to speak of the problems that harassed her and kept on interrupting Véronique:

"Look here, there are two things which I cannot understand. Who laid the trail with the clues that brought you from

Le Faouet to the exact spot where I always land? It almost makes one believe that someone had been from Le Faouet to the Isle of Sarek. And, on the other hand, how did old Maguennoc come to leave the island? Was it of his own free will? Or was it his dead body that they carried? If so, how?"

"Is it worth troubling about?" Véronique objected.

"Certainly it is. Just think! Besides me, who once a fortnight go either to Beg-Meil or Pont-F Abbe in my motor-boat for provisions, there are only two fishing-boats, which always go much higher up the coast, to Audieme, where they sell their catch. Then how did Maguennoc get across? Then again, did he commit suicide? But, if so, how did his body disappear?"

But Véronique protested:

"Please don't! It doesn't matter for the moment. It'll all be cleared up. Tell me about François. You were saying that he came to Sarek..."

Honorine yielded to Véronique's entreaties:

"He arrived in poor Maguennoc's arms, a few days after he was taken from you. Maguennoc, who had been taught his lesson by your father, said that a strange lady had entrusted him with the child; and he had it nursed by his daughter, who has since died. I was away, in a situation with a Paris family. When I came home again, François had grown into a fine little fellow, running about the moors and cliffs. It was then that I took service with your father, who had settled in Sarek. When Maguennoc's daughter died, we took the child to live with us."

"But under what name?"

"François, just François. M. d'Hergemont was known as Monsieur Antoine. François called him grandfather. No one ever made any remark upon it."

"And his character?" asked Véronique, with some anxiety.

"Oh, as far as that's concerned, he's a blessing!" replied Honorine. "Nothing of his father about him... nor of his grandfather either, as M. d'Hergemont himself admits. A gentle, lovable, most willing child. Never a sign of anger; always good-tempered. That's what got over his grandfather and made M. d'Hergemont come round to you again, because his grandson reminded him so of the daughter he had cast off. 'He's the very image of his mother,' he used to say. 'Véronique was gentle and affectionate like him, with the same fond and coaxing ways.' And then he began his search for you, with me to help him; for he had come to confide in me."

Véronique beamed with delight. Her son was like her! Her son was bright and kind-hearted!

"But does he know about me?" she said. "Does he know that I'm alive?"

"I should think he did! M. d'Hergemont tried to keep it from him at first. But I soon told him everything."

"Everything?"

"No. He believes that his father is dead and that, after the shipwreck in which he, I mean François, and M. d'Hergemont disappeared, you became a nun and have been lost sight of since. And he is so eager for news, each time I come back from one of my trips! He too is so full of hope! Oh, you can take my word for it, he adores his mother! And he's always singing that song you heard just now, which his grandfather taught him."

"My François, my own little François!"

"Ah, yes, he loves you! There's Mother Honorine. But you're mother, just that. And he's in a great hurry to grow up and finish his schooling, so that he may go and look for you."

"His schooling? Does he have lessons?"

"Yes, with his grandfather and, since two years ago, with such a nice fellow that I brought back from Paris, Stéphane Maroux, a wounded soldier covered with medals and restored to health after an internal operation. François dotes on him."

The boat was running quickly over the smooth sea, in which it ploughed a furrow of silvery foam. The clouds had dispersed on the horizon. The evening boded fair and calm.

"More, tell me more!" said Véronique, listening greedily. "What does my boy wear?"

"Knickerbockers and short socks, with his calves bare; a thick flannel shirt with gilt buttons; and a flat knitted cap, like his big friend, M. Stéphane; only his is red and suits him to perfection."

"Has he any friends besides M. Maroux?"

"All the growing lads of the island, formerly. But with the exception of three or four ship's boys, all the rest have left the island with their mothers, now that their fathers are at the war, and are working on the mainland, at Concameau or Lorient, leaving the old people at Sarek by themselves. We are not more than thirty on the island now."

"Whom does he play with? Whom does he go about with?"

"Oh, as for that, he has the best of companions!"

"Really? Who is it?"

"A little dog that Maguennoc gave him."

"A dog?"

"Yes; and the funniest dog you ever saw: an ugly ridiculous-looking thing, a cross between a poodle and a fox-terrier, but so comical and amusing! Oh, there's no one like Master All's Well!"

"All's Well?"

"That's what François calls him; and you couldn't have a better name for him. He always looks happy and glad to be alive. He's independent, too, and he disappears for hours and even days at a time; but he's always there when he's wanted, if you're feeling sad, or if things aren't going as you might like them to. All's Well hates to see anyone crying or scolding or quarrelling. The moment you cry, or pretend to cry, he comes and squats on his haunches in front of you, sits up, shuts one eye, half-opens the other and looks so exactly as if he was laughing that you begin to laugh yourself.

'That's right, old chap,' says François, 'you're quite right: all's well. There's nothing to take on about, is there?' And, when you're consoled, All's Well just trots away. His task is done."

Véronique laughed and cried in one breath. Then she was silent for a long time, feeling more and more gloomy and overcome by a despair which overwhelmed all her gladness. She thought of all the happiness that she had missed during the fourteen years of her childless motherhood, wearing her mourning for a son who was alive. All the cares that a mother lavishes upon the little creature new-born into the world, all the pride that she feels at seeing him grow and hearing him speak, all that delights a mother and uplifts her and makes her heart overflow with daily renewed affection: all this she had never known.

"We are half-way across," said Honorine.

They were running in sight of the Glenans Islands. On their right, the headland of Penmarch, whose coastline they were following at a distance of fifteen miles, marked a darker line which was not always differentiated from the horizon.

And Véronique thought of her sad past, of her mother, whom she hardly remembered, of her childhood spent with a selfish, disagreeable father, of her marriage, ah, above all of her marriage! She recalled her first meetings with Vorski, when she was only seventeen. How frightened she had been from the very beginning of that strange and unusual man, whom she dreaded while she submitted to his influence, as one does at that age submit to the influence of anything mysterious and incomprehensible!

Next came the hateful day of the abduction and the other days, more hateful still, that followed, the weeks during which he had kept her imprisoned, threatening her and dominating her with all his evil strength, and the promise of marriage which he had forced from her, a pledge against which all the girl's instincts and all her will revolted, but to which it seemed to her that she was bound to agree after so great a scandal and also because her father was giving his consent.

Her brain rebelled against the memories of her years of married life. Never that! Not even in the worst hours, when the nightmares of the past haunt one like spectres, never did she consent to revive, in the innermost recesses of her mind, that degrading past, with its mortifications, wounds and betrayals, and the disgraceful life led by her husband, who, shamelessly, with cynical pride, gradually revealed himself as the man he was, drinking, cheating at cards, robbing his boon companions, a swindler and blackmailer, giving his wife the impression, which she still retained and which made her shudder, of a sort of evil genius, cruel and unbalanced.

"Have done with dreams, Madame Véronique," said Honorine.

"It's not so much dreams and memories as remorse," she replied.

"Remorse, Madame Véronique? You, whose life has been one long martyrdom?"

"A martyrdom that was a punishment."

"But all that is over and done with, Madame Véronique, seeing that you are going to meet your son and your father again. Come, come, you must think of nothing but being happy."

"Happy? Can I be happy again?"

"I should think so! You'll soon see!... Look, there's Sarek."

Honorine took from a locker under her seat a large shell which she used as a trumpet, after the manner of the mariners of old, and, putting her lips to the mouthpiece and puffing out her cheeks, she blew a few powerful notes, which filled the air with a sound not unlike the lowing of an ox.

Véronique gave her a questioning look.

"It's him I'm calling," said Honorine.

"François? You're calling François?"

"Yes, it's the same every time I come back. He comes scrambling from the top of the cliffs where we live and runs down to the jetty."

"So I shall see him?" exclaimed Véronique, turning very pale.

"You will see him. Fold your veil double, so that he may not know you from your photographs. I'll speak to you as I would to a stranger who has come to look at Sarek."

They could see the island distinctly, but the foot of the cliffs was hidden by a multitude of reefs.

"Ah, yes, there's no lack of rocks! They swarm like a shoal of herring!" cried Honorine, who had been obliged to switch off the motor and was using two short paddles. "You know how calm the sea was just now. It's never calm here."

Thousands and thousands of little waves were dashing and clashing against one another and waging an incessant and implacable war upon the rocks. The boat seemed to be passing through the backwater of a torrent. Nowhere was a strip of blue or green sea visible amid the bubbling foam. There was nothing but white froth, whipped up by the indefatigable swirl of the forces which desperately assailed the pointed teeth of the reefs.

"And it's like that all round the island," said Honorine, "so much so that you may say that Sarek isn't accessible except in a small boat. Ah, the Huns could never have established a submarine base on our island! To make quite sure and remove all doubts, some officers came over from Lorient, two years ago, because of a few caves on the west, which can only be entered at low tide. It was waste of time. There was nothing doing here. Just think, it's like a sprinkle of rocks all around; and pointed rocks at that, which get at you treacherously from underneath. And, though these are the most dangerous, perhaps it is the others that are most to be feared, the big ones which you see and have got their name and their history from all sorts of crimes and shipwrecks. Oh, as to those!..."

Her voice grew hollow. With a hesitating hand, which seemed afraid of the half-completed gesture, she pointed to some reefs which stood up in powerful masses of different shapes, crouching animals, crenellated keeps, colossal needles, sphynx-heads, jagged pyramids, all in black granite stained with red, as though soaked in blood.

And she whispered:

"Oh, as to those, they have been guarding the island for centuries and centuries, but like wild beasts that only care for doing harm and killing. They... they... no, it's better never to speak about them or even think of them. They are the thirty wild beasts. Yes, thirty, Madame Véronique, there are thirty of them..."

She made the sign of the cross and continued, more calmly:

"There are thirty of them. Your father says that Sarek is called the island of the thirty coffins because the people instinctively ended in this case by confusing the two words *ecueils* and *cercueils*.* Perhaps... It's very likely... But, all the same, they are thirty real coffins, Madame Véronique; and, if we could open them, we should be sure to find them full of bones and bones and bones. M. d'Hergemont himself says that Sarek comes from the word Sarcophagus, which, according to him, is the learned way of saying coffin. Besides, there's more than that..."

Honorine broke off, as though she wanted to think of something else, and, pointing to a reef of rocks, said:

"Look, Madame Véronique, past that big one right in our way there, you will see, through an opening, our little harbour and, on the quay, François in his red cap."

Véronique had been listening absent-mindedly to Honorine's explanations. She leant her body farther out of the boat, in

---

* *"Reefs" and "coffins."*

order to catch sight the sooner of her son, while the Breton woman, once more a victim to her obsession, continued, in spite of herself:

"There's more than that. The Isle of Sarek—and that is why your father came to live here—contains a collection of dolmens which have nothing remarkable about them, but which are peculiar for one reason, that they are all nearly alike. Well, how many of them do you think there are? Thirty! Thirty, like the principal reefs. And those thirty are distributed round the islands, on the cliffs, exactly opposite the thirty reefs; and each of them bears the same name as the reef that corresponds to it: Dol-er-H'roeck, Dol-Kerlitu and so on. What do you say to that?"

She had uttered these names in the same timid voice in which she spoke of all these things, as if she feared to be heard by the things themselves, to which she was attributing a formidable and sacred life.

"What do you say to that, Madame Véronique? Oh, there's plenty of mystery about it all; and, once more, it's better to hold one's tongue! I'll tell you about it when we've left here, right away from the island, and when your little François is in your arms, between your father and you."

Véronique sat silent, gazing into space at the spot to which Honorine had pointed. With her back turned to her companion and her two hands gripping the gunwale, she stared distractedly before her. It was there, through that narrow opening, that she was to see her child, long lost and now found; and she did not want to waste a single second after the moment when she would be able to catch sight of him.

They reached the rock. One of Honorine's paddles grazed its side. They skirted and came to the end of it.

"Oh," said Véronique, sorrowfully, "he is not there!"

"François not there? Impossible!" cried Honorine.

She in her turn saw, three or four hundred yards in front of them, the few big rocks on the beach which served as a jetty. Three women, a little girl and some old seafaring men were waiting for the boat, but no boy, no red cap.

"That's strange," said Honorine, in a low voice. "It's the first time that he's failed to answer my call."

"Perhaps he's ill?" Véronique suggested.

"No, François is never ill."

"What then?"

"I don't know."

"But aren't you afraid?" asked Véronique, who was already becoming frightened.

"For him, no... but for your father. Maguennoc said that I oughtn't to leave him. It's he who is threatened."

"But François is there to defend him; and so is M. Maroux, his tutor. Come, answer me: what do you imagine?"

After a moment's pause, Honorine shrugged her shoulders.

"A pack of nonsense! I get absurd, yes, absurd things into my head. Don't be angry with me. I can't help it: it's the Breton in me. Except for a few years, I have spent all my life here, with legends and stories in the very air I breathed. Don't let's talk about it."

The Isle of Sarek appears in the shape of a long and undulating table-land, covered with ancient trees and standing on cliffs of medium height than which nothing more jagged could be imagined. It is as though the island were surrounded by a reef of uneven, diversified lacework, incessantly wrought upon by the rain, the wind, the sun, the snow, the frost, the mist and all the water that falls from the sky or oozes from the earth.

The only accessible point is on the eastern side, at the bottom of a depression where a few houses, mostly abandoned since the war, constitute the village. A break in the cliffs opens here, protected by the little jetty. The sea at this spot is perfectly calm.

Two boats lay moored to the quay.

Before landing, Honorine made a last effort:

"We're there, Madame Véronique, as you see. Now is it really worth your while to get out? Why not stay where you are? I'll bring your father and your son to you in two hours' time and we'll have dinner at Beg-Meil or at Pont-l'Abbé. Will that do?"

Véronique rose to her feet and leapt on to the quay without replying. Honorine joined her and insisted no longer:

"Well, children, where's young François? Hasn't he come?"

"He was here about twelve," said one of the women. "Only he didn't expect you until tomorrow."

"That's true enough... but still he must have heard me blow my horn. However, we shall see."

And, as the man helped her to unload the boat, she said:

"I shan't want all this taken up to the Priory. Nor the bags either. Unless... Look here, if I am not back by five o'clock, send a youngster after me with the bags."

"No, I'll come myself," said one of the seamen.

"As you please, Corréjou. Oh, by the way, where's Maguennoc?"

"Maguennoc's gone. I took him across to Pont-l'Abbé myself."

"When was that, Corréjou?"

"Why, the day after you went, Madame Honorine."

"What was he going over for?"

"He told us he was going... I don't know where... It had to do with the hand he lost... a pilgrimage..."

"A pilgrimage? To Le Faouet, perhaps? To St. Barbe's Chapel?"

"That's it... that's it exactly: St. Barbe's Chapel, that's what he said."

Honorine asked no more. She could no longer doubt that Maguennoc was dead. She moved away, accompanied by Véronique, who had lowered her veil; and the two went along a rocky path, cut into steps, which ran through the middle of an oak-wood towards the southernmost point of the island.

"After all," said Honorine, "I am not sure—and I may as well say so—that M. d'Hergemont will consent to leave. He treats all my stories as crotchets, though there's plenty of things that astonish even him..."

"Does he live far from here?" asked Véronique.

"It's forty minutes' walk. As you will see, it's almost another island, joined to the first. The Benedictines built an abbey there."

"But he's not alone there, is he, with François and M. Maroux?"

"Before the war, there were two men besides. Lately, Maguennoc and I used to do pretty well all the work, with the cook, Marie Le Goff."

"She remained, of course, while you were away?"

"Yes."

They reached the top of the cliffs. The path, which followed the coast, rose and fell in steep gradients. On every hand were old oaks with their bunches of mistletoe, which showed among the as yet scanty leaves. The sea, grey-green in the distance, girded the island with a white belt.

Véronique continued:

"What do you propose to do, Honorine?"

"I shall go in by myself and speak to your father. Then I shall come back and fetch you at the garden-gate; and in Franqois' eyes you will pass for a friend of his mother's. He will guess the truth gradually."

"And you think that my father will give me a good welcome?"

"He will receive you with open arms, Madame Véronique," cried the Breton woman, "and we shall all be happy, provided... provided nothing has happened... It's so funny that François doesn't run out to meet me! He can see our boat from every part of the island... as far off as the Glenans almost."

She relapsed into what M. d'Hergemont called her crotchets; and they pursued their road in silence. Véronique felt anxious and impatient.

Suddenly Honorine made the sign of the cross:

"You do as I'm doing, Madame Véronique," she said. "The monks have consecrated the place, but there's lots of bad, unlucky things remaining from the old days, especially in that wood, the wood of the Great Oak."

The old days no doubt meant the period of the Druids and their human sacrifices; and the two women were now entering a wood in which the oaks, each standing in isolation on a mound of moss-grown stones, had a look of ancient gods, each with his own altar, his mysterious cult and his formidable power.

Véronique, following Honorine's example, crossed herself and could not help shuddering as she said:

"How melancholy it is! There's not a flower on this desolate plateau."

"They grow most wonderfully when one takes the trouble. You shall see Maguennoc's, at the end of the island, to the right of the Fairies' Dolmen... a place called the Calvary of the Flowers."

"Are they lovely?"

"Wonderful, I tell you. Only he goes himself to get the mould from certain places. He prepares it. He works it up. He mixes it with some special leaves of which he knows the effect." And she repeated, "You shall see Maguennoc's flowers. There are no flowers like them in the world. They are miraculous flowers..."

After skirting a hill, the road descended a sudden declivity. A huge gash divided the island into two parts, the second of which now appeared, standing a little higher, but very much more limited in extent.

"It's the Priory, that part," said Honorine.

The same jagged cliffs surrounded the smaller islet with an even steeper rampart, which itself was hollowed out underneath like the hoop of a crown. And this rampart was joined to the main island by a strip of cliff fifty yards long and hardly thicker than a castle-wall, with a thin, tapering crest which looked as sharp as the edge of an axe.

There was no thoroughfare possible along this ridge, inasmuch as it was split in the middle with a wide fissure, for which reason the abutments of a wooden bridge had been anchored to the two extremities. The bridge started flat on the rock and subsequently spanned the intervening crevice.

They crossed it separately, for it was not only very narrow but also unstable, shaking under their feet and in the wind.

"Look, over there, at the extreme point of the island," said Honorine, "you can see a corner of the Priory."

The path that led to it ran through fields planted with small fir-trees arranged in quincunxes. Another path turned to the right and disappeared from view in some dense thickets.

Véronique kept her eyes upon the Priory, whose low-storied front was lengthening gradually, when Honorine, after a few minutes, stopped short, with her face towards the thickets on the right, and called out:

"Monsieur Stéphane!"

"Whom are you calling?" asked Véronique. "M. Maroux?"

"Yes, François' tutor. He was running towards the bridge: I caught sight of him through a clearing... Monsieur Stéphane!... But why doesn't he answer? Did you see a man running?"

"No."

"I declare it was he, with his white cap. At any rate, we can see the bridge behind us. Let us wait for him to cross."

"Why wait? If anything's the matter, if there's a danger of any kind, it's at the Priory."

"You're right. Let's hurry."

They hastened their pace, overcome with forebodings; and then, for no definite reason, broke into a run, so greatly did their fears increase as they drew nearer to the reality.

The islet grew narrower again, barred by a low wall which marked the boundaries of the Priory domain. At that moment, cries were heard, coming from the house.

Honorine exclaimed:

"They're calling! Did you hear? A woman's cries! It's the cook! It's Marie Le Goff!..."

She made a dash for the gate and grasped the key, but inserted it so awkwardly that she jammed the lock and was unable to open it.

"Through the gap!" she ordered. "This way, on the right!"

They rushed along, scrambled through the wall and crossed a wide grassy space filled with ruins, in which the winding and ill-marked path disappeared at every moment under trailing creepers and moss.

"Here we are! Here we are!" shouted Honorine. "We're coming!"

And she muttered:

"The cries have stopped! It's dreadful! Oh, poor Marie Le Goff!"

She grasped Véronique's arm:

"Let's go round. The front of the house is on the other side. On this side the doors are always locked and the window shutters closed."

But Véronique caught her foot in some roots, stumbled and fell to her knees. When she stood up again, the Breton woman had left her and was hurrying round the left wing. Unconsciously, Véronique, instead of following her, made straight for the house, climbed the step and was brought up short by the door, at which she knocked again and again.

The idea of going round, as Honorine had done, seemed to her a waste of time which nothing could ever make good.

However, realising the futility of her efforts, she was just deciding to go, when once more cries sounded from inside the house and above her head.

It was a man's voice, which Véronique seemed to recognize as her father's. She fell back a few steps. Suddenly one of the windows on the first floor opened and she saw M. d'Hergemont, his features distorted with inexpressible terror, gasping:

"Help! Help! Oh, the monster! Help!"

"Father! Father!" cried Véronique, in despair. "It's I!"

He lowered his head for an instant, appeared not to see his daughter and made a quick attempt to climb over the balcony. But a shot rang out behind him and one of the window-panes was blown into fragments.

"Murderer, murderer!" he shouted, turning back into the room.

Véronique, mad with fear and helplessness, looked around her. How could she rescue her father? The wall was too high and offered nothing to cling to. Suddenly, she saw a ladder, lying twenty yards away, beside the wall of the house. With a prodigious effort of will and strength, she managed to carry the ladder, heavy though it was, and to set it up under the open window.

At the most tragic moment in life, when the mind is no more than a seething confusion, when the whole body is shaken by the tremor of anguish, a certain logic continues to connect our ideas: and Véronique wondered why she had not heard Honorine's voice and what could have delayed her coming.

She also thought of François. Where was François? Had he followed Stéphane Maroux in his inexplicable flight? Had he gone in search of assistance? And who was it that M. d'Hergemont had apostrophized as a monster and a murderer?

The ladder did not reach the window; and Véronique at once became aware of the effort which would be necessary if she was to climb over the balcony. Nevertheless she did not hesitate.

They were fighting up there; and the struggle was mingled with stifled shouts uttered by her father. She went up the ladder. The most that she could do was to grasp the bottom rail of the balcony. But a narrow ledge enabled her to hoist herself on one knee, to put her head through and to witness the tragedy that was being enacted in the room.

At that moment, M. d'Hergemont had once more retreated to the window and even a little beyond it, so that she almost saw him face to face. He stood without moving, haggard-eyed and with his arms hanging in an undecided posture, as though waiting for something terrible to happen. He stammered:

"Murderer! Murderer!... Is it really you? Oh, curse you! François! François!"

He was no doubt calling upon his grandson for help; and François no doubt was also exposed to some attack, was perhaps wounded, was possibly dead!

Véronique summoned up all her strength and succeeded in setting foot on the ledge.

"Here I am! Here I am!" she meant to cry.

But her voice died away in her throat. She had seen! She saw! Facing her father, at a distance of five paces, against the opposite wall of the room, stood someone pointing a revolver at M. d'Hergemont and deliberately taking aim. And that someone was... oh, horror! Véronique recognized the red cap of which Honorine had spoken, the flannel shirt with the gilt buttons. And above all she beheld, in that young face convulsed with hideous emotions, the very expression which Vorski used to wear at times when his instincts, hatred and ferocity, gained the upper hand.

The boy did not see her. His eyes were fixed on the mark which he proposed to hit; and he seemed to take a sort of savage joy in postponing the fatal act.

Véronique herself was silent. Words or cries could not possibly avert the peril. What she had to do was to fling herself between her father and her son. She clutched hold of the railings, clambered up and climbed through the window.

It was too late. The shot was fired. M. d'Hergemont fell with a groan of pain.

And, at the same time, at that very moment, while the boy still had his arm outstretched and the old man was sinking into a huddled heap, a door opened at the back. Honorine appeared; and the abominable sight struck her, so to speak, full in the face.

"François!" she screamed. "You! You!"

The boy sprang at her. The woman tried to bar his way. There was not even a struggle. The boy took a step back, quickly raised his weapon and fired.

Honorine's knees gave way beneath her and she fell across the threshold. And, as he jumped over her body and fled, she kept on repeating:

"François... François... No, it's not true!... Oh, can it be possible?... François..."

There was a burst of laughter outside. Yes, the boy had laughed. Véronique heard that horrible, infernal laugh, so like Vorski's laugh; and it all agonized her with the same anguish which used to sear her in Vorski's days!

She did not run after the murderer. She did not call out.

A faint voice beside her was murmuring her name:

"Véronique... Véronique..."

M. d'Hergemont lay on the ground, staring at her with glassy eyes which were already filled with death.

She knelt down by his side; but, when she tried to unbutton his waistcoat and his bloodstained shirt, in order to dress the wound of which he was dying, he gently pushed her hand aside. She understood that all aid was useless and that he wished to speak to her. She stooped still lower.

"Véronique... forgive... Véronique..."

It was the first utterance of his failing thoughts.

She kissed him on the forehead and wept:

"Hush, father... Don't tire yourself..."

But he had something else to say; and his mouth vainly emitted syllables which did not form words and to which she listened in despair. His life was ebbing away. His mind was fading into the darkness. Véronique glued her ear to the lips which exhausted themselves in a supreme effort and she caught the words:

"Beware... beware... the God-Stone..."

Suddenly he half raised himself. His eyes flashed as though lit by the last flicker of an expiring flame. Véronique received the impression that her father, as he looked at her, now understood nothing but the full significance of her presence and foresaw all the dangers that threatened her; and, speaking in a hoarse and terrified but quite distinct voice, he said:

"You mustn't stay... It means death if you stay... Escape this island... Go... Go..."

His head fell back. He stammered a few more words which Véronique was just able to grasp:

"Oh, the cross!... The four crosses of Sarek!... My daughter... my daughter... crucified!..."

And that was all.

There was a great silence, a vast silence which Véronique felt weighing upon her like a burden that grows heavier second after second.

"You must escape from this island," a voice repeated. "Go, quickly. Your father bade you, Madame Véronique."

Honorine was beside her, livid in the face, with her two hands clasping a napkin, rolled into a plug and red with blood, which she held to her chest.

"But I must look after you first!" cried Véronique. "Wait a moment... Let me see..."

"Later on... they'll attend to me presently," spluttered Honorine. "Oh, the monster!... If I had only come in time! But the door below was barricaded..."

"Do let me see to your wound," Véronique implored. "Lie down."

"Presently... First Marie Le Goff, the cook, at the top of the staircase... She's wounded too... mortally perhaps... Go and see."

Véronique went out by the door at the back, the one through which her son had made his escape. There was a large landing here. On the top steps, curled into a heap, lay Marie Le Goff, with the death-rattle in her throat.

She died almost at once, without recovering consciousness, the third victim of the incomprehensible tragedy. As foretold by old Maguennoc, M. d'Hergemont had been the second victim.

4

THE POOR PEOPLE OF SAREK

Honorine's wound was deep but did not seem likely to prove fatal. When Véronique had dressed it and moved Marie Le Goff's body to the room filled with books and furnished like a study in which her father was lying, she closed M. d'Hergemont's eyes, covered him with a sheet and knelt down to pray. But the words of prayer would not come to her lips and her mind was incapable of dwelling on a single thought. She felt stunned by the repeated blows of misfortune. She sat down in a chair, holding her head in her hands. Thus she remained for nearly an hour, while Honorine slept a feverish sleep.

With all her strength she rejected her son's image, even as she had always rejected Vorski's. But the two images became mingled together, whirling around her and dancing before her eyes like those lights which, when we close our eyelids tightly, pass and pass again and multiply and blend into one. And it was always one and the same face, cruel, sardonic, hideously grinning.

She did not suffer, as a mother suffers when mourning the loss of a son. Her son had been dead these fourteen years; and the one who had come to life again, the one for whom all the wells of her maternal affection were ready to gush forth, had suddenly become a stranger and even worse: Vorski's son! How indeed could she have suffered?

But ah, what a wound inflicted in the depths of her being! What an upheaval, like those cataclysms which shake the whole of a peaceful country-side! What a hellish spectacle! What a vision of madness and horror! What an ironical jest, a jest of the most hideous destiny! Her son killing her father at the moment when, after all these years of separation and sorrow, she was on the point of embracing them both and living with them in sweet and homely intimacy! Her son a murderer! Her son dispensing death and terror broadcast! Her son levelling that ruthless weapon, slaying with all his heart and soul and taking a perverse delight in it!

The motives which might explain these actions interested her not at all. Why had her son done these things? Why had his tutor, Stéphane Maroux, doubtless an accomplice, possibly an instigator, fled before the tragedy? These were questions which she did not seek to solve. She thought only of the frightful scene of carnage and death. And she asked herself if death was not for her the only refuge and the only ending.

"Madame Véronique," whispered Honorine.

"What is it?" asked Véronique, roused from her stupor.

"Don't you hear?"

"What?"

"A ring at the bell below. They must be bringing your luggage."

She sprang to her feet.

"But what am I to say? How can I explain?... If I accuse that boy..."

"Not a word, please. Let me speak to them."

"You're very weak, my poor Honorine."

"No, no, I'm feeling better."

Véronique went downstairs, crossed a broad entrance-hall paved with black and white flags and drew the bolts of a great door.

It was, as they expected, one of the sailors:

"I knocked at the kitchen-door first," said the man. "Isn't Marie Le Goff there? And Madame Honorine?"

"Honorine is upstairs and would like to speak to you."

The sailor looked at her, seemed impressed by this young woman, who looked so pale and serious, and followed her without a word.

Honorine was waiting on the first floor, standing in front of the open door:

"Ah, it's you, Corréjou?... Now listen to me... and no silly talk, please."

"What's the matter, M'ame Honorine? Why, you're wounded! What is it?"

She stepped aside from the doorway and, pointing to the two bodies under their winding-sheets, said simply:

"Monsieur Antoine and Marie Le Goff... both of them murdered."

The man's face became distorted. He stammered:

"Murdered... you don't say so... Why?"

"I don't know; we arrived after it happened."

"But... young François?... Monsieur Stéphane?..."

"Gone... They must have been killed too."

"But... but... Maguennoc?"

"Maguennoc? Why do you speak of Maguennoc?"

"I speak of Maguennoc, I speak of Maguennoc... because, if he's alive... this is a very different business. Maguennoc always said that he would be the first. Maguennoc only says things of which he's certain. Maguennoc understands these things thoroughly."

Honorine reflected and then said:

"Maguennoc has been killed."

This time Corréjou lost all his composure: and his features expressed that sort of insane terror which Véronique had repeatedly observed in Honorine. He made the sign of the cross and said, in a low whisper:

"Then... then... it's happening, Ma'me Honorine?... Maguennoc said it would... Only the other day, in my boat, he was saying, 'It won't be long now... Everybody ought to get away.'"

And suddenly the sailor turned on his heel and made for the staircase.

"Stay where you are, Corréjou," said Honorine, in a voice of command.

"We must get away. Maguennoc said so. Everybody has got to go."

"Stay where you are," Honorine repeated.

Corréjou stopped, undecidedly. And Honorine continued:

"We are agreed. We must go. We shall start tomorrow, towards the evening. But first we must attend to Monsieur Antoine and to Marie Le Goff. Look here, you go to the sisters Archignat and send them to keep watch by the dead. They are bad women, but they are used to doing that. Say that two of the three must come. Each of them shall have double the ordinary fee."

"And after that, Ma'me Honorine?"

"You and all the old men will see to the coffins; and at daybreak we will bury the bodies in consecrated ground, in the cemetery of the chapel."

"And after that, Ma'me Honorine?"

"After that, you will be free and the others too. You can pack up and be off."

"But you, Ma'me Honorine?"

"I have the boat. That's enough talking. Are we agreed?"

"Yes, we're agreed. It means one more night to spend here. But I suppose that nothing fresh will happen between this and tomorrow?..."

"Why no, why no... Go, Corréjou. Hurry. And above all don't tell the others that Maguennoc is dead... or we shall never keep them here."

"That's a promise, Ma'me Honorine."

The man hastened away.

An hour later, two of the sisters Archignat appeared, two skinny, shrivelled old hags, looking like witches in their dirty, greasy caps with the black-velvet bows. Honorine was taken to her own room on the same floor, at the end of the left wing.

And the vigil of the dead began.

Véronique spent the first part of the night beside her father's body and then went and sat with Honorine, whose condition seemed to grow worse. She ended by dozing off and was wakened by the Breton woman, who said to her, in one of those accesses of fever in which the brain still retains a certain lucidity:

"François must be hiding... and M. Stéphane too... The island has safe hiding-places, which Maguennoc showed them. We shan't see them, therefore; and no one will know anything about them."

"Are you sure?"

"Quite. So listen to me. Tomorrow, when everybody has left Sarek and when we two are alone, I shall blow the signal with my horn and he will come here."

Véronique was horrified:

"But I don't want to see him!" she exclaimed, indignantly. "I loathe him!... Like my father, I curse him!... Have you forgotten? He killed my father, before our eyes! He killed Marie Le Goff! He tried to kill you!... No, what I feel for him is hatred and disgust! The monster!"

The Breton woman took her hand, as she had formed a habit of doing, and murmured:

"Don't condemn him yet... He did not know what he was doing."

"What do you mean? He didn't know? Why, I saw his eyes, Vorski's eyes!"

"He did not know... he was mad."

"Mad? Nonsense!"

"Yes, Madame Véronique. I know the boy. He's the kindest creature on earth. If he did all this, it was because he went mad suddenly... he and M. Stéphane. They must both be weeping in despair now."

"It's impossible. I can't believe it."

"You can't believe it because you know nothing of what is happening... and of what is going to happen... But, if you did know... Oh, there are things... there are things!"

Her voice was no longer audible. She was silent, but her eyes remained wide open and her lips moved without uttering a sound.

Nothing occurred until the morning. At five o'clock Véronique heard them nailing down the coffins; and almost immediately afterwards the door of the room in which she sat was opened and the sisters Archignat entered like a whirlwind, both greatly excited.

They had heard the truth from Corréjou, who, to give himself courage, had taken a drop too much to drink and was talking at random:

"Maguennoc is dead!" they screamed. "Maguennoc is dead and you never told us! Give us our money, quick! We're going!"

The moment they were paid, they ran away as fast as their legs would carry them; and, an hour later, some other women, informed by them, came hurrying to drag their men from their work. They all used the same words:

"We must go! We must get ready to start!... It'll be too late afterwards. The two boats can take us all."

Honorine had to intervene with all her authority and Véronique was obliged to distribute money. And the funeral was hurriedly conducted. Not far away was an old chapel, carefully restored by M. d'Hergemont, where a priest came once a month from Pont-l'Abbe to say mass. Beside it was the ancient cemetery of the abbots of Sarek. The two bodies were buried here; and an old man, who in ordinary times acted as sacristan, mumbled the blessing.

All the people seemed smitten with madness. Their voices and movements were spasmodic. They were obsessed with the fixed idea of leaving the island and paid no attention to Véronique, who knelt a little way off, praying and weeping.

It was all over before eight o'clock. Men and women made their way down across the island. Véronique, who felt as though she were living in a nightmare world where events followed upon one another without logic and with no connected sequence, went back to Honorine, whose feeble condition had prevented her from attending her master's funeral.

"I'm feeling better," said the Breton woman. "We shall go today or tomorrow and we shall go with François."

Véronique protested angrily; but Honorine repeated:

"With François, I tell you, and with M. Stéphane. And as soon as possible. I also want to go... and to take you with me... and François too. There is death in the island. Death is the master here. We must leave Sarek. We shall all go."

Véronique did not wish to thwart her. But at nine o'clock hurried steps were heard outside. It was Corréjou, coming from the village. On reaching the door he shouted:

"They've stolen your motor-boat, Ma'me Honorine! She's disappeared!"

"Impossible!" said Honorine.

But the sailor, all out of breath, declared:

"She's disappeared. I suspected something this morning early. But I expect I had had a glass too much; I did not give it another thought. Others have since seen what I did. The painter has been cut... It happened during the night. And they've made off. No one saw or heard them."

The two women exchanged glances; and the same thought occurred to both of them: François and Stéphane Maroux had taken to flight.

Honorine muttered between her teeth:

"Yes, yes, that's it: he understands how to work the boat."

Véronique perhaps felt a certain relief at knowing that the boy had gone and that she would not see him again. But Honorine, seized with a renewed fear, exclaimed:

"Then... then what are we to do?"

"You must leave at once, Ma'me Honorine. The boats are ready... everybody's packing up. There'll be no one in the village by eleven o'clock."

Véronique interposed:

"Honorine's not in a condition to travel."

"Yes, I am; I'm better," the Breton woman declared.

"No, it would be ridiculous. Let us wait a day or two... Come back in two days, Corréjou."

She pushed the sailor towards the door. He, for that matter, was only too anxious to go:

"Very well," he said, "that'll do: I'll come back the day after tomorrow. Besides, we can't take everything with us. We shall have to come back now and again to fetch our things... Goodbye, Ma'me Honorine; take care of yourself."

And he ran outside.

"Corréjou! Corréjou!"

Honorine was sitting up in bed and calling to him in despair:

"No, no, don't go away, Corréjou!... Wait for me and carry me to your boat."

She listened; and, as the man did not return, she tried to get up:

"I'm frightened," she said. "I don't want to be left alone."

Véronique held her down:

"You're not going to be left alone, Honorine. I shan't leave you."

There was an actual struggle between the two women; and Honorine, pushed back on her bed by main force, moaned, helplessly:

"I'm frightened... I'm frightened... The island is accursed... It's tempting Providence to remain behind... Maguennoc's death was a warning... I'm frightened..."

She was more or less delirious, but still retained a halflucidity which enabled her to intersperse a few intelligible and reasonable remarks among the incoherent phrases which revealed her superstitious Breton soul.

She gripped Véronique by her two shoulders and declared:

"I tell you, the island's cursed. Maguennoc confessed as much himself one day: 'Sarek is one of the gates of hell,' he said. 'The gate is closed now, but, on the day when it opens, every misfortune you can think of will be upon it like a squall.'"

She calmed herself a little, at Véronique's entreaty, and continued, in a lower voice, which grew fainter as she spoke:

"He loved the island, though... as we all do. At such times he would speak of it in a way which I did not understand: 'The gate is a double one, Honorine, and it also opens on Paradise.' Yes, yes, the island was good to live in... We loved it... Maguennoc made flowers grow on it... Oh, those flowers! They were enormous: three times as tall... and as beautiful. .

The minutes passed slowly. The bedroom was at the extreme left of the house, just above the rocks which overhung the sea and separated from them only by the width of the road.

Véronique sat down at the window, with her eyes fixed on the white waves which grew still more troubled as the wind blew more strongly. The sun was rising. In the direction of the village she saw nothing except a steep headland. But, beyond the belt of foam studded with the black points of the reefs, the view embraced the deserted plains of the Atlantic.

Honorine murmured, drowsily:

"They say that the gate is a stone... and that it comes from very far away, from a foreign country. It's the God-Stone. They also say that it's a precious stone... the colour of gold and silver mixed... The God-Stone... The stone that gives life or death... Maguennoc saw it... He opened the gate and put his arm through... And his hand... his hand was burnt to a cinder."

Véronique felt oppressed. Fear was gradually overcoming her also, like the oozing and soaking of stagnant water. The horrible events of the last few days, of which she had been a terrified witness, seemed to evoke others yet more dreadful, which she anticipated like an inevitable hurricane that is bound to carry off everything in its headlong course.

She expected them. She had no doubt that they would come, unloosed by the fatal power which was multiplying its terrible assaults upon her.

"Don't you see the boats?" asked Honorine.

"No," she said, "you can't see them from here."

"Yes, you can: they are sure to come this way. They are heavy boats: and there's a wider passage at the point."

The next moment, Véronique saw the bow of a boat project beyond the end of the headland. The boat lay low in the water, being very heavily laden, crammed with crates and parcels on which women and children were seated. Four men were rowing lustily.

"That's Corréjou's," said Honorine, who had left her bed, half-dressed. "And there's the other: look."

The second boat came into view, equally burdened. Only three men were rowing, with a woman to help them.

Both boats were too far away—perhaps seven or eight hundred yards—to allow the faces of the occupants to be seen. And no sound of voices rose from those heavy hulls with their cargoes of wretchedness, which were fleeing from death.

"Oh dear, oh dear!" moaned Honorine. "If only they escape this hell!"

"What can you be afraid of, Honorine? They are in no danger."

"Yes, they are, as long as they have not left the island."

"But they have left it."

"It's still the island all around the island. It's there that the coffins lurk and lie in wait."

"But the sea is not rough."

"There's more than the sea. It's not the sea that's the enemy."

"Then what is?"

"I don't know... I don't know..."

The two boats veered round at the southern point. Before them lay two channels, which Honorine pointed out by the name of two reefs, the Devil's Rock and the Sarek Tooth.

It at once became evident that Corréjou had chosen the Devil's Channel.

"They're touching it," said Honorine. "They are there. Another hundred yards and they are safe."

She almost gave a chuckle:

"Ah, all the devil's machinations will be thwarted, Madame Véronique! I really believe that we shall be saved, you and I and all the people of Sarek."

Véronique remained silent. Her depression continued and was all the more overwhelming because she could attribute it only to vague presentiments which she was powerless to fight against. She had drawn an imaginary line up to which the danger threatened, would continue to threaten, and where it still persisted; and this line Corréjou had not yet reached.

Honorine was shivering with fever. She mumbled:

"I'm frightened... I'm frightened..."

"Nonsense," declared Véronique, pulling herself together, "It's absurd! Where can the danger come from?"

"Oh," cried the Breton woman, "what's that? What does it mean?"

"What? What is it?"

They had both pressed their foreheads to the panes and were staring wildly before them. Down below, something had so to speak shot out from the Devil's Rock. And they at once recognized the motor-boat which they had used the day before and which according to Corréjou had disappeared.

"François! François!" cried Honorine, in stupefaction. "François and Monsieur Stéphane!"

Véronique recognized the boy. He was standing in the bow of the motor-boat and making signs to the people in the two rowing-boats. The men answered by waving their oars, while the women gesticulated. In spite of Véronique's opposition, Honorine opened both halves of the window; and they could hear the sound of voices above the throbbing of the motor, though they could not catch a single word.

"What does it mean?" repeated Honorine. "François and M. Stéphane!... Why did they not make for the mainland?"

"Perhaps," Véronique explained, "they were afraid of being observed and questioned on landing."

"No, they are known, especially François, who often used to go with me. Besides, the identity-papers are in the boat. No, they were waiting there, hidden behind the rock."

"But, Honorine, if they were hiding, why do they show themselves now?"

"Ah, that's just it, that's just it!... I don't understand... and it strikes me as odd... What must Corréjou and the others think?"

The two boats, of which the second was now gliding in the wake of the first, had almost stopped. All the passengers seemed to be looking round at the motor-boat, which came rapidly in their direction and slackened speed when she was level with the second boat. In this way, she continued on a line parallel with that of the two boats and fifteen or twenty yards away.

"I don't understand... I don't understand," muttered Honorine.

The motor had been cut off and the motor-boat now very slowly reached the space that separated the two fish-boats.

And suddenly the two women saw François stoop and then stand up again and draw his right arm back, as though he were going to throw something.

And at the same time Stéphane Maroux acted in the same way.

Then the unexpected, terrifying thing happened.

"Oh!" cried Véronique.

She hid her eyes for a second, but at once raised her head again and saw the hideous sight in all its horror.

Two things had been thrown across the little space, one from the bow, flung by François, the other from the stem, flung by Stéphane Maroux.

And two bursts of fire at once shot up from the two boats, followed by two whirls of smoke.

The explosions re-echoed. For a moment, nothing of what happened amid that black cloud was visible. Then the curtain parted, blown aside by the wind, and Véronique and Honorine saw the two boats swiftly sinking, while their occupants jumped into the sea.

The sight, the infernal sight, did not last long. They saw, standing on one of the buoys that marked the channel, a woman holding a child in her arms, without moving: then some motionless bodies, no doubt killed by the explosion; then two men fighting, mad perhaps. And all this went down with the boats.

A few eddies, some black specks floating on the surface; and that was all.

Honorine and Véronique, struck dumb with terror, had not uttered a single word. The thing surpassed the worst that their anguished minds could have conceived.

When it was all over, Honorine put her hand to her head and, in a hollow voice which Véronique was never to forget, said:

"My head's bursting. Oh, the poor people of Sarek! They were my friends, the friends of my childhood; and I shall never see them again... The sea never gives up its dead at Sarek: it keeps them. It has its coffins all ready: thousands and thousands of hidden coffins... Oh, my head is bursting!... I shall go mad... mad like François, my poor François!"

Véronique did not answer. She was grey in the face. With clutching fingers she clung to the balcony, gazing downwards as one gazes into an abyss into which one is about to fling oneself. What would her son do? Would he save those people, whose shouts of distress now reached her ears, would he save them without delay? One may have fits of madness; but the attacks pass away at the sight of certain things.

The motor-boat had backed at first to avoid the eddies. François and Stéphane, whose red cap and white cap were still visible, were standing in the same positions at the bow and the stern; and they held in their hands... what? The two women could not see clearly, because of the distance, what they held in their hands. It looked like two rather long sticks.

"Poles, to help them," suggested Véronique.

"Or guns," said Honorine.

The black specks were still floating. There were nine of them, the nine heads of the survivors, whose arms also the two women saw moving from time to time and whose cries for help they heard.

Some were hurriedly moving away from the motor-boat, but four were swimming towards it; and, of those four, two could not fail to reach it.

Suddenly François and Stéphane made the same movement, the movement of marksmen taking aim.

There were two flashes, followed by the sound of a single report.

The heads of the two swimmers disappeared.

"Oh, the monsters!" stammered Véronique, almost swooning and falling on her knees.

Honorine, beside her, began screaming:

"François! Franqois!"

Her voice did not carry, first because it was too weak and then the wind was in her face. But she continued:

"François! François!"

She next stumbled across the room and into the corridor, in search of something, and returned to the window, still shouting:

"François! François!"

She had ended by finding the shell which she used as a signal. But, on lifting it to her mouth, she found that she could produce only dull and indistinct sounds from it:

"Oh, curse the thing!" she cried, flinging the shell away. "I have no strength left... François! François!"

She was terrible to look at, with her hair all in disorder and her face covered with the sweat of fever. Véronique implored her:

"Please, Honorine, please!"

"But look at them, look at them!"

The motor-boat was drifting forward down below, with the two marksmen at their posts, holding their guns ready for murder.

The survivors fled. Two of them hung back in the rear.

These two were aimed at. Their heads disappeared from view.

"But look at them!" Honorine said, explosively, in a hoarse voice. "They're hunting them down! They're killing them like game!... Oh, the poor people of Sarek!..."

Another shot. Another black speck vanished.

Véronique was writhing in despair. She shook the rails of the balcony, as she might have shaken the bars of a cage in which she was imprisoned.

"Vorski! Vorski!" she groaned, stricken by the recollection of her husband. "He's Vorski's son!"

Suddenly she felt herself seized by the throat and saw, close to her own face, the distorted face of the Breton woman.

"He's your son!" spluttered Honorine. "Curse you! You are the monster's mother and you shall be punished for it!"

And she burst out laughing and stamping her feet, in an overpowering fit of hilarity.

"The cross, yes, the cross! You shall be crucified, with nails through your hands!... What a punishment, nails through your hands!"

She was mad.

Véronique released herself and tried to hold the other motionless: but Honorine, filled with malicious rage, threw her off, making her lose balance, and began to climb into the balcony.

She remained standing outside the window, lifting up her arms and once more shouting:

"François! François!"

The first floor was not so high on this side of the house, owing to the slope of the ground. Honorine jumped into the path below, crossed it, pushed her way through the shrubs that lined it and ran to the ridge of rocks which formed the cliff and overhung the sea.

She stopped for a moment, thrice called out the name of the child whom she had reared and flung herself headlong into the deep.

In the distance, the man-hunt drew to a finish.

The heads sank one by one. The massacre was completed.

Then the motor-boat with François and Stéphane on board fled towards the coast of Brittany, towards the beaches of Beg-Meil and Concameau.

Véronique was left alone on Coffin Island.

5

"FOUR WOMEN CRUCIFIED"

Véronique was left alone on Coffin Island. Until the sun sank among the clouds that seemed, on the horizon, to rest upon the sea, she did not move, but sat huddled against the window, with her head buried in her two arms resting on the sill.

The dread reality passed through the darkness of her mind like pictures which she strove not to see, but which at times became so clearly defined that she imagined herself to be living through those atrocious scenes again.

Still she sought no explanation of all this and formed no theories as to all the motives which might have thrown a light upon the tragedy. She admitted the madness of François and of Stéphane Maroux, being unable to suppose any other reasons for such actions as theirs. And, believing the two murderers to be mad, she did not even try to attribute to them any projects or definite wishes.

Moreover, Honorine's madness, of which she had, so to speak, observed the outbreak, impelled her to look upon all that had happened as provoked by a sort of mental upset to which all the people of Sarek had fallen victims. She herself at moments felt that her brain was reeling, that her ideas were fading away in a mist, that invisible ghosts were hovering around her.

She dozed off into a sleep which was haunted by these images and in which she felt so wretched that she began to sob. Also it seemed to her that she could hear a slight noise which, in her benumbed wits, assumed a hostile significance. Enemies were approaching. She opened her eyes.

A couple of yards in front of her, sitting upon its haunches, was a queer animal, covered with long mud-coloured hair and holding its fore-paws folded like a pair of arms.

It was a dog; and she at once remembered François' dog, of which Honorine had spoken as a dear, devoted, comical creature. She even remembered his name, All's Well.

As she uttered this name in an undertone, she felt an angry impulse and was almost driving away the animal endowed with such an ironical nickname. All's Well! And she thought of all the victims of the horrible nightmare, of all the dead people of Sarek, of her murdered father, of Honorine killing herself, of François going mad. All's Well, forsooth!

Meanwhile the dog did not stir. He was sitting up as Honorine had described, with his head a little on one side, one eye closed, the corners of his mouth drawn back to his ears and his arms crossed in front of him; and there was really something very like a smile flitting over his face.

Véronique now remembered: this was the manner in which All's Well displayed his sympathy for those in trouble. All's Well could not bear the sight of tears. When people wept, he sat up until they in their turn smiled and petted him.

Véronique did not smile, but she pressed him against her and said:

"No, my poor dog, all's not well; on the contrary, all's as bad as it can be. No matter: we must live, mustn't we, and we mustn't go mad ourselves like the others?"

The necessities of life obliged her to act. She went down to the kitchen, found some food and gave the dog a good share of it. Then she went upstairs again.

Night had fallen. She opened, on the first floor, the door of a bedroom which at ordinary times must have been unoccupied. She was weighed down with an immense fatigue, caused by all the efforts and violent emotions which she had undergone. She fell asleep almost at once. All's Well lay awake at the foot of her bed.

Next morning she woke late, with a curious feeling of peace and security. It seemed to her that her present life was somehow connected with her calm and placid life at Besançon. The few days of horror which she had passed fell away from her like distant events whose return she had no need to fear. The men and women who had gone under in the great horror became to her mind almost like strangers whom one has met and does not expect to see again. Her heart ceased bleeding. Her sorrow for them did not reach the depths of her soul.

It was due to the unforeseen and undisturbed rest, the consoling solitude. And all this seemed to her so pleasant that, when a steamer came and anchored on the spot of the disaster, she made no signal. No doubt yesterday, from the mainland, they had seen the flash of the explosions and heard the report of the shots. Véronique remained motionless.

She saw a boat put off from the steamer and supposed that they were going to land and explore the village. But not only did she dread an enquiry in which her son might be involved: she herself did not wish to be found, to be questioned, to have her name, her identity, her story discovered and to be brought back into the infernal circle from which she had escaped. She preferred to wait a week or two, to wait until chance brought within hailing-distance of the island some fishing-boat which could pick her up.

But no one came to the Priory. The steamer put off; and nothing disturbed her isolation.

And so she remained for three days. Fate seemed to have reconsidered its intention of making fresh assaults upon her.

She was alone and her own mistress. All's Well, whose company had done her a world of good, disappeared.

The Priory domain occupied the whole end of the island, on the site of a Benedictine abbey, which had been abandoned in the fifteenth century and gradually fallen into ruin and decay.

The house, built in the eighteenth century by a wealthy Breton ship-owner out of the materials of the old abbey and the stones of the chapel, was in no way interesting either outside or in. Véronique, for that matter, did not dare to enter any of the rooms. The memory of her father and son checked her before the closed doors.

But, on the second day, in the bright spring sunshine, she explored the park. It extended to the point of the island and, like the sward in front of the house, was studded with ruins and covered with ivy. She noticed that all the paths ran towards a steep promontory crowned with a clump of enormous oaks. When she reached the spot, she found that these oaks stood round a crescentshaped clearing which was open to the sea.

In the centre of the clearing was a cromlech with a rather short, oval table upheld by two supports of rock, which were almost square. The spot possessed an impressive magnificence and commanded a boundless view.

"The Fairies' Dolmen, of which Honorine spoke," thought Véronique. "I cannot be far from the Calvary and Maguennoc's flowers."

She walked round the megalith. The inner surface of the two uprights bore a few illegible engraved signs. But the two outer surfaces facing the sea formed as it were two smooth slabs prepared to receive an inscription; and here she saw something that caused her to shudder with anguish. On the right, deeply encrusted, was an unskilful, primitive drawing of four crosses with four female figures writhing upon them. On the left was a column of lines of writing, whose characters, inadequately carved in the stone, had been almost obliterated by the weather, or perhaps even deliberately effaced by human hands. A few words remained, however, the very words which Véronique had read on the drawing which she found beside Maguennoc's corpse:

"Four women crucified... Thirty coffins... The God-Stone which gives life or death."

Véronique moved away, staggering. The mystery was once more before her, as everywhere in the island, and she was determined to escape from it until the moment when she could leave Sarek altogether.

She took a path which started from the clearing and led past the last oak on the right. This oak appeared to have been struck by lightning, for all that remained of it was the trunk and a few dead branches.

Farther on, she went down some stone steps, crossed a little meadow in which stood four rows of menhirs and stopped suddenly with a stifled cry, a cry of admiration and amazement, before the sight that presented itself to her eyes.

"Maguennoc's flowers," she whispered.

The last two menhirs of the central alley which she was following stood like the posts of a door that opened upon the most glorious spectacle, a rectangular space, fifty yards long at most, which was reached by a short descending flight of steps and bordered by two rows of menhirs all of the same height and placed at accurately measured intervals, like the columns of a temple. The nave and side-aisles of this temple were paved with wide, irregular, broken granite flag-stones, which the grass, growing in the cracks, marked with patterns similar to those of the lead which frames the pieces of a stained-glass window.

In the middle was a small bed of flowers thronging around an ancient stone crucifix. But such flowers! Flowers which the wildest imagination or fancy never conceived, dream-flowers, miraculous flowers, flowers out of all proportion to ordinary flowers!

Véronique recognized all of them; and yet she stood dumbfounded at their size and splendour. There were flowers of many varieties, but few of each variety. It was like a nosegay made to contain every colour, every perfume and every beauty that flowers can possess.

And the strangest thing was that these flowers, which do not usually bloom at the same time and which open in successive months, were all growing and blossoming together! On one and the same day, these flowers, all perennial flowers whose time does not last much more than two or three weeks, were blooming and multiplying, full and heavy, vivid, sumptuous, proudly borne on their sturdy stems.

There were spiderworts, there were ranunculi, tiger-lilies, columbines, blood-red potentillas, irises of a brighter violet than a bishop's cassock. There were larkspurs, phlox, fuchsias, monk's-hoods, montbretias. And, above all this, to Véronique's intense emotion, above the dazzling flower-bed, standing a little higher in a narrow border around the pedestal of the crucifix, with all their blue, white and violet clusters seeming to lift themselves so as to touch the Saviour's very form, were veronicas!

She was faint with emotion. As she came nearer, she had read on a little label fastened to the pedestal these two words.

"Mother's flowers."

Véronique did not believe in miracles. She was obliged to admit that the flowers were wonderful, beyond all comparison with the flowers of our climes. But she refused to think that this anomaly was not to be explained except by supernatural causes or by magic recipes of which Maguennoc held the secret. No, there was some reason, perhaps a very simple one, of which events would afford a full explanation.

Meanwhile, amid the beautiful pagan setting, in the very centre of the miracle which it seemed to have wrought by its presence, the figure of Christ Crucified rose from the mass of flowers which offered Him their colours and their perfumes. Véronique knelt and prayed.

Next day and the day after, she returned to the Calvary of the Flowers. Here the mystery that surrounded her on every side had manifested itself in the most charming fashion; and her son played a part in it that enabled Véronique to think of him, before her own flowers, without hatred or despair.

But, on the fifth day, she perceived that her provisions were becoming exhausted; and in the middle of the afternoon she went down to the village.

There she noticed that most of the houses had been left open, so certain had their owners been, on leaving, of coming back again and taking what they needed in a second trip.

Sick at heart, she dared not cross the thresholds. There were geraniums on the window-ledges. Tall clocks with brass pendulums were ticking off the time in the empty rooms. She moved away.

In a shed near the quay, however, she saw the sacks and boxes which Honorine had brought with her in the motor-boat.

"Well," she thought, "I shan't starve. There's enough to last me for weeks; and by that time..."

She filled a basket with chocolate, biscuits, a few tins of preserved meat, rice and matches; and she was on the point of returning to the Priory, when it occurred to her that she would continue her walk to the other end of the island. She would fetch her basket on the way back.

A shady road climbed upwards on the right. The landscape seemed to be the same: the same flat stretches of moorland, without ploughed fields or pastures; the same clumps of ancient oaks. The island also became narrower, with no obstacle to block the view of the sea on either side or of the Penmarch headland in the distance.

There was also a hedge which ran from one cliff to the other and which served to enclose a property, a shabby property, with a straggling, dilapidated, tumbledown house upon it, some outhouses with patched roofs and a dirty, badly-kept yard, full of scrap-iron and stacks of firewood.

Véronique was already retracing her steps, when she stopped in alarm and surprise. It seemed to her that she heard someone moan. She listened, striving to plumb the vast silence, and once again the same sound, but this time more distinctly, reached her ears; and there were others: cries of pain, cries for help, women's cries. Then had not all the inhabitants taken to flight? She had a feeling of joy mingled with some sorrow, to know that she was not alone in Sarek, and of fear also, at the thought that events would perhaps drag her back again into the fatal cycle of death and horror.

So far as Véronique was able to judge, the noise came not from the house, but from the buildings on the right of the yard. This yard was closed with a simple gate which she had only to push and which opened with the creaking sound of wood upon wood.

The cries in the out-house at once increased in number. The people inside had no doubt heard Véronique approach. She hastened her steps.

Though the roof of the out-buildings was gone in places, the walls were thick and solid, with old arched doors strengthened with iron bars. There was a knocking against one of these doors from the inside, while the cries became more urgent:

"Help! Help!"

But there was a dispute; and another, less strident voice grated:

"Be quiet, Clémence, can't you? It may be them!"

"No, no, Gertrude, it's not! I don't hear them!... Open the door, will you? The key ought to be there."

Véronique, who was seeking for some means of entering, now saw a big key in the lock. She turned it; and the door opened.

She at once recognized the sisters Archignat, half-dressed, gaunt, evil-looking, witch-like. They were in a wash-house filled with implements; and Véronique saw at the back, lying on some straw, a third woman, who was bewailing her fate in an almost inaudible voice and who was obviously the third sister.

At that moment, one of the first two collapsed from exhaustion; and the other, whose eyes were bright with fever, seized Véronique by the arm and began to gasp:

"Did you see them, tell me?... Are they there?... How is it they didn't kill you?... They are the masters of Sarek since the others went off... And it's our turn next... We've been locked in here now for six days... Listen, it was on the day when everybody left. We three came here, to the wash-house, to fetch our linen, which was drying. And then *they* came... We didn't hear them... One never does hear them... And then, suddenly, the door was locked on us... A slam, a turn of the key... and the thing was done... We had bread, apples and best of all, brandy... We didn't do so badly... Only, were they going to come back and kill us? Was it our turn next?... Oh, my dear good lady, how we strained our ears! And how we trembled with fear!... My eldest sister's gone crazy... Hark, you can hear her raving... The other, Clémence, has borne all she can... And I... I... Gertrude..."

Gertrude had plenty of strength left, for she was twisting Véronique's arm:

"And Corréjou? He came back, didn't he, and went away again? Why didn't anyone come to look for us? It would have been easy enough: everybody knew where we were; and we called out at the least sound. So what does it all mean?"

Véronique hesitated what to reply. Still, why should she conceal the truth?

She replied:

"The two boats went down."

"What?"

"The two boats sank in view of Sarek. All on board were drowned. It was opposite the Priory... after leaving the Devil's Passage."

Véronique said no more, so as to avoid mentioning the names of François and his tutor or speaking of the part which these two had played. But Clémence now sat up, with distorted features. She had been leaning against the door and raised herself to her knees.

Gertrude murmured:

"And Honorine?"

"Honorine is dead."

"Dead!"

The two sisters both cried out at once. Then they were silent and looked at each other. The same thought struck them both. They seemed to be reflecting. Gertrude was moving her fingers as though counting. And the terror on their two faces increased.

Speaking in a very low voice, as though choking with fear, Gertrude, with her eyes fixed on Véronique, said:

"That's it... that's it... I've got the total... Do you know how many there were in the boats, without my sisters and me? Do you know? Twenty... Well, reckon it up: twenty... and Maguennoc, who was the first to die... and M. Antoine, who died afterwards... and little François and M. Stéphane, who vanished, but who are dead too... and Honorine and Marie Le Goff, both dead... So reckon it up: that makes twenty-six, twenty-six... The total's correct, isn't it?... Now take twenty-six from thirty... You understand, don't you? The thirty coffins: they have to be filled... So twenty-six from thirty... leaves four, doesn't it?"

She could no longer speak; her tongue faltered. Nevertheless the terrible syllables came from her mouth; and Véronique heard her stammering:

"Eh? Do you understand?... That leaves four... us four... the three sisters Archignat, who were kept behind and locked up...

and yourself... So—do you follow me?—the three crosses—you know, the 'four women crucified'—the number's there... it's our four selves... there's no one besides us on the island... four women..."

Véronique had listened in silence. She broke out into a slight perspiration.

She shrugged her shoulders, however:

"Well? And then? If there's no one except ourselves on the island, what are you afraid of?"

"*Them*, of course! *Them!*"

Véronique lost her patience:

"But if everybody has gone!" she exclaimed.

Gertrude took fright:

"Speak low. Suppose they heard you!"

"But who?"

"*They*, the people of old."

"The people of old?"

"Yes, those who used to make sacrifices... the people who killed men and women... to please their gods."

"But that's a thing of the past! The Druids: is that what you mean? Come, come; there are no Druids nowadays."

"Speak quietly! Speak quietly! There are still... there are evil spirits..."

"Then they're ghosts?" asked Véronique, horror-stricken by these superstitions.

"Ghosts, yes, but ghosts of flesh and blood... with hands that lock doors and keep you imprisoned... creatures that sink boats, the same, I tell you, that killed M. Antoine, Marie Le Goff and the others... that killed twenty-six of us..."

Véronique did not reply. There was no reply to make. She knew, she knew only too well who had killed M. d'Hergemont, Marie Le Goff and the others and sunk the two boats.

"What time was it when the three of you were locked in?" she asked.

"Half-past ten... We had arranged to meet Corréjou in the village at eleven."

Véronique reflected. It was hardly possible that François and Stéphane should have had time to be at half-past ten in this place and an hour later to be behind the rock from which they had darted out upon the two boats. Was it to be presumed that one or more of their accomplices were left on the island?

"In any case," she said, "you must come to a decision. You can't remain in this state. You must rest yourselves, eat something..."

The second sister had risen to her feet. She said, in the same hollow and violent tones as her sister:

"First of all, we must hide... and be able to defend ourselves against *them*."

"What do you mean?" asked Véronique.

She too, in spite of herself, felt this need of a refuge against a possible enemy.

"What do I mean? I'll tell you. The thing has been talked about a lot in the island, especially this year; and Maguennoc decided that, at the first attack, everybody should take shelter in the Priory."

"Why in the Priory?"

"Because we could defend ourselves there. The cliffs are perpendicular. You're protected on every side."

"What about the bridge?"

"Maguennoc and Honorine thought of everything. There's a little hut fifteen yards to the left of the bridge. That's the place they hit on to keep their stock of petrol in. Empty three or four cans over the bridge, strike a match... and the thing's done. You're just as in your own home. You can't be got at and you can't be attacked."

"Then why didn't they come to the Priory instead of taking to flight in the boats?"

"It was safer to escape in the boats. But we no longer have the choice."

"And when shall we start?"

"At once. It's daylight still; and that's better than the dark."

"But your sister, the one on her back?"

"We have a barrow. We've got to wheel her. There's a direct road to the Priory, without passing through the village."

Véronique could not help looking with repugnance upon the prospect of living in close intimacy with the sisters Archignat. She yielded, however, swayed by a fear which she was unable to overcome:

"Very well," she said. "Let's go. I'll take you to the Priory and come back to the village to fetch some provisions."

"Oh, you mustn't be away long!" protested one of the sisters. "As soon as the bridge is cut, we'll light a bonfire on Fairies' Dolmen Hill and they'll send a steamer from the mainland. Today the fog is coming up; but tomorrow..."

Véronique raised no objection. She now accepted the idea of leaving Sarek, even at the cost of an enquiry which would reveal her name.

They started, after the two sisters had swallowed a glass of brandy. The madwoman sat huddled in the wheel-barrow, laughing softly and uttering little sentences which she addressed to Véronique as though she wanted her to laugh too:

"We shan't meet them yet... They're getting ready..."

"Shut up, you old fool!" said Gertrude. "You'U bring us bad luck."

"Yes, yes, we shall see some sport... It'll be great fun... I have a cross of gold hung round my neck... and another cut into the skin of my head... Look!... Crosses everywhere... One ought to be comfortable on the cross... One ought to sleep well there..."

"Shut up, will you, you old fool?" repeated Gertrude, giving her a box on the ear.

"All right, all right!... But it's they who'll hit you; I see them hiding!..."

The path, which was pretty rough at first, reached the tableland formed by the west cliffs, which were loftier, but less rugged and worn away than the others. The woods were scarcer; and the oaks were all bent by the wind from the sea.

"We are coming to the heath which they call the Black Heath," said Clémence Archignat.

"*They* live underneath."

Véronique once more shrugged her shoulders:

"How do you know?"

"We know more than other people," said Gertrude. "They call us witches; and there's something in it. Maguennoc himself, who knew a great deal, used to ask our advice about anything that had to do with healing, lucky stones, the herbs you gather on St. John's Eve..."

"Mugwort and vervain," chuckled the madwoman. "They are picked at sunset."

"Or tradition too," continued Gertrude. "We know what's been said in the island for hundreds of years; and it's always been said that there was a whole town underneath, with streets and all, in which *they* used to live of old. And there are some left still, I've seen them myself."

Véronique did not reply.

"Yes, my sister and I saw one. Twice, when the June moon was six days old. He was dressed in white... and he was climbing the Great Oak to gather the sacred mistletoe... with a golden sickle. The gold glittered in the moonlight. I saw it, I tell you, and others saw it too... And he's not the only one. There are several of them left over from the old days to guard the treasure... Yes, as I say, the treasure... They say it's a stone which works miracles, which can make you die if you touch it and which makes you live if you lie down on it. That's all true, Maguennoc told us so, all perfectly true. *They* of old guard the stone, the God-Stone, and *they* are to sacrifice all of us this year... yes, all of us, thirty dead people for the thirty coffins..."

"Four women crucified," crooned the madwoman.

"And it will be soon. The sixth day of the moon is near at hand. We must be gone before *they* climb the Great Oak to gather the mistletoe. Look, you can see the Great Oak from here. It's in the wood on this side of the bridge. It stands out above the others."

"*They* are hiding behind it," said the madwoman, turning round in her wheel-barrow. "*They* are waiting for us."

"That'll do; and don't you stir... As I was saying, you see the Great Oak... over there... beyond the end of the heath. It is... it is..."

She dropped the wheel-barrow, without finishing her sentence.

"Well?" asked Clémence. "What's the matter?"

"I've seen something," stammered Gertrude. "Something white, moving about."

"Something? What do you mean? *They* don't show themselves in broad daylight! You've gone cross-eyed."

They both looked for a moment and then went on again. Soon the Great Oak was out of sight.

The heath which they were now crossing was wild and rough, covered with stones lying flat like tombstones and all pointing in the same direction.

"It's *their* burying-ground," whispered Gertrude.

They said nothing more. Gertrude repeatedly had to stop and rest. Clémence had not the strength to push the wheelbarrow. They were both of them tottering on their legs; and they gazed into the distance with anxious eyes.

They went down a dip in the ground and up again. The path joined that which Véronique had taken with Honorine on the first day; and they entered the wood which preceded the bridge.

Presently the growing excitement of the sisters Archignat made Véronique understand that they were approaching the Great Oak; and she saw it standing on a mound of earth and roots, bigger than the others and separated from them by wider intervals. She could not help thinking that it was possible for several men to hide behind that massive trunk and that perhaps several were hiding there now.

Notwithstanding their fears, the sisters had quickened their pace; and they kept their eyes turned from the fatal tree.

They left it behind. Véronique breathed more freely. All danger was passed; and she was just about to laugh at the sisters Archignat, when one of them, Clémence, spun on her heels and dropped with a moan.

At the same time something fell to the ground, something that had struck Clémence in the back. It was an axe, a stone axe.

"Oh, the thunder-stone, the thunder-stone!" cried Gertrude.

She looked up for a second, as if, in accordance with the inveterate popular belief, she believed that the axe came from the sky and was an emanation of the thunder.

But, at that moment, the madwoman, who had got out of her barrow, leapt from the ground and fell head forward. Something else had whizzed through the air. The madwoman was writhing with pain. Gertrude and Véronique saw an arrow which had been driven through her shoulder and was still vibrating.

Then Gertrude fled screaming.

Véronique hesitated. Clémence and the madwoman were rolling about on the ground. The madwoman giggled:

"Behind the oak! They're hiding... I see them."

Clémence stammered:

"Help!... Lift me up... carry me... I'm terrified!"

But another arrow whizzed past them and fell some distance farther.

Véronique now also took to her heels, urged not so much by panic, though this would have been excusable, as by the eager longing to find a weapon and defend herself. She remembered that in her father's study there was a glass case filled with guns and revolvers, all bearing the word "loaded," no doubt as a warning to François; and it was one of these that she wished to seize in order to face the enemy. She did not even turn round. She was not interested to know whether she was being pursued. She ran for the goal, the only profitable goal.

Being lighter and swifter of foot, she overtook Gertrude, who panted:

"The bridge... We must burn it... The petrol's there..."

Véronique did not reply. Breaking down the bridge was a secondary matter and would even have been an obstacle to her plan of taking a gun and attacking the enemy.

But, when she reached the bridge, Gertrude whirled about in such a way that she almost fell down the precipice. An arrow had struck her in the back.

"Help! Help!" she screamed. "Don't leave me!"

"I'm coming back," replied Véronique, who had not seen the arrow and thought that Gertrude had merely caught her foot in running. "I'm coming back, with two guns. You join me."

She imagined in her mind that, once they were both armed, they would go back to the wood and rescue the other sisters. Redoubling her efforts, therefore, she reached the wall of the estate, ran across the grass and went up to her father's study. Here she stopped to recover her breath; and, after she had taken the two guns, her heart beat so fast that she had to go back at a slower pace.

She was astonished at not meeting Gertrude, at not seeing her. She called her. No reply. And it was not till then that the thought occurred to her that Gertrude had been wounded like her sisters.

She once more broke into a run, But, when she came within sight of the bridge, she heard shrill cries pierce through the buzzing in her ears and, on coming into the open opposite the sharp ascent that led to the wood of the Great Oak, she saw...

What she saw rivetted her to the entrance to the bridge. On the other side, Gertrude was sprawling upon the ground, struggling, clutching at the roots, digging her nails into the grass and slowly, slowly, with an imperceptible and uninterrupted movement, moving along the slope.

And Véronique became aware that the unfortunate woman was fastened under the arms and round the waist by a cord which was hoisting her up, like a bound and helpless prey, and which was pulled by invisible hands above.

Véronique raised one of the guns to her shoulder. But at what enemy was she to take aim? What enemy was she to fight? Who was hiding behind the trees and stones that crowned the hill like a rampart?

Gertrude slipped between those stones, between those trees. She had ceased screaming, no doubt she was exhausted and swooning. She disappeared from sight.

Véronique had not moved. She realized the futility of any venture or enterprise. By rushing into a contest in which she was beaten beforehand she would not be able to rescue the sisters Archignat and would merely offer herself to the conqueror as a new and final victim.

Besides, she was overcome with fear. Everything was happening in accordance with the ruthless logic of facts of which she did not grasp the meaning but which all seemed connected like the links of a chain. She was afraid, afraid of those beings, afraid of those ghosts, instinctively and unconsciously afraid, afraid like the sisters Archignat, like Honorine, like all the victims of the terrible scourge.

She stooped, so as not to be seen from the Great Oak, and, bending forward and taking the shelter offered by some bramblebushes, she reached the little hut of which the sisters Archignat had spoken, a sort of summer-house with a pointed roof and coloured tiles. Half the summer-house was filled with cans of petrol.

From here she overlooked the bridge, on which no one could step without being seen by her. But no one came down from the wood.

Night fell, a night of thick fog silvered by the moon which just allowed Véronique to see the opposite side.

After an hour, feeling a little reassured, she made a first trip with two cans which she emptied on the outer beams of the bridge.

Ten times, with her ears pricked up, carrying her gun slung over her shoulder and prepared at any moment to defend herself, she repeated the journey. She poured the petrol a little at random, groping her way and yet as far as possible selecting the places where her sense of touch seemed to tell her that the wood was most rotten.

She had a box of matches, the only one that she had found in the house. She took out a match and hesitated a moment, frightened at the thought of the great light it would make:

"Even so," she reflected, "if it could be seen from the mainland... But, with this fog..."

Suddenly she struck the match and at once lit a paper torch which she had prepared by soaking it in petrol.

A great flame blazed and burnt her fingers. Then she threw the paper in a pool of petrol which had formed in a hollow and fled back to the summer-house.

The fire flared up immediately and, at one flash, spread over the whole part which she had sprinkled. The cliffs on the two islands, the strip of granite that united them, the big trees around, the hill, the wood of the Great Oak and the sea at the bottom of the ravine: these were all lit up.

"*They* know where I am... *They* are looking at the summer-house where I am hiding," thought Véronique, keeping her eyes fixed on the Great Oak.

But not a shadow passed through the wood. Not a sound of voices reached her ears. Those concealed above did not leave their impenetrable retreat.

In a few minutes, half the bridge collapsed, with a great crash and a gush of sparks. But the other half went on burning; and at every moment a piece of timber tumbled into the precipice, lighting up the depths of the night.

Each time that this happened, Véronique had a sense of relief and her overstrung nerves grew relaxed. A feeling of security crept over her and became more and more justified as the gulf between her and her enemies widened. Nevertheless she remained inside the summer-house and resolved to wait for the dawn in order to make sure that no communication was henceforth possible.

The fog increased. Everything was shrouded in darkness. About the middle of the night, she heard a sound on the other side, at the top of the hill, so far as she could judge. It was the sound of woodcutters felling trees, the regular sound of an axe biting into branches which were finally removed by breaking.

Véronique had an idea, absurd though she knew it to be, that they were perhaps building a footbridge; and she clutched her gun resolutely.

About an hour later, she seemed to hear moans and even a stifled cry, followed, for some time, by the rustle of leaves and the sound of steps coming and going. This ceased. Once more there was a great silence which seemed to absorb in space every stirring, every restless, every quivering, every living thing.

The numbness produced by the fatigue and hunger from which she was beginning to suffer left Véronique little power of thought. She remembered above all that, having failed to bring any provisions from the village, she had nothing to eat.

She did not distress herself, for she was determined, as soon as the fog lifted—and this was bound to happen before long—to light bonfires with the cans of petrol. She reflected that the best place would be at the end of the island, at the spot where the dolmen stood.

But suddenly a dreadful thought struck her: had she not left her box of matches on the bridge? She felt in her pockets but could not find it. All search was in vain.

This also did not perturb her unduly. For the time being, the feeling that she had escaped the attacks of the enemy filled her with such delight that it seemed to her that all the difficulties would disappear of their own accord.

The hours passed in this way, endlessly long hours, which the penetrating fog and the cold made more painful as the morning approached.

Then a faint gleam overspread the sky. Things emerged from the gloom and assumed their actual forms. And Véronique now saw that the bridge had collapsed throughout its length. An interval of fifty yards separated the two islands, which were only joined below by the sharp, pointed, inaccessible ridge of the cliff.

She was saved.

But, on raising her eyes to the hill opposite, she saw, right at the top of the slope, a sight that made her utter a cry of horror. Three of the nearest trees of those which crowned the hill and belonged to the wood of the Great Oak had been stripped of their lower branches. And, on the three bare trunks, with their arms strained backward, with their legs bound, under the tatters of their skirts, and with ropes drawn tight beneath their livid faces, half-hidden by the black bows of their caps, hung the three sisters Archignat.

They were crucified.

6

ALL'S WELL

Walking erect, with a stiff and mechanical gait, without turning round to look at the abominable spectacle, without recking of what might happen if she were seen, Véronique went back to the Priory.

A single aim, a single hope sustained her: that of leaving the Isle of Sarek. She had had her fill of horror. Had she seen three corpses, three women who had had their throats cut, or been shot, or even hanged, she would not have felt, as she did now, that her whole being was in revolt. But this, this torture, was too much. It involved an ignominy, it was an act of sacrilege, a damnable performance which surpassed the bounds of wickedness.

And then she was thinking of herself, the fourth and last victim. Fate seemed to be leading her towards that catastrophe as a person condemned to death is pushed on to the scaffold. How could she do other than tremble with fear? How could she fail to read a warning in the choice of the hill of the Great Oak for the torture of the three sisters Archignat?

She tried to find comfort in words:

"Everything will be explained. At the bottom of these hideous mysteries are quite simple causes, actions apparently fantastic but in reality performed by beings of the same species as myself, who behave as they do from criminal motives and in accordance with a determined plan. No doubt all this is only possible because of the war; the war brings about a peculiar state of affairs in which events of this kind are able to take place. But, all the same, there is nothing miraculous about it nor anything inconsistent with the rules of ordinary life."

Useless phrases! Vain attempts at argument which her brain found difficulty in following! In reality, upset as she was by violent nervous shocks, she came to think and feel like all those people of Sarek whose death she had witnessed. She shared their weakness, she was shaken by the same terrors, besieged by the same nightmares, unbalanced by the persistence within her of the instincts of bygone ages and lingering superstitions ever ready to rise to the surface.

Who were these invisible beings who persecuted her? Whose mission was it to fill the thirty coffins of Sarek? Who was it that was wiping out all the inhabitants of the luckless island? Who was it that lived in caverns, gathering at the fateful hours the sacred mistletoe and the herbs of St. John, using axes and arrows and crucifying women? And in view of what horrible task, of what monstrous duty? In accordance with what inconceivable plans? Were they spirits of darkness, malevolent genii, priests of a dead religion, sacrificing men, women and children to their blood-thirsty gods?

"Enough, enough, or I shall go mad!" she said, aloud. "I must go! That must be my only thought: to get away from this hell!"

But it was as though destiny were taking special pains to torture her! On beginning her search for a little food, she suddenly noticed, in her father's study, at the back of a cupboard, a drawing pinned to the wall, representing the same scene as the roll of paper which she had found near Maguennoc's body in the deserted cabin.

A portfolio full of drawings lay on one of the shelves in the cupboard. She opened it. It contained a number of sketches of the same scene, likewise in red chalk. Each of them bore above the head of the first woman the inscription, "V. d'H." One of them was signed, "Antoine d'Hergemont."

So it was her father who had made the drawing on Maguennoc's paper! It was her father who had tried in all these sketches to give the tortured woman a closer and closer resemblance to his own daughter!

"Enough, enough!" repeated Véronique. "I won't think, I won't reflect!"

Feeling very faint, she pursued her search but found nothing with which to stay her hunger.

Nor did she find anything that would allow her to light a fire at the point of the island, though the fog had lifted and the signals would certainly have been observed.

She tried rubbing two flints against each other, but she did not understand how to go to work and she did not succeed.

For three days she kept herself alive with water and wild grapes gathered among the ruins. Feverish and utterly exhausted, she had fits of weeping which nearly every time produced the sudden appearance of All's Well; and her physical suffering was such that she felt angry with the poor dog for having that ridiculous name and drove him away. All's Well, greatly surprised, squatted on his haunches farther off and began to sit up again. She felt exasperated with him, as though he could help being François' dog!

The least sound made her shake from head to foot and covered her with perspiration. What were the creatures in the Great Oak doing? From which side were they preparing to attack her? She hugged herself nervously, shuddering at the thought of falling into those monsters' hands, and could not keep herself from remembering that she was a beautiful woman and that they might be tempted by her good looks and her youth.

But, on the fourth day, a great hope uplifted her. She had found in a drawer a powerful reading-glass. Taking advantage of the bright sunshine, she focussed the rays upon a piece of paper which ended by catching fire and enabling her to light a candle.

She believed that she was saved. She had discovered quite a stock of candles, which allowed her, to begin with, to keep the precious flame alive until the evening. At eleven o'clock, she took a lantern and went towards the summer-house, intending to set fire to it. It was a fine night and the signal would be perceived from the coast.

Fearing to be seen with her light, fearing above all the tragic vision of the sisters Archignat, whose tragic Calvary was flooded by the moonlight, she took, on leaving the Priory, another road, more to the left and bordered with thickets. She walked anxiously, taking care not to rustle the leaves or stumble over the roots. When she reached open country, not far from the summer-house, she felt so tired that she had to sit down. Her head was buzzing. Her heart almost refused to beat.

She could not see the place of execution from here either. But, on turning her eyes, despite herself, in the direction of the hill, she received the impression that something resembling a white figure had moved. It was in the very heart of the wood, at the end of an avenue which intersected the thick mass of trees on that side.

The figure appeared again, in the full moonlight; and Véronique saw, notwithstanding the considerable distance, that it was the figure of a person clad in a robe and perched amid the branches of a tree which stood alone and higher than the others.

She remembered what the sisters Archignat had said:

"The sixth day of the moon is near at hand. *They* will climb the Great Oak and gather the sacred mistletoe."

And she now remembered certain descriptions which she had read in books and different stories which her father had told her; and she felt as if she were present at one of those Druid ceremonies which had appealed to her imagination as a child. But at the same time she felt so weak that she was not convinced that she was awake or that the strange sight before her eyes was real. Four other figures formed a group at the foot of the tree and raised their arms as though to catch the bough ready to fall. A light flashed above. The high-priest's golden sickle had cut off the bunch of mistletoe.

Then the high-priest climbed down from the oak; and all five figures glided along the avenue, skirted the wood and reached the top of the knoll.

Véronique, who was unable to take her haggard eyes from those creatures, bent forward and saw the three corpses hanging each from its tree of torment. At the distance where she stood, the black bows of the caps looked like crows. The figures stopped opposite the victims as though to perform some incomprehensible rite. At last the high-priest separated himself from the group and, holding the bunch of mistletoe in his hand, came down the hill and went towards the spot where the first arch of the bridge was anchored.

Véronique was almost fainting. Her wavering eyes, before which everything seemed to dance, fastened on to the glittering sickle which swung from side to side on the priest's chest, below his long white beard. What was he going to do? Though the bridge no longer existed, Véronique was convulsed with anguish. Her legs refused to carry her. She lay down on the ground, keeping her eyes fixed upon the terrifying sight.

On reaching the edge of the chasm, the priest again stopped for a few seconds. Then he stretched out the arm in which he carried the mistletoe and, preceded by the sacred plant as by a talisman which altered the laws of nature in his favour, he took a step forward above the yawning gulf.

And he walked thus in space, all white in the moonlight.

What happened Véronique did not know, nor was she quite sure what had been happening, if she had not been the sport of an hallucination, nor at what stage of the strange ceremony this hallucination had originated in her enfeebled brain.

She waited with closed eyes for events which did not take place and which, for that matter, she did not even try to foresee. But other, more real things preoccupied her mind. Her candle was going out inside the lantern. She was aware of this; and yet she had not the strength to pull herself together and return to the Priory. And she said to herself that, if the sun should not shine again within the next few days, she would not be able to light the flame and that she was lost.

She resigned herself, weary of fighting and realizing that she was defeated beforehand in this unequal contest. The only ending that was not to be endured was that of being captured. But why not abandon herself to the death that offered, death from starvation, from exhaustion? If you suffer long enough, there must come a moment when the suffering decreases and when you pass, almost unconsciously, from life, which has grown too cruel, to death, which Véronique was gradually beginning to desire.

"That's it, that's it," she murmured. "To go from Sarek or to die: it's all the same. What I want is to get away."

A sound of leaves made her open her eyes. The flame of the candle was expiring. But behind the lantern All's Well was sitting, beating the air with his fore-paws.

And Véronique saw that he carried a packet of biscuits, fastened round his neck by a string.

"Tell me your story, you dear old All's Well," said Véronique, next morning, after a good night's rest in her bedroom at the Priory. "For, after all, I can't believe that you came to look for me and bring me food of your own accord. It was an accident, wasn't it? You were wandering in that direction, you heard me crying and you came to me. But who tied that little box of biscuits round your neck? Does it mean that we have a friend in the island, a friend who takes an interest in us? Why doesn't he show himself? Speak and tell me, All's Well."

She kissed the dog and went on:

"And whom were those biscuits intended for? For your master, for François? Or for Honorine? No? Then for Monsieur Stéphane perhaps?"

The dog wagged his tail and moved towards the door. He really seemed to understand. Véronique followed him to Stéphane Maroux's room. All's Well slipped under the tutor's bed. There were three more cardboard boxes of biscuits, two packets of chocolate and two tins of preserved meat. And each parcel was supplied with a string ending in a wide loop, from which All's Well must have released his head.

"What does it mean?" asked Véronique, bewildered. "Did you put them under there? But who gave them to you? Have we actually a friend in the island, who knows us and knows Stéphane Maroux? Can you take me to him? He must live on this side of the island, because there is no means of communicating with the other and you can't have been there."

Véronique stopped to think. But, in addition to the provisions stowed away by All's Well, she also noticed a small canvas-covered satchel under the bed; and she wondered why Stéphane Maroux had hidden it. She thought that she had the right to open it and to look for some clue to the part played by the tutor, to his character, to his past perhaps, to his relations with M. d'Hergemont and François:

"Yes," she said, "it is my right and even my duty."

Without hesitation, she took a pair of big scissors and forced the frail lock.

The satchel contained nothing but a manuscript-book, with a rubber band round it. But, the moment she opened the book, she stood amazed.

On the first page was her own portrait, her photograph as a girl, with her signature in full and the inscription:

"To my friend Stéphane."

"I don't understand, I don't understand," she murmured. "I remember the photograph: I must have been sixteen. But how did I come to give it to him? I must have known him!"

Eager to learn more, she read the next page, a sort of preface worded as follows:

"Véronique, I wish to lead my life under your eyes. In undertaking the education of your son, of that son whom I ought to loathe, because he is the son of another, but whom I love because he is your son, my intention is that my life shall be in full harmony with the secret feeling that has swayed it so long. One day, I have no doubt, you will resume your place as François' mother. On that day you will be proud of him. I shall have effaced all that may survive in him of his father and I shall have exalted all the fine and noble qualities which he inherits from you. The aim is great enough for me to devote myself to it body and soul. I do so with gladness. Your smile shall be my reward."

Véronique's heart was flooded with a singular emotion. Her life was lit with a calmer radiance; and this new mystery, which she was unable to fathom any more than the others, was at least, like that of Maguennoc's flowers, gentle and comforting.

As she continued to turn the pages, she followed her son's education from day to day. She beheld the pupil's progress and the master's methods. The pupil was engaging, intelligent, studious, zealous loving, sensitive, impulsive and at the same time thoughtful. The master was affectionate, patient and borne up by some profound feeling which showed through every line of the manuscript.

And, little by little, there was a growing enthusiasm in the daily confession, which expressed itself in terms less and less restrained:

"François, my dearly-beloved son—for I may call you so, may I not?—François, your mother lives once again in you. Your eyes are pure and limpid as hers. Your soul is grave and simple as her soul. You are unacquainted with evil; and one might almost say that you are unacquainted with good, so closely is it blended with your beautiful nature."

Some of the child's exercises were copied into the book, exercises in which he spoke of his mother with passionate affection and with the persistent hope that he would soon see her again.

"We shall see her again, François," Stéphane added, "and you will then understand better what beauty means and light and the charm of life and the delight of beholding and admiring."

Next came anecdotes about Véronique, minor details which she herself did not remember or which she thought that she alone knew:

"One day, at the Tuileries—she was only sixteen—a circle was formed round her... by people who looked at her and wondered at her loveliness. Her girlfriends laughed, happy at seeing her admired..."

"Open her right hand, François. You will see a long, white scar in the middle of the palm. When she was quite a little girl, she ran the point of an iron railing into her hand..."

But the last pages were not written for the boy and had certainly not been read by him. The writer's love was no longer disguised beneath admiring phrases. It displayed itself without reserve, ardent, exalted, suffering, quivering with hope, though always respectful.

Véronique closed the book. She could read no more.

"Yes, I confess, All's Well," she said to the dog, who was already sitting up, "my eyes are wet with tears. Devoid of feminine weaknesses as I am, I will tell you what I would say to nobody else: that really touches me. Yes, I must try to recall the unknown features of the man who loves me like this... some friend of my childhood whose affection I never suspected and whose name has not left even a trace in my memory."

She drew the dog to her:

"Two kind hearts, are they not, All's Well? Neither the master nor the pupil is capable of the crimes which I saw them commit. If they are the accomplices of our enemies here, they are so in spite of themselves and without knowing it. I cannot believe in philtres and incantations and plants which deprive you of your reason. But, all the same, there is something, isn't there, you dear little dog? The boy who planted veronicas round the Calvary of Flowers and who wrote, 'Mother's flowers,' is not guilty, is he? And Honorine was right, when she spoke of a fit of madness, and he will come back to look for me, won't he? Stéphane and he are sure to come back."

The hours that went by were full of soothing quiet. Véronique was no longer lonely. The present had no terrors for her; and she had faith in the future.

Next morning, she said to All's Well, whom she had locked up to prevent his running away:

"Will you take me there now my man? Where? Why, to the friend, of course, who sent provisions to Stéphane Maroux. Come along."

All's Well was only waiting for Véronique's permission. He dashed off in the direction of the grassy sward that led to the dolmen; and he stopped half way. Véronique came up with him. He turned to the right and took a path which brought them to a huddle of ruins near the edge of the cliffs. Then he stopped again.

"Is it here?" asked Véronique.

The dog lay down flat. In front of him, at the foot of two blocks of stones leaning against each other and covered with the same growth of ivy, was a tangle of brambles with under it a little passage like the entrance to a rabbit-warren. All's Well slipped in, disappeared and then returned in search of

Véronique, who had to go back to the Priory and fetch a bill-hook to cut down the brambles.

She managed in half an hour to uncover the top step of a staircase, which she descended, feeling her way and preceded by All's Well, and which took her to a long tunnel, cut in the body of the rock and lighted on the left by little openings. She raised herself on tip-toe and saw that these openings overlooked the sea.

She walked on the level for ten minutes and then went down some more steps. The tunnel grew narrower. The openings, which all looked towards the sky, no doubt so as not to be seen from below, now gave light from both the right and the left. Véronique began to understand how All's Well was able to communicate with the other part of the island. The tunnel followed the narrow strip of cliff which joined the Priory estate to Sarek. The waves lapped the rocks on either side.

They next climbed by steps under the knoll of the Great Oak. Two tunnels opened at the top. All's Well chose the one on the left, which continued to skirt the sea.

Then on the right there were two more passages, both quite dark. The island appeared to be riddled in this way with invisible communications; and Véronique felt something clutch at her heart as she reflected that she was making for the part which the sisters Archignat had described as the enemy's subterranean domains, under the Black Heath.

All's Well trotted in front of her, turning round from time to time to see if she was following.

"Yes, yes, dear, I'm coming," she whispered, "and I am not a bit afraid: I am sure that you are leading me to a friend... a friend who has taken shelter down here. But why has he not left his shelter? Why did you not show him the way?"

The passage had been chipped smooth throughout, with a rounded ceiling and a very dry granite floor, which was amply ventilated by the openings. There was not a mark, not a scratch of any kind on the walls. Sometimes the point of a black flint projected.

"Is it here?" asked Véronique, when All's Well stopped.

The tunnel went no farther and widened into a chamber into which the light filtered more thinly through a narrower window.

All's Well seemed undecided. He listened, with his ears pricked up, standing on his hind-legs and resting his fore-paws against the end wall of the tunnel.

Véronique noticed that the wall, at this spot, was not formed throughout its length of the bare granite but consisted of an accumulation of stones of unequal size set in cement. The work evidently belonged to a different, doubtless more recent period.

A regular partition-wall had been built, closing the underground passage, which was probably continued on the other side.

She repeated:

"It's here, isn't it?"

But she said nothing more. She had heard the stifled sound of a voice.

She went up to the wall and presently gave a start. The voice was raised higher. The sounds became more distinct. Someone, a child, was singing, and she caught the words:

"And the mother said,
Rocking her child abed:
'Weep not. If you do,
The Virgin Mary weeps with you.'"

Véronique murmured:

"The song... the song..."

It was the same that Honorine had hummed at Beg-Meil. Who could be singing it now? A child, imprisoned in the island? A boyfriend of François'?

And the voice went on:
"'Babes that laugh and sing
Smiles to the Blessed Virgin bring.
Fold your hands this way
And to sweet Mary pray.'"

The last verse was followed by a silence that lasted for a few minutes. All's Well appeared to be listening with increasing attention, as though something, which he knew of, was about to take place.

Thereupon, just where he stood, there was a slight noise of stones carefully moved. All's Well wagged his tail frantically and barked, so to speak, in a whisper, like an animal that understands the danger of breaking the silence. And suddenly, about his head, one of the stones was drawn inward, leaving a fairly large aperture.

All's Well leapt into the hole at a bound, stretched himself out and, helping himself with his hind-legs, twisting and crawling, disappeared inside.

"Ah, there's Master All's Well!" said the young voice. "How are we, Master All's Well? And why didn't we come and pay our master a visit yesterday? Serious business, was it? A walk with Honorine? Oh, if you could talk, my dear old chap, what stories you would have to tell! And, first of all, look here..."

Véronique, thrilled with excitement, had knelt down against the wall. Was it her son's voice that she heard? Was she to believe that he was back and in hiding? She tried in vain to see. The wall was thick; and there was a bend in the opening. But how clearly each syllable uttered, how plainly each intonation reached her ears!

"Look here," repeated the boy, "why doesn't Honorine come to set me free? Why don't you bring her here? You managed to find me all right. And grandfather must be worried about me...

But *what* an adventure!... So you're still of the same mind, eh, old chap? All's well, isn't it? All's as well as well can be!"

Véronique could not understand. Her son—for there was no doubt that it was François—her son was speaking as if he knew nothing of what had happened. Had he forgotten? Had his memory lost every trace of the deeds done during his fit of madness?

"Yes, a fit of madness," thought Véronique, obstinately. "He was mad. Honorine was quite right: he was undoubtedly mad. And his reason has returned. Oh, François, François!..."

She listened, with all her tense being and all her trembling soul, to the words that might bring her so much gladness or such an added load of despair. Either the darkness would close in upon her more thickly and heavily than ever, or daylight was to pierce that endless night in which she had been struggling for fifteen years.

"Why, yes," continued the boy, "I agree with you, All's Well. But all the same, I should be jolly glad if you could bring me some real proof of it. On the one hand, there's no news of grandfather or Honorine, though I've given you lots of messages for them; on the other hand, there's no news of Stéphane. And that's what alarms me. Where is he? Where have they locked him up? Won't he be starving by now? Come, All's Well, tell me: where did you take the biscuits yesterday?... But, look here, what's the matter with you? You seem to have something on your mind. What are you looking at over there? Do you want to go away? No? Then what is it?"

The boy stopped. Then, after a moment, in a much lower voice:

"Did you come with someone?" he asked. "Is there anybody behind the wall?"

The dog gave a dull bark. Then there was a long pause, during which François also must have been listening.

Véronique's emotion was so great that it seemed to her that François must hear the beating of her heart.

He whispered:

"Is that you, Honorine?"

There was a fresh pause; and he continued:

"Yes, I'm sure it's you... I can hear you breathing... Why don't you answer?"

Véronique was carried away by a sudden impulse. Certain gleams of light had flashed upon her mind since she had understood that Stéphane was a prisoner, no doubt like François, therefore a victim of the enemy; and all sorts of vague suppositions flitted through her brain. Besides, how could she resist the appeal of that voice? Her son was asking her a question... her son!

"François... François!" she stammered.

"Ah," he said, "there's an answer! I knew it! Is it you, Honorine?"

"No, François," she said.

"Then who is it?"

"A friend of Honorine's."

"I don't know you, do I?"

"No... but I am your friend."

He hesitated. Was he on his guard?

"Why didn't Honorine come with you?"

Véronique was not prepared for this question, but she at once realized that, if the involuntary suppositions that were forcing themselves upon her were correct, the boy must not yet be told the truth.

She therefore said:

"Honorine came back from her journey, but has gone away again."

"Gone to look for me?"

"That's it, that's it," she said, quickly. "She thought that you had been carried away from Sarek and your tutor with you."

"But grandfather?"

"He's gone too: so have all the inhabitants of the island."

"Ah! The old story of the coffins and the crosses, I suppose?"

"Just so. They thought that your disappearance meant the beginning of the disasters; and their fear made them take to flight."

"But you, madame?"

"I have known Honorine for a long time. I came from Paris with her to take a holiday at Sarek. I have no reason to go away. All these superstitions have no terrors for me."

The child was silent. The improbability and inadequacy of the replies must have been apparent to him: and his suspicions increased in consequence. He confessed as much, frankly:

"Listen, madame, there's something I must tell you. It's ten days since I was imprisoned in this cell. During the first part of that time, I saw and heard nobody. But, since the day before yesterday, every morning a little wicket opens in the middle of my door and a woman's hand comes through and gives a fresh supply of water. A woman's hand... so... you see?"

"So you want to know if that woman is myself?"

"Yes, I am obliged to ask you."

"Would you recognize that woman's hand?"

"Yes, it is lean and bony, with a yellow arm."

"Here's mine," said Véronique. "It can pass where All's Well did."

She pulled up her sleeve; and by flexing her bare arm she easily passed it through.

"Oh," said François, at once, "that's not the hand I saw!"

And he added, in a lower voice:

"How pretty this one is!"

Suddenly Véronique felt him take it in his own with a quick movement; and he exclaimed:

"Oh, it can't be true, it can't be true!"

He had turned her hand over and was separating the fingers so as to uncover the palm entirely. And he whispered:

"The scar!... It's there!... The white scar!..."

Then Véronique became greatly agitated. She remembered Stéphane Maroux's diary and certain details set down by him which François must have heard. One of these details was this scar, which recalled an old and rather serious injury.

She felt the boy's lips pressed to her hand, first gently and then with passionate ardour and a great flow of tears, and heard him stammering:

"Oh, mother, mother darling!... My dear, dear mother!..."

7

FRANÇOIS AND STÉPHANE

Long the mother and son remained thus, kneeling against the wall that divided them, yet as close together as though they were able to see each other with their frenzied eyes and to mingle their tears and kisses. They spoke both at once, asking each other questions and answering them at random. They were in a transport of delight. The life of each flowed over into the other's life and became swallowed up in it. No power on earth could now dissolve their union or break the bonds of love and confidence which unite mothers and sons.

"Yes, All's Well, old man," said Franqois, "you may sit up as much and as long as you like. We are really crying this time... and you will be the first to get tired, for one doesn't mind shedding such tears as these, does one, mother?"

As for Véronique, her mind retained not a vestige of the terrible visions which had dismayed it. Her son a murderer, her son killing and massacring people: she no longer admitted any of that. She did not even admit the excuse of madness. Everything would be explained in some other way which she was not even in a hurry to understand. She thought only of her son. He was there. His eyes saw her through the wall. His heart beat against hers. He lived; and he was the same gentle, affectionate, pure and charming child that her maternal dreams had pictured.

"My son, my son!" she kept on repeating, as though she could not utter those marvellous words often enough. "My son, it's you, it's you! I believed you dead, a thousand times dead, more dead than it is possible to be... And you are alive! And you are here! And I am touching you! O Heaven, can it be true! I have a son... and my son is alive!..."

And he, on his side, took up the refrain with the same passionate fervour:

"Mother! Mother! I have waited for you so long!... To me you were not dead, but it was so sad to be a child and to have no mother... to see the years go by and to waste them in waiting for you."

For an hour they talked at random, of the past, of the present, of a hundred subjects which at first appeared to them the most interesting things in the world and which they forthwith dropped to ask each other more questions and to try to know each other a little better and to enter more deeply into the secret of their lives and the privacy of their souls.

It was François who first attempted to impart some little method to their conversation:

"Listen, mother; we have so much to say to each other that we must give up trying to say it all today and even for days and days. Let us speak now of what is essential and in the fewest possible words, for we have perhaps not much time before us."

"What do you mean?" said Véronique, instantly alarmed. "I have no intention of leaving you!"

"But, mother, if we are not to leave each other, we must first be united. Now there are many obstacles to be overcome, even if it were only the wall that separates us. Besides, I am very closely watched; and I may be obliged at any moment to send you away, as I do All's Well, at the first sound of footsteps approaching."

"Watched by whom?"

"By those who fell upon Stéphane and me on the day when we discovered the entrance to these caves, under the heath on the table-land, the Black Heath."

"Did you see them?"

"No, it was too dark."

"But who are they? Who are those enemies?"

"I don't know."

"You suspect, of course?"

"The Druids?" he said, laughing. "The people of old of whom the legends speak? Rather not! Ghosts? Not that either. They were just simply creatures of today, creatures of flesh and blood."

"They live down here, though?"

"Most likely."

"And you took them by surprise?"

"No, on the contrary. They seemed even to be expecting us and to be lying in wait for us. We had gone down a stone staircase and a very long passage, lined with perhaps eighty caves, or rather eighty cells. The doors, which were of wood, were open; and the cells overlooked the sea. It was on the way back, as we were going up the staircase again in the dark, that we were seized from one side, knocked down, bound, blindfolded and gagged. The whole thing did not take a minute. I suspect that we were carried back to the end of the long passage. When I succeeded in removing my bonds and my bandage, I found that I was locked in one of the cells, probably the last in the passage; and I have been here ten days."

"My poor darling, how you must have suffered!"

"No, mother, and in any case not from hunger. There was a whole stack of provisions in one corner and a truss of straw in another to lie on. So I waited quietly."

"For whom?"

"You promise not to laugh, mother?"

"Laugh at what, dear?"

"At what I'm going to tell you?"

"How can you think...?"

"Well, I was waiting for someone who had heard of all the stories of Sarek and who promised grandfather to come."

"But who was it?"

The boy hesitated:

"No, I am sure you will make fun of me, mother, I'll tell you later. Besides, he never came... though I thought for a moment... Yes, fancy, I had managed to remove two stones from the wall and to open this hole of which my gaolers evidently didn't know. All of a sudden, I heard a noise, someone scratching..."

"It was All's Well?"

"It was Master All's Well coming by the other road. You can imagine the welcome he received! Only what astonished me was that nobody followed him this way, neither Honorine nor grandfather. I had no pencil or paper to write to them; but, after all, they had only to follow All's Well."

"That was impossible," said Véronique, "because they believed you to be far away from Sarek, carried off no doubt, and because your grandfather had left."

"Just so: why believe anything of the sort? Grandfather knew, from a lately discovered document, where we were, for it was he who told us of the possible entrance to the underground passage. Didn't he speak to you about it?"

Véronique had been very happy in listening to her son's story. As he had been carried off and imprisoned, he was not the atrocious monster who had killed M. d'Hergemont, Marie Le Goff, Honorine and Correjou and his companions. The truth which she had already vaguely surmised now assumed a more definite form and, though still thickly shrouded, was visible in its essential part. François was not guilty. Someone had put on his clothes and impersonated him, even as someone else, in the semblance of Stéphane, had pretended to be

Stéphane. Ah, what did all the rest matter, the improbabilities and inconsistencies, the proofs and certainties! Véronique did not even think about it. The only thing that counted was the innocence of her beloved son.

And so she still refused to tell him anything that would sadden him and spoil his happiness; and she said:

"No, I have not seen your grandfather. Honorine wanted to prepare him for my visit, but things happened so hurriedly..."

"And you were left alone on the island, poor mother? So you hoped to find me here?"

"Yes," she said, after a moment's hesitation.

"Alone, but with All's Well, of course."

"Yes. I hardly paid any attention to him during the first days. It was not until this morning that I thought of following him."

"And where does the road start from that brought you here?"

"It's an underground passage the outlet of which is concealed between two stones near Maguennoc's garden."

"What! Then the two islands communicate?"

"Yes, by the cliff underneath the bridge."

"How strange! That's what neither Stéphane not I guessed, nor anybody else, for that matter... except our dear All's Well, when it came to finding his master."

He interrupted himself and then whispered:

"Hark!"

But, the next moment, he said:

"No, it's not that yet. Still, we must hurry."

"What am I to do?"

"It's quite simple, mother. When I made this hole, I saw that it could be widened easily enough, if it were possible also to take out the three or four stones next to it. But these are firmly fixed; and we should need an implement of some kind."

"Well, I'll go and..."

"Yes, do, mother. Go back to the Priory. To the left of the house, in a basement, is a sort of workshop where Maguennoc kept his garden-tools. You will find a small pick-axe there, with a very short handle. Bring it me in the evening. I will work during the night; and tomorrow morning I shall give you a kiss, mother."

"Oh, it sounds too good to be true!"

"I promise you I shall. Then all that we shall have to do will be to release Stéphane."

"Your tutor? Do you know where he is shut up?"

"I do almost know. According to the particulars which grandfather gave us, the underground passages consist of two floors one above the other; and the last cell of each is fitted as a prison. I occupy one of them. Stéphane should occupy the other, below mine. What worries me..."

"What is it?"

"Well, it's this: according to grandfather again, these two cells were once torture-chambers... 'death chambers' was the word grandfather used."

"Oh, but how alarming!"

"Why alarm yourself, mother? You see that they are not thinking of torturing me. Only, on the off chance and not knowing what sort of fate was in store for Stéphane, I sent him something to eat by All's Well, who is sure to have found a way of getting to him."

"No," she said, "All's Well did not understand."

"How do you know, mother?"

"He thought you were sending him to Stéphane Maroux's room and he heaped it all under the bed."

"Oh!" said the boy, anxiously. "What can have become of Stéphane?" And he at once added, "You see, mother, that we must hurry, if we would save Stéphane and save ourselves."

"What are you afraid of?"

"Nothing, if you act quickly."

"But still..."

"Nothing, I assure you. I feel certain that we shall get the better of every obstacle."

"And, if any others present themselves... dangers which we cannot foresee?..."

"It is then," said François, laughing, "that the man whom I am expecting will come and protect us."

"You see, my darling, you yourself admit the need of assistance..."

"Why, no, mother, I am trying to ease your mind, but nothing will happen. Come, how would you have a son who has just found his mother lose her again at once? It isn't possible. In real life, may be... but we are not living in real life. We are absolutely living in a romance; and in romances things always come right. You ask All's Well. It's so, old chap, isn't it: we shall win and be united and live happy ever after? That's what you think, All's Well? Then be off, old chap, and take mother with you. I'm going to fill up the hole, in case they come and inspect my cell. And be sure not to try and come in when the hole is stopped, eh, All's Well? That's when the danger is. Go, mother, and don't make a noise when you come back."

Véronique was not long away. She found the pick-axe; and, forty minutes after, brought it and managed to slip it into the cell.

"No one has been yet," said François, "but they are certain to come soon and you had better not stay. I may have a night's work before me, especially as I shall have to stop because of likely visits. So I shall expect you at seven o'clock tomorrow... By the way, talking of Stéphane: I have been thinking it over. Some noises which I heard just now confirmed my notion that he is shut up more or less underneath me. The opening that lights my cell is too narrow for me to pass through. Is there a fairly wide window at the place where you are now?"

"No, but it can be widened by removing the little stones round it."

"Capital. You will find in Maguennoc's workshop a bamboo ladder, with iron hooks to it, which you can easily bring with you tomorrow morning. Next, take some provisions and some rugs and leave them in a thicket at the entrance to the tunnel."

"What for, darling?"

"You'll see. I have a plan. Goodbye, mother. Have a good night's rest and pick up your strength. We may have a hard day before us."

Véronique followed her son's advice. The next morning, full of hope, she once more took the road to the cell. This time, All's Well, reverting to his instincts of independence, did not come with her.

"Keep quite still, mother," said François, in so low a whisper that she could scarcely hear him. "I am very closely watched; and I think there's someone walking up and down in the passage. However, my work is nearly done; the stones are all loosened. I shall have finished in two hours. Have you the ladder?"

"Yes."

"Remove the stones from the window... that will save time... for really I am frightened about Stéphane... And be sure not to make a noise..."

Véronique moved away.

The window was not much more than three feet from the floor: and the small stones, as she had supposed, were kept in place only by their own weight and the way in which they were arranged. The opening which she thus contrived to make was very wide; and she easily passed the ladder which she had brought with her through and secured it by its iron hooks to the lower ledge.

She was some hundred feet or so above the sea, which lay all white before her, guarded by the thousand reefs of Sarek. But she could not see the foot of the cliff, for there was under the window a slight projection of granite which jutted forward and on which the ladder rested instead of hanging perpendicularly.

"That will help François," she thought.

Nevertheless, the danger of the undertaking seemed great; and she wondered whether she herself ought not to take the risk, instead of her son, all the more so as François might be mistaken, as Stéphane's cell was perhaps not there at all and as perhaps there was no means of entering it by a similar opening. If so, what a waste of time! And what a useless danger for the boy to run!

At that moment she felt so great a need of self-devotion, so intense a wish to prove her love for him by direct action, that she formed her resolution without pausing to reflect, even as one performs immediately a duty which there is no question of not performing. Nothing deterred her: neither her inspection of the ladder, whose hooks were not wide enough to grip the whole thickness of the ledge, nor the sight of the precipice, which gave an impression that everything was about to fall away from under her. She had to act; and she acted.

Pinning up her skirt, she stepped across the wall, turned round, supported herself on the ledge, groped with her foot in space and found one of the rungs. Her whole body was trembling. Her heart was beating furiously, like the clapper of a bell. Nevertheless she had the mad courage to catch hold of the two uprights and go down.

It did not take long. She knew that there were twenty rungs in all. She counted them. When she reached the twentieth, she looked to the left and murmured, with unspeakable joy:

"Oh, François... my darling!"

She had seen, three feet away at most, a recess, a hollow which appeared to be the entrance to a cavity cut in the rock itself.

"Stéphane... Stéphane," she called, but in so faint a voice that Stéphane Maroux, if he were there, could not hear her.

She hesitated a few seconds, but her legs were giving way and she no longer had the strength either to climb up again or to remain hanging where she was. Taking advantage of a few irregularities in the rock and thus shifting the ladder, at the risk of unhooking it, she succeeded, by a sort of miracle of which she was quite aware, in catching hold of a flint which projected from the granite and setting foot in the cave. Then, with fierce energy, she made one supreme effort and, recovering her balance with a jerk, she entered.

She at once saw someone, fastened with cords, lying on a truss of straw.

The cave was small and not very deep, especially in the upper portion, which pointed towards the sky rather than the sea and which must have looked, from a distance, like a mere fold in the cliff. There was no projection to bound it at the edge. The light entered freely.

Véronique went nearer. The man did not move. He was asleep.

She bent over him; though she did not recognize him for certain, it seemed to her that a memory was emerging from that dim past in which all the faces of our childhood gradually fade away. This one was surely not unknown to her: a gentle visage, with regular features, fair hair flung well back, a broad, white forehead and a slightly feminine countenance, which reminded Véronique of the charming face of a convent friend who had died before the war.

She deftly unfastened the bonds with which the wrists were fastened together.

The man, without waking immediately, stretched his arms, as though submitting himself to a familiar operation, not effected for the first time, which did not necessarily interfere with his sleep. Presumably he was released like this at intervals, perhaps in order to eat and at night, for he ended by muttering:

"So early?... But I'm not hungry... and it's still light!"

This last reflection astonished the man himself. He opened his eyes and at once sat up where he lay, so that he might see the person who was standing in front of him, no doubt for the first time in broad daylight.

He was not greatly surprised, for the reason that the reality could not have been manifest to him at once. He probably thought that he was the sport of a dream or an hallucination; and he said, in an undertone:

"Véronique... Véronique..."

She felt a little embarrassed by his gaze, but finished releasing his bonds; and, when he distinctly felt her hand on his own hands and on his imprisoned limbs, he understood the wonderful event which her presence implied and he said, in a faltering voice:

"You! You!... Can it be?... Oh, speak just one word, just one!... Can it possibly be you?" He continued, almost to himself, "Yes, it is she... it is certainly she... She is here!" And, anxiously, aloud, "You... at night... on the other nights... it wasn't you who came then? It was another woman, wasn't it? An enemy?... Oh, forgive me for asking you!... It's because... because I don't understand... How did you come here?"

"I came this way," she said, pointing to the sea.

"Oh," he said, "how wonderful!"

He stared at her with dazed eyes, as he might have stared at some vision descended from Heaven; and the circumstances were so unusual that he did not think of suppressing the eagerness of his gaze.

She repeated, utterly confused:

"Yes, this way... François suggested it."

"I did not mention him," he said, "because, with you here, I felt sure that he was free."

"Not yet," she said, "but he will be in an hour."

A long pause ensued. She interrupted it to conceal her agitation:

"He will be free... You shall see him... But we must not frighten him: there are things which he doesn't know."

She perceived that he was listening not to the words uttered but to the voice that uttered them and that this voice seemed to plunge him into a sort of ecstasy, for he was silent and smiled. She thereupon smiled too and questioned him, thus obliging him to answer:

"You called me by my name at once. So you knew me? I also seem to... Yes, you remind me of a friend of mine who died."

"Madeleine Ferrand?"

"Yes, Madeleine Ferrand."

"Perhaps I also remind you of her brother, a shy schoolboy who used often to visit the parlour at the convent and who used to look at you from a distance."

"Yes, yes," she declared. "I remember. We even spoke to each other sometimes; you used to blush. Yes, that's it: your name was Stéphane. But how do you come to be called Maroux?"

"Madeleine and I were not children of the same father."

"Ah," she said, "that was what misled me!"

She gave him her hand:

"Well, Stéphane," she said, "as we are old friends and have renewed our acquaintance, let us put off all our remembrances until later. For the moment, the most urgent matter is to get away. Have you the strength?"

"The strength, yes: I have not had such a very bad time. But how are we to go from here?"

"By the same road by which I came, a ladder communicating with the upper passage of cells."

He was now standing up:

"You had the courage, the pluck?" he asked, at last realizing what she had dared to do.

"Oh, it was not very difficult!" she declared. "François was so anxious! He maintained that you were both occupying old torture-chambers... death-chambers..."

It was as though these words aroused him violently from a dream and made him suddenly see that it was madness to converse in such circumstances.

"Go away!" he cried. "François is right! Oh, if you knew the risk you are running. Please, please go!"

He was beside himself, as though convulsed by the thought of an immediate peril. She tried to calm him, but he entreated her:

"Another second may be your undoing. Don't stay here... I am condemned to death and to the most terrible death. Look at the ground on which we are standing, this sort of floor... But it's no use talking about it. Oh, please do go!"

"With you," she said.

"Yes, with me. But save yourself first."

She resisted and said, firmly:

"For us both to be saved, Stéphane, we must above all things remain calm. What I did just now we can do again only by calculating all our actions and controlling our excitement. Are you ready?"

"Yes," he said, overcome by her magnificent confidence.

"Then follow me."

She stepped to the very edge of the precipice and leant forward:

"Give me your hand," she said, "to help me keep my balance."

She turned round, flattened herself against the cliff and felt the surface with her free hand.

Not finding the ladder, she leant outward slightly.

The ladder had become displaced. No doubt, when Véronique, perhaps with too abrupt a movement, had set foot in the cave, the iron hook of the right-hand upright had slipped and the ladder, hanging only by the other hook, had swung like a pendulum.

The bottom rungs were now out of reach.

8

ANGUISH

Had Véronique been alone, she would have yielded to one of those moods of despondency which her nature, brave though it was, could not escape in the face of the unrelenting animosity of fate. But in the presence of Stéphane, who she felt to be the weaker and who was certainly exhausted by his captivity, she had the strength to restrain herself and announce, as though mentioning quite an ordinary incident:

"The ladder has swung out of our reach."

Stéphane looked at her in dismay:

"Then... then we are lost!"

"Why should we be lost?" she asked, with a smile.

"There is no longer any hope of getting away."

"What do you mean? Of course there is. What about François?"

"François?"

"Certainly. In an hour at most, François will have made his escape; and, when he sees the ladder and the way I came, he will call to us. We shall hear him easily. We have only to be patient."

"To be patient!" he said, in terror. "To wait for an hour! But they are sure to be here in less than that. They keep a constant watch."

"Well, we will manage somehow."

He pointed to the wicket in the door:

"Do you see that wicket?" he said. "They open it each time. They will see us through the grating."

"There's a shutter to it. Let's close it."

"They will come in."

"Then we won't close it and we'll keep up our confidence, Stéphane."

"I'm frightened for you, not for myself."

"You mustn't be frightened either for me or for yourself... If the worst comes to the worst, we are able to defend ourselves," she added, showing him a revolver which she had taken from her father's rack of arms and carried on her ever since.

"Ah," he said, "what I fear is that we shall not even be called upon to defend ourselves! They have other means."

"What means?"

He did not answer. He had flung a quick glance at the floor; and Véronique for a moment examined its curious structure.

All around, following the circumference of the walls, was the granite itself, rugged and uneven. But outlined in the granite was a large square. They could see, on each of the four sides, the deep crevice that divided it from the rest. The timbers of which it consisted were worn and grooved, full of cracks and gashes, but nevertheless massive and powerful. The fourth side almost skirted the edge of the precipice, from which it was divided by eight inches at most.

"A trap-door?" she asked, with a shudder.

"No, not that," he said. "It would be too heavy."

"Then what?"

"I don't know. Very likely it is nothing but a remnant of some past contrivance which no longer works. Still..."

"Still what?"

"Last night... or rather this morning there was a creaking sound down below there. It seemed to suggest attempts, but they stopped at once... it's such a long time since!... No, the thing no longer works and they can't make use of it."

"Who's *they*?"

Without waiting for his answer, she continued:

"Listen, Stéphane, we have a few minutes before us, perhaps fewer than we think. François will be free at any moment now and will come to our rescue. Let us make the most of the interval and tell each other the things which both of us ought to know. Let us discuss matters quietly. We are threatened with no immediate danger; and the time will be well employed."

Véronique was pretending a sense of security which she did not feel. That François would make his escape she refused to doubt; but who could tell that the boy would go to the window and notice the hook of the hanging ladder? On failing to see his mother, would he not rather think of following the underground tunnel and running to the Priory?

However, she mastered herself, feeling the need of the explanation for which she had asked, and, sitting down on a granite projection which formed a sort of bench, she at once began to tell Stéphane the events which she had witnessed and in which she had played a leading part, from the moment when her investigations led her to the deserted cabin containing Maguennoc's dead body.

Stéphane listened to the terrifying narrative without attempting to interrupt her but with an alarm marked by his gestures of abhorrence and the despairing expression of his face. M. d'Hergemont's death in particular seemed to crush him, as did Honorine's. He had been greatly attached to both of them.

"There, Stéphane," said Véronique, when she had described the anguish which she suffered after the execution of the sisters Archignat, the discovery of the underground passage and her interview with François. "That is all that I need absolutely tell you. I thought that you ought to know what I have kept from François, so that we may fight our enemies together."

He shook his head:

"Which enemies?" he said. "I, too, in spite of your explanations, am asking the very question which you asked me. I have a feeling that we are flung into the midst of a great tragedy which has continued for years, for centuries, and in which we have begun to play our parts only at the moment of the crisis, at the moment of the terrific cataclysm prepared by generations of men. I may be wrong. Perhaps there is nothing more than a disconnected series of sinister, weird and horrible coincidences amid which we are tossed from side to side, without being able to appeal to any other reasons than the whim of chance. In reality I know no more than you do. I am surrounded by the same obscurity, stricken by the same sorrows and the same losses. It's all just insanity, extravagant convulsions, unprecedent shocks, the crimes of savages, the fury of the barbaric ages."

Véronique agreed:

"Yes, of the barbaric ages; and that is what baffles me most and impresses me so much! What is the connection between the present and the past, between our persecutors of today and the men who lived in these caves in days of old and whose actions are prolonged into our own time, in a manner so impossible to understand? To what do they all refer, those legends of which I know nothing except from Honorine's delirium and the distress of the sisters Archignat?"

They spoke low, with their ears always on the alert. Stéphane listened for sounds in the corridor, Véronique concentrated her attention on the cliff, in the hope of hearing François' signal.

"They are very complicated legends," said Stéphane, "very obscure traditions in which we must abandon any attempt to distinguish between what is superstition and what might be truth. Out of this jumble of old wives' tales, the most that we can disentangle is two sets of ideas, those referring to the prophecy of the thirty coffins and those relating to the existence of a treasure, or rather of a miraculous stone."

"Then they take as a prophecy," said Véronique, "the words which I read on Maguennoc's drawing and again on the Fairies' Dolmen?"

"Yes, a prophecy which dates back to an indeterminate period and which for centuries has governed the whole history and the whole life of Sarek. The belief has always prevailed that a day would come when, within a space of twelve months, the thirty principal reefs which surround the island and which are called the thirty coffins would receive their thirty victims, who were to die a violent death, and that those thirty victims would include four women who were to die crucified. It is an established and undisputed tradition, handed down from father to son: and everybody believes in it. It is expressed in the line and part of a line inscribed on the Fairies' Dolmen: 'Four women crucified,' and 'For thirty coffins victims thirty times!'"

"Very well; but people have gone on living all the same, normally and peaceably. Why did the outburst of terror suddenly take place this year?"

"Maguennoc was largely responsible. Maguennoc was a fantastic and rather mysterious person, a mixture of the wizard and the bone-setter, the healer and the charlatan, who had studied the stars in their courses and whom people liked to consult about the most remote events of the past as well as the future. Now Maguennoc announced not long ago that 1917 would be the fateful year."

"Why?"

"Intuition perhaps, presentiment, divination, or subconscious knowledge: you can choose any explanation that you please. As for Maguennoc, who did not despise the practices of the most antiquated magic, *he* would tell you that he knew it from the flight of a bird or the entrails of a fowl. However, his prophecy was based on something more serious. He pretended, quoting evidence collected in his childhood among the old people of Sarek, that, at the beginning of the last century, the first line of the inscription on the Fairies' Dolmen was not yet obliterated and that it formed this, which would rhyme with 'Four women shall be crucified on tree:' 'In Sarek's isle, in year fourteen and three.' The year fourteen and three is the year seventeen; and the prediction became more impressive for Maguennoc and his friends of late years, because the total number was divided into two numbers and the war broke out in 1914. From that day, Maguennoc grew more and more important and more and more sure of the truth of his previsions. For that matter, he also grew more and more anxious; and he even announced that his death, followed by the death of M. d'Hergemont, would give the signal for the catastrophe. Then the year 1917 arrived and produced a genuine terror in the island. The events were close at hand."

"And still," said Véronique, "and still it was all absurd."

"Absurd, yes; but it all acquired a curiously disturbing significance on the day when Maguennoc was able to compare the scraps of prophecy engraved on the dolmen with the complete prophecy."

"Then he succeeded in doing so?"

"Yes. He discovered *under* the abbey ruins, in a heap of stones which had formed a sort of protecting chamber round it, an old worn and tattered missal, which had a few of its pages in good condition, however, and one in particular, the one which you saw, or rather of which you saw a copy in the deserted cabin."

"A copy made by my father?"

"By your father, as were all those in the cupboard in his study. M. d'Hergemont, you must remember, was fond of drawing, of painting water-colours. He copied the illuminated page, but of the prophecy that accompanied the drawing he reproduced only the words inscribed on the Fairies' Dolmen."

"How do you account for the resemblance between the crucified woman and myself?"

"I never saw the original, which Maguennoc gave to M. d'Hergemont and which your father kept jealously in his room. But M. d'Hergemont maintained that the resemblance was there. In any case, he accentuated it in his drawing, in spite of himself, remembering all that you had suffered... and through his fault, he said."

"Perhaps," murmured Véronique, "he was also thinking of the other prophecy that was once made to Vbrski: 'You will perish by the hand of a friend and your wife will be crucified.' So I suppose the strange coincidence struck him... and even made him write the initials of my maiden name, 'V. d'H.', at the top." And she added, "And all this happened in accordance with the wording of the inscription..."

They were both silent. How could they do other than think of that inscription, of the words written ages ago on the pages of the missal and on the stone of the dolmen? If destiny had as yet provided only twenty-seven victims for the thirty coffins of Sarek, were the last three not there, ready to complete the sacrifice, all three imprisoned, all three captive and in the power of the sacrificial murderers? And if, at the top of the knoll, near the Grand Oak, there were as yet but three crosses, would the fourth not soon be prepared, to receive a fourth victim?

"François is a very long time," said Véronique, presently.

She went to the edge and looked over. The ladder had not moved and was still out of reach.

"The others will soon be coming to my door," said Stéphane. "I am surprised that they haven't been yet."

But they did not wish to confess their mutual anxiety; and Véronique put a further question, in a calm voice:

"And the treasure? The God-Stone?"

"That riddle is hardly less obscure," said Stéphane, "and also depends entirely on the last line of the inscription: 'The

God-Stone which gives life or death.' What is this God-Stone? Tradition says that it is a miraculous stone; and, according to M. d'Hergemont, this belief dates back to the remotest periods. People at Sarek have always had faith in the existence of a stone capable of working wonders. In the middle ages they used to bring puny and deformed children and lay them on the stone for days and nights together, after which the children got up strong and healthy. Barren women resorted to this remedy with good results, as did old men, wounded men and all sorts of degenerates. Only it came about that the place of pilgrimage underwent changes, the stone, still according to tradition, having been moved and even, according to some, having disappeared. In the eighteenth century, people venerated the Fairies' Dolmen and used still sometimes to expose scrofulous children there."

"But," said Véronique, "the stone also had harmful properties, for it gave death as well as life?"

"Yes, if you touched it without the knowledge of those whose business it was to guard it and keep it sacred. But in this respect the mystery becomes still more complicated, for there is the question also of a precious stone, a sort of fantastic gem which shoots out flames, burns those who wear it and makes them suffer the tortures of the damned."

"That's what happened to Maguennoc, by Honorine's account," said Véronique.

"Yes," replied Stéphane, "but here we are entering upon the present. So far I have been speaking of the fabled past, the two legends, the prophecy and the God-Stone. Maguennoc's adventure opens up the period of the present day, which for that matter is hardly less obscure than the ancient period. What happened to Maguennoc? We shall probably never know. He had been keeping in the background for a week, gloomy and doing no work, when suddenly he burst into M. d'Hergemont's study roaring, 'I've touched it! I'm done for! I've touched it!...

I took it in my hand... It burnt me like fire, but I wanted to keep it... Oh, it's been gnawing into my bones for days! It's hell, it's hell!' And he showed us the palm of his hand. It was all burnt, as though eaten up with cancer. We tried to dress it for him, but he seemed quite mad and kept rambling on, 'I'm the first victim... the fire will go to my heart... And after me the others' turn will come...' That same evening, he cut off his hand with a hatchet. And a week later, after infecting the whole island with terror, he went away."

"Where did he go to?"

"To the village of Le Faouet, on a pilgrimage to the Chapel of St. Barbe, near the place where you found his dead body."

"Who killed him, do you think?"

"Undoubtedly one of the creatures who used to correspond by means of signs written along the road, one of the creatures who live hidden in the cells and who are pursuing some purpose which I don't understand."

"Those who attacked you and François, therefore?"

"Yes; and immediately afterwards, having stolen and put on our clothes, played the parts of François and myself."

"With what object?"

"To enter the Priory more easily and then, if their attempt failed, to balk enquiry."

"But haven't you seen them since they have kept you here?"

"I have seen only a woman, or rather caught a glimpse of her. She comes at night. She brings me food and drink, unties my hands, loosens the fastenings round my legs a little and comes back two hours after."

"Has she spoken to you?"

"Once only, on the first night, in a low voice, to tell me that, if I called out or uttered a sound or tried to escape, François would pay the penalty."

"But, when they attacked you, couldn't you then make out...?"

"No, I saw no more than François did."

"And the attack was quite unexpected?"

"Yes, quite. M. d'Hergemont had that morning received two important letters on the subject of the investigation which he was making into all these facts. One of the letters, written by an old Breton nobleman well-known for his royalist leanings, was accompanied by a curious document which he had found among his great-grandfather's papers, a plan of some underground cells which the Chouans used to occupy in Sarek. It was evidently the same Druid dwellings of which the legends tell us. The plan showed the entrance on the Black Heath and marked two stories, each ending in a torture-chamber. François and I went out exploring together; and we were attacked on our way back."

"And you have made no discovery since?"

"No, none at all."

"But François spoke of a rescue which he was expecting, someone who had promised his assistance."

"Oh, a piece of boyish nonsense, an idea of François', which, as it happened, was connected with the second letter which M. d'Hergemont received that morning!"

"And what was it about?"

Stéphane did not reply at once. Something made him think that they were being spied on through the door. But, on going to the wicket, he saw no one in the passage outside.

"Ah," he said, "if we are to be rescued, the sooner it happens the better. *They* may come at any moment now."

"Is any help really possible?" asked Véronique.

"Well," Stéphane answered, "we must not attach too much importance to it, but it's rather curious all the same. You know, Sarek has often been visited by officers or inspectors with a view to exploring the rocks and beaches around the island, which were quite capable of concealing a submarine base. Last time, the special delegate sent from Paris, a wounded officer, Captain

Patrice Belval,* became friendly with M. d'Hergemont, who told him the legend of Sarek and the apprehension which we were beginning to feel in spite of everything; it was the day after Maguennoc went away. The story interested Captain Belval so much that he promised to speak of it to one of his friends in Paris, a Spanish or Portuguese nobleman, Don Luis Perenna,* an extraordinary person, it would seem, capable of solving the most complicated mysteries and of succeeding in the most reckless enterprises. A few days after Captain Belval's departure, M. d'Hergemont received from Don Luis Perenna the letter of which I spoke to you and of which he read us only the beginning. 'Sir,' it said, 'I look upon the Maguennoc incident as more than a little serious; and I beg you, at the least fresh alarm, to telegraph to Patrice Belval. If I can rely upon certain indications, you are standing on the brink of an abyss. But, even if you were at the bottom of that abyss, you would have nothing to fear, if only I hear from you in time. From that moment, I make myself responsible, whatever happens, even though everything may seem lost and though everything may be lost. As for the riddle of the God-Stone, it is simply childish and I am astonished that, with the very ample data which you gave Belval, it should for an instant be regarded as impossible of explanation. I will tell you in a few words what has puzzled so many generations of mankind...'"

"Well?" said Véronique, eager to know more.

"As I said, M. d'Hergemont did not tell us the end of the letter. He read it in front of us, saying, with an air of amazement, 'Can that be it?... Why, of course, of course it is... How wonderful!' And, when we asked him, he said, 'I'll tell you all about it this evening, when you come back from the Black Heath. Meanwhile you may like to know that this most extraordinary man—it's the only word for him—discloses to me, without

---

* See *The Golden Triangle*, by Maurice Leblanc.

more ado or further particulars, the secret of the God-Stone and the exact spot where it is to be found. And he does it so logically as to leave no room for doubt.'"

"And in the evening?"

"In the evening, François and I were carried off and M. d'Hergemont was murdered."

Véronique paused to think:

"I should not be surprised," she said, "if they wanted to steal that important letter from him. For, after all, the theft of the God-Stone seems to me the only motive that can explain all the machinations of which we are the victims."

"I think so too: but M. d'Hergemont, on Don Luis Perenna's recommendation, tore up the letter before our eyes."

"So, after all, Don Luis Perenna has not been informed?"

"No."

"Yet François..."

"François does not know of his grandfather's death and does not suspect that M. d'Hergemont never heard of our disappearance and therefore never sent a message to Don Luis Perenna. If he had done so, Don Luis, to François' mind, must be on his way. Besides, François has another reason for expecting something..."

"A serious reason?"

"No. François is still very much of a child. He has read a lot of books of adventure, which have worked upon his imagination. Now Captain Belval told him such fantastic stories about his friend Perenna and painted Perenna in such strange colours that François firmly believes Perenna to be none other than Arsène Lupin. Hence his absolute confidence and his certainty that, in case of danger, the miraculous intervention will take place at the very minute when it becomes necessary."

Véronique could not help smiling:

"He is a child, of course; but children sometimes have intuitions which we have to take into account. Besides, it keeps up his courage and his spirits. How could he have endured this ordeal, at his age, if he had not had that hope?"

Her anguish returned. In a very low voice, she said:

"No matter where the rescue comes from, so long as it comes in time and so long as my son is not the victim of those dreadful creatures!"

They were silent for a long time. The enemy, present, though invisible, oppressed them with his formidable weight. He was everywhere; he was master of the island, master of the subterranean dwellings, master of the heaths and woods, master of the sea around them, master of the dolmens and the coffins. He linked together the monstrous ages of the past and the no less monstrous hours of the present. He was continuing history according to the ancient rites and striking blows which had been foretold a thousand times.

"But why? With what object? What does it all mean?" asked Véronique, in a disheartened tone. "What connection can there be between the people of today and those of long ago? What is the explanation of the work resumed by such barbarous methods?"

And, after a further pause, she said, for in her heart of hearts, behind every question and reply and every insoluble problem, the obsession never ceased to torment her:

"Ah, if François were here! If we were all three fighting together! What has happened to him? What keeps him in his cell? Some obstacle which he did not foresee?"

It was Stéphane's turn to comfort her:

"An obstacle? Why should you suppose so? There is no obstacle. But it's a long job..."

"Yes, yes, you are right; a long, difficult job. Oh, I'm sure that he won't lose heart! He has such high spirits! And such confidence! 'A mother and son who have been brought together cannot be parted again,' he said. 'They may still persecute us, but separate us, never! We shall win in the end.

He was speaking truly, wasn't he, Stéphane? I've not found my son again, have I, only to lose him? No, no, it would be too unjust and it would be impossible..."

Stéphane looked at her, surprised to hear her interrupt herself. Véronique was listening to something.

"What is it?" asked Stéphane.

"I hear sounds," she said.

He also listened:

"Yes, yes, you're right."

"Perhaps it's François," she said. "Perhaps it's up there."

She moved to rise. He held her back:

"No, it's the sound of footsteps in the passage."

"In that case... in that case...?" said Véronique.

They exchanged distraught glances, forming no decision, not knowing what to do.

The sound came nearer. The enemy could not be suspecting anything, for the steps were those of one who is not afraid of being heard.

Stéphane said, slowly:

"They must not see me standing up. I will go back to my place. You must fasten me again as best you can."

They remained hesitating, as though cherishing the absurd hope that the danger would pass of its own accord. Then, suddenly, releasing herself from the sort of stupor that seemed to paralyse her, Véronique made up her mind:

"Quick!... Here they come!... Lie down!"

He obeyed. In a few seconds, she had replaced the cords on and around him as she had found them, but without tying them.

"Turn your face to the rock," she said. "Hide your hands. Your hands might betray you."

"And you?"

"I shall be all right."

She stooped and stretched herself at full length against the door, in which the spy-hole, barred with strips of iron, projected inwardly in such a way as to hide her from sight.

At the same moment, the enemy stopped outside. Notwithstanding the thickness of the door, Véronique heard the rustle of a dress.

And, above her, someone looked in.

It was a terrible moment. The least indication would give the alarm.

"Oh, why does she stay?" thought Véronique. "Is there anything to betray my presence? My clothes?..."

She thought that it was more likely Stéphane, whose attitude did not appear natural and whose bonds did not wear their usual aspect.

Suddenly there was a movement outside, followed by a whistle and a second whistle.

Then from the far end of the passage came another sound of steps, which increased in the solemn silence and stopped, like the first, behind the door. Words were spoken. Those outside seemed to be concerting measures.

Véronique managed to reach her pocket. She took out her revolver and put her finger on the trigger. If anyone entered, she would stand up and fire shot after shot, without hesitating. Would not the least hesitation have meant François' death?

9

THE DEATH-CHAMBER

Véronique's estimate was correct, provided that the door opened outwards and that her enemies were at once revealed to view. She therefore examined the door and suddenly observed that, against all logical expectation, it had a large strong bolt at the bottom. Should she make use of it?

She had no time to weigh the advantages or drawbacks of this plan. She had heard a jingle of keys and, almost at the same time, the sound of a key grating in the lock.

Véronique received a very clear vision of what was likely to happen. When the assailants burst in, she would be thrust aside, she would be hampered in her movements, her aim would be inaccurate and her shots would miss, whereupon *they* would shut the door again and promptly hurry off to François' cell. The thought of it made her lose her head; and her action was instinctive and immediate. First, she pushed the bolt at the foot of the door. Next, half rising, she slammed the iron shutter over the wicket. A latch clicked. It was no longer possible either to enter or to look in.

Then at once she realized the absurdity of her action, which had not opposed any obstacle to the menace of the enemy. Stéphane, leaping to her side, said:

"Good heavens, what have you done? Why, they saw that I was not moving and they now know that I am not alone!"

"Exactly," she answered, striving to defend herself. "They will try to break down the door, which will give us the time we want."

"The time we want for what?"

"To make our escape."

"Which way?"

"François will call out to us. François will.."

She did not complete her sentence. They now heard the sound of footsteps moving swiftly down the passage. There was no doubt about it; the enemy, without troubling about Stéphane, whose flight appeared impossible, was making for the upper floor of cells. Moreover, might he not suppose that the two friends were acting in agreement and that it was the boy who was in Stéphane's cell and who had barred the door?

Véronique therefore had precipitated events and given them a turn which she had so many reasons to dread; and François, up above, would be caught at the very moment when he was preparing to escape.

She was utterly overwhelmed:

"Why did I come here?" she muttered. "It would have been so simple to wait! The two of us would have saved you to a certainty."

One idea flashed through the confusion of her mind: had she not sought to hasten Stéphane's release because of what she knew of this man's love for her? And was it not an unworthy curiosity that had prompted her to make the attempt? A horrible idea, which she at once rejected, saying:

"No, I had to come. It is fate which is persecuting us."

"Don't believe it," said Stéphane. "Everything will come right."

"Too late!" said she, shaking her head.

"Why? How do we know that François has not left his cell? You yourself thought so just now..."

She did not reply. Her face became drawn and very pale. By virtue of her sufferings she had acquired a kind of intuition of the evil that threatened her. This evil now surrounded her on every hand. A second series of ordeals was before her, more terrible than the first.

"There's death all about us," she said.

He tried to smile:

"You are talking like the people of Sarek. You have the same fears..."

"They were right to be afraid. And you yourself feel the horror of it all."

She rushed to the door, drew the bolt, tried to open it; but what could she do against that massive, iron-clad door?

Stéphane seized her by the arm:

"One moment... Listen... It sounds as if..."

"Yes," she said, "it's up there that they are knocking... above our heads... in François' cell..."

"Not at all, not at all: listen..."

There was a long silence; and then blows were heard in the thickness of the cliff. The sound came from below them.

"The same blows that I heard this morning," said Stéphane, in dismay. "The same attempt of which I spoke to you... Ah, I understand!..."

"What? What do you mean?"

The blows were repeated, at regular intervals, and then ceased, to be followed by a dull, continuous sound, pierced by shriller creakings and sudden cracks, like the straining of machinery newly started, or of one of those capstans which are used for hoisting boats up a beach.

Véronique listened, desperately expectant of what was coming, trying to guess, seeking to find some clue in Stéphane's eyes. He stood in front of her, looking at her as a man, in the hour of danger, looks at the woman he loves.

And suddenly she staggered and had to press her hand against the wall. It was as though the cave and indeed the whole cliff were bodily moving from its place.

"Oh," she murmured, "is it I who am trembling like this? Is it from fear that I am shaking from head to foot?"

Seizing Stéphane's hands, she said:

"Tell me! I want to know!..."

He did not answer. There was no fear in his eyes bedewed with tears, there was nothing but immense love and unbounded despair. He was thinking only of her.

Besides, was it necessary for him to explain what was happening? Did not the reality itself become more and more apparent as the seconds passed? A strange reality indeed, having no connection with commonplace facts, a reality quite beyond anything that the imagination might invent in the domain of evil, a strange reality which Véronique, who was beginning to grasp its indication, still refused to believe.

Acting like a trap-door, but like a trap-door working the reverse way, the square of enormous joists which was set in the middle of the cave rose, pivoting on the fixed axis by which it was hinged parallel with the cliff. The almost imperceptible movement was that of an enormous lid opening; and the thing already formed a sort of spring-board reaching from the edge to the back of the cave, a spring-board with as yet a very slight slope, on which it was easy enough to keep one's balance.

At the first moment, Véronique thought that the enemy's object was to crush them between the implacable floor and the granite of the ceiling. But, almost immediately afterwards, she understood that the hateful mechanism, by standing erect like a draw-bridge when hoisted up, was intended to hurl them over the precipice. And it would carry out that intention inexorably. The result was fatal and inevitable. Whatever they might try, whatever efforts they might make to hold on, a minute would come when the floor of that draw-bridge would be absolutely vertical, forming an integral part of the perpendicular cliff.

"It's horrible, it's horrible," she muttered.

Their hands were still clasped. Stéphane was weeping silent tears.

Presently she moaned:

"There's nothing to be done, is there?"

"Nothing," he replied.

"Still, there is room beyond that wooden floor. The cave is round. We might..."

"The space is too small. If we tried to stand between the sides of the square and the wall, we should be crushed to death. That has all been planned. I have often thought about it."

"Then...?"

"We must wait."

"For what? For whom?"

"For François."

"Oh, François!" she said, with a sob. "Perhaps he too is doomed... Or perhaps he is looking for us and will fall into some trap. In any case, I shall not see him... And he will know nothing... And he will not even have seen his mother before dying..."

She pressed Stéphane's hands and said:

"Stéphane, if one of us escapes death—and I hope it may be you..."

"It will be you," he said, in a tone of conviction. "I am even surprised that the enemy should condemn you to the same torture as myself. But no doubt he doesn't know that it's you who are here with me."

"It surprises me too!" said Véronique. "A different torture is set aside for me. But what does it matter, if I am not to see my son again!... Stéphane, I can safely leave him in your charge, can't I? I know all that you have already done for him."

The floor continued to rise very slowly, with an uneven vibration and sudden jerks. The slope became more accentuated. A few minutes more and they would no longer be able to speak freely and quietly.

Stéphane replied:

"If I survive, I swear to fulfil my task to the end. I swear it in memory..."

"In memory of me," she said, in a firm voice, "in memory of the Véronique whom you knew... and loved."

He looked at her passionately:

"So you know?"

"Yes; and I tell you frankly, I have read your diary. I know your love for me... and I accept it." She gave a sad smile. "That poor love which you offered to the woman who was absent... and which you are now offering to the woman who is about to die."

"No, no," he said, eagerly, "don't believe that... Salvation may be near at hand... I feel it. My love does not belong to the past but to the future."

He stooped to put his lips to her hands.

"Kiss me," she said, offering him her forehead.

Each of them had been obliged to place one foot on the brink of the precipice, on the straight edge of granite which ran parallel with the fourth side of the spring-board.

They kissed gravely.

"Hold me firmly," said Véronique.

She leant back as far as she could, raising her head, and called in a muffled voice:

"François... François..."

But there was no one at the upper opening, from which the ladder was still hanging by one of its hooks, well out of reach.

Véronique bent over the sea. At this spot, the swell of the cliff did not project as much as elsewhere; and she saw, in between the foam-topped reefs, a little pool of still water, very calm and so deep that she could not see the bottom. She thought that death would be gentler there than on the sharp-pointed rocks and, yielding to a sudden longing to have done with it all and to avoid a lingering agony, she said to Stéphane:

"Why wait for the end? Better die than suffer this torture."

"No, no!" he exclaimed, horrified at the thought that Véronique might disappear from his sight.

"Then you are still hoping?"

"Until the last second, since it's your life that's at stake."

"I have no longer any hope."

Nor was he borne up by hope; but he would have given anything to lull Véronique's sufferings and to bear the whole weight of the supreme ordeal himself.

The floor continued to rise. The vibration had ceased and the slope became much more marked, already reaching the bottom of the wicket, half way up the door. Then there was a sound like a sudden stoppage of machinery, followed by a violent jolt, and the whole wicket was covered. It was becoming impossible for them to stand erect.

They lay down on the slanting floor, bracing their feet against the granite edge.

Two more jerks occurred, each time pushing the upper end still higher. The top of the inner wall was reached; and the enormous mechanism moved slowly forward, along the ceiling, towards the opening of the cave. They could see very plainly that it would fit this opening exactly and close it hermetically, like a draw-bridge. The rock had been hewn in such a way that the deadly task might be accomplished without leaving any loophole for chance.

They did not utter a word. With hands tight-clasped, they resigned themselves to the inevitable. Their death was assuming the aspect of an event decreed by destiny. The machine had been constructed far back in the centuries and had no doubt been reconstructed, repaired and put in order at a more recent date; and during those centuries, worked by invisible executioners, it had caused the death of culprits, of guilty men and innocent, of men of Armorica, Gaul, France or foreign lands. Prisoners of war, sacrilegious monks, persecuted peasants, renegade Chouans and soldiers of the Revolution; one by one the monster had hurled them over the cliff.

Today it was their turn.

They had not even the bitter solace of rage and hatred. Whom were they to hate? They were dying in the deepest obscurity, with no hostile face emerging from that implacable night. They were dying in the accomplishment of a task unknown to themselves, to make up a total, so to speak, and for the fulfilment of absurd prophecies, of imbecile intentions, such as the orders given by the barbarian gods and formulated by fanatical priests. They were—it was a thing unheard of—the victims of some expiatory sacrifice, of some holocaust offered to the divinities of a blood-thirsty creed!

The wall stood behind them. In a few more minutes it would be perpendicular. The end was approaching.

Time after time Stéphane had to hold Véronique back. An increasing terror distracted her mind. She yearned to fling herself down.

"Please, please," she stammered, "do let me... I am suffering more than I can bear."

Had she not found her son again, she would have retained her self-control to the end. But the thought of François was unsettling her. The boy must also be a prisoner, they must be torturing him too and immolating him, like his mother, on the altars of the execrable gods.

"No, no, he will come," Stéphane declared. "You will be saved... I will have it so... I know it."

She replied, wildly:

"He is imprisoned as we are... They are burning him with torches, driving arrows into him, tearing his flesh... Oh, my poor little son!..."

"He will come, dear, he told you he would. Nothing can separate a mother and son who have been brought together again."

"We have found each other in death; we shall be united in death. I wish it might be at once! I don't want him to suffer!"

The agony was too great. With an effort she released her hands from Stéphane's and made a movement to fling herself down. But she immediately threw herself back against the draw-bridge, with a cry of amazement which was echoed by Stéphane.

Something had passed before their eyes and disappeared again. It came from the left.

"The ladder!" exclaimed Stéphane. "It's the ladder, isn't it?"

"Yes, it's François," said Véronique, catching her breath with joy and hope. "He is saved. He is coming to rescue us."

At that moment, the wall of torment was almost upright, vibrating implacably beneath their shoulders. The cave no longer existed behind them. The depths had already claimed them; at most they were clinging to a narrow ledge.

Véronique leant outwards again. The ladder swung back and then became stationary, fixed by its two hooks.

Above them, at the opening in the cliff, was a boy's face; and the boy was smiling and making gestures:

"Mother, mother... quick!"

The call was eager and urgent. The two arms were outstretched towards the pair below. Véronique moaned:

"Oh, it's you, it's you, my darling!"

"Quick, mother, I'm holding the ladder!... Quick!... It's quite safe!"

"I'm coming, darling, I'm coming."

She had seized the nearest upright. This time, with Stéphane's assistance, she had no difficulty in placing her foot on the bottom rung. But she said:

"And you, Stéphane? You're coming with me, aren't you?"

"I have plenty of time," he said. "Hurry."

"No, you must promise."

"I swear. Hurry."

She climbed four rungs and stopped:

"Are you coming, Stéphane?"

He had already turned towards the cliff and slipped his left hand into a narrow fissure which remained between the drawbridge and the rock. His right hand reached the ladder and he was able to set foot on the lowest rung. He too was saved.

With what delight Véronique covered the rest of the distance! What mattered the void below her, now that her son was there, waiting for her to clasp him to her breast at last!

"Here I am, here I am," she said. "Here I am, my darling."

She swiftly put her head and shoulders in the window. He pulled her through; and she climbed over the ledge. At last she was with her son.

They flung themselves into each other's arms:

"Oh, mother, mother, is it really true? Mother!"

But she had no sooner closed her arms about him than she drew back a little, she did not know why. An inexplicable discomfort checked her first outburst.

"Come here," she said, dragging him to the light of the window. "Come and let me look at you."

The boy did as she wished. She examined him for two or three seconds, no longer, and suddenly, giving a start of terror, ejaculated:

"Then it's you? It's you, the murderer?"

Oh, horror! She was once more looking on the face of the monster who had killed her father and Honorine before her eyes!

"So you know me?" he chuckled.

Véronique realised her mistake from the boy's very tone. This was not François but the other, the one who had played his devilish part in the clothes which François usually wore.

He gave another chuckle:

"Ah, you're beginning to see things as they are, M'ame! You know me now, don't you?"

The hateful face contracted, became wicked and cruel, animated by the vilest expression.

"Vorski! Vorski!" stammered Véronique. "It's Vorski I recognise in you."

He burst out laughing:

"Why not? Do you think I'm going to disown my father as you did?"

"Vorski's son! His son!" Véronique repeated.

"Lord bless me, yes, his son: why shouldn't I be? Surely the good fellow had the right to have two sons! Me first and dear François next!"

"Vorski's son!" Véronique exclaimed once more.

"And one of the best, I tell you, M'ame, a worthy son of his father and brought up on the highest principles. I've shown you as much already, haven't I? But it's not finished, we're only at the beginning... Here, would you like me to give you a fresh proof? Just take a squint at that stick-in-the-mud of a tutor!... No, but look how things go when I take a hand in them."

He sprang to the window. Stéphane's head appeared. The boy picked up a stone and struck with all his might, throwing him backwards.

Véronique, who at the first moment had hesitated, not realising the danger, now rushed and seized the boy's arm. It was too late. The head vanished. The hooks of the ladder slipped off the ledge. There was a loud cry, followed by the sound of a body falling into the water below.

Véronique ran to the window. The ladder was floating on the part of the little pool which she was able to see, lying motionless in its frame of rocks. There was nothing to point to the place where Stéphane had fallen, not an eddy, not a ripple.

She called out;

"Stéphane! Stéphane!..."

No reply, nothing but the great silence of space in which the winds are still and the sea asleep.

"You villain, what have you done?" she cried.

"Don't take on, missus," he said. "Master Stéphane brought up your kid to be a duffer. Come it's a laughing matter, it is, really. Give us a kiss, won't you, daddy's missus? But, I say, what a face you're pulling! Surely you don't hate me as much as all that?"

He went up to her, with his arms outstretched. Véronique swiftly covered him with her revolver:

"Be off, be off, or I'll kill you as I would a mad dog! Be off!"

The boy's face became more inhuman than ever. He fell back step by step, snarling:

"Oh, I'll make you pay for this, my pretty lady!... What do you mean by it? I come up to give you a kiss... I'm full of kindly feelings... and you want to shoot me! You shall pay for it in blood... in nice red flowing blood... blood... blood..."

He seemed to love the sound of the word. He repeated it time after time, then once more gave a burst of evil laughter and fled down the tunnel which led to the Priory, shouting:

"The blood of your son, Mother Véronique!... The blood of your darling François!"

10

THE ESCAPE

Shuddering, uncertain how to act next, Véronique listened till she no longer heard the sound of his footsteps. What should she do? The murder of Stéphane had for a moment turned her thoughts from François; but she now once more fell a prey to anguish. What had become of her son? Should she go to him at the Priory and defend him against the dangers that threatened him?

"Come, come," she said, "I'm losing my head... Let me think things out... A few hours ago, François was speaking to me through the wall of his prison... for it was certainly he then, it was certainly François who yesterday took my hand and covered it with his kisses... A mother cannot be deceived; and I was quivering with love and tenderness... But since... since this morning has he not left his prison?"

She stopped to think and then said, slowly:

"That's it... that's what happened... Stéphane and I were discovered below, on the floor underneath. The alarm was given at once. The monster, Vorski's son, had gone up expressly to watch François. He found the cell empty and, seeing the opening which had been made, crawled out here. Yes, that's it... If not, by what way did he come?... When he got here, it occurred to him to run to the window, knowing that it overlooked the sea and suspecting that François had chosen it to make his escape. He at once saw the hooks of the ladder. Then, on leaning over, he saw me, knew who I was and called out to me... And now... now he is on his way to the Priory, where he is bound to meet François..."

Nevertheless Véronique did not stir. She had an instinct that the danger lay not at the Priory but here, by the cells. And she wondered whether François had really succeeded in escaping and whether, before his task was done, he had not been surprised by the other and attacked by him.

It was a horrible doubt! She stooped quickly and, perceiving that the hole had been widened, tried to pass through it herself. But the outlet, at most large enough for a child, was too narrow for her; and her shoulders became fixed. She persisted in the attempt, however, tearing her bodice and bruising her skin against the rock, and at last, by dint of patience and wriggling, succeeded in slipping through.

The cell was empty. But the door was open on the passages facing her; and Véronique had an impression—merely an impression, for the window admitted only a faint light—that someone was just leaving the cell through the open door. And from this confused impression of something that she had not absolutely seen she retained the certainty that it was a woman who was hiding there, in the passage, a woman surprised by her unexpected entrance.

"It's their accomplice," thought Véronique. "She came up with the boy who killed Stéphane, and she has no doubt taken François away... Perhaps François is even there still, quite near me, while she's watching me..."

Meanwhile Véronique's eyes were growing accustomed to the semidarkness and she distinctly saw a woman's hand upon the door, which opened inwardly. The hand was slowly pulling.

"Why doesn't she shut it at once," Véronique wondered, "since she obviously wants to put a barrier between us?"

Véronique received her answer when she heard a pebble grating under the door and interfering with its movement. If the pebble were not there, the door would be closed. Without hesitating, Véronique went up, took hold of a great iron handle and pulled it towards her. The hand disappeared, but the opposition continued. There was evidently a handle on the other side as well.

Suddenly she heard a whistle. The woman was summoning assistance. And almost at the same time, in the passage, at some distance from the woman, there was a cry:

"Mother! Mother!"

Ah, with what deep emotion Véronique heard that cry! Her son, her real son was calling to her, her son, still a captive but alive! Oh, the superhuman delight of it!

"I'm here, darling!"

"Quick, mother! I'm tied up; and the whistle is their signal... they'll be coming."

"I'm here... I shall save you before they come!"

She had no doubt of the result. It seemed to her as though her strength knew no limits and as though nothing could resist the exasperated tension of her whole being.

Her adversary was in fact weakening and giving ground by inches. The opening became wider; and suddenly the contest was over. Véronique walked through.

The woman had already fled down the passage and was dragging the boy by a rope in order to make him walk despite the cords with which he was bound. It was a vain attempt and she abandoned it forthwith. Véronique was close to her, with her revolver in her hand.

The woman let go the boy and stood up in the light from the open cells. She was dressed in white serge, with a knotted girdle round her waist. Her arms were half bare. Her face was still young, but faded, thin and wrinkled. Her hair was fair, interspersed with strands of white. Her eyes gleamed with a feverish hatred.

The two women looked at each other without a word, like two adversaries who have met before and are about to fight again. Véronique almost smiled, with a smile of mingled triumph and defiance. In the end she said:

"If you dare to lay a finger on my child, I'll kill you. Go! Be off!"

The woman was not frightened. She seemed to be reflecting and to be listening in the expectation of assistance. None come. Then she lowered her eyes to François and made a movement as though to seize upon her prey again.

"Don't touch him!" Véronique exclaimed, violently. "Don't touch him, or I fire!"

The woman shrugged her shoulders and said, in measured accents:

"No threats, please! If I had wanted to kill that child of yours, I should have done so by now. But his hour has not came; and it is not by my hand that he is to die."

Véronique, trembling all over, could not help asking:

"By whose hand is he to die?"

"By my son's: you know... the one you've seen."

"Is he your son, the murderer, the monster?"

"He's the son of..."

"Silence! Silence!" Véronique commanded. She understood that the woman had been Vorski's mistress and feared that she would make some disclosure in François' presence. "Silence: that name is not to be spoken."

"It will be when it has to be," said the woman. "Ah, I've suffered enough through you, Véronique: it's your turn now; and you're only at the beginning of it!"

"Go!" cried Véronique, pointing her revolver.

"Once more, no threats, please."

"Go, or I fire! I swear it on the head of my son."

The woman retreated, betraying a certain anxiety in spite of herself. But she was seized with a fresh access of rage.

Impotently she raised her clenched fists and shouted, in a raucous, broken voice:

"I will be revenged... You shall see. Véronique... The cross— do you understand?—the cross is ready... You are the fourth... What, oh, what a revenge!"

She shook her gnarled, bony fists. And she continued:

"Oh, how I hate you! Fifteen years of hatred! But the cross will avenge me... I shall string you up on it myself... The cross is ready... you'll see... the cross is ready for you!..."

She walked away slowly, holding herself erect under the threat of the revolver.

"Don't kill her, mother, will you?" whispered François, suspecting the contest in his mother's mind.

Véronique seemed to wake from a dream:

"No, no," she replied, "don't be afraid... And yet perhaps I ought to..."

"Oh, please let her be, mother, and let us go away."

She lifted him in her arms, even before the woman was out of sight, pressed him to her and carried him to the cell as though he weighed no more than a little child.

"Mother, mother," he said.

"Yes, darling, your own mother; and no one shall take you from me again, that I swear to you."

Without troubling about the wounds inflicted by the stone she slipped, this time almost at the first attempt, through the gap made by François, drew him after her and then, but not before, released him from his bonds.

"There is no danger here," she said, "at least for the moment, because they can hardly get at us except by the cell and I shall be able to defend the entrance."

Mother and son exchanged the fondest of embraces. There was now no barrier to part their lips and their arms. They could see each other, could gaze into each other's eyes.

"How handsome you are, my darling!" said Véronique.

She saw no resemblance between him and the boy murderer and was astonished that Honorine could have taken one for the other. And she felt as if she would never weary of admiring the breeding, the frankness and the sweetness which she read in his face.

"And you, mother," he said, "do you think that I ever pictured a mother as beautiful as you? No, not even in my dreams, when you seemed as lovely as a fairy. And yet Stéphane often used to tell me..."

She interrupted him:

"We must hurry, dearest, and take refuge from their pursuit. We must go."

"Yes," he said, "and above all we must leave Sarek. I have invented a plan of escape which is bound to succeed. But, first of all, Stéphane: what has become of him? I heard the sound of which I spoke to you underneath my cell and I fear..."

She dragged him along by the hand, without answering his question:

"I have many things to tell you, darling, painful things which I must no longer keep from you. But presently will do... For the moment we must take refuge in the Priory. That woman will go in search of help and come after us."

"But she was not alone, mother, when she entered my cell suddenly and caught me in the act of digging at the wall. There was someone with her."

"A boy, wasn't it? A boy of your own size?"

"I could hardly see. He and the woman fell upon me, bound me and carried me into the passage. Then the woman left me for a moment and he went back to the cell. He therefore knows about this tunnel by now and about the exit in the Priory grounds."

"Yes, I know. But we shall easily get the better of him; and we'll block up the exit."

"But there remains the bridge which joins the two islands," François objected.

"No," she said, "I burnt it down and the Priory is absolutely cut off."

They were walking very quickly, Véronique pressing her pace, François a little anxious at the words spoken by his mother.

"Yes, yes," he said, "I see that there is a good deal which I don't know and which you have kept from me, mother, in order not to frighten me. For instance, when you burnt down the bridge... It was with the petrol set aside for the purpose, wasn't it, and as arranged with Maguennoc in case of danger? So you were threatened too; and the first attack was made on you, mother?... And then there was something that woman said with such a hateful look on her face!... And then... and then, above all, what has become of Stéphane? They were whispering about him just now in my cell... All this worries me... Then again I don't see the ladder which you brought..."

"Please, dearest, don't let us wait a moment. The woman will have found assistance..."

The boy stopped short:

"Mother."

"What? Do you hear anything?"

"Someone walking."

"Are you sure?"

"Someone coming this way."

"Oh," she said, in a hollow voice, "it's the murderer coming back from the Priory!"

She felt her revolver and prepared herself for anything that might happen. But suddenly she pushed François towards a dark corner on her left, formed by the entry to one of those tunnels, probably blocked, which she had noticed when she came.

"Get in there," she said. "We shall be all right here: he will not see us."

The sound approached.

"Stand well back," she said, "and don't stir."

The boy whispered:

"What's that in your hand? A revolver? Mother, you're not going to fire?"

"I ought to, I ought to," said Véronique. "He's such a monster!... It's as with his mother... I ought to have... we shall perhaps regret it." And she added, almost unconsciously, "He killed your grandfather."

"Oh, mother, mother!"

She supported him, to prevent his falling, and amid the silence she heard the boy sobbing on her breast and stammering:

"Never mind... don't fire, mother..."

"Here he comes, darling, here he comes; look at him."

The other passed. He was walking slowly, a little bent, listening for the least sound. He appeared to Véronique to be the exact same size as her son; and this time, when she looked at him with more attention, she was not so much surprised that Honorine and M. d'Hergemont had been taken in, for there were really some points of resemblance, which would have been accentuated by the fact that he was wearing the red cap stolen from François.

He walked on.

"Do you know him?" asked Véronique.

"No, mother."

"Are you sure that you never saw him?"

"Sure."

"And it was he who fell upon you, with the woman, in your cell?"

"I haven't a doubt of it, mother. He even hit me in the face, for no reason, with absolute hatred."

"Oh," she said, "this is all incomprehensible! When shall we escape this awful nightmare?"

"Quick, mother, the road's clear. Let's make the most of it."

On returning to the light, she saw that he was very pale and felt his hand in hers like a lump of ice. Nevertheless he looked up at her with a smile of happiness.

They set out again; and soon, after passing the strip of cliff that joined the two islands and climbing the staircases, they emerged in the open air, to the right of Maguennoc's garden. The daylight was beginning to wane.

"We are saved," said Véronique.

"Yes," replied the boy, "but only on condition that they cannot reach us by the same road. We shall have to bar it, therefore."

"How?"

"Wait for me here; I'll go and fetch some tools at the Priory."

"Oh, don't let us leave each other, François!"

"You can come with me, mother."

"And suppose the enemy arrives in the meantime? No, we must defend this outlet."

"Then help me, mother."

A rapid inspection showed them that one of the two stones which formed a roof above the entrance was not very firmly rooted in its place. They found no difficulty in first shifting and then clearing it. The stone fell across the staircase and was at once covered by an avalanche of earth and pebbles which made the passage, if not impracticable, at least very hard to manage.

"All the more so," said François, "as we shall stay here until we are able to carry out my plan. And be easy, mother; it's a sound scheme and we have nearly managed it."

For that matter, they recognized above all, that rest was essential. They were both of them worn out.

"Lie down, mother... look, just here: there's a bed of moss under this overhanging rock which makes a regular nest. You'll be as cosy as a queen there and sheltered from the cold."

"Oh, my darling, my darling!" murmured Véronique, overcome with happiness.

It was now the time for explanations; and Véronique did not hesitate to give them. The boy's grief at hearing of the death of all those whom he had known would be mitigated by the great joy which he felt at recovering his mother. She therefore spoke without reserve, cradling him in her lap, wiping away his tears, feeling plainly that she was enough to make up for all the lost affections and friendships. He was particularly afflicted by Stéphane's death.

"But is it quite certain?" he asked. "For, after all, there is nothing to tell us that he is drowned. Stéphane is a perfect swimmer; and so... Yes, yes, mother, we must not despair... on the contrary... Look, here's a friend who always comes at the worst times, to declare that everything is not lost."

All's Well came trotting along. The sight of his master did not appear to surprise him. Nothing unduly surprised All's Well. Events, to his mind, always followed one another in a natural order which did not disturb either his habits or his occupations. Tears alone seemed to him worthy of special attention. And Véronique and François were not crying.

"You see, mother? All's Well agrees with me; nothing is lost... But, upon my word, All's Well, you're a sharp little fellow! What would you have said, eh, if we'd left the island without you?"

Véronique looked at her son:

"Left the island?"

"Certainly: and the sooner the better. That's my plan. What do you say to it?"

"But how are we to get away?"

"In a boat."

"Is there one here?"

"Yes, mine."

"Where?"

"Close by, at Sarek Point."

"But how are we to get down? The cliff is perpendicular."

"She's at the very place where the cliff is steepest, a place known as the Postern. The name puzzled Stéphane and myself. A postern suggests an entrance, a gate. Well, we ended by learning that, in the middle ages, at the time of the monks, the little isle on which the Priory stands was surrounded by ramparts. It was therefore to be presumed that there was a postern here which commanded an outlet on the sea. And in fact, after hunting about with Maguennoc, we discovered, on the flat top of the cliff, a sort of gully, a sandy depression reinforced at intervals by regular walls made of big building-stones. A path winds down the middle, with steps and windows on the side of the sea, and leads to a little bay. That is the Postern outlet. We repaired it: and my boat is hanging at the foot of the cliff."

Véronique's features underwent a transformation:

"Then we're safe now!"

"There's no doubt of that."

"And the enemy can't get there?"

"How could he?"

"He has the motor-boat at his disposal."

"He has never been there, because he doesn't know of the bay nor of the way down to it either: you can't see them from the open sea. Besides, they are protected by a thousand sharp-pointed rocks."

"And what's to prevent us from leaving at once?"

"The darkness, mother. I'm a good mariner and accustomed to navigate all the channels that lead away from Sarek, but I should not be at all sure of not striking some reef or other. No, we must wait for daylight."

"It seems so long!"

"A few hours' patience, mother. And we are together, you and I! At break of dawn, we'll take the boat and begin by hugging the foot of the cliff till we are underneath the cells. Then we'll pick up Stéphane, who of course will be waiting for us on some strip of beach, and we'll all be off, won't we, All's Well? We'll land at Pont-l'Abbé at twelve o'clock or so. That's my plan."

Véronique could not contain her delight and admiration. She was astonished to find so young a boy giving proofs of such self-possession.

"It's splendid, darling, and you're right in everything. Luck is decidedly coming our way."

The evening passed without incidents. An alarm, however, a noise under the rubbish which blocked the underground passage and a ray of light trickling through a slit obliged them to mount guard until the minute of their departure. But it did not affect their spirits.

"Why, of course I'm easy in my mind," said François. "From the moment when I found you again, I felt that it was for good. Besides, if the worst came to the worst, have we not a last hope left? Stéphane spoke to you about it, I expect. And it makes you laugh, my confidence in a rescuer whom I have never seen... Well, I tell you, mother, if I were to see a dagger about to strike me, I should be certain, absolutely certain, mind you, that a hand would come and ward off the blow."

"Alas," she said, "that providential hand did not prevent all the misfortunes of which I told you!"

"It will keep off those which threaten my mother," declared the boy.

"How? This unknown friend has not been warned."

"He will come all the same. He doesn't need to be warned to know how great the danger is. He will come. And, mother, promise me one thing: whatever happens, you must have confidence."

"I will have confidence, darling, I promise you."

"And you will be right," he said, laughing, "for I shall be the leader. And what a leader, eh, mother? Why, yesterday evening I foresaw that, to carry the enterprise through successfully and so that my mother should be neither cold nor hungry, in case we were not able to take the boat this afternoon, we must have food and rugs! Well, they will be of use to us tonight, seeing that for prudence's sake we mustn't abandon our post here and sleep at the Priory. Where did you put the parcel, mother?"

They ate gaily and with a good appetite. Then François wrapped his mother up and tucked her in: and they both fell asleep, lying close together, happy and unafraid.

When the keen air of the morning woke Véronique, a belt of rosy light streaked the sky. François was sleeping the peaceful sleep of a child that feels itself protected and is untroubled by dreams. For a long time she just sat gazing at him without wearying: and she was still looking at him when the sun was high above the horizon.

"To work, mother," he said, after he had opened his eyes and given her a kiss. "No one in the tunnel? No. Then we have plenty of time to go on board."

They took the rugs and provisions and, with brisk steps, went towards the descent leading to the Postern, at the extreme end of the island. Beyond this point the rocks were heaped up in formidable confusion: and the sea, though calm, lapped against them noisily.

"I hope your boat's there still!" said Véronique.

"Lean over a little, mother. You can see her down there, hanging in that crevice. We have only to work the pulley to get her afloat. Oh, it's all very well thought out, mother darling! We have nothing to fear... Only... only..."

He had interrupted himself and was thinking.

"What? What is it?" asked Véronique.

"Oh, nothing! A slight delay."

"But..."

He began to laugh:

"Really, for the leader of an expedition, it's rather humiliating, I admit. Just fancy, I've forgotten one thing: the oars. They are at the Priory."

"But this is terrible!" cried Véronique.

"Why? I'll run to the Priory and I shall be back in ten minutes."

All Véronique's apprehensions returned:

"And suppose they make their way out of the tunnel meanwhile?"

"Come, come, mother," he laughed, "you promised to have confidence. To get out of the tunnel would take them an hour's hard work; and we should hear them. Besides, what's the use of talking, mother? I'll be back at once."

He ran off.

"François! François!"

He did not reply.

"Oh," she thought, once more assailed by forebodings. "I had sworn not to leave him for a second!"

She followed him at a distance and stopped on a hillock between the Fairies' Dolmen and the Calvary of the Flowers. From here she could see the entrance to the tunnel and also saw her son jogging along the grass.

He first went into the basement of the Priory. But the oars seemed not to be there, for he came out almost at once and went to the main door, which he opened and disappeared from sight.

"One minute ought to be plenty for him," said Véronique to herself. "The oars must be in the hall... or at any rate on the ground-floor... Say two minutes, at the outside."

She counted the seconds while watching the entrance to the tunnel.

But three minutes, four minutes, five minutes passed: and the front door did not open again.

All Véronique's confidence vanished. She thought that it was mad of her not to have gone with her son and that she ought never to have submitted to a child's will. Without troubling about the tunnel or the dangers from that side, she began to walk towards the Priory. But she had the horrible feeling which people sometimes experience in dreams, when their legs seem paralysed and when they are unable to move, while the enemy advances to attack them.

And suddenly, on reaching the Dolmen, she beheld a sight the meaning of which was immediately clear to her. The ground at the foot of the oaks round the right-hand part of the semi-circle was littered with lately cut branches, which still bore their green leaves.

She raised her eyes and stood stupefied and dismayed.

One oak alone had been stripped. And on the huge trunk, bare to a height of twelve or fifteen feet, there was a paper, transfixed by an arrow and bearing the inscription, "V. d'H."

"The fourth cross," Véronique faltered, "the cross marked with my name!"

She supposed that, as her father was dead, the initials of her maiden name must have been written by one of her enemies, the chief of them, no doubt; and for the first time, under the influence of recent events, remembering the woman and the boy who were persecuting her, she involuntarily attributed a definite set of features to that enemy.

It was a fleeting impression, an improbable theory, of which she was not even conscious. She was overwhelmed by something much more terrible. She suddenly understood that the monsters, those creatures of the heath and the cells, the accomplices of the woman and the boy, must have been there, since the cross was prepared. No doubt they had built a footbridge and thrown it over the chasm to take the place of the bridge to which she had set fire. They were masters of the Priory. And François was once more in their hands!

Then she rushed straight along, collecting all her strength. She in her turn ran over the turf, dotted with ruins, that sloped towards the front of the house.

"François! François! François!"

She called his name in a piercing voice. She announced her coming with loud cries. Thus did she reach the Priory.

One half of the door stood ajar. She pushed it and darted into the hall, crying:

"François! François!"

The call rang from floor to attic and throughout the house, but remained unanswered:

"François! François!"

She went upstairs, opening doors at random, running into her son's room, into Stéphane's, into Honorine's. She found nobody.

"François! François!... Don't you hear me? Are they hurting you?... Oh, François, do answer!"

She went back to the landing. Opposite her was M. d'Hergemont's study. She flung herself upon the door and at once recoiled, as though stricken by a vision from hell.

A man was standing there, with arms crossed and apparently waiting for her. And it was the man whom she had pictured for an instant when thinking of the woman and the boy. It was the third monster!

She said, simply, but in a voice filled with inexpressible horror:

"Vorski!... Vorski!..."

11

THE SCOURGE OF GOD

Vorski! Vorski! The unspeakable creature, the thought of whom filled her with shame and horror, the monstrous Vorski, was not dead! The murder of the spy by one of his colleagues, his burial in the cemetery at Fontainebleau; all this was a fable, a delusion! The only real fact was that Vorski was alive!

Of all the visions that could have haunted Véronique's brain, there was none so abominable as the sight before her; Vorski standing erect, with his arms crossed and his head up, alive! Vorski alive!

She would have accepted anything with her usual courage, but not this. She had felt strong enough to face and defy no matter what enemy, but not this one. Vorski stood for ignominious disgrace, for insatiable wickedness, for boundless ferocity, for method mingled with madness in crime.

And this man loved her.

She suddenly blushed. Vorski was staring with greedy eyes at the bare flesh of her shoulders and arms, which showed through her tattered bodice, and looking upon this bare flesh as upon a prey which nothing could snatch from him. Nevertheless Véronique did not budge. She had no covering within reach. She pulled herself together under the insult of the man's desire and defied him with such a glance that he was embarrassed and for a moment turned away his eyes.

Then she cried, with an uncontrollable outburst of feeling:

"My son! Where's François? I want to see him."

"*Our* son is sacred, madame," he replied. "He has nothing to fear from his father."

"I want to see him."

He lifted his hand as one taking an oath:

"You shall see him, I swear."

"Dead, perhaps!" she said, in a hollow voice.

"As much alive as you and I, madame."

There was a fresh pause. Vorski was obviously seeking his words and preparing the speech with which the implacable conflict between them was to open.

He was a man of athletic stature, with a powerful frame, legs slightly bowed, an enormous neck swollen by great bundles of muscles and a head unduly small, with fair hair plastered down and parted in the middle. That in him which at one time produced an impression of brute strength, combined with a certain distinction, had become with age the massive and vulgar aspect of a professional wrestler posturing on the hustings at a fair. The disquieting charm which once attracted the women had vanished; and all that remained was a harsh and cruel expression of which he tried to correct the hardness by means of an impassive smile.

He unfolded his arms, drew up a chair and, bowing to Véronique, said:

"Our conversation, madame, will be long and at times painful. Won't you sit down?"

He waited for a moment and, receiving no reply, without allowing himself to be disconcerted, continued:

"Perhaps you would rather first take some refreshment at the sideboard. Would you care for a biscuit and a thimbleful of old claret or a glass of champagne?"

He affected an exaggerated politeness, the essentially Teutonic politeness of the semi-barbarians who are anxious to prove that they are familiar with all the niceties of civilization and that they have been initiated into every refinement of courtesy, even towards a woman whom the right of conquest would permit them to treat more cavalierly. This was one of the points of detail which in the past had most vividly enlightened Véronique as to her husband's probable origin.

She shrugged her shoulders and remained silent.

"Very well," he said, "but you must then authorize me to stand, as behoves a man of breeding who prides himself on possessing a certain amount of *savoir faire*. Also pray excuse me for appearing in your presence in this more than careless attire. Internment-camps and the caves of Sarek are hardly places in which it is easy to renew one's wardrobe."

He was in fact wearing a pair of old patched trousers and a torn red-flannel waistcoat. But over these he had donned a white linen robe which was half-closed by a knotted girdle. It was a carefully studied costume; and he accentuated its eccentricity by adopting theatrical attitudes and an air of satisfied negligence.

Pleased with his preamble, he began to walk up and down, with his hands behind his back, like a man who is in no hurry and who is taking time for reflection in very serious circumstances. Then he stopped and, in a leisurely tone:

"I think, madame, that we shall gain time in the end by devoting a few indispensable minutes to a brief account of our past life together. Don't you agree?"

Véronique did not reply. He therefore began, in the same deliberate tone:

"In the days when you loved me..."

She made a gesture of revolt. He insisted:

"Nevertheless, Véronique..."

"Oh," she said, in an accent of disgust, "I forbid you!... That name from your lips!... I will not allow it..."

He smiled and continued, in a tone of condescension:

"Don't be annoyed with me, madame. Whatever formula I employ, you may be assured of my respect. I therefore resume my remarks. In the days when you loved me, I was, I must admit, a heartless libertine, a debauchee, not perhaps without a certain style and charm, for I always made the most of my advantages, but possessing none of the qualities of a married man. These qualities I should easily have acquired under your influence, for I loved you to distraction. You had about you a purity that enraptured me, a charm and a simplicity which I have never met with in any woman. A little patience on your part, an effort of kindness would have been enough to transform me. Unfortunately, from the very first moment, after a rather melancholy engagement, during which you thought of nothing but your father's grief and anger, from the first moment of our marriage there was a complete and irretrievable lack of harmony between us. You had accepted in spite of yourself the bridegroom who had thrust himself upon you. You entertained for your husband no feeling save hatred and repulsion. These are things which a man like Vorski does not forgive. So many women and among them some of the proudest had given me proof of my perfect delicacy that I had no cause to reproach myself. That the little middle-class person that you were chose to be offended was not my business. Vorski is one of those who obey their instincts and their passions. Those instincts and passions failed to meet with your approval. That, madame, was your affair; it was purely a matter of taste. I was free; I resumed my own life. Only..."

He interrupted himself for a few seconds and then went on:

"Only, I loved you. And, when, a year later, certain events followed close upon one another, when the loss of your son drove you into a convent, I was left with my love unassuaged, burning and torturing me. What my existence was you can guess for yourself; a series of orgies and violent adventures in which I vainly strove to forget you, followed by sudden fits of hope, clues which were suggested to me, in the pursuit of which I flung myself headlong, only to relapse into everlasting discouragement and loneliness. That was how I discovered the whereabouts of your father and your son, that was how I came to know their retreat here, to watch them, to spy upon them, either personally or with the aid of people who were entirely devoted to me. In this way I was hoping to reach yourself, the sole object of my efforts and the ruling motive of all my actions, when war was declared. A week later, having failed in an attempt to cross the frontier, I was imprisoned in an internment-camp."

He stopped. His face became still harder; and he growled:

"Oh, the hell that I went through there! Vorski! Vorski, the son of a king, mixed up with all the waiters and pickpockets of the Fatherland! Vorski a prisoner, scoffed at and loathed by all! Vorski unwashed and eaten up with vermin! My God, how I suffered!... But let us pass on. What I did, to escape from death, I was entitled to do. If someone else was stabbed in my stead, if someone else was buried in my name in a corner of France, I do not regret it. The choice lay between him and myself; I made my choice. And it was perhaps not only my persistent love of life that inspired my action; it was also—and this above all is a new thing—an unexpected dawn which broke in the darkness and which was already dazzling me with its glory. But this is my secret. We will speak of it later, if you force me to. For the moment..."

In the face of all this rhetoric delivered with the emphasis of an actor rejoicing in his eloquence and applauding his own periods, Véronique had retained her impassive attitude. Not one of those lying declarations was able to touch her. She seemed to be thinking of other things.

He went up to her and, to compel her attention, continued, in a more aggressive tone:

"You do not appear to suspect, madame, that my words are extremely serious. They are, however, and they will become even more so. But, before approaching more formidable matters and in the hope of avoiding them altogether, I should like to make an appeal, not to your spirit of conciliation, for there is no conciliation possible with you, but to your reason, to your sense of reality. After all, you cannot be ignorant of your present position, of the position of your son..."

She was not listening, he was absolutely convinced of it. Doubtless absorbed by the thought of her son, she read not the least meaning into the words that reached her ears. Nevertheless, irritated and unable to conceal his impatience, he continued:

"My offer is a simple one; and I hope and trust that you will not reject it. In François' name and because of my feelings of humanity and compassion, I ask you to link the present to the past of which I have sketched the main features. From the social point of view, the bond that unites us has never been shattered. You are still in name and in the eyes of the law..."

He ceased, stared at Véronique and then, clapping his hand violently on her shoulder, shouted:

"Listen, you baggage, can't you! It's Vorski speaking!"

Véronique lost her balance, saved herself by catching at the back of a chair and once more stood erect before her adversary, with her arms folded and her eyes full of scorn.

This time Vorski again succeeded in controlling himself. He had acted under impulse and against his will. His voice retained an imperious and malevolent intonation:

"I repeat that the past still exists. Whether you like it or not, madame, you are Vorski's wife. And it is because of this undeniable fact that I am asking you, if you please, to consider yourself so today. Let us understand each other; if I do not aim at obtaining your love or even your friendship, I will not accept either that we should return to our former hostile relations.

I do not want the scornful and distant wife that you have been. I want... I want a woman... a woman who will submit herself... who will be the devoted, attentive, faithful companion..."

"The slave," murmured Véronique.

"Yes," he exclaimed, "the slave; you have said it. I don't shrink from words any more than I do from deeds. The slave; and why not? A slave understands her duty, which is blindly to obey, bound hand and foot, *perinde ac cadaver*, does the part appeal to you? Will you belong to me body and soul? As for your soul, I don't care a fig about that. What I want... what I want... you know well enough, don't you? What I want is what I have never had. Your husband? Ha, ha, have I ever been your husband? Look back into my life as I will, amid all my seething emotions and delights, I do not find a single memory to remind me that there was ever between us anything but the pitiless struggle of two enemies. When I look at you, I see a stranger, a stranger in the past as in the present. Well, since my luck has turned, since I once more have you in my clutches, it shall not be so in the future. It shall not be so tomorrow, nor even tonight, Véronique. I am the master; you must accept the inevitable. Do you accept?"

He did not wait for her answer and, raising his voice still higher, roared:

"Do you accept? No subterfuges or false promises. Do you accept? If so, go on your knees, make the sign of the cross and say, in a firm voice, 'I accept. I will be a consenting wife. I will submit to all your orders and to all your whims. You are the master.'"

She shrugged her shoulders and made no reply. Vorski gave a start. The veins in his forehead swelled up. However, he still contained himself:

"Very well. For that matter, I was expecting this. But the consequences of your refusal will be so serious for you that I propose to make one last attempt. Perhaps, after all, your refusal is addressed to the fugitive that I am, to the poor beggar that I seem to be; and perhaps the truth will alter your ideas. That truth is dazzling and wonderful. As I told you, an unforeseen dawn has broken through my darkness; and Vorski, son of a king, is bathed in radiant light."

He had a trick of speaking of himself in the third person which Véronique knew of old and which was the sign of his insupportable vanity. She also observed and recognized in his eyes a peculiar gleam which was always there at moments of exaltation, a gleam which was obviously due to his drinking habits but in which she seemed to see besides a sign of temporary aberration. Was he not indeed a sort of madman and had his madness not increased as the years passed?

He continued, and this time Véronique listened.

"I had therefore left here, at the time when the war broke out, a person who is attached to me and who continued the work of watching your father which I had begun. An accident revealed to us the existence of the caves dug under the heath and also one of the entrances to the caves. It was in this safe retreat that I took refuge after my last escape; and it was here that I learnt, through some intercepted letters, of your father's investigations into the secret of Sarek and the discoveries which he had made. You can understand how my vigilance was redoubled! Particularly because I found in all this story, as it became more and more clear to me, the strangest coincidences and an evident connection with certain details in my own life. Presently doubt was no longer possible. Fate had sent me here to accomplish a task which I alone was able to fulfil... and more, a task in which I alone had the right to assist. Do you understand what I mean? Long centuries ago, Vorski was predestined. Vorski was the man appointed by fate, Vorski's name was written in the book of time. Vorski had the necessary qualities, the indispensable means, the requisite titles... I was ready, I set to work without delay, conforming ruthlessly to the decrees of destiny. There was no hesitation as to the road to be followed to the end; the beacon was lighted. I therefore followed the path marked out for me. Vorski has now only to gather the reward of his efforts. Vorski has only to put out his hand. Within reach of his hand fortune, glory, unlimited power. In a few hours, Vorski, son of a king, will be king of the world. It is this kingdom that he offers you."

He was becoming more and more declamatory, more and more of the emphatic and pompous play-actor.

He bent towards Véronique:

"Will you be a queen, an empress, and soar above other women even as Vorski will dominate other men? Queen by right of gold and power even as you are already queen by right of beauty? Will you?... Vorski's slave, but mistress of all those over whom Vorski holds sway? Will you?... Understand me clearly; it is not a question of your making a single decision; you have to choose between two. There is, mark you, the alternative to your refusal. Either the kingdom which I am offering, or else..."

He paused and then, in a grating tone, completed his sentence:

"Or else the cross!"

Véronique shuddered. The dreadful word, the dreadful thing appeared once more. And she now knew the name of the unknown executioner!

"The cross!" he repeated, with an atrocious smile of content. "It is for you to choose. On the one hand all the joys and honours of life. On the other hand, death by the most barbarous torture. Choose. There is nothing between the two alternatives. You must select one or the other. And observe that there is no unnecessary cruelty on my part, no vain ostentation of authority. I am only the instrument. The order comes from a higher power than mine, it comes from destiny. For the divine will to be accomplished, Véronique d'Hergemont must die and die on the cross. This is explicitly stated. There is no remedy against fate. There is no remedy unless one is Vorski and, like Vorski, is capable of every audacity, of every form of cunning. If Vorski was able, in the forest of Fontainebleau, to substitute a sham Vorski for the real one, if Vorski thus succeeded in escaping the fate which condemned him, from his childhood, to die by the knife of a friend, he can certainly discover some stratagem by which the divine will is accomplished, while the woman he loves is left alive. But in that case she will have to submit. 1 offer safety to my bride or death to my foe. Which are you, my foe or my bride? Which do you choose? Life by my side, with all the joys and honours of life... or death?"

"Death," Véronique replied, simply.

He made a threatening gesture:

"It is more than death. It is torture. Which do you choose?"

"Torture."

He insisted, malevolently:

"But you are not alone! Pause to reflect! There is your son. When you are gone, he will remain. In dying, you leave an orphan behind you. Worse than that; in dying, you bequeath him to me. I am his father. I possess full rights. Which do you choose?"

"Death," she said, once more.

He became incensed:

"Death for you, very well. But suppose it means death for him? Suppose I bring him here, before you, your François, and put the knife to his throat and ask you for the last time, what will your answer be?"

Véronique closed her eyes. Never before had she suffered so intensely, and Vorski had certainly found the vulnerable spot. Nevertheless she murmured:

"I wish to die."

Vorski flew into a rage, and, resorting straightway to insults, throwing politeness and courtesy to the winds, he shouted:

"Oh, the hussy, how she must hate me! Anything, anything, she accepts anything, even the death of her beloved son, rather than yield to me! A mother killing her son! For that's what it is; you're killing your son, so as not to belong to me. You are depriving him of his life, so as not to sacrifice yours to me. Oh, what hatred! No, no, it is impossible. I don't believe in such hatred. Hatred has its limits. A mother like you! No, no, there's something else... some love-affair, perhaps? No, no, Véronique's not in love... What then? My pity, a weakness on my part? Oh, how little you know me! Vorski show pity! Vorski show weakness! Why, you've seen me at work! Did I flinch in the performance of my terrible mission? Was Sarek not devastated as it was written? Were the boats not sunk and the people not drowned? Were the sisters Archignat not nailed to the ancient oak-trees? I, I flinch! Listen, when I was a child, with these two hands of mine I wrung the necks of dogs and birds, with these two hands I flayed goats alive and plucked the live chickens in the poultry-yard. Pity indeed! Do you know what my mother called me? Attila! And, when she was mystically inspired and read the future in these hands of mine or on the tarot-cards, 'Attila Vorski,' that great seer would say, 'you shall be the instrument of Providence. You shall be the sharp edge of the blade, the point of the dagger, the bullet in the rifle, the noose in the rope. Scourge of God! Scourge of God, your name is written at full length in the books of time! It blazes among the stars that shone at your birth. Scourge of God! Scourge of God!' And you, you hope that my eyes will be wet with tears? Nonsense! Does the hangman weep? It is the weak who weep, those who fear lest they be punished, lest their crimes be turned against themselves. But I, I! Our ancestors feared but one thing, that the sky should fall upon their heads. What have *I* to fear? I am God's accomplice! He has chosen me among all men. It is God that has inspired me, the God of the fatherland, the old German God, for whom good and evil do not count where the greatness of his sons is at stake. The spirit of evil is within me. I love evil, I thirst after evil. So you shall die, Véronique, and I shall laugh when I see you suffering on the cross!"

He was already laughing. He walked with great strides, stamping noisily on the floor. He lifted his arms to the ceiling; and Véronique, quivering with anguish, saw the red frenzy in his bloodshot eyes.

He took a few more steps and then came up to her and, in a restrained voice, snarling with menace:

"On your knees, Véronique, and beseech my love! It alone can save you. Vorski knows neither pity nor fear. But he loves you; and his love will stop at nothing. Take advantage of it, Véronique. Appeal to the past. Become the child that you once were; and perhaps one day I shall drag myself at your feet. Véronique, do not repel me; a man like me is not to be repelled. One who loves as I love you, Véronique, as I love you, is not to be defied."

She suppressed a cry. She felt his hated hands on her bare arms. She tried to release herself; but he, much stronger than she, did not let go and continued, in a panting voice:

"Do not repel me... it is absurd... it is madness... You must know that I am capable of anything... Well?... The cross is horrible... To see your son dying before your eyes; is that what you want?... Accept the inevitable. Vorski will save you. Vorski will give you the most beautiful life... Oh, how you hate me! But no matter: I accept your hatred, I love your hatred, I love your disdainful mouth... I love it more than if it offered itself of its own accord..."

He ceased speaking. An implacable struggle took place between them. Véronique's arms vainly resisted his closer and closer grip. Her strength was failing her; she felt helpless, doomed to defeat. Her knees gave way beneath her. Opposite her and quite close, Vorski's eyes seemed filled with blood; and she was breathing the monster's breath.

Then, in her terror, she bit him with all her might; and, profiting by a second of discomfiture, she released herself with one great effort, leapt back, drew her revolver, and fired once and again.

The two bullets whistled past Vorski's ears and sent fragments flying from the wall behind him. She had fired too quickly, at random.

"Oh, the jade!" he roared. "She nearly did for me."

In a second he had his arms round her body and, with an irresistible effort, bent her backwards, turned her round and laid her on a sofa. Then he took a cord from his pocket and bound her firmly and brutally.

There was a moment's respite and silence. Vorski wiped the perspiration from his forehead, filled himself a tumbler of wine and drank it down at a gulp.

"That's better," he said, placing his foot on his victim, "and confess that this is best all round. Each one in his place, my beauty; you trussed like a fowl and I treading on you at my pleasure. Aha, we're no longer enjoying ourselves so much! We're beginning to understand that it's a serious matter. Ah, you needn't be afraid, you baggage: Vorski's not the man to take advantage of a woman! No, no, that would be to play with fire and to burn with a longing which this time would kill me. I'm not such a fool as that. How should I forget you afterwards? One thing only can make me forget and give me my peace of mind; your death. And, since we understand each other on that subject, all's well. For it's settled, isn't it; you want to die?"

"Yes," she said, as firmly as before.

"And you want your son to die?"

"Yes," she said.

He rubbed his hands:

"Excellent! We are agreed; and the time is past for words that mean nothing. The real words remain to be spoken, those which count; for you admit that, so far, all that I have said is mere verbiage, what? Just as all the first part of the adventure, all that you saw happening at Sarek, is only child's play. The real tragedy is beginning, since you are involved in it body and soul; and that's the most terrifying part, my pretty one. Your beautiful eyes have wept, but it is tears of blood that are wanted, you poor darling! But what would you have? Once again, Vorski is not cruel. He obeys a higher power; and destiny is against you. Your tears? Nonsense! You've got to shed a thousand times as many as another. Your death? Fudge! You've got to die a thousand deaths before you die for good. Your poor heart must bleed as never woman's and mother's poor heart bled before. Are you ready, Véronique? You shall hear really cruel words, to be followed perhaps by words more cruel still. Oh, fate is not spoiling you, my pretty one!..."

He poured himself out a second glass of wine and emptied it in the same gluttonous fashion; then he sat down beside her and, stooping, said, almost in her ear:

"Listen, dearest, I have a confession to make to you. I was already married when I met you. Oh, don't be upset! There are greater catastrophes for a wife and greater crimes for a husband than bigamy. Well, by my first wife I had a son... whom I think you know; you exchanged a few amicable remarks with him in the passage of the cells... Between ourselves, he's a regular bad lot, that excellent Raynold, a rascal of the worst, in whom I enjoy the pride of discovering, raised to their highest degree, some of my best instincts and some of my chief qualities. He is a second edition to myself, but he already outstrips me and now and then alarms me. Whew, what a devil! At his age, a little over fifteen, I was an angel compared with him. Now it so happens that this fine fellow has to take the field against my other son, against our dear François. Yes, such is the whim of destiny, which, once again, gives orders and of which, once again, I am the clear-sighted and subtle interpreter. Of course it is not a question of a protracted and daily struggle. On the contrary, something short, violent and decisive: a duel, for instance. That's it, a duel; you understand, a serious duel. Not a turn with the fists, ending in a few bruises; no, what you call a duel to the death, because one of the two adversaries must be left, on the ground, because there must be a victor and a victim, in short, a living combatant and a dead one."

Véronique had turned her head a little and she saw that he was smiling. Never before had she so plainly perceived the madness of that man, who smiled at the thought of a mortal contest between two children both of whom were his sons. The whole thing was so extravagant that Véronique, so to speak, did not suffer. It was all outside the limits of suffering.

"There is something better, Véronique," he said, gloating over every syllable. "There's something better. Yes, destiny has devised a refinement which I dislike, but to which, as a faithful servant, I have to give effect. It has devised that you should be present at the duel. Capital; you, François' mother, must see him fight. And, upon my word, I wonder whether that apparent malevolence is not a mercy in disguise. Let us say that you owe it to me, shall we, and that I myself am granting you this unexpected, I will even say, this unjust favour? For, when all is said, though Raynold is more powerful and experienced than François and though, logically, François ought to be beaten, how it must add to his courage and strength to know that he is fighting before his mother's eyes! He will feel like a knight errant who stakes all his pride on winning. He will be a son whose victory will save his mother... at least, so he will think. Really the advantage is too great; and you can thank me, Véronique, if this duel, as I am sure it will, does not—and I am sure that it will not—make your heart beat a little faster... Unless... unless I carry out the infernal programme to the end... Ah, in that case, you poor little thing!..."

He gripped her once more and, lifting her to her feet in front of him, pressing his face against hers, he said, in a sudden fit of rage:

"So you won't give in?"

"No, no!" she cried.

"You will never give in?"

"Never! Never! Never!" she repeated, with increasing vehemence.

"You hate me more than everything?"

"I hate you more than I love my son."

"You lie, you lie!" he snarled. "You lie! Nothing comes above your son!"

"Yes, my hatred for you."

All Véronique's passion of revolt, all the detestation which she had succeeded in restraining now burst forth; and, indifferent to what might come of it, she flung the words of hatred full in his face:

"I hate you! I hate you! I would have my son die before my eyes, I would witness his agony, anything rather than the horror of your sight and presence. I hate you! You killed my father! You are an unclean murderer, a half-witted, savage idiot, a criminal lunatic! I hate you!"

He lifted her with an effort, carried her to the window and threw her on the ground, spluttering:

"On your knees! On your knees! The punishment is beginning. You would scoff at me, you hussy, would you? Well, you shall see!"

He forced her to her knees and then, pushing her against the lower wall and opening the window, he fastened her head to the rail of the balcony by means of a cord round her neck and under her arms. He ended by gagging her with a scarf:

"And now look!" he cried. "The curtain's going up! Boy François doing his exercises!... Oh, you hate me, do you? Oh, you would rather have hell than a kiss from Vorski? Well, my darling, you shall have hell; and I'm arranging a little performance for you, one of my own composing and a highly original one at that!... Also, I may tell you, it's too late now to change your mind. The thing's irrevocable. You may beg and entreat for mercy as much as you like; it's too late! The duel, followed by the cross; that's the programme. Say your prayers, Véronique, and call on Heaven. Shout for assistance if it amuses you... Listen, I know that your brat is expecting a rescuer, a professor of clap-trap, a Don Quixote of adventure. Let him come! Vorski will give him the reception he deserves! The more the merrier! We shall see some fun!... And, if the very gods join in the game and take up your defence, I shan't care! It's no longer their business, it's my business. It's no longer a question of Sarek and the treasure and the great secret and all the humbug of the God-Stone! It's a question of yourself! You have spat in Vorski's face and Vorski is taking his revenge. He is taking his revenge! It is the glorious hour. What exquisite joy!... To do evil as others do good, lavishly and profusely! To do evil! To kill, torture, break, ruin and destroy!... Oh, the fierce delight of being a Vorski!"

He stamped across the room, striking the floor at each step and hustling the furniture. His haggard eyes roamed in all directions. He would have liked to begin his work of destruction at once, strangling some victim, giving work to his greedy fingers, executing the incoherent orders of his insane imagination.

Suddenly, he drew a revolver and, brutishly, stupidly, fired bullets into the mirrors, the pictures, the window-panes.

And, still gesticulating, still capering about, an ominous and sinister figure, he opened the door, bellowing:

"Vorski's having his revenge! Vorski's having his revenge!"

12

THE ASCENT OF GOLGOTHA

Twenty or thirty minutes elapsed. Véronique was still alone. The cords cut into her flesh; and the rails of the balcony bruised her forehead. The gag choked her. Her knees, bent in two and doubled up beneath her, carried the whole weight of her body. It was an intolerable position, an unceasing torture... Still, though she suffered, she was not very clearly aware of it. She was unconscious of her physical suffering; and she had already undergone such mental suffering that this supreme ordeal did not awaken her drowsing senses.

She hardly thought. Sometimes she said to herself that she was about to die; and she already felt the repose of the after-life, as one sometimes, amidst a storm, feels in advance the wide peace of the harbour. Hideous things were sure to happen between the present moment and the conclusion which would set her free; but her brain refused to dwell on them; and her son's fate in particular elicited only momentary thoughts, which were immediately dispersed.

At heart, as there was nothing to enlighten her as to her frame of mind, she was hoping for a miracle. Would the miracle occur in Vorski? Incapable of generosity though he was, would not the monster hesitate none the less in the presence of an utterly unnecessary crime? A father does not kill his son, or at least the act must be brought about by imperative reasons; and Vorski had no such reasons to allege against a mere child whom he did not know and whom he could not hate except with an artificial hatred.

Her torpor was lulled by this hope of a miracle. All the sounds which re-echoed through the house, sounds of discussions, sounds of hurrying footsteps, seemed to her to indicate not so much the preparations for the events foretold as the sign of interruptions which would ruin all Vorski's plans. Had not her dear François said that nothing could any longer separate them from each other and that, at the moment when everything might seem lost and even when everything would be really lost, they must keep their faith intact?

"My François," she repeated, "my darling François, you shall not die... we shall see each other again... you promised me!"

Out of doors, a blue sky, flecked with a few menacing clouds, hung outspread above the tall oaks. In front of her, beyond that same window at which her father had appeared to her, in the middle of the grass which she had crossed with Honorine on the day of her arrival, a site had been recently cleared and covered with sand, like an arena. Was it here that her son was to fight? She received the sudden intuition that it must be; and her heart contracted.

"François," she said, "François, have no fear... I shall save you... Oh, forgive me, François darling, forgive me!... All this is a punishment for the wrong I once did... It is the atonement... The son is atoning for the mother... Forgive me, forgive me!..

At that moment a door opened on the ground-floor and voices ascended from the doorstep. She recognized Vorski's voice among them.

"So it's understood," he said. "We shall each go our own way; you two on the left, I on the right. You'll take this kid with you, I'll take the other and we'll meet in the lists. You'll be the seconds, so to speak, of yours and I'll be the second of mine, so that all the rules will be observed."

Véronique shut her eyes, for she did not wish to see her son, who would no doubt be maltreated, led out to fight like a slave. She could hear the creaking of two sets of footsteps following the two circular paths. Vorski was laughing and speechifying.

The groups turned and advanced in opposite directions.

"Don't come any nearer," Vorski ordered. "Let the two adversaries take their places. Halt, both of you. Good. And not a word, do you hear? If either of you speaks, I shall cut him down without mercy. Are you ready? Begin!"

So the terrible thing was commencing. In accordance with Vorski's will, the duel was about to take place before the mother, the son was about to fight before her face. How could she do other than look? She opened her eyes.

She at once saw the two come to grips and hold each other off. But she did not at once understand what she saw, or at least she failed to understand its exact meaning. She saw the two boys, it was true; but which of them was François and which was Raynold?

"Oh," she stammered, "it's horrible!... And yet... no, I must be mistaken... It's not possible..."

She was not mistaken. The two boys were dressed alike, in the same velvet knickerbockers, the same white-flannel shirts, the same leather belts. But each had his head wrapped in a red-silk scarf, with two holes for the eyes, as in a highwayman's mask.

Which was François? Which was Raynold?

Now she remembered Vorski's inexplicable threat. This was what he meant by the programme drawn up by himself, this was to what he alluded when he spoke of a little play of his composing. Not only was the son fighting before the mother, but she did not know which was her son.

It was an infernal refinement of cruelty; Vorski himself had said so. No agony could add to Véronique's agony.

The miracle which she had hoped for lay chiefly in herself and in the love which she bore her son. Because her son was fighting before her eyes, she felt certain that her son could not die. She would protect him against the blows and against the ruses of the foe. She would make the dagger swerve, she would ward off death from the head which she adored. She would inspire her boy with dauntless energy, with the will to attack, with indefatigable strength, with the spirit that foretells and seizes the propitious moment. But now that both of them were veiled, on which was she to exercise her good influence, for which to pray, against which to rebel?

She knew nothing. There was no clue to enlighten her. One of them was taller, slimmer and lither in his movements. Was this François? The other was more thick-set, stronger and stouter in appearance. Was this Raynold? She could not tell. Nothing but a glimpse of a face, or even a fleeting expression, could have revealed the truth to her. But how was she to pierce the impenetrable mask?

And the fight continued, more terrible for her than if she had seen her son with his face uncovered.

"Bravo!" cried Vorski, applauding an attack.

He seemed to be following the duel like a connoisseur, with the affectation of impartiality displayed by a good judge of fighting who above all things wants the best man to win. And yet it was one of his sons that he had condemned to death.

Facing her stood the two accomplices, both of them men with brutal faces, pointed skulls and big noses with spectacles. One of them was extremely thin; the other was also thin, but with a swollen paunch like a leather bottle. These two did not applaud and remained indifferent, or perhaps even hostile, to the sight before them.

"Capital!" cried Vorski, approvingly. "Well parried! Oh, you're a couple of sturdy fellows and I'm wondering to whom to award the palm."

He pranced around the adversaries, urging them on in a hoarse voice in which Véronique, remembering certain scenes in the past, seemed to recognize the effects of drink. Nevertheless the poor thing made an effort to stretch out her bound hands towards him; and she moaned under her gag:

"Mercy! Mercy! I can't bear it. Have pity!"

It was impossible for her martyrdom to last. Her heart was beating so violently that it shook her from head to foot; and she was on the point of fainting when an incident occurred that gave her fresh life. One of the boys, after a fairly stubborn tussle, had jumped back and was swiftly bandaging his right wrist, from which a few drops of blood were trickling. Véronique seemed to remember seeing in her son's hand the small blue-and-white handkerchief which the boy was using.

She was immediately and irresistibly convinced. The boy—it was the more slender and agile of the two—had more grace than the other, more distinction, greater elegance of movement.

"It's François," she murmured. "Yes, yes, it's he... It's you, isn't it, my darling? I recognize you now... The other is common and heavy... It's you, my darling!... Oh, my François, my dearest François!"

In fact, though both were fighting with equal fierceness, this one displayed less savage fury and blind rage in his efforts. It was as though he were trying not so much to kill his adversary as to wound him and as though his attacks were directed rather to preserving himself from the death that lay in wait for him. Véronique felt alarmed and stammered, as though he could hear her:

"Don't spare him, my darling! He's a monster, too!... Oh, dear, if you're generous, you're lost!... François, François, mind what you're doing!"

THE ASCENT OF GOLGOTHA

The blade of the dagger had flashed over the head of the one whom she called her son; and she had cried out, under her gag, to warn him. François having avoided the blow, she felt persuaded that her cry had reached his ears; and she continued instinctively to put him on his guard and advise him:

"Take a rest... Get your breath... Whatever you do, keep your eyes on him... He's getting ready to do something... He's going to rush at you... Here he comes! Oh, my darling, another inch and he would have stabbed you in the neck!... Be careful, darling, he's treacherous... there's no trick too mean for him to play..."

But the unhappy mother felt, however reluctant she might yet be to admit it, that the one whom she called her son was beginning to lose strength. Certain signs proclaimed a reduced power of resistance, while the other, on the contrary, was gaining in eagerness and vigour. François retreated until he reached the edge of the arena.

"Hi, you, boy!" grinned Vorski. "You're not thinking of running away, are you? Keep your nerve, damn it! Show some pluck! Remember the conditions!"

The boy rushed forward with renewed zest; and it was the other's turn to fall back. Vorski clapped his hands, while Véronique murmured:

"It's for me that he's risking his life. The monster must have told him, 'Your mother's fate depends on you. If you win, she's saved.' And he has sworn to win. He knows that I am watching him. He guesses that I am here. He hears me. Bless you, my darling!"

It was the last phase of the duel. Véronique trembled all over, exhausted by her emotion and by the too violent alternation of hope and anguish. Once again her son lost ground and once again he leapt forward. But, in the final struggle that followed, he lost his balance and fell on his back, with his right arm caught under his body.

His adversary at once stooped, pressed his knee on the other's chest and raised his arm. The dagger gleamed in the air.

"Help! Help!" Véronique gasped, choking under her gag.

She flattened her breast against the wall, without thinking of the cords which tortured her. Her forehead was bleeding, cut by the sharp corner of the rail, and she felt that she was about to die of the death of her son. Vorski had approached and stood without moving, with a merciless look on his face.

Twenty seconds, thirty seconds passed. With his outstretched left hand, François checked his adversary's attempt. But the victorious arm sank lower and lower, the dagger descended, the point was only an inch or two from the neck.

Vorski stooped. Just then, he was behind Raynold, so that neither Raynold nor François could see him; and he was watching most attentively, as though intending to intervene at some given moment. But in whose favour would he intervene? Was it his plan to save François?

Véronique no longer breathed; her eyes were enormously dilated; she hung between life and death.

The point of the dagger touched the neck and must have pricked the flesh, but only very slightly, for it was still held back by François' resistance.

Vorski bent lower. He stood over the fighters and did not take his eyes from the deadly point. Suddenly he took a pen-knife from his pocket, opened it and waited. A few more seconds elapsed. The dagger continued to descend. Then quickly he gashed Raynold's shoulder with the blade of his knife.

The boy uttered a cry of pain. His grip at once became relaxed; and, at the same time, François, set free, his right arm released, half rose, resumed the offensive and, without seeing Vorski or understanding what had happened, in an instinctive impulse of his whole being escaped from death and revolting against his adversary, struck him full in the face. Raynold in his turn fell like a log.

THE ASCENT OF GOLGOTHA

All this had certainly lasted no longer than ten seconds. But the incident was so unexpected and took Véronique so greatly aback that, not realizing, not knowing that she ought to rejoice, believing rather that she was mistaken and that the real François was dead, murdered by Vorski, the poor thing sank into a huddled heap and lost consciousness.

A long, long time elapsed. Then, gradually, Véronique became aware of certain sensations. She heard the clock strike four; and she said:

"It's two hours since François died. For it was he who died."

She had not a doubt that the duel had ended in this way. Vorski would never have allowed François to be the victor and his other son to be killed. And so it was against her own child that she had sent up wishes and for the monster that she had prayed!

"François is dead," she repeated. "Vorski has killed him."

The door opened and she heard Vorski's voice. He entered, with an unsteady gait:

"A thousand pardons, dear lady, but I think Vorski must have fallen asleep. It's your father's fault, Véronique! He had hidden away in his cellar some confounded Saumur which Conrad and Otto discovered and which has fuddled me a bit! But don't cry; we shall make up for lost time... Besides everything must be settled by midnight. So..."

He had come nearer; and he now exclaimed:

"What! Did that rascal of a Vorski leave you tied up? What a brute that Vorski is! And how uncomfortable you must be!... Hang it all, how pale you are! I say, look here, you're not dead, are you? That would be a nasty trick to play us!"

He took Véronique's hand, which she promptly snatched away.

"Capital! We still loathe our little Vorski! Then that's all right and there's plenty of reserve strength. You'll hold out to the end, Véronique."

He listened:

"What is it? Who's calling me? Is it you, Otto? Come up... Well, Otto, what news? I've been asleep, you know. That damned Saumurwine!..."

Otto, one of the two accomplices, entered the room at a run. He was the one whose paunch bulged so oddly.

"What news?" he exclaimed. "Why, this: I've seen someone on the island!"

Vorski began to laugh:

"You're drunk, Otto. That damned Saumur wine..."

"I'm not drunk. I saw... and so did Conrad..."

"Oho," said Vorski, more seriously, "if Conrad was with you! Well, what did you see?"

"A white figure, which hid when we came along."

"Where?"

"Between the village and the heath, in a little wood of chestnut trees."

"On the other side of the island then?"

"Yes."

"All right. We'll take our precautions."

"How? There may be several of them."

"I don't care if there are ten of them; it would make no difference. Where's Conrad?"

"By the footbridge which we put in the place of the bridge that was burnt down. He's keeping watch from there."

"Conrad is a clever one. When the bridge was burnt, we were kept on the other side; if the footbridge is burnt, it'll produce the same hindrance. Véronique, I really believe they're coming to rescue you. It's the miracle you expected, the assistance you hoped for. But it's too late, my beauty."

He untied the bonds that fastened her to the balcony, carried her to the sofa and loosened the gag slightly:

"Sleep, my wench," he said. "Get what rest you can. You're only half-way to Golgotha yet; and the last bit of the ascent will be the hardest."

He went away jesting; and Véronique heard the two men exchange a few sentences which proved to her that Otto and Conrad were only supers who knew nothing of the business in hand:

"Who's this wretched woman whom you're persecuting?" asked Otto.

"That doesn't concern you."

"Still, Conrad and I would like to know something about it."

"Lord, why?"

"Oh, just because!"

"Conrad and you are a pair of fools," replied Vorski. "When I took you into my service and helped you to escape with me, I told you all I could of my plans. You accepted my conditions. It was your lookout. You've got to see this thing through now."

"And if we don't?"

"If you don't, beware of the consequences. I don't like shirkers..."

More hours passed. Nothing, it seemed to Véronique, could any longer save her from the end for which she craved with all her heart. She no longer hoped for the intervention of which Otto had spoken. In reality she was not thinking at all. Her son was dead; and she had no other wish than to join him without delay, even at the cost of the most dreadful suffering. What did that suffering matter to her? There are limits to the strength of those who are tortured; and she was so near to reaching those limits that her agony would not last long.

She began to pray. Once more the memory of the past forced itself on her mind; and the fault which she had committed seemed to her the cause of all the misfortunes heaped upon her.

And, while praying, exhausted, harassed, in a state of nervous extenuation which left her indifferent to anything that might happen, she fell asleep.

Vorski's return did not even rouse her. He had to shake her:

"The hour is at hand, my girl. Say your prayers."

He spoke low, so that his assistants might not hear what he said; and, whispering in her ear, he told her things of long ago, insignificant trifles which he dribbled out in a thick tone. At last he called out:

"It's still too light, Otto. Go and see what you can find in the larder, will you? I'm hungry."

They sat down to table, but Vorski stood up again at once:

"Don't look at me, my girl. Your eyes worry me. What do you expect? My conscience doesn't worry me when I'm alone, but it gets worked up when a fine pair of eyes like yours go right through me. Lower your lids, my pretty one."

He bound Véronique's eyes with a handkerchief which he knotted behind her head. But this did not satisfy him; and he unhooked a muslin curtain from the window, wrapped her whole head in it and wound it round her neck. Then he sat down again to eat and drink.

The three of them hardly spoke and said not a word of their trip across the island, nor of the duel of the afternoon. In any case, these were details which did not interest Véronique and which, even if she had paid attention to them, would not have aroused her. Everything had become indifferent to her. The words reached her ears but assumed no definite meaning. She thought of nothing but dying.

When it was dark, Vorski gave the signal for departure.

"Then you're still determined?" asked Otto, in a voice betraying a certain hostility.

"More so than ever. What's your reason for asking?"

"Nothing... But, all the same..."

"All the same what?"

THE ASCENT OF GOLGOTHA

"Well, I may as well out with it, we only half like the job."

"You don't mean to say so! And you only discover it now, my man, after stringing up the sisters Archignat and treating it as a lark!"

"I was drunk that day. You made us drink."

"Well, get boozed if you want to, old cock. Here, take the brandy-bottle. Fill your flask and shut up... Conrad, is the stretcher ready?"

He turned to his victim:

"A polite attention for you, my dear... Two old stilts of your brat's, fastened together with straps... It's very practical and comfortable."

At half-past eight, the grim procession set out, with Vorski at the head, carrying a lantern. The accomplices followed with the litter.

The clouds which had been threatening all the afternoon had now gathered and were rolling, thick and black, over the island. The night was falling swiftly. A stormy wind was blowing and made the candle flicker in the lantern.

"Brrrr!" muttered Vorski. "Dismal work! A regular Golgotha evening."

He swerved and grunted at the sight of a little black shape bounding along by his side:

"What's that? Look. It's a dog, isn't it?"

"It's the boy's mongrel," said Otto.

"Oh, of course, the famous All's Well! The brute's come in the nick of time. Everything's going jolly well! Just wait a bit, you mangy beast!"

He aimed a kick at the dog. All's Well avoided it and keeping out of reach, continued to accompany the procession, giving a muffled bark at intervals.

It was a rough ascent; and every moment one of the three men, leaving the invisible path that skirted the grass in front of the house and led to the open space by the Fairies' Dolmen, tripped in the brambles or in the runners of ivy.

"Halt!" Vorski commanded. "Stop and take breath, my lads. Otto, hand us your flask. My heart's turning upside down."

He took a long pull:

"Your turn, Otto... What, don't you want to? What's the matter with you?"

"I'm thinking that there are people on the island who are looking for us."

"Let them look!"

"And suppose they come by boat and climb that path in the cliffs which the woman and the boy were trying to escape by this morning, the path we found?"

"What we have to fear is an attack by land, not by sea. Well, the footbridge is burnt. There's no means of communication."

"Unless they find the entrance to the cells, on the Black Heath, and follow the tunnel to this place."

"Have they found the entrance?"

"I don't know."

"Well, granting that they do find it, haven't we just blocked the exit on this side, broken down the staircase, thrown everything topsy-turvy? To clear it will take them half a day and more. Whereas at midnight the thing'll be done and by daybreak we shall be far away from Sarek."

"It'll be done, it'll be done; that is to say, we shall have one more murder on our conscience. But..."

"But what?"

"What about the treasure?"

"Ah, the treasure! You've got it out at last! Well, make your mind easy: your shares of it are as good as in your pockets."

"Are you sure of that?"

"Rather! Do you imagine that I'm staying here and doing all this dirty work for fun?"

They resumed their progress. After a quarter of an hour, a few drops of rain began to fall. There was a clap of thunder. The storm still appeared to be some distance away.

They had difficulty in completing the rough ascent: and Vorski had to help his companions.

"At last!" he said. "We're there. Otto, hand me the flask. That's it. Thanks."

They had laid their victim at the foot of the oak which had had its lower branches removed. A flash of light revealed the inscription, "V. d'H." Vorski picked up a rope, which had been left there in readiness, and set a ladder against the trunk of the tree:

"We'll do as we did with the sisters Archignat," he said. "I'll pass the cord over the big branch which we left intact. That will serve as a pulley."

He interrupted himself and jumped to one side. Something extraordinary had just happened.

"What's that?" he whispered. "What was it? Did you hear that whistling sound?"

"Yes," said Conrad, "it grazed my ear. One would have said it was a bullet."

"You're mad."

"I heard it too," said Otto, "and it seems to me that it hit the tree."

"What tree?"

"The oak, of course! It was as though somebody had fired at us."

"There was no report."

"A stone, then; a stone that must have hit the oak."

"We'll soon see," said Vorski.

He turned his lantern and at once let fly an oath:

"Damn it! Look, there, under the lettering."

They looked. An arrow was fixed at the spot to which he pointed. Its feathered end was still quivering.

"An arrow!" gasped Conrad. "How is it possible? An arrow!"

And Otto spluttered:

"We're done for! It's us they were aiming at!"

"The man who took aim at us can't be far off," Vorski observed.

"Keep your eyes open. We'll have a look."

He swung the light in a circle which penetrated the surrounding darkness.

"Stop," said Conrad, eagerly. "A little more to the right. Do you see?"

"Yes, yes, I see."

Thirty yards from where they stood, in the direction of the Calvary of the Flowers, just beyond the blasted oak, they saw something white, a figure which was trying, at least so it seemed, to hide behind a clump of bushes.

"Not a word, not a movement," Vorski ordered. "Do nothing to let him think that we've discovered him. Conrad, come with me.

You, Otto, stay here, with your revolver in your hand, and keep a good watch. If they try to come near and to release her ladyship, fire two shots and we'll run back at once. Is that understood?"

"Quite."

Vorski bent over Véronique and loosened the veil slightly. Her eyes and mouth were still concealed by their bandages. She was breathing with difficulty; the pulse was weak and slow.

"We have time," he muttered, "but we must hurry if we want her to die according to plan. In any case she doesn't seem to be in pain. She has lost all consciousness."

He put down the lantern and then softly, followed by his assistant, stole towards the white figure, both of them choosing the places where the shadow was densest.

But he soon became aware, on the one hand, that the figure, which had seemed stationary, was moving as he himself moved forward, so that the space between them remained the same, and, on the other hand, that it was escorted by a small black figure frisking by its side.

"It's that filthy mongrel!" growled Vorski.

He quickened his pace: the distance did not decrease. He ran: the figure in front of him ran likewise. And the strangest part of it was that they heard no sound of leaves disturbed or of ground trampled by the mysterious person running ahead of them.

"Damn it!" swore Vorski. "He's laughing at us. Suppose we fired at him, Conrad?"

"He's too far. The bullets wouldn't reach him."

"All the same, we're not going to..."

The unknown individual led them to the end of the island and then down to the entrance of the tunnel, passed close to the Priory, skirted the west cliff and reached the foot-bridge, some of the planks of which were still smouldering. Then he branched off, passed back by the other side of the house and went up the grassy slope.

From time to time the dog barked gaily.

Vorski could not control his rage. However hard he tried, he was unable to gain an inch of ground: and the pursuit had lasted fifteen minutes. He ended by vituperating the enemy:

"Stop, can't you? Show yourself a man!... What are you trying to do? Lead us into a trap? What for?... Is it her ladyship you're trying to save? It's not worthwhile, in the state she's in. Oh, you damned, smart bounder, if I could only get hold of you!"

Suddenly Conrad seized him by the skirt of his robe.

"What is it, Conrad?"

"Look. He seems to be stopping."

As Conrad suggested, the white figure for the first time was becoming more and more clearly visible in the darkness and they were able to distinguish, through the leaves of a thicket, its present attitude, with the arms slightly opened, the back bowed, the legs bent and apparently crossed on the ground.

"He must have fallen," said Conrad.

Vorski, after running forward, shouted:

"Am I to shoot, you scum? I've got the drop on you. Hands up, or I fire."

Nothing stirred.

"It's your own lookout! If you show fight, you're a dead man. I shall count three and fire."

He walked to twenty yards of the figure and counted, with outstretched arm:

"One... two... Are you ready, Conrad? Fire!"

The two bullets were discharged at the same time.

There was a cry of distress. The figure seemed to collapse. The two men rushed forward:

"Ah, now you've got it, you rascal! I'll show you the stuff that Vorski's made of! You've given me a pretty run, you oaf! Well, your account's settled!"

After the first few steps, he slackened his speed, for fear of a surprise. The figure did not move; and Vorski, on coming close, saw that it had the limp and misshapen look of a dead man, of a corpse. Nothing remained but to fall upon it. This was what Vorski did, laughing and jesting:

"A good bag, Conrad! Let's pick up the game."

But he was greatly surprised, on picking up the game, to feel in his hands nothing but an almost impalpable quarry, consisting, to tell the truth, of just a white robe, with no one inside it, the owner of the robe having taken flight in good time, after hooking it to the thorns of a thicket. As for the dog, he had disappeared.

"Damn and blast it!" roared Vorski. "He's cheated us, the ruffian! But why, hang it, why?"

Venting his rage in the stupid fashion that was his habit, he was stamping on the piece of stuff, when a thought struck him:

"Why? Because, damn it, as I said just now, it's a trap: a trap to get us away from her ladyship while his friends went for Otto! Oh, what an ass I've been!"

He started to go back in the dark and, as soon as he was able to see the dolmen, he called out:

"Otto! Otto!"

"Halt! Who goes there?" answered Otto, in a scared voice.

"It's me... Damn you, don't fire!"

"Who's there? You?"

"Yes, yes, you fool."

"But the two shots?"

"Nothing... A mistake... We'll tell you about it..."

He was now close to the oak and, at once, taking up the lantern, turned its rays upon his victim. She had not moved and lay stretched at the foot of the tree, with her head wrapped in the veil.

"Ah!" he said. "I breathe again! Hang it, how frightened I was!"

"Frightened of what?"

"Of their taking her from us, of course!"

"Well, wasn't I here?"

"Oh, you! You've got no more pluck than a louse... and, if they had gone for you..."

"I should have fired, at any rate. You'd have heard the signal."

"May be. Well, did nothing happen?"

"Nothing at all."

"Her ladyship didn't carry on too much?"

"She did at first. She moaned and groaned under her hood, until I lost all patience."

"And then?"

"Oh, then! It didn't last long: I stunned her with a good blow of my fist."

"You brute!" exclaimed Vorski. "If you've killed her, you're a dead man."

He plumped down and glued his ear to his unfortunate victim's breast.

"No," he said, presently, "her heart is still beating. But that may not last long. To work, lads. It must all be over in ten minutes."

13

"ELOI, ELOI, LAMA SABACHTHANI!"

The preparations were soon made; and Vorski himself took an active part in them. Resting the ladder against the trunk of the tree, he passed one end of the rope round his victim and the other over one of the upper branches. Then, standing on the bottom rung, he instructed his accomplices:

"Here, all you've got to do now is to pull. Get her on her feet first and one of you keep her from falling."

He waited a moment. But Otto and Conrad were whispering to each other; and he exclaimed:

"Look here, hurry up, will you?... Remember I'm making a pretty easy target, if they took it into their heads to send a bullet or an arrow at me. Are you ready?"

The two assistants did not reply.

"Well, this is a bit thick! What's the matter with you? Otto! Conrad!"

He leapt to the ground and shook them:

"You're a pair of nice ones, you are! At this rate, we should still be at it tomorrow morning... and the whole thing will miscarry... Answer me, Otto, can't you?" He turned the light full on Otto's face. "Look here, what's all this about? Are you wriggling out of it? If so, you'd better say so! And you, Conrad? Are you both going on strike?"

Otto wagged his head:

"On strike... that's saying a lot. But Conrad and I would like a word or two of explanation?"

"Explanation? What about, you pudding-head? About the lady we're executing? About either of the two brats? It's no use taking that line, my man. I said to you, when I first mentioned the business, 'Will you go to work blindfold? There'll be a tough job and plenty of bloodshed. But there's big money at the end of it.'"

"That's the whole question," said Otto.

"Say what you mean, you jackass!"

"It's for you to say and repeat the terms of our agreement What are they?"

"You know as well as I do."

"Exactly, it's to remind you of them that I'm asking you to repeat them."

"I remember them exactly. I get the treasure; and out of the treasure I pay you two hundred thousand francs between the two of you."

"That's so and it's not quite so. We'll come back to that. Let's begin by talking of this famous treasure. Here have we been grinding away for weeks, wallowing in blood, living in a nightmare of every sort of crime... and not a thing in sight!"

Vorski shrugged his shoulders:

"You're getting denser and denser, my poor Otto! You know there were certain things to be done first. They're all done, except one. In a few minutes, this will be finished too and the treasure will be ours!"

"How do we know?"

"Do you think I'd have done all that I have done, if I wasn't sure of the result... as sure as I am that I'm alive? Everything has happened in a certain given order. It was all predetermined. The last thing will come at the hour foretold and will open the gate for me."

"The gate of hell," sneered Otto, "as I heard Maguennoc call it."

"Call it by that name or another, it opens on the treasure which I shall have won."

"Very well," said Otto, impressed by Vorski's tone of conviction, "very well. I'm willing to believe you're right. But what's to tell us that we shall have our share?"

"You shall have your share for the simple reason that the possession of the treasure will provide me with such indescribable wealth that I'm not likely to risk having trouble with you two fellows for the sake of a couple of hundred thousand francs."

"So we have your word?"

"Of course."

"Your word that all the clauses of our agreement shall be respected."

"Of course. What are you driving at?"

"This, that you've begun to trick us in the meanest way by breaking one of the clauses of the agreement."

"What's that? What are you talking about? Do you realize whom you're speaking to?"

"I'm speaking to you, Vorski."

Vorski laid violent hands on his accomplice:

"What's this? You dare to insult me? To call me by my name, me, me?"

"What of it, seeing that you've robbed me of what's mine by rights?"

Vorski controlled himself and, in a voice trembling with anger:

"Say what you have to say and be careful, my man, for you're playing a dangerous game. Speak out."

"It's this," said Otto. "Apart from the treasure, apart from the two hundred thousand francs, it was arranged between us—

you held up your hand and took your oath on it — that any loose cash found by either of us in the course of the business would be divided in equal shares: half for you, half for Conrad and myself. Is that so?"

"That's so."

"Then pay up," said Otto, holding out his hand.

"Pay up what? I haven't found anything."

"That's a lie. While we were settling the sisters Archignat, you discovered on one of them, tucked away in her bodice, the hoard which we couldn't find in their house."

"Well, that's a likely story!" said Vorski, in a tone which betrayed his embarrassment.

"It's absolutely the truth."

"Prove it."

"Just fish out that little parcel, tied up with string, which you've got pinned inside your shirt, just there," said Otto, touching Vorski's chest with his finger. "Fish it out and let's have a look at those fifty thousand-franc notes."

Vorski made no reply. He was dazed, like a man who does not understand what is happening to him and who is trying to guess how his adversary procured a weapon against him.

"Do you admit it?" asked Otto.

"Why not?" he re-joined. "I meant to square up later, in the lump."

"Square up now. We'd rather have it that way."

"And suppose I refuse?"

"You won't refuse."

"Suppose I do?"

"In that case, look out for yourself!"

"I have nothing to fear. There's only two of you."

"There's three of us, at least."

"Where's the third?"

"The third is a gentleman who seems cleverer than most, from what Conrad tells me: brrr!... The one who fooled you just now, the one with the arrow and the white robe!"

"You propose to call him?"

"Rather!"

Vorski felt that the game was not equal. The two assistants were standing on either side of him and pressing him hard. He had to yield:

"Here, you thief! Here, you robber!" he shouted, taking out the parcel and unfolding the notes.

"It's not worthwhile counting," said Otto, snatching the bundle from him unawares.

"Hi!..."

"We'll do it this way: half for Conrad, half for me."

"Oh, you blackguard! Oh, you double-dyed thief! I'll make you pay for this. I don't care a button about the money. But to rob me as though you'd decoyed me into a wood, so to speak! I shouldn't like to be in your skin, my lad!"

He continued to insult the other and then, suddenly, burst into a laugh, a forced, malicious laugh:

"After all, Otto, upon my word, well played! But where and how did you come to know it? You'll tell me that, won't you?... Meanwhile, we've not a minute to lose. We're agreed all round, aren't we? And you'll get on with the work?"

"Willingly, since you're taking the thing so well," said Otto. And he added, obsequiously, "After all... you have a style about you, sir! You're a fine gentleman, you are!"

"And you, you're a varlet whom I pay. You've had your money, so hurry up. The business is urgent."

The "business," as the frightful creatures called it, was soon done. Climbing on his ladder, Vorski repeated his orders, which were executed in docile fashion by Conrad and Otto.

They raised the victim to her feet and then, keeping her upright, hauled at the rope. Vorski seized the poor woman and, as her knees were bent, violently forced them straight. Thus flattened against the trunk of the tree, with her skirt tightened round her legs, her arms hanging to right and left at no great distance from her body, she was bound round the waist and under the arms.

She seemed not to have recovered from her blow and uttered no sound of complaint. Vorski tried to speak a few words, but spluttered them, incapable of utterance. Then he tried to raise her head, but abandoned the attempt, lacking the courage to touch her who was about to die: and the head dropped low on the breast.

He at once got down and stammered:

"The brandy, Otto. Have you the flask? Oh, damn it, what a beastly business!"

"There's time yet," Conrad suggested.

Vorski took a few sips and cried:

"Time... for what? To let her off? Listen to me, Conrad. Rather than let her off, I'd sooner... yes, I'd sooner die in her stead. Give up my task? Ah, you don't know what my task or what my object is! Besides..."

He drank some more:

"It's excellent brandy, but, to settle my heart, I'd rather have rum. Have you any, Conrad?"

"A drain at the bottom of a flask."

"Hand it over."

They had screened the lantern lest they should be seen; and they sat close up to the tree, determined to keep silence. But this fresh drink went to their heads. Vorski began to hold forth very excitedly:

"You've no need of any explanations. The woman who's dying up there, it's no use your knowing her name. It's enough if you know that she's the fourth of the women who were to die on the cross and was specially appointed by fate. But there's one thing I can say to you, now that Vorski's triumph is about to shine forth before your eyes. In fact I take a certain pride in telling you, for, while all that's happened so far has depended on me and my will, the thing that's going to happen directly depends on the mightiest of will, wills working for Vorski!"

He repeated several times, as though smacking his lips over the name:

"For Vorski... For Vorski!"

And he stood up, impelled by the exuberance of his thoughts to walk up and down and wave his arms:

"Vorski, son of a king, Vorski, the elect of destiny, prepare yourself! Your time has come! Either you are the lowest of adventurers and the guiltiest of all the great criminals dyed in the blood of their fellow-men, or else you are really the inspired prophet whom the gods crown with glory. A superman or a highwayman: that is fate's decree. The last heartbeats of the sacred victim sacrificed to the gods are marking the supreme seconds. Listen to them, you two!"

Climbing the ladder, he tried to hear those poor beats of an exhausted heart. But the head, drooping to the left, prevented him from putting his ear to the breast; and he dared not touch it. The silence was broken only by a hoarse and irregular breath.

He said, in a low whisper:

"Véronique, do you hear me? Véronique... Véronique..."

After a moment's hesitation:

"I want you to know it... yes, I myself am terrified at what I'm doing. But it's fate... You remember the prophecy? 'Your wife shall die on the cross.' Why, your very name, Véronique, demands it!... Remember St. Veronica wiping Christ's face with a handkerchief and the Saviour's sacred image remaining on the handkerchief... Véronique, you can hear me, surely? Véronique..."

He ran down hurriedly, snatched the flask of rum from Conrad's hands and emptied it at a draught.

He was now seized with a sort of delirium which made him rave for a few moments in a language which his accomplices did not understand. Then he began to challenge the invisible enemy, to challenge the gods, to hurl forth imprecations and blasphemies:

"Vorski is the mightiest of all men, Vorski governs fate. The elements and the mysterious powers of nature are compelled to obey him. Everything will fall out as he has determined; and the great secret will be declared to him in the mystic forms and according to the rules of the Kabala. Vorski is awaited as the prophet. Vorski will be welcomed with cries of joy and ecstasy; and one whom I know not, one whom I can only half see, will come to meet him with palms and benedictions. Let the unknown make ready! Let him arise from the darkness and ascend from hell! Here stands Vorski. To the sound of bells, to the singing of alleluias, let the fateful sign be revealed upon the face of the heavens, while the earth opens and sends forth whirling flames!"

He fell silent, as though he had descried in the air the signs which he foretold. The hopeless death-rattle of the dying woman sounded from overhead. The storm growled in the distance; and the black clouds were rent by lightning. All nature seemed to be responding to the ruffian's appeal.

His grandiloquent speech and his play-acting made a great impression on the two accomplices.

"He frightens me," Otto muttered.

"It's the rum," Conrad replied. "But all the same he's foretelling terrible things."

"Things which prowl round us," shouted Vorski, whose ears noticed the least sound, "things which make part of the present moment and have been bequeathed to us by the pageant of the centuries. It's like a prodigious childbirth. And I tell the two of you, you will be the amazed witnesses of these things! Otto and Conrad, be prepared as I am: the earth will shake; and, at the very spot where Vorski is to win the God-Stone, a column of fire will rise up to the sky."

"He doesn't know what he's saying," mumbled Conrad.

"And there he is on the ladder again," whispered Otto. "It'll serve him right if he gets an arrow through him."

But Vorski's exaltation knew no bounds. The end was at hand. Extenuated by pain, the victim was in her death-agony.

Beginning very low, so as to be heard by none save her, but raising his voice gradually, Vorski said:

"Véronique... Véronique... You are fulfilling your mission... You are nearing the top of the ascent... All honour to you! You deserve a share in my triumph... All honour to you! Listen! You hear it already, don't you? The artillery of the heavens is drawing near. My enemies are vanquished; you can no longer hope for rescue! Here is the last beat of your heart... Here is your last cry: *'Eloi, Eloi, lama sabachthani?* My God, my God, why hast Thou forsaken me?'"

He screamed with laughter, like a man laughing at the most riotous adventure. Then came silence. The roars of thunder ceased. Vorski bent forward and suddenly, from the top of the ladder, shouted:

"*Eloi, Eloi, lama sabachthani!* The gods have forsaken her. Death has done its work. The last of the four women is dead. Véronique is dead!"

He was silent once again and then roared twice over:

"Véronique is dead! Véronique is dead!"

Once again there was a great, deep silence.

And all of a sudden the earth shook, not with a vibration produced by the thunder, but with a deep inner convulsion, which came from the very bowels of the earth and was repeated several times, like a noise re-echoing through the woods and hills.

And almost at the same time, close by, at the other end of the semicircle of oaks, a fountain of fire shot forth and rose to the sky, in a whirl of smoke in which flared red, yellow and violet flames.

Vorski did not speak a word. His companions stood aghast. One of them stammered:

"It's the old rotten oak, the one which has already been struck by lightning."

Though the fire had disappeared almost instantly, the three men retained the fantastic vision of the old oak, all aglow, vomiting flames and smoke of many colours.

"This is the entrance leading to the God-Stone," said Vorski, solemnly. "Destiny has spoken, as I said it would: and it has spoken at the bidding of me who was once its servant and who am now its master."

He advanced, carrying the lantern. They were surprised to see that the tree showed no trace of fire and that the mass of dry leaves, held as in a bowl where a few lower branches were outspread, had not caught fire.

"Yet another miracle," said Vorski. "It is all an inconceivable miracle."

"What are we going to do?" asked Conrad.

"Go in by the entrance revealed to us... Take the ladder, Conrad, and feel with your hand in that heap of leaves. The tree is hollow and we shall soon see..."

"A tree can be as hollow as you please," said Otto, "but there are always roots to it; and I can hardly believe in a passage through the roots."

"I repeat, we shall see. Move the leaves, Conrad, clear them away."

"No, I won't," said Conrad, bluntly.

"What do you mean, you won't? Why not?"

"Have you forgotten Maguennoc? Have you forgotten that he tried to touch the God-Stone and had to cut his hand off?"

"But this isn't the God-Stone!" Vorski snarled.

"How do you know? Maguennoc was always speaking of the gate of hell. Isn't this what he meant when he talked like that?"

Vorski shrugged his shoulders:

"And you, Otto, are you afraid too?"

Otto did not reply, and Vorski himself did not seem eager to risk the attempt, for he ended by saying:

"After all, there's no hurry. Let's wait till daylight comes. We will cut down the tree with an axe: and that will show us better than anything how things stand and how to go to work."

They agreed accordingly. But, as the signal had been seen by others besides themselves and as they must not allow themselves to be forestalled, they resolved to sit down opposite the tree, under the shelter offered by the huge table of the Fairies' Dolmen.

"Otto," said Vorski, "go to the Priory, fetch us something to drink and also bring an axe, some ropes and anything else that we're likely to want."

The rain was beginning to pour in torrents. They settled themselves under the dolmen and each in turn kept watch while the other slept.

Nothing happened during the night. The storm was very violent. They could hear the waves roaring. Then gradually everything grew quiet.

At daybreak they attacked the oak-tree, which they soon overthrew by pulling upon the ropes.

They now saw that, inside the tree itself, amid the rubbish and the dry rot, a sort of trench had been dug, which extended through the mass of sand and stones packed about the roots.

They cleared the ground with a pick-axe. Some steps at once came into sight: there was a sudden drop of earth: and they saw a staircase which followed a perpendicular wall and led down into the darkness. They threw the light of their lantern before them. A cavern opened beneath their feet.

Vorski was the first to venture down. The others followed him cautiously.

The steps, which at first consisted of earthen stairs reinforced by flints, were presently hewn out of the rock. The cave which they entered was in no way peculiar and seemed rather to be a vestibule. It communicated, in fact, with a sort of crypt, which had a vaulted ceiling and walls of rough masonry of unmortared stones.

All around, like shapeless statues, stood twelve small menhirs, each of which was surmounted by a horse's skull. Vorski touched one of these skulls; it crumbled into dust.

"No one has been to this crypt," he said, "for twenty centuries. We are the first men to tread the floor of it, the first to behold the traces of the past which it contains."

He added, with increasing emphasis:

"It is the mortuary-chamber of a great chieftain. They used to bury his favourite horses with him... and his weapons too. Look, here are axes... and a flint knife; and we also find the remains of certain funeral rites, as this piece of charcoal shows and, over there, those charred bones..."

His voice was husky with emotion. He muttered: "I am the first to enter here. I was expected. A whole world awakens at my coming."

Conrad interrupted him:

"There are other doorways, another passage; and there's a sort of light showing in the distance."

A narrow corridor brought them to a second chamber, through which they reached yet a third. The three crypts were exactly alike, with the same masonry, the same upright stones, the same horses' skulls.

"The tombs of three great chieftains," said Vorski. "They evidently lead to the tomb of a king; and the chieftains must have been the king's guards, after being his companions during his lifetime. No doubt it's the next crypt."

He hesitated to go farther, not from fear, but from excessive excitement and a sense of inflamed vanity which he was enjoying to the full:

"I am on the verge of knowledge," he declaimed, in dramatic tones. "Vorski is approaching the goal and has only to put out his hand to be regally rewarded for his labours and his struggles. The God-Stone is there. For ages and ages men have sought to fathom the secret of the island and not one has succeeded. Vorski came and the God-Stone is his. So let it show itself to me and give me the promised power. There is nothing between it and Vorski, nothing but my will. And I declare my will! The prophet has risen out of the night. He is here. If there be, in this kingdom of the dead, a shade whose duty it is to lead me to the divine stone and place the golden crown upon my head, let that shade arise! Here stands Vorski."

He went in.

The fourth room was much larger and shaped like a dome with a slightly flattened summit. In the middle of the flattened part was a round hole, no wider than the hole left by a very small flue; and from it there fell a shaft of half-veiled light which formed a very plainly-defined disk on the floor.

The centre of this disk was occupied by a little block of stones set together. And on this block, as though purposely displayed, lay a metal rod.

In other respects, this crypt did not differ from the first three. Like them it was adorned with menhirs and horses' heads, like them it contained traces of sacrifices.

Vorski did not take his eyes off the metal rod. Strange to say, the metal gleamed as though no dust had ever covered it. He put out his hand.

"No, no," said Conrad, quickly.

"Why not?"

"It may be the one Maguennoc touched and burnt his hand with."

"You're mad."

"Still..."

"Oh, I'm not afraid of anything!" Vorski declared taking hold of the rod.

It was a leaden sceptre, very clumsily made, but nevertheless revealing a certain artistic intention. Round the handle was a snake, here encrusted in the lead, there standing out in relief. Its huge, disproportionate head formed the pommel and was studded with silver nails and little green pebbles transparent as emeralds.

"Is it the God-Stone?" Vorski muttered.

He handled the thing and examined it all over with respectful awe; and he soon observed that the pommel shifted almost loose. He fingered it, turned it to the left, to the right, until at length it gave a click and the snake's head became unfastened.

There was a space inside, containing a stone, a tiny, pale-red stone, with yellow streaks that looked like veins of gold.

"It's the God-Stone, it's the God-Stone!" said Vorski, greatly agitated.

"Don't touch it!" Conrad repeated, filled with alarm.

"What burnt Maguennoc will not burn me," replied Vorski, solemnly.

And, in bravado, swelling with pride and delight, he kept the mysterious stone in the hollow of his hand, which he clenched with all his strength:

"Let it burn me! I will let it! Let it sear my flesh! I shall be glad if it will!"

Conrad made a sign to him and put his finger to his lips.

"What's the matter?" asked Vorski. "Do you hear anything?"

"Yes," said the other.

"So do I," said Otto.

What they heard was a rhythmical, measured sound, which rose and fell and made a sort of irregular music.

"Why, it's close by!" mumbled Vorski. "It sounds as if it were in the room."

"ELOI, ELOI, LAMA SABACHTHANI!"

It was in the room, as they soon learnt for certain; and there was no doubt that the sound was very like a snore.

Conrad, who had ventured on this suggestion, was the first to laugh at it; but Vorski said:

"Upon my word, I'm inclined to think you're right. It *is* a snore... There must be someone here then?"

"It comes from over there," said Otto, "from that corner in the dark."

The light did not extend beyond the menhirs. Behind each of them opened a small, shadowy chapel. Vorski turned his lantern into one of these and at once uttered a cry of amazement:

"Someone... yes... there is someone... Look..."

The two accomplices came forward. On a heap of rubble, piled up in an angle of the wall, a man lay sleeping, an old man with a white beard and long white hair. A thousand wrinkles furrowed the skin of his face and hands. There were blue rings round his closed eyelids. At least a century must have passed over his head.

He was dressed in a patched and torn linen robe, which came down to his feet. Round his neck and hanging over his chest was a string of those sacred beads which the Gauls called serpents' eggs and which are actually sea-eggs or sea-urchins. Within reach of his hand was a handsome jadeite axe, covered with illegible symbols. On the ground, in a row, lay sharp-edged flints, some large, flat rings, two ear-drops of green jasper and two necklaces of fluted blue enamel.

The old man went on snoring.

Vorski muttered:

"The miracle continues... It's a priest... a priest like those of the olden time... of the time of the Druids."

"And then?" asked Otto.

"Why, then he's waiting for me!"

Conrad expressed his brutal opinion:

"I suggest we break his head with his axe."

But Vorski flew into a rage:

"If you touch a single hair of his head, you're a dead man!"

"Still..."

"Still what?"

"He may be an enemy... he may be the one whom we were pursuing last night... Remember... the white robe."

"You're the biggest fool I ever met! Do you think that, at his age, he could have kept us on the run like that?"

He bent over and took the old man gently by the arm, saying:

"Wake up!... It's I!"

There was no answer. The man did not wake up.

Vorski insisted.

The man moved on his bed of stones, mumbled a few words and went to sleep again.

Vorski, growing a little impatient, renewed his attempts, but more vigorously, and raised his voice:

"I say, what about it? We can't hang about all day, you know. Come on!"

He shook the old man more roughly. The man made a movement of irritation, pushed away his importunate visitor, clung to sleep a few seconds longer and, in the end, turned round wearily and, in an angry voice, growled:

"Oh, rats!"

14

THE ANCIENT DRUID

The three accomplices, who were perfectly acquainted with all the niceties of the French language and familiar with every slang phrase, did not for a moment mistake the true sense of that unexpected exclamation. They were astounded.

Vorski put the question to Conrad and Otto.

"Eh? What does he say?"

"What you heard... That's right," said Otto.

Vorski ended by making a fresh attack on the shoulder of the stranger, who turned on his couch, stretched himself, yawned, seemed to fall asleep again, and, suddenly admitting himself defeated, half sat up and shouted:

"When you've quite finished, please! Can't a man have a quiet snooze these days, in this beastly hole?"

A ray of light blinded his eyes: and he spluttered, in alarm:

"What is it? What do you want with me?"

Vorski put down his lantern on a projection in the wall; and the face now stood clearly revealed. The old man, who had continued to vent his ill temper in incoherent complaints, looked at his visitor, became gradually calmer, even assumed an amiable and almost smiling expression and, holding out his hand, exclaimed:

"Well, I never! Why, it's you, Vorski! How are you, old bean?"

Vorski gave a start. That the old man should know him and call him by his name did not astonish him immensely, since he had the half-mystic conviction that he was expected as a prophet might be. But to a prophet, to a missionary clad in light and glory, entering the presence of a stranger crowned with the double majesty of age and sacerdotal rank, it was painful to be hailed by the name of "old bean!"

Hesitating, ill at ease, not knowing with whom he was dealing, he asked:

"Who are you? What are you here for? How did you get here?"

And, when the other stared at him with a look of surprise, he repeated, in a louder voice:

"Answer me, can't you? Who are you?"

"Who am I?" replied the old man, in a husky and bleating voice. "Who am I? By Teutatès, god of the Gauls, is it you who ask me that question? Then you don't know me? Come, try and remember... Good old Ségenax—eh, do you get me now—Velléda's father, good old Ségenax, the law-giver venerated by the Rhedons of whom Chateaubriand speaks in the first volume of his *Martyrs*?... Ah, I see your memory's reviving!"

"What are you gassing about!" cried Vorski.

"I'm not gassing. I'm explaining my presence here and the regrettable events which brought me here long ago. Disgusted by the scandalous behaviour of Velléda, who had gone wrong with that dismal blighter Eudorus, I became what we should call a Trappist nowadays, that is to say, I passed a brilliant exam, as a bachelor of Druid laws. Since that time, in consequence of a few sprees—oh, nothing to speak of: three or four jaunts to Paris, where I was attracted by Mabille and afterwards by the Moulin Rouge—I was obliged to accept the little berth which I fill here, a cushy job, as you see: guardian of the God-Stone, a shirker's job, what!"

Vorski's amazement and uneasiness increased at each word. He consulted his companions.

"Break his head," Conrad repeated. "That's what I say: and I stick to it."

"And you, Otto?"

"I think we ought to be on our guard."

"Of course we must be on our guard."

But the old Druid caught the word. Leaning on a staff, he helped himself up and exclaimed:

"What's the meaning of this? Be on your guard... against me! That's really a bit thick! Treat me as a fake! Why, haven't you seen my axe, with the pattern of the swastika? The swastika, the leading cabalistic symbol, eh, what?... And this? What do you call this?" He lifted his string of beads. "What do you call it? Horse-chestnuts? You've got some cheek, you have, to give a name like that to serpents' eggs, 'eggs which they form out of slaver and the froth of their bodies mingled and which they cast into the air, hissing the while.' It's Pliny's own words I'm quoting! You're not going to treat Pliny also as a fake, I hope!... You're a pretty customer! Putting yourself on your guard against me, when I have all my degrees as an ancient Druid, all my diplomas, all my patents, all my certificates signed by Pliny and Chateaubriand! The cheek of you!... Upon my word, you won't find many ancient Druids of my sort, genuine, of the period, with the bloom of age upon them and a beard of centuries! I a fake, I, who boast every tradition and who juggle with the customs of antiquity!... Shall I dance the ancient Druid dance for you, as I did before Julius Caesar? Would you like me to?"

And, without waiting for a reply, the old man, flinging aside his staff, began to cut the most extravagant capers and to execute the wildest of jigs with perfectly astounding agility. And it was the most laughable sight to see him jumping and twisting about, with his back bent, his arms outstretched, his legs shooting to right and left from under his robe, his beard following the evolutions of his frisking body, while the bleating voice announced the successive changes in the performance:

"The ancient Druids' dance, or Caesar's delight! Hi-tiddly, hi-tiddly, hi-ti, hi!... The mistletoe dance, vulgarly known as the tickletoe!... The serpents' egg waltz, music by Pliny! Hullo there! Begone, dull care!... The Vorska, or the tango of the thirty coffins!... The hymn of the Red Prophet! Hallelujah! Hallelujah! Glory be to the prophet!"

He continued his furious jig a little longer and then suddenly halted before Vorski and, in a solemn tone, said:

"Enough of this prattle! Let us talk seriously, I am commissioned to hand you the God-Stone. Now that you are here, are you ready to take delivery of the goods?"

The three accomplices were absolutely flabbergasted. Vorski did not know what to do, was unable to make out who the infernal fellow was:

"Oh, shut up!" he shouted, angrily. "What do you want? What's your object?"

"What do you mean, my object? I've just told you; to hand you the God-Stone!"

"But by what right? In what capacity?"

The ancient Druid nodded his head:

"Yes, I see what you're after. Things are not happening in the least as you thought they would. Of course, you came here feeling jolly spry, glad and proud of the work you had done. Just think; furnishings for thirty coffins, four women crucified, shipwrecks, hands steeped in blood, murders galore. Those things are no small beer; and you were expecting an imposing reception, with an official ceremony, solemn pomp and state, antique choirs, processions of bards and minstrels, human sacrifices and what not; the whole Gallic bag of tricks! Instead of which, a poor beggar of a Druid, snoozing in a corner, who just simply offers you the goods. What a come down, my lords! Can't be helped, Vorski; we do what we can and every man acts according to the means at his disposal. I'm not a millionaire, you know; and I've already advanced you, in addition to the washing of a few white robes, some thirty francs forty for Bengal lights, fountains of fire and a nocturnal earthquake."

Vorski started, suddenly understanding and beside himself with rage:

"What! So it was..."

"Of course it was me! Who did you think it was? St. Augustine? Unless you believed in an intervention of the gods and supposed that they took the trouble last night to send an archangel to the island, arrayed in a white robe, to lead you to the hollow oak!... Really, you're asking too much!"

Vorski clenched his fists. So the man in white whom he had pursued the night before was no other than this impostor!

"Oh," he growled, "I'm not fond of having my leg pulled!"

"Having your leg pulled!" cried the old man. "You've got a cheek, old chap! Who hunted me like a wild beast, till I was quite out of breath? And who drove bullets through my best Sunday robe? I never knew such a fellow! It'll teach me to put my back into a job again!"

"That'll do!" roared Vorski. "That'll do. Once more and for the last time... what do you want with me?"

"I'm sick of telling you. I am commissioned to hand you the God-Stone."

"Commissioned by whom?"

"Oh, hanged if I know! I've always been brought up to believe that someday a prince of Almain would appear at Sarek, one Vorski, who would slay his thirty victims and to whom I was to make an agreed signal when his thirtieth victim had breathed her last. Therefore, as I'm a slave to orders, I got together my little parcel, bought two Bengal lights at three francs seventy-five apiece at a hardware shop in Brest, *plus* a few choice crackers, and, at the appointed hour, took up my perch in my observatory, taper in hand, all ready for work. When you started howling, in the top of the tree, 'She's dead! She's dead!', I thought that was the right moment, set fire to the lights and with my crackers shook the bowels of the earth. There! Now you know all about it."

Vorski stepped forward, with his fists raised to strike. That torrent of words, that imperturbable composure, that calm, bantering voice put him beside himself.

"Another word and I'll knock you down!" he cried. "I've had enough of it."

"Is your name Vorski?"

"Yes; and then?"

"Are you a prince of Almain?"

"Yes, yes; and then?"

"Have you slain your thirty victims?"

"Yes, yes, yes!"

"Well, then you're my man. I have a God-Stone to hand you and I mean to hand it you, come what may. That's the sort of hairpin I am. You've got to pocket it, your miracle-stone."

"But I don't care a hang for the God-Stone!" roared Vorski, stamping his foot. "And I don't care a hang for you! I want nobody. The God-Stone! Why, I've got it, it's mine. I've got it on me."

"Let's have a look."

"What do you call that?" said Vorski, taking from his pocket the little stone disk which he had found in the pommel of the sceptre.

"That?" asked the old man, with an air of surprise. "Where did you get that from?"

"From the pommel of this sceptre, when I unfastened it."

"And what do you call it?"

"It's a piece of the God-Stone."

"You're mad."

"Then what do you say it is?"

"That's a trouser-button."

"A what?"

"A trouser-button."

"How do you make that out?"

"A trouser-button with the shaft broken off, a button of the sort which the niggers in the Sahara wear. I've a whole set of them."

"Prove it, damn you!"

"I put it there."

"What for?"

"To take the place of the precious stone which Maguennoc sneaked, the one which burnt him and obliged him to cut off his hand."

Vorski was silent. He was nonplussed. He had no notion what to do next or how to behave towards this strange adversary.

The ancient Druid went up to him and, gently, in a fatherly voice:

"No, my lad," he said, "you can't do without me, you see. I alone hold the key of the safe and the secret of the casket. Why do you hesitate?"

"I don't know you."

"You baby! If I were suggesting something indelicate and incompatible with your honour, I could understand your scruples. But my offer is one of those which can't offend the nicest conscience. Well, is it a bargain? No? Not yet? But, by Teutatès, what more do you want, you unbelieving Vorski? A miracle perhaps? Lord, why didn't you say so before? Miracles, forsooth: I turn 'em out thirteen to the dozen. I work a little miracle before breakfast every morning. Just think, a Druid! Miracles? Why, I've got my shop full of 'em! I can't find room to sit down for them. Where will you try first? Resurrection department? Hair-restoring department? Revelation of the future department? You can choose where you like. Look here, at what time did your thirtieth victim breathe her last?"

"How should I know?"

"Eleven fifty-two. Your excitement was so great that it stopped your watch. Look and see."

It was ridiculous. The shock produced by excitement has no effect on the watch of the man who experiences the excitement. Nevertheless, Vorski involuntarily took out his watch: it marked eight minutes to twelve. He tried to wind it up: it was broken.

The ancient Druid, without giving him time to recover his breath and reply, went on:

"That staggers you, eh? And yet there's nothing simpler for a Druid who knows his business. A Druid sees the invisible. He does more: he makes anyone else see it if he wants to. Vorski, would you like to see something that doesn't exist? What's your name? I'm not speaking of your name Vorski, but of your real name, your governor's name."

"Silence on that subject!" Vorski commanded. "It's a secret I've revealed to nobody."

"Then why do you write it down?"

"I've never written it down."

"Vorski, your father's name is written in red pencil on the fourteenth page of the little note-book you carry on you. Look and see."

Acting mechanically, like an automaton whose movements are controlled by an alien will, Vorski took from his inside pocket a case containing a small notebook. He turned the pages till he came to the fourteenth, when he muttered, with indescribable dismay:

"Impossible! Who wrote this? And you know what's written here?"

"Do you want me to prove it to you?"

"Once more, silence! I forbid you..."

"As you please, old chap! All that I do is meant for your edification. And it's no trouble to me! Once I start working miracles, I simply can't stop. Here's another funny little trick.

You carry a locket hanging from a silver chain round your shirt, don't you?"

"Yes," said Vorski, his eyes blazing with fever.

"The locket consists of a frame, without the photograph which used to be set in it."

"Yes, yes, a portrait of..."

"Of your mother, I know: and you lost it."

"Yes, I lost it last year."

"You mean you *think* you've lost the portrait."

"Nonsense, the locket is empty."

"You *think* the locket's empty. It's not. Look and see."

Still moving mechanically, with his eyes starting from his head, Vorski unfastened the button of his shirt and pulled out the chain. The locket appeared. There was the portrait of a woman in a round gold frame.

"It's she, it's she," he muttered, completely taken aback.

"Quite sure?"

"Yes."

"Then what do you say to it all, eh? There's no fake about it, no deception. The ancient Druid's a smart chap and you're coming with him, aren't you?"

"Yes."

Vorski was beaten. The man had subjugated him. His superstitious instincts, his inherited belief in the mysterious powers, his restless and unbalanced nature, all imposed absolute submission on him. His suspicion persisted, but did not prevent him from obeying.

"Is it far?" he asked.

"Next door, in the great hall."

Otto and Conrad had been the astounded witnesses of this dialogue. Conrad tried to protest. But Vorski silenced him:

"If you're afraid, go away. Besides," he added, with an affectation of assurance, "besides, we shall walk with our revolvers ready. At the slightest alarm, fire."

"Fire on me?" chuckled the ancient Druid.

"Fire on any enemy, no matter who it may be."

"Well, you go first, Vorski... What, won't you?"

He had brought them to the very end of the crypt, in the darkest shadow, where the lantern showed them a recess hollowed at the foot of the wall and plunging into the rocks in a downward direction.

Vorski hesitated and then entered. He had to crawl on his hands and knees in this narrow, winding passage, from which he emerged, a minute later, on the threshold of a large hall.

The others joined him.

"The hall of the God-Stone," the ancient Druid declared, solemnly.

It was lofty and imposing, similar in shape and size to the broad walk under which it lay. The same number of upright stones, which seemed to be the columns of an immense temple, stood in the same place and formed the same rows as the menhirs on the walk overhead: stones hewn in the same uncouth way, with no regard for art or symmetry. The floor was composed of huge irregular flagstones, intersected with a network of gutters and covered with round patches of dazzling light, falling from above at some distance one from the other.

In the centre, under Maguennoc's garden, rose a platform of unmortared stones, fourteen or fifteen feet high, with sides about twenty yards long. On the top was a dolmen with two sturdy supports and a long, oval granite table.

"Is that it?" asked Vorski, in a husky voice.

Without giving a direct answer, the ancient Druid said:

"What do you think of it? They were dabs at building, those ancestors of ours! And what ingenuity they displayed! What precautions against prying eyes and profane enquiries! Do you know where the light comes from? For we are in the bowels of the island and there are no windows opening on to the sky. The light comes from the upper menhirs. They are pierced from the top to bottom with a channel which widens as it goes down and which sheds floods of light below. In the middle of the day, when the sun is shining, it's like fairyland. You, who are an artist, would shout with admiration."

"Then that's *it?*" Vorski repeated.

"At any rate, it's a sacred stone," declared the ancient Druid, impassively, "since it used to overlook the place of the underground sacrifices, which were the most important of all. But there is another one underneath, which is protected by the dolmen and which you can't see from here; and that is the one on which the selected victims were offered up. The blood used to flow from the platform and along all these gutters to the cliff's and down to the sea."

Vorski muttered, more and more excited:

"Then that's it? If so, let's go on."

"No need to stir," said the old man, with exasperating coolness. "It's not that one either. There's a third; and to see that one you have only to lift your head a little."

"Where? Are you sure?"

"Of course! Take a good look... above the upper table, yes, in the very vault which forms the ceiling and which is like a mosaic made of great flagstones... You can twig it from here, can't you? A flagstone forming a separate oblong, long and narrow like the lower table and shaped like it... They might be two sisters... But there's only one good one, stamped with the trademark..."

Vorski was disappointed. He had expected a more elaborate introduction to a more mysterious hiding-place.

"Is that the God-Stone?" he asked. "Why, it has nothing particular about it."

"From a distance, no; but wait till you see it close by. There are coloured veins in it, glittering lodes, a special grain: in short, the God-Stone. Besides, it's remarkable not so much for its substance as for its miraculous properties."

"What are the miracles in question?" asked Vorski.

"It gives life and death, as you know, and it gives a lot of other things."

"What sort of things?"

"Oh, hang it, you're asking me too much! I don't know anything about it."

"How do you mean, you don't know?"

The ancient Druid leant over and, in a confidential tone:

"Listen, Vorski," he said, "I confess that I have been boasting a bit and that my function, though of the greatest importance—keeper of the God-Stone, you know, a first-class berth—is limited by a power which in a manner of speaking is higher than my own."

"What power?"

"Velléda's."

Vorski eyed him with renewed uneasiness:

"Velléda?"

"Yes, or at least the woman whom I call Velléda, the last of the Druidesses: I don't know her real name."

"Where is she?"

"Here."

"Here?"

"Yes, on the sacrificial stone. She's asleep."

"What, she's asleep?"

"She's been sleeping for centuries, since all time. I've never seen her other than sleeping: a chaste and peaceful slumber. Like the Sleeping Beauty, Velléda is waiting for him whom the gods have appointed to awake her; and that is..."

"Who?"

"You, Vorski, you."

Vorski knitted his brows. What was the meaning of this improbable story and what was his impenetrable interlocutor driving at?

The ancient Druid continued:

"That seems to ruffle you! Come, there's no reason, just because your hands are red with blood and because you have thirty coffins on your mind, why you shouldn't have the right to act as Prince Charming. You're too modest, my young friend. Look here, Velléda is marvellously beautiful: I tell you, hers is a superhuman beauty. Ah, my fine fellow, you're getting excited! What? Not yet?"

Vorski hesitated. Really he was feeling the danger increase around him and rise like a swelling wave that is about to break. But the old man would not leave him alone:

"One last word, Vorski; and I'm speaking low so that your friends shan't hear me. When you wrapped your mother in her shroud, you left on her fore-finger, in obedience to her formal wish, a ring which she had always worn, a magic ring made of a large turquoise surrounded by a circle of smaller turquoises set in gold. Am I right?"

"Yes," gasped Vorski, taken aback, "yes, you're right: but I was alone and it is a secret which nobody knew."

"Vorski, if that ring is on Velléda's finger, will you trust me and will you believe that your mother, in her grave, appointed Velléda to receive you, that she herself might hand you the miraculous stone?"

Vorski was already walking towards the tumulus. He quickly climbed the first few steps. His head passed the level of the platform.

"Oh," he said, staggering back, "the ring... the ring is on her finger!"

Between the two supports of the dolmen, stretched on the sacrificial table and clad in a spotless gown that came down to her feet, lay the Druidess. Her body and face were turned the other way; and a veil hanging over her forehead hid her hair. Almost bare, her shapely arm lay along the table. On the forefinger was a turquoise ring.

"Is that your mother's ring all right?" asked the ancient Druid.

"Yes, there's no doubt about it."

Vorski had hurried across the space between himself and the dolmen and, stooping, almost kneeling, was examining the turquoises.

"The number is complete," he whispered. "One of them is cracked. Another is half covered by the gold setting which has worked down over it."

"You needn't be so cautious," said the old man. "She won't hear you; and your voice can't wake her. What you had better do is to stand up and pass your hand lightly over her forehead. That is the magic caress which will rouse her from her slumber."

Vorski stood up. Nevertheless he hesitated to approach the woman, who inspired him with ungovernable fear and respect.

"Don't come any nearer, you two," said the ancient Druid, addressing Otto and Conrad. "When Velléda's eyes open, they must rest on no one but Vorski and behold no other sight. Well, Vorski, are you afraid?"

"No, I'm not afraid."

"Only you're not feeling comfortable. It's easier to murder people than to bring them to life, what? Come, show yourself a man! Put aside her veil and touch her forehead. The God-Stone is within your reach. Act and you will be the master of the world."

Vorski acted. Standing against the sacrificial altar, he looked down upon the Druidess. He bent over the motionless bust. The white gown rose and fell to the regular rhythm of the breathing. With an undecided hand he drew back the veil and then stooped lower, so that his other hand might touch the uncovered forehead.

But at that moment his action remained, so to speak, suspended and he stood without moving, like a man who does not understand but is vainly trying to understand.

"Well, what's up, old chap?" exclaimed the Druid. "You look petrified. Another squabble? Something gone wrong? Must I come and help you?"

Vorski did not answer. He was staring wildly, with an expression of stupefaction and affright which gradually changed into one of mad terror. Drops of perspiration trickled over his face. His haggard eyes seemed to be gazing upon the most horrible vision.

The old man burst out laughing:

"Lord love us, how ugly you are! I hope the last of the Druidesses won't raise her divine eyelids and see that hideous mug of yours! Sleep, Velléda, sleep your pure and dreamless sleep."

Vorski stood muttering between his teeth incoherent words which conveyed the menace of an increasing anger. The truth became partly revealed to him in a series of flashes. A word rose to his lips which he refused to utter, as though, in uttering it, he feared lest he should give life to a being who was no more, to that woman who was dead, yes, dead though she lay breathing before him: she could not but be dead, because he had killed her. However, in the end and in spite of himself, he spoke; and every syllable cost him intolerable suffering:

"Véronique... Véronique..."

"So you think she's like her?" chuckled the ancient Druid. "Upon my word, may be you are right: there is a sort of family resemblance... I dare say, if you hadn't crucified the other with your own hands and if you hadn't yourself received her last breath, you would be ready to swear that the two women are one and the same person... and that Véronique d'Hergemont is alive and that she's not even wounded... not even a scar... not so much as the mark of the cords round her wrists... But just look, Vorski, what a peaceful face, what comforting serenity! Upon my word, I'm beginning to believe that you made a mistake and that it was another woman you crucified! Just think a bit!...

Hullo, you're going to go for me now! Come to my rescue, O Teutatès! The prophet wants to have my blood!"

Vorski had drawn himself up and was now facing the ancient Druid. His features, fashioned for hatred and fury, had surely never expressed more of either than at this moment. The ancient Druid was not merely the man who for an hour had been toying with him as with a child. He was the man who had performed the most extraordinary feat and who suddenly appeared to him as the most ruthless and dangerous foe. A man like that must be got rid of on the spot, since the opportunity presented itself.

"I'm done!" said the old man. "He's going to eat me up! Crikey, what an ogre!... Help! Murder! Help!... Oh, look at his iron fingers! He's going to strangle me!... Unless he uses a dagger... or a rope... No, a revolver! I prefer that, it's neater... Fire away, Alexis. Two of the seven bullets have already made holes in my best Sunday robe. That leaves five. Fire away, Alexis."

Each word aggravated Vorski's fury. He was eager to get the work over and he shouted:

"Otto... Conrad... are you ready?"

He raised his arm. The two assistants likewise took aim. Four paces in front of them stood the old man, laughingly pleading for mercy:

"Please, kind gentlemen, have pity on a poor beggar... I won't do it again... I'll be a good boy... Kind gentlemen, please..."

Vorski repeated:

"Otto... Conrad... attention!... I'm counting three: one... two... three... fire!"

The three shots rang out together. The Druid whirled round with one leg in the air, then drew himself up straight, opposite his adversaries, and cried, in a tragic voice:

"A hit, a palpable hit! Shot through the body! Dead, for a ducat!... The ancient Druid's *kaput*!... A tragic development! Oh, the poor old Druid, who was so fond of his joke!"

"Fire!" roared Vorski. "Shoot, can't you, you idiots? Fire!"

"Fire! Fire!" repeated the Druid. "Bang! Bang! A bull's eye!... Two!... Three bull's eyes!... Your shot, Conrad: bang!... Yours, Otto: bang!"

The shots rattled and echoed through the great resounding hall. The bewildered and furious accomplices were gesticulating before their target, while the invulnerable old man danced and kicked, now almost squatting on his heels, now leaping up with astounding agility:

"Lord, what fun one can have in a cave! And what a fool you are, Vorski, my own! You blooming old prophet!... What a mug! But, I say, however could you take it all in? The Bengal lights! The crackers! And the trouser-button! And your old mother's ring!... You silly juggins! What a spoof!"

Vorski stopped. He realized that the three revolvers had been made harmless, but how? By what unprecedented marvel? What was at the bottom of all this fantastic adventure? Who was that demon standing in front of him?

He flung away his useless weapon and looked at the old man. Was he thinking of seizing him in his arms and crushing the life out of him? He also looked at the woman and seemed ready to fall upon her. But he obviously no longer felt equal to facing those two strange creatures, who appeared to him to be remote from the world and from actuality.

Then, quickly, he turned on his heel and, calling to his accomplices, made for the crypts, followed by the ancient Druid's jeers:

"Look at that now! He's slinging his hook! And the God-Stone, what about it? What do you want me to do with it?... I say, isn't he showing a clean pair of heels!... Hi! Are your trousers on fire? Yoicks, tally-ho, tally-ho! Proph—et Proph—et!..."

15

THE HALL OF THE UNDERGROUND SACRIFICES

Vorski had never known fear and he was perhaps not yielding to an actual sense of fear in taking to flight now. But he no longer knew what he was doing. His bewildered brain was filled with a whirl of contradictory and incoherent ideas in which the intuition of an irretrievable and to some extent supernatural defeat held the first place.

Believing as he did in witchcraft and wonders, he had an impression that Vorski, the man of destiny, had fallen from his mission and been replaced by another chosen favourite of destiny. There were two miraculous forces opposed to each other, one emanating from him, Vorski, the other from the ancient Druid; and the second was absorbing the first. Véronique's resurrection, the ancient Druid's personality, the speeches, the jokes, the leaps and bounds, the actions, the invulnerability of that spring-heeled individual, all this seemed to him magical and fabulous; and it created, in these caves of the barbaric ages, a peculiar atmosphere which stifled and demoralized him.

He was eager to return to the surface of the earth. He wanted to breathe and see. And what he wanted above all to see was the tree stripped of its branches to which he had tied Véronique and on which Véronique had expired.

"For she *is* dead," he snarled, as he crawled through the narrow passage which communicated with the third and largest of the crypts. "She *is* dead. I know what death means. I have often held it in my hands and I make no mistakes. Then how did that demon manage to bring her to life again?"

He stopped abruptly near the block on which he had picked up the sceptre:

"Unless..." he said.

Conrad, following him, cried:

"Hurry up, instead of chattering."

Vorski allowed himself to be pulled along; but, as he went, he continued:

"Shall I tell you what I think, Conrad? Well, the woman he showed us, the one asleep, wasn't that one at all. Was she even alive? Oh, the old wizard is capable of anything! He'll have modelled a figure, a wax doll, and given it her likeness."

"You're mad. Get on!"

"I'm not mad. That woman was not alive. The one who died on the tree is properly dead. And you'll find her again up there, I warrant you. Miracles, yes, but not such a miracle as that!"

Having left their lantern behind them, the three accomplices kept bumping against the wall and the upright stones. Their footsteps echoed from vault to vault. Conrad never ceased grumbling:

"I warned you... We ought to have broken his head."

Otto, out of breath with walking, said nothing.

Thus, groping their way, they reached the lobby which preceded the entrance-crypt; and they were not a little surprised to find that this first hall was dark, though the passage which they had dug in the upper part, under the roots of the dead oak, ought to have given a certain amount of light.

"That's funny," said Conrad.

"Pooh!" said Otto. "We've only got to find the ladder hooked to the wall. Here, I have it... here's a step... and the next..."

He climbed the rungs, but was pulled up almost at once:

"Can't get any farther... It's as if there had been a fall of earth."

"Impossible!" Vorski protested. "However, wait a bit, I was forgetting: I have my pocket-lighter."

He struck a light; and the same cry of anger escaped all three of them: the whole of the top of the staircase and half the room was buried under a heap of stones and sand, with the trunk of the dead oak fallen in the middle. Not a chance of escape remained.

Vorski gave way to a fit of despair and collapsed on the stairs:

"We're tricked. It's that old brute who has played us this trick... which shows that he's not alone."

He bewailed his fate, raving, lacking the strength to continue the unequal struggle. But Conrad grew angry:

"I say, Vorski, this isn't like you, you know."

"There's nothing to be done against that fellow."

"Nothing to be done! In the first place, there's this, as I've told you twenty times: wring his neck. Oh, why did I restrain myself?"

"You couldn't even have laid a hand on him. Did any of our bullets touch him?"

"Our bullets... our bullets," muttered Conrad. "All this strikes me as mighty queer. Hand me your lighter. I have another revolver, which comes from the Priory: and I loaded it myself yesterday morning. I'll soon see."

He examined the weapon and was not long in discovering that the seven cartridges which he had put in the cylinder had been replaced by seven cartridges from which the bullets had been extracted and which could therefore fire nothing except blank shots.

"That explains it," he said, "and your ancient Druid is no more of a wizard than I am. If our revolvers had been really loaded, we'd have shot him down like a dog."

But the explanation only increased Vorski's alarm:

"And how did he unload them? At what moment did he manage to take our revolvers from our pockets and put them back after drawing the charges? I did not leave go of mine for an instant."

"No more did I," Conrad admitted.

"And I defy anyone to touch it without my knowing. So what then? Doesn't it prove that that demon has a special power? After all, we must look at things as they are. He's a man who possesses secrets of his own... and who has means at his disposal, means which..."

Conrad shrugged his shoulders:

"Vorski, this business has shattered you. You were within reach of the goal and yet you let go at the first obstacle. You're turned into a dish-cloth. Well, I don't bow my head like you. Tricked? Why so? If he comes after us, there are three of us."

"He won't come. He'll leave us here shut up in a burrow with no way out of it."

"Then, if he doesn't come, I'll go back there, I will! I've got my knife; that's enough for me."

"You're wrong, Conrad."

"How am I wrong? I'm a match for any man, especially for that old blighter; and he's only got a sleeping woman to help him."

"Conrad, he's not a man and she's not a woman. Be careful."

"I'm careful and I'm going."

"You're going, you're going; but what's your plan?"

"I've no plan. Or rather, if I have, it's to out that beggar."

"All the same, mind what you're doing. Don't go for him bull-headed; try to take him by surprise."

"Well, of course!" said Conrad, moving away. "I'm not ass enough to risk his attacks. Be easy, I've got the bounder!"

Conrad's daring comforted Vorski.

"After all," he said, when his accomplice was gone, "he's right. If that old Druid didn't come after us, it's because he's got other ideas in his head. He certainly doesn't expect us to return on the offensive; and Conrad can very well take him by surprise. What do you say, Otto?"

Otto shared his opinion:

"He has only to bide his time," he replied.

Fifteen minutes passed. Vorski gradually recovered his assurance. He had yielded to the reaction, after an excess of hope followed by disappointment too great for him to bear and also because of the weariness and depression produced by his drinking-bout. But the fighting spirit stimulated him once more; and he was anxious to have done with his adversary.

"I shouldn't be surprised," he said, "if Conrad had finished him off by now."

By this time he had acquired an exaggerated confidence which proved his unbalanced state of mind; and he wanted to go back again at once.

"Come along, Otto, it's the last trip. An old beggar to get rid of; and the thing's done. You've got your dagger? Besides, it won't be wanted. My two hands will do the trick."

"And suppose that blasted Druid has friends?"

"We'll see."

He once more went towards the crypts, moving cautiously and watching the opening of the passages which led from one to the other. No sound reached their ears. The light in the third crypt showed them the way.

"Conrad must have succeeded," Vorski observed. "If not, he would have shirked the fight and come back to us."

Otto agreed.

THE HALL OF THE UNDERGROUND SACRIFICES 233

"It's a good sign, of course, that we don't see him. The ancient Druid must have had a bad time of it. Conrad is a scorcher."

They entered the third crypt. Things were in the places where they had left them: the sceptre on the block and the pommel, which Vorski had unfastened, a little way off, on the ground. But, when he cast his eyes towards the shadowy recess where the ancient Druid was sleeping when they first arrived, he was astounded to see the old fellow, not exactly at the same place, but between the recess and the exit to the passage.

"Hang it, what's he doing?" he stammered, at once upset by that unexpected presence. "One would think he was asleep!"

The ancient Druid, in fact, appeared to be asleep. Only, why on earth was he sleeping in that attitude, flat on his stomach, with his arms stretched out on either side and his face to the floor? No man on his guard, or at least aware that he was in some sort of danger, would expose himself in this way to the enemy's attack. Moreover—Vorski's eyes were gradually growing accustomed to the half-darkness of the end crypt— moreover the white robe was marked with stains which looked red, which undoubtedly were red. What did it mean?

Otto said, in a low voice:

"He's lying in a queer attitude."

Vorski was thinking the same thing and put it more plainly:

"Yes, the attitude of a corpse."

"The attitude of a corpse," Otto agreed. "That's it, exactly."

Vorski presently fell back a step:

"Oh," he exclaimed, "can it be?"

"What?" asked the other.

"Between the two shoulders... Look."

"Well?"

"The knife."

"What knife?"

"Conrad's," Vorski declared. "Conrad's dagger. I recognise it. Driven in between the shoulders." And he added, with a shudder, "That's where the red stains come from... It's blood... blood flowing from the wound."

"In that case," Otto remarked, "he is dead?"

"He's dead, yes, the ancient Druid is dead... Conrad must have surprised him and killed him... The ancient Druid is dead."

Vorski remained undecided for a while, ready to fall upon the lifeless body and to stab it in his turn. But he dared no more touch it now that it was dead than when it was alive; and all that he had the courage to do was to run and wrench the dagger from the wound.

"Ah," he cried, "you scoundrel, you've got what you deserve! And Conrad is a champion. I shan't forget you, Conrad, be sure of that."

"Where can Conrad be?"

"In the hall of the God-Stone. Ah, Otto, I'm itching to get back to the woman whom the ancient Druid put there and to settle her hash too!"

"Then you believe that she's a live woman?" chuckled Otto.

"And very much alive at that... like the ancient Druid! That wizard was only a fake, with a few tricks of his own, perhaps, but no real power. There's the proof!"

"A fake, if you like," the accomplice objected. "But, all the same, he showed you by his signals the way to enter these caves. Now what was his object in that? And what was he doing here? Did he really know the secret of the God-Stone, the way to get possession of it and exactly where it is?"

"You're right. It's all so many riddles," said Vorski, who preferred not to examine the details of the adventure too closely. "But it's so many riddles which'll answer themselves and which I'm not troubling about for the moment, because it's no longer that creepy individual who's putting them to me."

For the third time they went through the narrow communicating passage. Vorski entered the great hall like a conqueror, with his head high and a confident glance. There was no longer any obstacle, no longer any enemy to overcome. Whether the God-Stone was suspended between the stones of the ceiling, or whether the God-Stone was elsewhere, he was sure to discover it. There remained the mysterious woman who looked like Véronique, but who could not be Véronique and whose real identity he was about to unmask.

"Always presuming that she's still there," he muttered. "And I very much suspect that she's gone. She played her part in the ancient Druid's obscure schemes: and the ancient Druid, thinking me out of the way..."

He stepped forward and climbed a few steps.

The woman was there. She was there, lying on the lower table of the dolmen, shrouded in veils as before. The arm no longer hung towards the ground. There was only the hand emerging from the veils. The turquoise ring was on the finger.

"She hasn't moved," said Otto. "She's still asleep."

"Perhaps she is asleep," said Vorski. "I'll watch her. Leave me alone."

He went nearer. He still had Conrad's dagger in his hand: and perhaps it was this that suggested killing to him, for his eyes fell upon the weapon and it was not till then that he seemed to realise that he was carrying it and that he might make use of it.

He was not more than three paces from the woman, when he perceived that the wrist which was uncovered was all bruised and as it were mottled with black patches, which evidently came from the cords with which she had been bound. Now the ancient Druid had remarked, an hour ago, that the wrists showed no signs of a bruise!

This detail confounded him anew, first, because it proved to him that this was really the woman whom he had crucified, who had been taken down and who was now before his eyes and, secondly, because he was suddenly re-entering the domain of miracles; and Véronique's arm appeared to him, alternately, under two different aspects, as the arm of a living, uninjured woman and as the arm of a lifeless, tortured victim.

His trembling hand clutched the dagger, clinging to it, in a manner of speaking, as the only instrument of salvation. Once more in his confused brain the idea arose of striking, not to kill, because the woman must be dead, but of striking the invisible enemy who persisted in thwarting him and of conjuring all the evil spells at one blow.

He raised his arm. He chose the spot. His face assumed an expression of extreme savagery, lit up with the joy of murder. And suddenly he swooped down, striking, like a madman, at random, ten times, twenty times, with a frenzied unbridling of all his instincts.

"Take that and die!" he spluttered. "Another!... Die!... And let's have an end of this... You are the evil genius that's been resisting me... and now I'm killing you... Die and leave me free!... Die so that I shall be the only master!"

He stopped to take breath. He was exhausted. And while his haggard eyes stared blindly at the horrible spectacle of the lacerated corpse, he received the strange impression that a shadow was placing itself between him and the sunlight which came through the opening overhead.

"Do you know what you remind me of?" said a voice.

He was dumbfounded. The voice was not Otto's voice. And the voice continued, while he stood with his head lowered and stupidly holding his dagger planted in the dead woman's body:

"Do you know what you remind me of, Vorski? You remind me of the bulls of my country. Let me tell you that I am a Spaniard and a great frequenter of the bull-ring. Well, when our bulls have gored some poor old cab-horse that is only fit for the knacker's yard, they go back to the body, from time to time, turn it over, gore it again, keep on killing it and killing it. You're like them, Vorski. You're seeing red. In order to defend yourself against the living enemy, you fall desperately on the enemy who is no longer alive; and it is death itself that you are trying to kill. What a silly beast you're making of yourself."

Vorski raised his head. A man was standing in front of him, leaning against one of the uprights of the dolmen. The man was of the average height, with a slender, well-built figure, and seemed to be still young, notwithstanding his hair, which was turning grey at the temples. He wore a blue-serge jacket with brass buttons and a yachting-cap with a black peak.

"Don't trouble to rack your brains," he said. "You don't know me. Let me introduce myself: Don Luis Perenna, grandee of Spain, a noble of many countries and Prince of Sarek. Yes, don't be surprised: I've taken the title of Prince of Sarek, having a certain right to it."

Vorski looked at him without understanding. The man continued:

"You don't seem very familiar with the Spanish nobility. Still, just test your memory: I am the gentleman who was to come to the rescue of the d'Hergemont family and the people of Sarek, the one whom your son Francois was expecting with such simple faith... Well, are you there?... Look, your companion, the trusty Otto, he seems to remember!... But perhaps my other name will convey more to you? It is well and favourably known. Lupin... Arsène Lupin..."

Vorski watched him with increasing terror and with a misgiving which became more accentuated at each word and movement of this new adversary. Though he recognized neither the man nor the man's voice, he felt himself dominated by a will of which he had already felt the power and lashed by the same sort of implacable irony. But was it possible?

"Everything is possible," Don Luis Perenna went on, "including even what you think. But I repeat, what a silly beast you're making of yourself! Here are you playing the bold highwayman, the dashing adventurer; and you're frightened the moment you set eyes on one of your crimes! As long as it was just a matter of happy-go-lucky killing, you went straight ahead. But the first little jolt throws you off the track. Vorski kills; but whom has he killed? He has no idea. Is Véronique d'Hergemont dead or alive? Is she fastened to the oak on which you crucified her? Or is she lying here, on the sacrificial table? Did you kill her up there or down here? You can't tell. You never even thought, before you stabbed, of looking to see what you were stabbing. The great thing for you is to slash away with all your might, to intoxicate yourself with the sight and smell of blood and to turn live flesh into a hideous pulp. But look, can't you, you idiot? When a man kills, he's not afraid of killing and he doesn't hide the face of his victim. Look, you idiot!"

He himself stopped over the corpse and unwrapped the veil around the head.

Vorski had closed his eyes. Kneeling, with his chest pressed against the dead woman's legs, he remained without moving and kept his eyes obstinately shut.

"Are you there now?" chuckled Don Luis. "If you daren't look, it's because you've guessed or because you're on the point of guessing, you wretch: am I right? Your idiot brain is working it out: am I right? There were two women in the Isle of Sarek and two only, Véronique and the other... the other whose name was Elfride, I understand: am I right? Elfride and Véronique, your two wives, one the mother of Raynold, the other the mother of Francois. So, if it's not Francois' mother whom you tied on the cross and whom you've just stabbed, then it's Raynold's mother. If the woman lying here, with her wrists bruised by the torture, is not Véronique, then she's Elfride. There's no mistake possible: Elfride, your wife and your accomplice; Elfride, your willing and subservient tool. And you know it so well that you would rather take my word for it than risk a glance and see the livid face of that dead woman, of your obedient accomplice tortured by yourself. You miserable poltroon!"

THE HALL OF THE UNDERGROUND SACRIFICES 239

Vorski had hidden his head in his folded arms. He was not weeping. Vorski could not weep. Nevertheless, his shoulders were jerking convulsively; and his whole attitude expressed the wildest despair.

This lasted for some time. Then the shaking of the shoulders ceased. Still Vorski did not stir.

"Upon my word, you move me to pity, you poor old buffer!" said Don Luis. "Were you so fond of your Elfride as all that? She had become a habit, what? A mascot? Well, what can I say? People as a rule aren't such fools as you! They know what they're doing. They look before they leap! Hang it all, they stop to think! Whereas you go floundering about in crime like a new-born babe struggling in the water! No wonder you sink and go to the bottom... The ancient Druid, for instance: is he dead or alive? Did Conrad stick a dagger into his back, or was I playing the part of that diabolical personage? In short, are there an ancient Druid and a Spanish grandee, or are the two individuals one and the same?

This is all a sealed book to you, my poor fellow. And yet you'll want an explanation. Shall I help you?"

If Vorski had acted without thinking, it was easy to see, when he raised his head, that on this occasion he had taken time to reflect; that he knew very well the desperate resolve which circumstances called upon him to take. He was certainly ready for an explanation, as Don Luis suggested, but he wanted it dagger in hand, with the implacable intention of using it. Slowly, with his eyes fixed on Don Luis and without concealing his purpose, he had freed his weapon and was rising to his feet.

"Take care," said Don Luis. "Your knife is faked as your revolver was. It's made of tin-foil."

Useless pleasantry! Nothing could either hasten or delay the methodical impulse which urged Vorski to the supreme contest. He walked round the sacred table and took up his stand in front of Don Luis.

"You're sure it's you who have been thwarting all my plans these last few days?"

"The last twenty-four hours, no longer. I arrived at Sarek twenty-four hours ago."

"And you're determined to go on to the end?"

"Yes; and farther still, if possible."

"Why? And in what capacity?"

"As a sportsman; and because you fill me with disgust."

"So there's no arrangement to be made?"

"No."

"Would you refuse to go shares with me?"

"Ah, now you're talking!"

"You can have half, if you like."

"I'd rather have the lot."

"Meaning that the God-Stone…"

"The God-Stone belongs to me."

Further speech was idle. An adversary of that quality has to be made away with; if not, he makes away with you. Vorski had to choose between the two endings; there was not a third.

Don Luis remained impassive, leaning against the pillar. Vorski towered a head above him: and at the same time Vorski had the profound impression that he was equally Don Luis' superior in every other respect, in strength, muscular power and weight. In these conditions, there was no need to hesitate. Moreover, it seemed out of the question that Don Luis could even attempt to defend himself or to evade the blow before the dagger fell. His parry was bound to come late unless he moved at once. And he did not move. Vorski therefore struck his blow with all certainty, as one strikes a quarry that is doomed beforehand.

And yet—it all happened so quickly and so inexplicably that he could not tell what occurred to bring about his defeat—and yet, three or four seconds later, he was lying on the ground, disarmed, defeated, with his two legs feeling as though they had been broken with a stick and his right arm hanging limp and paining him till he cried out.

Don Luis did not even trouble to bind him. With one foot on the big, helpless body, half-bending over his adversary, he said:

"For the moment, no speeches. I'm keeping one in reserve for you. It'll strike you as a bit long, but it'll show you that I understand the whole business from start to finish, that is to say, much better than you do. There's one doubtful point: and you're going to clear it up. Where's your son Francois d'Hergemont?"

Receiving no reply, he repeated:

"Where's Francois d'Hergemont?"

Vorski no doubt considered that chance had placed an unexpected trump in his hands and that the game was perhaps not absolutely lost, for he maintained an obstinate silence.

"You refuse to answer?" asked Don Luis. "One... two... three times: do you refuse?... Very well!"

He gave a low whistle.

Four men appeared from a corner of the hall, four men with swarthy faces, resembling Moors. Like Don Luis, they wore jackets and sailor's caps with shiny peaks.

A fifth person arrived almost immediately afterwards, a wounded French officer, who had lost his right leg and wore a wooden leg in its place.

"Ah, is that you, Patrice?" said Don Luis.

He introduced him formally:

"Captain Patrice Belval, my greatest friend; Mr Vorski, a Hun."

Then he asked:

"No news, captain? You haven't found François?"

"No."

"We shall have found him in an hour and then we'll be off. Are all our men on board?"

"Yes."

"Everything all right there?"

"Quite."

He turned to the three Moors:

"Pick up the Hun," he ordered, "and carry him up to the dolmen outside. You needn't bind him: he couldn't move a limb if he tried. Oh, one minute!"

He leant over Vorski's ear:

"Before you start, have a good look at the God-Stone, between the flags in the ceiling. The ancient Druid wasn't lying to you. It *is* the miraculous stone which people have been seeking for centuries... and which I discovered from a distance... by correspondence. Say goodbye to it, Vbrski! You will never see it again, if indeed you are ever to see anything in this world."

He made a sign with his hand.

The four Moors briskly took up Vorski and carried him to the back of the hall, on the side opposite the communicating passage.

Turning to Otto, who had stood throughout this scene without moving:

"I see that you're a reasonable fellow, Otto, and that you understand the position. You won't get up to any tricks?"

"No."

"Then we shan't touch you. You can come along without fear."

He slipped his arm through Belval's and the two walked away, talking.

They left the hall of the God-Stone through a series of three crypts, each of which was on a higher level than the one before. The last of them also led to a vestibule. At the far side of the vestibule, a ladder stood against a lightly-built wall in which an opening had been newly made. Through this they emerged into the open air, in the middle of a steep path, cut into steps, which wound about as it climbed upwards in the rock and which brought them to that part of the cliff to which

THE HALL OF THE UNDERGROUND SACRIFICES

François had taken Véronique on the previous morning. It was the Postern path. From above they saw, hanging from two iron davits, the boat in which Véronique and her son had intended to take flight. Not far away, in a little bay, was the long, tapering outline of a submarine.

Turning their backs to the sea, Don Luis and Patrice Belval continued on their way towards the semicircle of oaks and stopped near the Fairies' Dolmen, where the Moors were waiting for them. They had set Vorski down at the foot of the tree on which his last victim had died. Nothing remained on the tree to bear witness to the abominable torture except the inscription, "V. d'H."

"Not too tired, Vorski?" asked Don Luis. "Legs feeling better?"

Vorski gave a contemptuous shrug of the shoulders.

"Yes, I know," said Don Luis. "You're pinning your faith to your last card. Still, I would have you know that I also hold a few trumps and that I have a rather artistic way of playing them. The tree behind you should be more than enough to tell you so. Would you like another instance? While you're getting muddled with all your murders and are no longer sure of the number of your victims, I bring them to life again. Look at that man coming from the Priory. Do you see him? He's wearing a blue reefer with brass buttons, like myself. He's one of your dead men, isn't he? You locked him up in one of the torture-chambers, intending to cast him into the sea; and it was your sweet cherub of a Raynold who hurled him down before Véronique's eyes. Do you remember? Stéphane Maroux his name was. He's dead, isn't he? No, not a bit of it! A wave of my magic wand; and he's alive again. Here he is. I take him by the hand. I speak to him."

Going up to the newcomer, he shook hands with him and said:

"You see, Stéphane? I told you that it would be all over at twelve o'clock precisely and that we should meet at the dolmen. Well, it is twelve o'clock precisely."

Stéphane seemed in excellent health. He showed not a sign of a wound. Vorski looked at him in dismay and stammered:

"The tutor... Stéphane Maroux..."

"The man himself," said Don Luis. "What did you expect? Here again you behaved like an idiot. The adorable Raynold and you throw a man into the sea and don't even think of leaning over to see what becomes of him. I pick him up... And don't be too badly staggered, old chap. It's only the beginning; and I have a few more tricks in my bag. Remember, I'm a pupil of the ancient Druid's!... Well, Stéphane, where do we stand? What's the result of your search?"

"Nothing."

"François?"

"Not to be found."

"And All's Well? Did you send him on his master's tracks, as we arranged?"

"Yes, but he simply took me down the Postern path to François' boat."

"There's no hiding-place on that side?"

"Not one."

Don Luis was silent and began to pace up and down before the dolmen. He seemed to be hesitating at the last moment, before beginning the series of actions upon which he had resolved. At last, addressing Vorski, he said:

"I have no time to waste. I must leave the island in two hours. What's your price for setting François free at once?"

"François fought a duel with Raynold," Vorski replied, "and was beaten."

"You lie. François won."

"How do you know? Did you see them fight?"

"No, or I should have interfered. But I know who was the victor."

"No one knows except myself. They were masked."

"Then, if François is dead, it's all up with you."

Vorski took time to think. The argument allowed of no debate. He put a question in his turn:

"Well, what do you offer me?"

"Your liberty."

"And with it?"

"Nothing."

"Yes, the God-Stone."

"*Never!*"

Don Luis shouted the word, accompanying it with a vehement gesture of the hand, and he explained:

"Never! Your liberty, yes, if the worst comes to the worst and because I know you and know that, denuded of all resources, you will simply go and get yourself hanged somewhere else. But the God-Stone would spell safety, wealth, the power to do evil..."

"That's exactly why I want it," said Vorski; "and, by telling me what it's worth, you make me all the more difficult in the matter of François."

"I shall find François all right. It's only a question of patience; and I shall stay two or three days longer, if necessary."

"You will not find him; and, if you do, it will be too late."

"Why?"

"Because he has had nothing to eat since yesterday."

This was said coldly and maliciously. There was a silence; and Don Luis retorted:

"In that case, speak, if you don't want him to die."

"What do I care? Anything rather than fail in my task and stop midway when I've got so far. The end is within sight: those who get in my way must look out for themselves."

"You lie. You won't let that boy die."

"I let the other die right enough!"

Patrice and Stéphane made a movement of horror, while Don Luis laughed frankly:

"Capital! There's no hypocrisy about you. Plain and convincing arguments. By Jingo, how beautiful to see a Hun laying bare his soul! What a glorious mixture of vanity and cruelty, of cynicism and mysticism! A Hun has always a mission to fulfil, even when he's satisfied with plundering and murdering. Well, you're better than a Hun: you're a Superhun!"

And he added, still laughing:

"So I propose to treat you as Superhun. Once more, will you tell me where François is?"

"No."

"All right."

He turned to the four Moors and said, very calmly:

"Go ahead, lads."

It was a matter of a second. With really extraordinary precision of gesture and as though the act had been separated into a certain number of movements, learnt and rehearsed beforehand like a military drill, they picked up Vorski, fastened him to the rope which hung to the tree, hoisted him up without paying attention to his cries, his threats or his shouts and bound him firmly, as he had bound his victim.

"Howl away, old chap," said Don Luis, serenely, "howl as much as you like! You can only wake the sisters Archignat and the others in the thirty coffins! Howl away, my lad! But, good Lord, how ugly you are! What a face!"

He took a few steps back, to appreciate the sight better:

"Excellent! You look very well there; it couldn't be better. Even the inscription fits: 'V. d'H.,' Vorski de Hohenzollern! For I presume that, as the son of a king, you are allied to that noble house. And now, Vorski, all you have to do is to lend me an attentive ear: I'm going to make you the little speech I promised you."

Vorski was wriggling on the tree and trying to burst his bonds. But, since every effort merely served to increase his suffering, he kept still and, to vent his fury, began to swear and blaspheme most hideously and to inveigh against Don Luis:

"Robber! Murderer! It's you that are the murderer, it's you that are condemning François to death! François was wounded by his brother; it's a bad wound and may be poisoned..."

Stéphane and Patrice pleaded with Don Luis. Stéphane expressed his alarm:

"You can never tell," he said. "With a monster like that, anything is possible. And suppose the boy's ill?"

"It's bunkum and blackmail!" Don Luis declared. "The boy's quite well."

"Are you sure?"

"Well enough, in any case, to wait an hour. In an hour the Superhun will have spoken. He won't hold out any longer. Hanging loosens the tongue."

"And suppose he doesn't hold out at all?"

"What do you mean?"

"Suppose he himself expires, from too violent an effort, heart failure, a clot of blood to the head?"

"Well?"

"Well, his death would destroy the only hope we have of learning where François is hidden, his death would be François' undoing!"

But Don Luis was inflexible:

"He won't die!" he cried. "Vorski's sort doesn't die of a stroke! No, no, he'll talk, he'll talk within an hour. Just time enough to deliver my lecture."

Patrice Belval began to laugh in spite of himself:

"Have you a lecture to deliver?"

"Rather! And such a lecture!" exclaimed Don Luis. "The whole adventure of the God-Stone! An historical treatise, a comprehensive view extending from prehistoric times to the thirty murders committed by the Superhun! By Jove, it's not every day that one has the opportunity of reading a paper like that; and I wouldn't miss it for a kingdom! Mount the platform, Don Luis, and fire away with your speech!"

He took his stand opposite Vorski:

"You lucky dog, you! You're in the front seats and you won't lose a word. I expect you're glad, eh, to have a little light thrown upon your darkness? We've been floundering about so long that it's time we had a definite lead. I assure you I'm beginning not to know where I am. Just think, a riddle which has lasted for centuries and centuries and which you've merely muddled still further."

"Thief! Robber!" snarled Vorski.

"Insults? Why? If you're not comfortable, let's talk about François."

"Never! He shall die."

"Not at all, you'll talk. I give you leave to interrupt me. When you want me to stop, all you've got to do is to whistle a tune: *'En r'venant de la r'vue'* or *Tipperary*. I'll at once send to see; and, if you've told the truth, we'll leave you here quietly, Otto will untie you and you can be off in François' boat. Is it agreed?"

He turned to Stéphane and Patrice Belval:

"Sit down, my friends," he said, "for it will take rather long. But, if I am to be eloquent, I need an audience... and an audience who will also act as judges."

"We're only two," said Patrice.

"You're three."

"With whom?"

"Here's your third."

It was All's Well. He came trotting along, without hurrying more than usual. He frisked round Stéphane, wagged his tail to Don Luis, as though to say, "I know you: you and I are pals," and squatted on his hind-quarters, with the air of one who does not wish to disturb people.

THE HALL OF THE UNDERGROUND SACRIFICES 249

"That's right, All's Well!" cried Don Luis. "You also want to hear all about the adventure. Your curiosity does you honour; and I won't disappoint you."

Don Luis appeared to be delighted. He had an audience, a full bench of judges. Vorski was writhing on his tree. It was an exquisite moment.

He cut a sort of caper which must have reminded Vorski of the ancient Druid's pirouettes and, drawing himself up, bowed, imitated a lecturer taking a sip of water from a tumbler, rested his hands on an imaginary table and at last began, in a deliberate voice:

"Ladies and Gentlemen:

"On the twenty-fifth of July, in the year seven hundred and thirty-two B. C...."

16

THE HALL OF THE KINGS OF BOHEMIA

Don Luis interrupted himself after delivering his opening sentence and stood enjoying the effect produced. Captain Belval, who knew his friend, was laughing heartily. Stéphane continued to look anxious. All's Well had not budged.

Don Luis continued:

"Let me begin by confessing, ladies and gentlemen, that my object in fixing my date so precisely was to some extent to stagger you. In reality I could not tell you within a few centuries the exact date of the scene which I shall have the honour of describing to you. But what I can guarantee is that it is laid in that country of Europe which today we call Bohemia and at the spot where the little industrial town of Joachimsthal now stands. That, I hope, is fairly circumstantial. Well, on the morning of the day when my story begins, there was great excitement among one of those Celtic tribes which had settled a century or two earlier between the banks of the Danube and the sources of the Elbe, amidst the Hyrcanian forests. The warriors, assisted by their wives, were striking their tents, collecting the sacred axes, the bows and arrows, gathering up the pottery, the bronze and tin implements, loading the horses and the oxen.

"The chiefs were here, there and everywhere, attending to the smallest details. There was neither tumult nor disorder.

They started early in the direction of a tributary of the Elbe, the Eger, which they reached towards the end of the day. Here boats were waiting, guarded by a hundred of the picked warriors who had been sent ahead. One of these boats was conspicuous for its size and the richness of its decoration. A long yellow cloth was stretched from side to side. The chief of chiefs, the King, if you prefer, climbed on the stem thwart and made a speech which I will spare you, because I do not wish to shorten my own, but which may be summed up as follows: the tribe was emigrating to escape the cupidity of the neighbouring populations. It is always sad to leave the places where one has dwelt. But it made no difference to the men of the tribe, because they were carrying with them their most valuable possession, the sacred inheritance of their ancestors, the divinity that protected them and made them formidable and great among the greatest, in short, the stone that covered the tomb of their kings.

"And the chief of chiefs, with a solemn gesture, drew the yellow cloth and revealed a block of granite in the shape of a slab about two yards by one, granular in appearance and dark in colour, with a few glittering scales gleaming in its substance.

"There was a single shout raised by the crowd of men and women; and all, with outstretched arms, fell flat on their faces in the dust.

"Then the chief of chiefs took up a metal sceptre with a jewelled handle, which lay on the block of granite, brandished it on high and spoke:

"'The all-powerful staff shall not leave my hand until the miraculous stone is in a place of safety. The all-powerful staff is born of the miraculous stone. It also contains the fire of heaven, which gives life or death. While the miraculous stone was the tomb of my forefathers, the all-powerful staff never left their hands on days of disaster or of victory. May the fire of heaven lead us! May the Sun-god light our way!'

"He spoke: and the whole tribe set out upon its journey."

Don Luis struck an attitude and repeated, in a self-satisfied tone:

"He spoke: and the whole tribe set out upon its journey."

Patrice Belval was greatly amused; and Stéphane, infected by his hilarity, began to feel more cheerful. But Don Luis now addressed his remarks to them:

"There's nothing to laugh at! All this is very serious. It's not a story for children who believe in conjuring tricks and sleight of hand, but a real history, all the details of which will, as you shall see, give rise to precise, natural and, in a sense, scientific explanations. Yes, ladies and gentlemen, scientific: I am not afraid of the word. We are here on scientific ground; and Vorski himself will regret his cynical merriment."

Don Luis took a second sip of water and continued:

"For weeks and months the tribe followed the course of the Elbe; and one evening, on the stroke of half-past nine, reached the seaboard, in the country which afterwards became the country of the Frisians. It remained there for weeks and months, without finding the requisite security. It therefore determined upon a fresh exodus.

"This time it was a naval exodus. Thirty boats put out to sea—observe this number thirty, which was that of the families composing the tribe—and for weeks and months they wandered from shore to shore, settling first in Scandinavia, next among the Saxons, driven off, putting to sea again and continuing their voyage. And I assure you it was really a strange, moving, impressive sight to see this vagrant tribe dragging in its wake the tombstone of its kings and seeking a safe, inaccessible and final refuge in which to conceal its idol, protect it from the attack of its enemies, celebrate its worship and employ it to consolidate the tribal power.

"The last stage was Ireland; and it was here that, one day, after they had dwelt in the green isle for half a century or perhaps a century, after their manners had acquired a certain softening by contact with nations which were already less barbarous, the grandson or great-grandson of the great chief, himself a great chief, received one of the emissaries whom he maintained in the neighbouring countries. This one came from the continent. He had discovered the miraculous refuge. It was an almost unapproachable island, protected by thirty rocks and having thirty granite monuments to guard it.

"Thirty! The fateful number! It was an obvious summons and command from the mysterious deities. The thirty galleys were launched once more and the expedition set forth.

"It succeeded. They took the island by assault. The natives they simply exterminated. The tribe settled down; and the tombstone of the Kings of Bohemia was installed... in the very place which it occupies today and which I showed to our friend Vorski. Here I must interpolate a few historical data of the greatest significance. I will be brief."

Adopting a professorial tone, Don Luis explained:

"The island of Sarek, like all France and all the western part of Europe, had been inhabited for thousands of years by a race known as the Liguri, the direct descendants of the cave-dwellers part of whose manners and customs they had retained. They were mighty builders, those Liguri, who, in the neolithic period, perhaps under the influence of the great civilizations of the east, had erected their huge blocks of granite and built their colossal funeral chambers.

"It was here that our tribe found and made great use of a system of caves and natural crypts adapted by the patient hand of man and of a cluster of enormous monuments which struck the mystic and superstitious imagination of the Celts.

"We find therefore that, after the first or wandering phase, there begins for the God-Stone a period of rest and worship which we will call the Druidical period. It lasted for a thousand or fifteen hundred years. The tribe became mingled with the neighbouring tribes and probably lived under the protection of some Breton king. But, little by little, the ascendancy had passed from the chiefs to the priests; and these priests, that is to say, the Druids, assumed an authority which increased in the course of the generations that followed.

"They owed this authority, beyond all doubt, to the miraculous stone. True, they were the priests of a religion accepted by all and also the instructors of Gallic childhood (it seems certain, incidentally, that the cells under the Black Heath were those of a Druid convent, or rather a sort of university); true, in obedience to the practices of the time, they presided over human sacrifices and ordained the gathering of the mistletoe, the vervain and all the magic herbs; but, before all, in the island of Sarek, they were the guardians and the possessors of the stone which gave life or death. Placed above the hall of the underground sacrifices, it was at that time undoubtedly visible in the open air; and I have every reason to believe that the Fairies' Dolmen, which we now see here, then stood in the place known as the Calvary of the Flowers and sheltered the God-Stone. It was there that ailing and crippled persons and sickly children were laid to recover their health and strength. It was on the sacred slab that barren women became fruitful, on the sacred slab that old men felt their energies revive.

"In my eyes it dominates the whole of the legendary and fabled past of Brittany. It is the radiating centre of all the superstitions, all the beliefs, all the fears and hopes of the country. By virtue of the stone or of the magic sceptre which the archdruid wielded and with which he burnt men's flesh or healed their sores at will, we see the beautiful tales of romance springing spontaneously into being, tales of the knights of the Round Table, tales of Merlin the wizard. The stone is at the bottom of every mystery, at the heart of every symbol. It is darkness and light in one, the great riddle and the great explanation."

Don Luis uttered these last words with a certain exaltation. He smiled:

"Don't let yourself be carried away, Vorski. We'll keep our enthusiasm for the narrative of your crimes. For the moment, we are at the climax of the Druidical period, a period which lasted far beyond the Druids through long centuries during which, after the Druids had gone, the miraculous stone was exploited by the sorcerers and soothsayers. And thus we come gradually to the third period, the religious period, that is to say, actually to the progressive decline of all that constituted the glory of Sarek: pilgrimages, commemorative festivals and so forth.

"The Church in fact was unable to put up with that crude fetish-worship. As soon as she was strong enough, she was bound to fight against the block of granite which attracted so many believers and perpetuated so hateful a religion. The fight was an unequal one; and the past succumbed. The dolmen was moved to where we stand, the slab of the kings of Bohemia was buried under a layer of earth and a Calvary rose at the very spot where the sacrilegious miracles were once wrought.

"And, over and above that, there was the great oblivion!

"Let me explain. The practices were forgotten. The rites were forgotten and all that constituted the history of a vanished cult. But the God-Stone was not forgotten. Men no longer knew where it was. In time they even no longer knew what it was. But they never ceased to speak of and believe in the existence of something which they called the God-Stone. From mouth to mouth, from generation to generation, they handed down on to one another fabulous and terrible stories, which became farther and farther removed from reality, which formed a more and more vague and, for that matter, a more and more frightful legend, but which kept alive in their imaginations the recollection of the God-Stone and, above all, its name.

"This persistence of an idea in men's memories, this survival of a fact in the annals of a country had the logical result that, from time to time, some enquiring person would try to reconstruct the prodigious truth. Two of these enquiring persons, Brother Thomas, a member of the Benedictine Order, who lived in the middle of the fifteenth century, and the man Maguennoc, in our own time, played an important part. Brother Thomas was a poet and an illuminator about whom we possess not many details, a very bad poet, to judge by his verses, but as an illuminator ingenuous and not devoid of talent. He left a sort of missal in which he related his life at Sarek Abbey and drew the thirty dolmens of the island, the whole accompanied by instances, religious quotations and predictions after the manner of Nostradamus. It was this missal, discovered by Maguennoc aforesaid, that contained the famous page with the crucified women and the prophecy relating to Sarek; it was this missal that I myself found and consulted last night in Maguennoc's bedroom.

"He was an odd person, this Maguennoc, a belated descendant of the sorcerers of old; and I strongly suspect him of playing the ghost on more than one occasion. You may be sure that the white-robed, white-bearded Druid whom people declared that they had seen on the sixth day of the moon, gathering the mistletoe, was none other than Maguennoc. He too knew all about the good old recipes, the healing herbs, the way to work up the soil so as to make it yield enormous flowers. One thing is certain, that he explored the mortuary crypts and the hall of the sacrifices, that it was he who purloined the magic stone contained in the knob of the sceptre and that he used to enter these crypts by the opening through which we have just come, in the middle of the Postern path, of which he was obliged each time to replace the screen of stones and pebbles. It was he also who gave M. d'Hergemont the page from the missal. Whether he confided the result of his last explorations to him and how much exactly M. d'Hergemont knew does not matter now. Another figure looms into sight, one who is henceforth the embodiment of the whole affair and claims all our attention, an emissary dispatched by fate to solve the riddle of the centuries, to carry out the orders of the mysterious powers and to pocket the God-Stone. I am speaking of Vorski."

Don Luis swallowed his third glass of water and, beckoning to the accomplice, said:

"Otto, you had better give him a drink, if he's thirsty. Are you thirsty, Vorski?"

Vorski on his tree seemed exhausted, incapable of further effort or resistance. Stéphane and Patrice once more intervened on his behalf, fearing an immediate consummation.

"Not at all, not at all!" cried Don Luis. "He's all right and he'll hold out until I've finished my speech, if it were only because he wants to know. You're tremendously interested, aren't you, Vorski?"

"Robber! Murderer!" spluttered the wretched man.

"Splendid! So you still refuse to tell us where François is hidden?"

"Murderer! Highwayman!"

"Then stay where you are, old chap. As you please. There's nothing better for the health than a little suffering. Besides, you have caused so much suffering to others, you dirty scum!"

Don Luis uttered these words harshly and in accents of anger which one would hardly have expected from a man who had already beheld so many crimes and battled with so many criminals. But then this last one was out of all proportion.

Don Luis continued:

"About thirty-five years ago, a very beautiful woman, who came from Bohemia but who was of Hungarian descent, visited the watering-places that swarm around the Bavarian lakes and soon achieved a great reputation as a fortune-teller palmist, seer and medium. She attracted the attention of King Louis

II, Wagner's friend, the man who built Bayreuth, the crowned mad-man famed for his extravagant fancies. The intimacy between the king and the clairvoyant lasted for some years. It was a violent, restless intimacy, interrupted by the frequent whims of the king; and it ended tragically on the mysterious evening when Louis of Bavaria threw himself out of his boat into the Stambergersee. Was it really, as the official version stated, suicide following on a fit of madness? Or was it a case of murder, as some have held? Why suicide? Why murder? These are questions that have never been answered. But one fact remains: the Bohemian woman was in the boat with Louis II and next day was escorted to the frontier and expelled from the country after her money and jewellery had been taken from her.

"She brought back with her from this adventure a young monster, four years old, Alex Vorski by name, which young monster lived with his mother near the village of Joachimsthal in Bohemia. Here, in course of time, she instructed him in all the practices of hypnotic suggestion, extra lucidity and trickery. Endowed with a character of unexampled violence but a very weak intellect, a prey to hallucinations and nightmares, believing in spells, in predictions, in dreams, in occult powers, he took legends for history and falsehoods for reality. One of the numerous legends of the mountains in particular had impressed his imagination: it was the one that describes the fabulous power of a stone which, in the dim recesses of the past, was carried away by evil genii and which was one day to be brought back by the son of a king. The peasants still show the cavity left by the stone in the side of a hill.

"'The king's son is yourself,' his mother used to say. 'And, if you find the missing stone, you will escape the dagger that threatens you and will yourself become a king.'

"This ridiculous prophecy and another, no less fantastic, in which the Bohemian woman announced that her son's wife would perish on the cross and that he himself would die by the hand of a friend, were among those which exercised the most direct influence on Vorski when the fateful hour struck. And I will go straight on to this fateful hour, without saying any more of what our conversations of yesterday and last night revealed to the three of us or of what we have been able to reconstruct. There is no reason to repeat in full the story which you, Stéphane, told Véronique d'Hergemont in your cell. There is no need to inform you, Patrice, you, Vorski, or you, All's Well, of events with which you are familiar, such as your marriage, Vorski, or rather your two marriages, first with Elfride and next with Véronique d'Hergemont, the kidnapping of François by his grandfather, the disappearance of Véronique, the searches which you set on foot to find her, your conduct at the outbreak of the war and your life in the internmentcamps. These are mere trifles besides the events which are on the point of taking place. We have cleared up the history of the God-Stone. It is the modem adventure, which you, Vorski, have woven around the God-Stone, that we are now about to unravel.

"In the beginning it appears like this: Vorski is imprisoned in an internment-camp near Pontivy in Brittany. He no longer calls himself Vorski, but Lauterbach. Fifteen months before, after a first escape and at the moment when the court martial was about to sentence him to death as a spy, he escaped again, spent some time in the Forest of Fontainebleau, there found one of his former servants, a man called Lauterbach, a German like himself and like himself an escaped prisoner, killed him, dressed the body in his clothes and made the face up in such a way as to give him the appearance of his murderer, Vorski. The military police were taken in and had the sham Vorski buried at Fontainebleau. As for the real Vorski, he had the bad luck to be arrested once more, under his new name of Lauterbach, and to be interned in the camp at Pontivy.

"So much for Vorski. On the other hand, Elfride, his first wife, the formidable accomplice in all his crimes and herself a German—I have some particulars about her and their past life in common which are of no importance and need not be mentioned here—Elfride, I was saying, his accomplice, was hidden with their son Raynold in the cells of Sarek. He had left her there to spy on M. d'Hergemont and through him to ascertain Véronique d'Hergemont's whereabouts. The reasons which prompted the wretched woman's actions I do not know. It may have been blind devotion, fear of Vorski, an instinctive love of evil-doing, hatred of the rival who supplanted her. It doesn't matter. She has suffered the most terrible punishment. Let us speak only of the part she played, without seeking to understand how she had the courage to live for three years underground, never going out except at night, stealing food for herself and her son and patiently awaiting the day when she could serve and save her lord and master.

"I am also ignorant of the series of events that enabled her to take action, nor do I know how Vorski and Elfride managed to communicate. But what I know most positively is that Vorski's escape was long and carefully prepared by his first wife. Every detail arranged. Every precaution was taken. On the fourteenth of September of last year, Vorski escaped, taking with him the two accomplices with whom he had made friends during his captivity and whom he had, so to speak, enrolled: the Otto and Conrad whom you know of.

"It was an easy journey. At every cross-roads, an arrow, accompanied by a number, one of a series, and surmounted by the initials 'V. d'H.,' which initials were evidently selected by Vorski, pointed out the road which he was to follow. At intervals, in a deserted cabin, some provisions were hidden under a stone or in a truss of hay. The way led through Guémené, Le Faouet and Rosporden and ended on the beach at Beg-Meil.

"Here Elfride and Raynold came by night to fetch the three fugitives in Honorine's motor-boat and to land them near the Druid cells under the Black Heath. They clambered up. Their lodgings were ready for them and, as you have seen, were fairly comfortable. The winter passed; and Vorski's plan, which as yet was very vague, became more precisely outlined from day to day.

"Strange to say, at the time of his first visit to Sarek, before the war, he had not heard of the secret of the island. It was Elfride who told him the legend of the God-Stone in the letters which she wrote to him at Pontivy. You can imagine the effect produced by this revelation on a man like Vorski. The God-Stone was bound to be the miraculous stone wrested from the soil of his native land, the stone which was to be discovered by the son of a king and which, from that time onward, would give him power and royalty. Everything that he learnt later confirmed his conviction. But the great fact that dominates his subterranean life at Sarek was the discovery of Brother Thomas' prophecy in the course of the last month. Fragments of this prophecy were lingering on every hand, which he was able to pick up by listening to the conversations of the fisherfolk in the evenings, lurking under the windows of the cottages or on the roofs of the barns. Within mortal memory, the people of Sarek have always feared some terrible events, connected with the discovery and the disappearance of the invisible stone. There was likewise always a question of wrecks and of women crucified. Besides, Vorski was acquainted with the inscription on the Fairies' Dolmen, about the thirty victims destined for the thirty coffins, the martyrdom of the four women, the God-Stone which gives life or death. What a number of disturbing coincidences for a mind as weak as his!

"But the prophecy itself, found by Maguennoc in the illuminated missal, constitutes the essential factor of the whole story. Remember that Maguennoc had torn out the famous page and that M. d'Hergemont, who was fond of drawing, had copied it several times and had unconsciously given to the principal woman the features of his daughter Véronique. Vorski became aware of the existence of the original and of one of the copies when he saw Maguennoc one night looking at them by the light of his lamp. Immediately, in the darkness, he contrived somehow to pencil in his note-book the fifteen lines of this precious document. He now knew and understood everything. He was dazzled by a blinding light. All the scattered elements were gathered into a whole, forming a compact and solid truth. There was no doubt possible: the prophecy concerned *him*! And it was *his* mission to realize it!

"This, I repeat, is the essence of the whole matter. From that moment, Vorski's path was lighted by a beacon. He held in his hand Ariadne's clue of thread. The prophecy represented to him an unimpeachable text. It was one of the Tables of the Law. It was the Bible. And yet think of the stupidity, of the unspeakable silliness of those fifteen lines scribbled at a venture, with no other motive than rhyme! Not a phrase showing a sign of inspiration! Not a spark, not a gleam! Not a trace of the sacred madness that uplifted the Delphian pythoness or provoked the delirious visions of a Jeremiah or an Ezekiel! Nothing! Syllables, rhymes! Nothing! Less than nothing! But quite enough to enlighten the gentle Vorski and to make him burn with all the enthusiasm of a neophyte!

"Stéphane, Patrice, listen to the prophecy of Brother Thomas. The Superhun wrote it down on ten different pages of his notebook, so that he might wear it ten times next to his skin and engrave it in the very substance of his being. Here's one of the pages. Stéphane, Patrice, listen! Listen, O faithful Otto! And you yourself, Vorski, for the last time listen to the doggerel of Brother Thomas! Listen as I read!

"In Sarek's isle, in year fourteen and three,
There will be shipwrecks, terrors, grief and crimes,
Death-chambers, arrows, poison there will be
And woe, four women crucified on tree!
For thirty coffins victims thirty times.

"Before his mother's eyes, Abel kills Cain.
The father then, coming forth of Almain,
A cruel prince, obeying destiny,
By thousand deaths and lingering agony,
His wedded wife one night of June hath slain.

"Fire and loud noise will issue from the earth
In secrecy where the great treasure lies
And man again will on the stone set eyes
Once stolen from wild men in bygone days
O'er the sea; the God-Stone which gives life or death."

Don Luis Perenna had begun to read in emphatic tones, bringing out the imbecility of the words and the triteness of the rhythm. He ended in a hollow voice, without resonance, which died away in an anguished silence. The whole adventure appeared in all its horror.

He continued:

"You understand how the facts are linked together, don't you Stéphane, you who were one of the victims and who knew or know the others? So do you, Patrice, don't you? In the fifteenth century, a poor monk, with a disordered imagination and a brain haunted by infernal visions, expresses his dreams in a prophecy which we will describe as bogus, which rests on no serious data, which consists of details depending on the exigencies of the rhyme or rhythm and which certainly, both in the poet's mind and from the standpoint of originality, possesses no more value than if the poet had drawn the words at random out of a bag. The story of the God-Stone, the legends and traditions, none of all this provides him with the least element of prophecy. The worthy man evolved the prophecy from his own consciousness, not intending any harm and simply to add a text of some sort to the margin of the devilish drawing which he had so painstakingly illuminated. And he is so pleased with it that he takes the trouble to take a pointed implement and engrave a few lines of it on one of the stones of the Fairies' Dolmen.

"Well, four or five centuries later, the prophetic page falls into the hands of a Superhun, a criminal lunatic, a madman eaten up with vanity. What does the Superhun see in it? A diverting puerile fantasy? A meaningless caprice? Not a bit of it! He regards it as a document of the highest interest, one of those documents which the most Superhunnish of his fellow countrymen love to pore over, with this difference, that the document to his mind possesses a miraculous origin. He looks upon it as the Old and New Testament, the Scriptures which explain and expound the Sarek law, the very gospel of the God-Stone. And this gospel designates him, Vorski, him, the Superhun, as the Messiah appointed to execute the decrees of Providence.

"To Vorski, there is no possibility of mistake. No doubt he enjoys the business, because it is a matter of stealing wealth and power. But this question occupies a secondary position. He is above all obeying the mystic impulse of a race which believes itself to be marked out by destiny and which flatters itself that it is always fulfilling missions, a mission of regeneration as well as a mission of pillage, arson and murder. And Vorski reads his mission set out in full in Brother Thomas' prophecy. Brother Thomas says explicitly what has to be done and names him, Vorski, in the plainest terms, as the man of destiny. Is he not a king's son, in other words a 'prince of Almain?' Does he not come from the country where the stone was stolen from the 'wild men o'er the sea?' Has he not also a wife who is doomed, in the seer's prophecies, to the torture of the cross? Has he not two sons, one gentle and gracious as Abel, and the other wicked and uncontrolled as Cain?

"These proofs are enough for him. He now has his mobilization papers, his marching-orders in his pocket. The gods have indicated the objective upon which he is to march; and he marches. True, there are a few living people in his path. So much the better; it is all part of the programme. For it is after all these living people have been killed and, moreover, killed in the manner announced by Brother Thomas that the task will be done, the God-Stone released and Vorski, the instrument of destiny, crowned king. Therefore, let's turn up our sleeves, take our trusty butcher's knife in hand, and get to work! Vorski will translate Brother Thomas' nightmare into real life!"

17

"CRUEL PRINCE, OBEYING DESTINY"

Don Luis once more addressed himself to Vorski:

"We're agreed, aren't we, Kamerad? All that I'm saying exactly expresses the truth?"

Vorski had closed his eyes, his head was drooping, and the veins on his temple were immoderately swollen. To prevent any interference by Stéphane, Don Luis exclaimed:

"You will speak, my fine fellow! Ah, the pain is beginning to grow serious, is it? The brain is giving way?... Remember, just one whistle, a bar or two of *Tipperary* and I interrupt my speech... You won't? You're not ripe yet? So much the worse for you!... And you, Stéphane, have no fear for François. I answer for everything. But no pity for this monster, please! No, no and again no! Don't forget that he prepared and contrived everything of his own free will! Don't forget... But I'm getting angry. What's the use?"

Don Luis unfolded the page of the note-book on which Vorski had written down the prophecy and, holding it under his eyes, continued:

"What remains to be said is not so important, once the general explanation is accepted. Nevertheless, we must go into detail to some slight extent, show the mechanism of the affair imagined and built up by Vorski and lastly come to the part played by our attractive ancient Druid... So we are now in the month of June. This is the season fixed for the execution of the thirty victims. It was evidently appointed by Brother Thomas because the rhythm of his verse called for a month in one syllable, just as the year fourteen and three was selected because three rhymes with be and tree and just as Brother Thomas decided upon the number of thirty victims because thirty is the number of the Sarek reefs and coffins. But Vorski takes it as a definite command. Thirty victims are needed in June '17. They will be provided. They will be provided on condition that the twenty-nine inhabitants of Sarek—we shall see presently that Vorski has his thirtieth victim handy—consent to stay on the island and await their destruction. Well, Vorski suddenly hears of the departure of Honorine and Maguennoc. Honorine will come back in time. But how about Maguennoc? Vorski does not hesitate: he sends Elfride and Conrad on his tracks, with instructions to kill him and to wait. He hesitates the less because he believes, from certain words which he has overheard, that Maguennoc has taken with him the precious stone, the miraculous gem which must not be touched but which must be left in its leaden sheath (this is the actual phrase used by Maguennoc)!

"Elfride and Conrad therefore set out. One morning, at an inn, Elfride mixes poison with the coffee which Maguennoc is drinking (the prophecy has stated that there will be poison). Maguennoc continues his journey. But in an hour or two he is seized with intolerable pain and dies, almost immediately, on the bank by the roadside. Elfride and Conrad come up and go through his pockets. They find nothing, no gem, no precious stone. Vbrski's hopes have not been realized. All the same, the corpse is there. What are they to do with it? For the time being, they fling it into a half-demolished hut, which Vorski and his accomplices had visited some months before. Here Véronique d'Hergemont discovers the body... and an hour later fails to find it there. Elfride and Conrad, keeping watch close at hand, have taken it away and hidden it, still for the time being, in the cellars of a little empty country-house.

"There's one victim accounted for. We may observe, in passing, that Maguennoc's predictions relating to the order in which the thirty victims are to be executed—beginning with himself—have no basis. The prophecy doesn't mention such a thing. In any case, Vorski goes to work at random. At Sarek he carries off François and Stéphane Maroux and then, both as a measure of precaution and in order to cross the island without attracting attention and to enter the Priory more easily, he dresses himself in Stéphane's clothes, while Raynold puts on François'. The job before them is an easy one. The only people in the house are an old man, M. d'Hergemont, and a woman, Marie Le Goff. As soon as these are got rid of, the rooms and Maguennoc's in particular will be searched. Vorski, as yet unaware of the result of Elfride's expedition, would not be surprised if Maguennoc had left the miraculous jewel at the Priory.

"The first to fall is the cook, Marie Le Goff, whom Vorski takes by the throat and stabs with a knife. But it so happens that the ruffian's face gets covered with blood; and, seized with one of those fits of cowardice to which he is subject, he runs away, after loosing Raynold upon M. d'Hergemont.

"The fight between the boy and the old man is a long one. It is continued through the house and, by a tragic chance, ends before Véronique d'Hergemont's eyes. M. d'Hergemont is killed. Honorine arrives at the same moment. She drops, making the fourth victim.

"Matters now begin to go quickly. Panic sets in during the night. The people of Sarek, frightened out of their wits, seeing that Maguennoc's predictions are being fulfilled and that the hour of the disaster which has so long threatened their island is about to strike, make up their minds to go. This is what Vorski and his son are waiting for. Taking up their position in the motor-boat which they have stolen, they rush after the runaways and the abominable hunt begins, the great disaster foretold by Brother Thomas:

"'There will be shipwrecks, terrors, grief and crimes.'

"Honorine, who witnesses the scene and whose brain is already greatly upset, goes mad and throws herself from the cliff.

"Thereupon we have a lull of a few days, during which Véronique d'Hergemont explores the Priory and the island without being disturbed. As a matter of fact, after their successful hunt, leaving only Otto, who spends his time drinking in the cells, the father and son have gone off in the boat to fetch Elfride and Conrad and to bring back Maguennoc's body and fling it in the water within sight of Sarek, since Maguennoc of necessity has one of the thirty coffins earmarked for his reception.

"At that moment, that is when he returns to Sarek, Vorski's bag numbers twenty-four victims. Stéphane and François are prisoners, guarded by Otto. The rest consists of four women reserved for crucifixion, including the three sisters Archignat, all locked up in their wash-house. It is their turn next. Véronique d'Hergemont tries to release them, but it is too late. Waylaid by the band, shot at by Raynold, who is an expert archer, the sisters Archignat are wounded by arrows (for arrows, see the prophecy) and fall into the enemy's hands. That same evening they are strung up on the three oaks, after Vorski has first relieved them of the fifty thousand-franc notes which they carried concealed on their persons. Total: twenty-nine victims. Who will be the thirtieth? Who will be the fourth woman?"

Don Luis paused and continued:

"As to this, the prophecy speaks very plainly in two places, each of which complements the other:

"'Before his mother's eyes, Abel kills Cain.'

"And, a few lines lower down:

"'His wedded wife one night in June hath slain.'

"Vorski, from the moment when he became aware of this document, had interpreted the two lines in his own fashion. Being, in fact, unable at that time to dispose of Véronique, for whom he has vainly been hunting all over France, he temporizes with the decrees of destiny. The fourth woman to be tortured shall be a wife, but she shall be his first wife, Elffide. And this will not be absolutely contrary to the prophecy, which, if need be, can apply to the mother of Cain just as well as to the mother of Abel. And observe that the other prophecy, that which was communicated to him by word of mouth in the old days, also failed to specify the woman who was to die:

"'Vorski's wife shall perish on the cross.'

"Which wife? Elfride.

"So his dear, devoted accomplice is to perish. It's terrible for Vorski; it breaks his heart. But the god Moloch must be obeyed; and, considering that Vorski, to accomplish his task, decided to sacrifice his son Raynold, it would be inexcusable if he refused to sacrifice his wife Elfride. So all will be well.

"But, suddenly, a dramatic incident occurs. While pursuing the sisters Archignat, he sees and recognizes Véronique d'Hergemont!

"A man like Vorski could not fail to behold in this yet another favour vouchsafed by the powers above. The woman whom he has never forgotten is sent to him at the very moment when she is to take her place in the great adventure. She is given to him as a miraculous victim which he can destroy... or conquer. What a prospect! And how the heavens brighten with unexpected light! Vorski loses his head. He becomes more and more convinced that he is the Messiah, the chosen one, the apostle, missionary, the man who is 'obeying destiny.' He is linked up with the line of the high-priests, the guardians of the God-Stone. He is a Druid, an archdruid; and, as such, on the night when Véronique d'Hergemont burns the bridge, on the sixth night after the moon, he goes and cuts the sacred mistletoe with a golden sickle!

"And the siege of the Priory begins. I will not linger over this. Véronique d'Hergemont has told you the whole story, Stéphane, and we know her sufferings, the part played by the delightful All's Well, the discovery of the underground passage and the cells, the fight for François, the fight for you, Stéphane, whom Vorski imprisoned in one of the torture-cells called 'death-chambers' in the prophecy. Here you are surprised with Madame d'Hergemont. The young monster, Raynold, hurls you into the sea. François and his mother escape. Unfortunately, Vorski and his band succeed in reaching the Priory. François is captured. His mother joins him. And then... and then the most tragic scenes ensue, scenes upon which I will not enlarge: the interview between Vorski and Véronique d'Hergemont, the duel between the two brothers, between Cain and Abel, before Véronique d'Hergemont's very eyes. For the prophecy insists upon it:

"'Before his mother's eyes, Abel kills Cain.'

"And the prophecy likewise demands that she shall suffer beyond expression and that Vorski shall be subtle in doing evil. 'A cruel prince,' he puts marks on the two combatants; and, when Abel is on the point of being defeated, he himself wounds Cain so that Cain may be killed.

"The monster is mad. He's mad and drunk. The climax is close at hand. He drinks and drinks; for Véronique d'Hergemont's martyrdom is to take place that evening:

"'By thousand deaths and lingering agony,
His wedded wife one night of June hath slain.'

"The thousand deaths Véronique has already undergone; and the agony will be lingering. The hour comes. Supper, funeral procession, preparations, the setting up of the ladder, the binding of the victim and then... and then the ancient Druid!"

Don Luis gave a hearty laugh as he uttered the last words:

"Here, upon my word, things begin to get amusing! From this moment onward, tragedy goes hand in hand with comedy, the gruesome with the burlesque. Oh, that ancient Druid, what a caution! To you, Stéphane, and you, Patrice, who were behind the scenes, the story is devoid of interest. But to you, Vorski, what exciting revelations!... I say, Otto, just put the ladder against the trunk of the tree, so that your employer can rest his feet on the top rung. Is that easier for you, Vorski? Mark you, my little attention does not come from any ridiculous feeling of pity. Oh, dear, no! But I'm afraid that you might go phut; and besides I want you to be in a comfortable position to listen to the ancient Druid's confession."

He had another burst of laughter. There was no doubt about it: the ancient Druid was a great source of entertainment to Don Luis.

"The ancient Druid's arrival," he said, "introduces order and reason into the adventure. What was loose and vague becomes more compact. Incoherent crime turns into logical punishment. We have no longer blind obedience to Brother Thomas' doggerel, but the submission to common sense, the rigorous method of a man who knows what he wants and who has no time to lose. Really, the ancient Druid deserves all our admiration.

"The ancient Druid, whom we may call either Don Luis Perenna or Arsène Lupin—you suspect that, don't you?—knew very little of the story when the periscope of his submarine, the *Crystal Stopper*, emerged in sight of the coast of Sarek at midday yesterday."

"Very little?" Stéphane Maroux cried, in spite of himself.

"One might say, nothing," Don Luis declared.

"What! All those facts about Vorski's past, all those precise details about what he did at Sarek, about his plans and the part played by Elfride and the poisoning of Maguennoc?"

"I learnt all that here, yesterday," said Don Luis.

"But from whom? We never left one another?"

"Believe me when I say that the ancient Druid, when he landed yesterday on the coast of Sarek, knew nothing at all. But the ancient Druid lays claim to be at least as great a favourite of the gods as you are, Vorski. And in fact he at once had the luck to see, on a lonely little beach, our friend Stéphane, who himself had had the luck to fall into a pretty deep pool of water and thus to escape the fate which you and your son had prepared for him. Rescue-work, conversation. In half an hour, the ancient Druid had the facts. Forthwith, investigations. He ended by reaching the cells, where he found in yours, Vorski, a white robe which he needed for his own use and a scrap of paper with a copy of the prophecy written by yourself. Excellent. The ancient Druid knows the enemy's plans.

"He begins by following the tunnel down which François and his mother fled, but is unable to pass because of the subsidence which has been produced. He retraces his steps and comes out on the Black Heath. Exploration of the island. Meeting with Otto and Conrad. The enemy burns the footbridge. It is six o'clock in the evening. Query; how to get to the Priory? Stéphane suggests, by the Postern path. The ancient Druid returns to the *Crystal Stopper*. They circumnavigate the island under the direction of Stéphane, who knows all the channels—and besides, my dear Vorski, the *Crystal Stopper* is a very docile submarine. She can slip in anywhere; the ancient Druid had her built to his own designs—and at last they land at the spot where François' boat is hanging. Here, meeting with All's Well, who is sleeping under the boat, the ancient Druid introduces himself. Immediate display of sympathy. They make a start. But, half-way up the ascent, All's Well branches off. At this place the wall is the cliff is, so to speak, patched with movable blocks of stone. In the middle of these stones is an opening, an opening made by Maguennoc, as the ancient Druid discovered later, in order to enter the hall of sacrifices and the mortuary crypts. Thus, the ancient Druid finds himself in the thick of the plot, master above ground and below. Only, it is eight o'clock in the evening.

"As regards François, there is no immediate anxiety. The prophecy says, 'Abel kills Cain.' But Véronique d'Hergemont was to perish 'one night of June.' Had she undergone the horrible martyrdom? Was it too late to rescue her?"

Don Luis turned to Stéphane:

"You remember, Stéphane, the agony through which you and the ancient Druid passed and your relief at discovering the tree prepared with the inscription, 'V. d'H.' The tree has no victim on it yet. Véronique will be saved; and in fact we hear a sound of voices coming from the Priory. It is the grim procession. It slowly climbs the grassy slope amid the thickening darkness. The lantern is waved. A halt is called. Vorski spouts and holds forth. The last scene is at hand. Soon we shall rush to the assault and Véronique will be delivered.

"But here an incident occurs which will amuse you, Vorski. Yes, we make a strange discovery, my friends and I: we find a woman prowling round the dolmen, who hides as we come up. We seize her. Stéphane recognizes her by the light of an electric torch. Do you know who it was, Vorski? I give you a hundred guesses. Elfride! Yes, Elfride, your accomplice, the one whom you meant to crucify at first! Curious, wasn't it? In an extreme state of excitement, half crazy, she tells us that she consented to the duel between the two boys on your promise that her son would be the victor and kill Véronique's son. But you had locked her up, in the morning; and, in the evening, when she succeeded in making her escape, it was Raynold's dead body that she found. She has now come to be present at the torture of the rival whom she detests and then to avenge herself on you and kill you, my poor old chap.

"A capital idea! The ancient Druid approves; and, while you go up to the dolmen and Stéphane keeps an eye on you, he continues to question Elfride. But, lo and behold, Vorski, at the sound of your voice, the jade begins to kick! She veers round unexpectedly. Her master's voice stimulates her to an unparalleled display of ardour. She wants to see you, to warn you of your danger, to save you; and suddenly she makes a rush at the ancient Druid with a dagger in her hand. The ancient Druid is obliged, in self-defence, to knock her down, half-stunning her; and the sight of this moribund woman at once suggests to him a means of turning the incident to good account. The wretched creature is tied up in the twinkling of an eye. The ancient Druid intends you yourself to punish her, Vorski, and make her undergo the fate which you had reserved for her before. So he slips his robe on Stéphane, gives him his instructions, shoots an arrow in your direction the moment you come up and, while you go running in pursuit of a white robe, does a conjuring-trick and substitutes Elfride for Véronique, the first wife for the second. How? That's my business. All you need know is that the trick was played and succeeded to perfection!" Don Luis stopped to draw breath. One would really have thought, from his familiar and confidential tone, that he was telling Vorski an amusing story, a good joke, which Vorski ought to be the first to laugh at.

"That's not all," he continued. "Patrice Belval and some of my Moors—you may as well know that we have eighteen of them on board—have been working in the underground rooms. There's no getting away from the prophecy. The moment the wife has expired

"'Fire and loud noise will issue from the earth.
In secrecy where the great treasure lies.'

"Of course, Brother Thomas never knew where the great treasure lay, nor did anyone else. But the ancient Druid has guessed; and he wants Vorski to receive his signal and to drop ready-roasted into his mouth. For this he needs an outlet issuing near the Fairies' Dolmen. Captain Belval looks for one and finds it. They clear an old stairway. They clear the inside of the dead tree. They take from the submarine some dynamite-cartridges and signal-rockets and place them in position. And, when you, Vorski, from your perch, start proclaiming like a herald, 'She's dead! The fourth woman has died upon the cross!' Bang, bang, bang! Thunder, flame, uproar, the whole bag of tricks. That does it: you are more and more the darling of the gods, the pet of destiny, and you burn with the noble longing to fling yourself down the chimney and gobble up the God-Stone. Next day, therefore, after sleeping off your brandy and your rum, you start to work again, smiling. You killed your thirty victims, according to the rites prescribed by Brother Thomas. You have surmounted every obstacle. The prophecy is fulfilled.

"'And man again will on the stone set eyes
Once stolen from wild men in bygone days
O'er sea: the God-stone which gives life or death.'

"The ancient Druid has no choice but to give in and to hand you the key of Paradise. But first, of course, a little interlude, a few capers and wizard's tricks, just for a bit of fun. And then hey for the God-Stone guarded by the Sleeping Beauty!"

Don Luis nimbly cut a few of those capers of which he seemed so fond. Then he said to Vorski:

"Well, old chap, I have a vague impression that you've had enough of my speech and that you would prefer to reveal François' hiding-place to me at once, rather than stay here any longer. I'm awfully sorry, but you really must learn how the matter stands with the Sleeping Beauty and the unexpected presence of Véronique d'Hergemont. However, two minutes will be sufficient. Pardon me."

Dropping the character of the ancient Druid and speaking in his own name, Don Luis continued:

"What you want to know is why I took Véronique d'Hergemont to that place after snatching her from your clutches. The answer is very simple. Where would you have me take her? To the submarine? An absurd suggestion! The sea was rough that night and Véronique needed rest. To the Priory? Never! That would have been too far from the scene of operations and I should have had no peace of mind. In reality there was only one place sheltered from the storm and sheltered from attack; and that was the hall of sacrifices. That was why I took her there and why she was sleeping there, quietly, under the influence of a strong narcotic, when you saw her. I confess that the pleasure of treating you to this spectacle counted for something in my decision. And how splendidly I was rewarded! Oh, if you could have seen the face you pulled! Such a ghastly sight! Véronique raised from the dead! Véronique brought back to life! So horrible was the vision that you ran away helter-skelter.

"But to cut a long story short: you find the exit blocked. Thereupon you change your mind. Conrad returns to the offensive. He attacks me by stealth while I am preparing to move Véronique d'Hergemont to the submarine. Conrad receives a mortal blow from one of the Moors. Second comic interlude. Conrad, dressed up in the ancient Druid's robe, is laid on the floor in one of the crypts; and of course your first thought is to leap on him and wreak your vengeance on him. And, when you see Elfride's body, which has taken the place of Véronique d'Hergemont in the sacred table, whoosh... you jump on that too and reduce the woman whom you have already crucified to a bleeding pulp! Blunder upon blunder! And the end of the whole story likewise strikes a comic note.

You are strung up on the pillory while I deliver straight at you a speech which does for you and which proves that, if you have won the God-Stone by virtue of your thirty coffins, I am taking possession of it by my own intrinsic virtue. There's the whole adventure for you, my dear Vorski. Except for a few secondary incidents, or some others, of greater importance, which there is no need for you to know, you know as much as I do. You've been quite comfortable and have had lots of time to think. So I am confidently expecting your answer about François. Come, out with your little song:

"'It's a long, long way to Tipperary.

It's a long way to go…'

"Well? Are you feeling in a chatty mood?"

Don Luis had climbed a few rungs. Stéphane and Patrice had come near and were anxiously listening. It was evident that Vorski meant to speak.

He had opened his eyes and was staring at Don Luis with a look of mingled hatred and fear. This extraordinary man must have appeared to him as one of those persons against whom it is absolutely useless to fight and to whom it is equally useless to appeal for compassion. Don Luis represented the conqueror; and, in the presence of one stronger than yourself, there is nothing for it but to yield in all humility. Besides, Vorski was incapable of further resistance. The torture was becoming intolerable.

He spoke a few words in an unintelligible voice.

"A little louder, please," said Don Luis. "I can't hear. Where's François?"

He climbed the ladder. Vorski stammered:

"Shall I be free?"

"On my word of honour. We shall all leave this place, except Otto, who will release you."

"At once?"

"At once."

"Then..."

"Then what?"

"Well, François is alive."

"You mutton-head. I know that. But where is he?"

"Tied into the boat."

"The one hanging at the foot of the cliff?"

"Yes."

Don Luis struck his forehead with his hand:

"Idiot! Idiot! Idiot!... Don't mind: I'm speaking of myself. Yes, I ought to have guessed that! Why, All's Well was sleeping under the boat, peacefully, like a good dog sleeping beside his master! Why, when we sent All's Well on François' trail, he led Stéphane straight to the boat. It's true enough, there are times when the cleverest of us behave like simpletons! But you, Vorski, did you know that there was a way down there and a boat?"

"I knew it since yesterday."

"And, you artful dog, you intended to skedaddle in her?"

"Yes."

"Well, Vorski, you shall skedaddle in her, with Otto. I'll leave her for you. Stéphane!"

But Stéphane Maroux was already running towards the cliff, escorted by All's Well.

"Release him, Stéphane," cried Don Luis.

And he added, addressing the Moors:

"Help him, you others. And get the submarine under way. We shall sail in ten minutes."

He turned to Vorski:

"Goodbye, my dear chap... Oh, just one more word! Every well-regulated adventure contains a love story. Ours appears to be without one, for I should never dare to allude to the feelings that urged you towards the sainted woman who bore your name. And yet I must tell you of a very pure and noble affection. Did you notice the eagerness with which Stéphane flew to François' assistance? Obviously he loves his young pupil, but he loves the mother still more. And, since everything that pleases Véronique d'Hergemont is bound to please you, I wish to admit that he is not indifferent to her, that his wonderful love has touched her heart, that it was with real joy that she saw him restored to her this morning and that this will all end in a wedding... as soon as she's a widow, of course. You follow me, don't you? The only obstacle to their happiness is yourself. Therefore, as you are a perfect little gentleman, you will not like to... But I need not go on. I rely on your good manners to die as soon as you can. Goodbye, old fellow, I won't offer you my hand, but my heart's with you. Otto, in ten minutes, unless you hear to the contrary, release your employer. You'll find the boat at the bottom of the cliff. Good luck, my friends!"

It was finished. The battle between Don Luis and Vorski was ended: and the issue had not been in doubt for a single instant. From the first minute, one of the two adversaries had so consistently dominated the other, that the latter, in spite of all his daring and his training as a criminal, had been nothing more than a grotesque, absurd, disjointed puppet in his opponent's hands. After succeeding in the entire execution of his plan, after attaining and surpassing his object, he, the master of events, in the moment of victory, found himself suddenly strung up on the tree of torture; and there he remained, gasping and captive like an insect pinned to a strip of cork.

Without troubling any further about his victims, Don Luis went off with Patrice Belval, who could not help saying to him:

"All the same, you're letting those vile scoundrels down very lightly!"

"Pooh, it won't be long before they get themselves nabbed elsewhere," said Don Luis, chuckling. "What do you expect them to do?"

"Well, first of all, to take the God-Stone."

"Out of the question! It would need twenty men to do that, with a scaffolding and machinery. I myself am giving up the idea for the present. I shall come back after the war."

"But, look here, Don Luis, what is this miraculous stone?"

"Ah, now you're asking something!" said Don Luis, without making further reply.

They set out; and Don Luis, rubbing his hands, said:

"I worked the thing well. It's not much over twenty-four hours since we landed at Sarek. And the riddle had lasted twenty-four centuries. One century an hour. My congratulations, Lupin."

"I should be glad to offer you mine, Don Luis," said Patrice Belval, "but they are not worth as much as those of an expert like yourself."

When they reached the sands of the little beach, François' boat had already been lowered and was empty. Farther away, on the right, the *Crystal Stopper* was floating on the calm sea. François came running up to them, stopped a few yards from Don Luis and looked at him with wide-open eyes:

"I say," he murmured, "then it's you? It's you I was expecting?"

"Faith," said Don Luis, laughing. "I don't know if you were expecting me... but I'm sure it's me!"

"You... you... Don Luis Perenna!... That is to say..."

"Hush, no other names! Perenna's enough for me... Besides, we won't talk about me, if you don't mind. I was just a chance, a gentleman who happened to drop in at the right moment. Whereas you... by Jove, youngster, but you've done jolly well!... So you spent the night in the boat?"

"Yes, under the tarpaulin, lashed to the bottom and tightly gagged."

"Uncomfortable?"

"Not at all. I hadn't been there ten minutes when All's Well appeared. So..."

"But the man, the scoundrel: what had he threatened to do to you?"

"Nothing. After the duel, while the others were attending to my opponent, he brought me down here, pretending that he was going to take me to mother and put us both on board the boat. Then, when we got to the boat, he laid hold of me without a word."

"Do you know the man? Do you know his name?"

"I know nothing about him. All I can say is that he was persecuting us, mother and me."

"For reasons which I shall explain to you, François. In any case, you have nothing to fear from him now."

"Oh, but you haven't killed him?"

"No, but I have put it out of his power to do any more harm. This will all be explained to you; but I think that, for the moment, the most urgent thing is that we should go to your mother."

"Stéphane told me that she was resting over there, in the submarine, and that you had saved her too. Does she expect me?"

"Yes; we had a talk last night, she and I, and I promised to find you. I felt that she trusted me. All the same, Stéphane, you had better go ahead and prepare her."

The *Crystal Stopper* lay at the end of a reef of rocks which formed a sort of natural jetty. Some ten or twelve Moors were running to and fro. Two had drawn apart and were whispering together. Two of them were holding a gangway which Don Luis and François crossed a minute later.

In one of the cabins, arranged as a drawing-room, Véronique lay stretched on a couch. Her pale face bore the marks of the unspeakable suffering which she had undergone. She seemed very weak, very weary. But her eyes, full of tears, were bright with happiness.

François rushed into her arms. She burst into sobs, without speaking a word.

Opposite them, All's Well, seated on his haunches, beat the air with his fore-paws and looked at them, with his head a little on one side:

"Mother," said François, "Don Luis is here."

She took Don Luis' hand and pressed a long kiss upon it, while François murmured:

"You saved mother... You saved us both..."

Don Luis interrupted him:

"Will you give me pleasure, François? Well, don't thank me. If you really want to thank somebody, there, thank your friend All's Well. He does not look as if he had played a very important part in the piece. And yet, compared with the scoundrel who persecuted you, he was the good genius, always discreet, intelligent, modest and silent."

"So are you!"

"Oh, I am neither modest nor silent; and that's why I admire All's Well. Here, All's Well, come along with me and, for goodness' sake, stop sitting up! You might have to do it all night, for they will be shedding tears together for hours, the mother and son..."

18

THE GOD-STONE

The *Crystal Stopper* was running on the surface of the water. Don Luis sat talking, with Stéphane, Patrice and All's Well, who were gathered round him:

"What a swine that Vorski is!" he said. "I've seen that breed of monster before, but never one of his calibre."

"Then, in that case..." Patrice Belval objected.

"In that case?" echoed Don Luis.

"I repeat what I've said already. You hold a monster in your hands and you let him go free! To say nothing of its being highly immoral, think of all the harm that he can do, that he inevitably will do! It's a heavy responsibility to take upon yourself, that of the crimes which he will still commit."

"Do you think so too, Stéphane?" asked Don Luis.

"I'm not quite sure what I think," replied Stéphane, "because, to save François, I was prepared to make any concession. But, all the same..."

"All the same, you would rather have had another solution?"

"Frankly, yes. So long as that man is alive and free, Madame d'Hergemont and her son will have everything to fear from him."

"But what other solution was there? I promised him his liberty in return for François' immediate safety. Ought I to have promised him only his life and handed him over to the police?"

"Perhaps," said Captain Belval.

"Very well. But, in that case, the police would institute enquiries, and by discovering the fellow's real identity bring back to life the husband of Véronique d'Hergemont and the father of François. Is that what you want?"

"No, no!" cried Stéphane, eagerly.

"No, indeed," confessed Patrice Belval, a little uneasily. "No, that solution is no better; but what astonishes me is that you, Don Luis, did not hit upon the right one, the one which would have satisfied us all."

"There was only one solution," Don Luis Perenna said, plainly.

"There was only one."

"Which was that?"

"Death."

There was a pause. Then Don Luis resumed:

"My friends, I did not form you into a court simply as a joke; and you must not think that your parts as judges are played because the trial seems to you to be over. It is still going on; and the court has not risen. That is why I want you to answer me honestly: do you consider that Vorski deserves to die?"

"Yes," declared Patrice.

And Stéphane approved:

"Yes, beyond a doubt."

"My friends," Don Luis continued, "your verdict is not sufficiently solemn. I beseech you to utter it formally and conscientiously, as though you were in the presence of the culprit. I ask you once more: what penalty did Vorski deserve?"

They raised their hands and, one after the other, answered:

"Death."

Don Luis whistled. One of the Moors ran up.

"Two pairs of binoculars, Hadji."

The man brought the glasses and Don Luis handed them to Stéphane and Patrice:

"We are only a mile from Sarek," he said. "Look towards the point: the boat should have started."

"Yes," said Patrice, presently.

"Do you see her, Stéphane?"

"Yes, only..."

"Only what?"

"There's only one passenger."

"Yes," said Patrice, "only one passenger."

They put down their binoculars and one of them said:

"Only one has got away: Vorski evidently. He must have killed Otto, his accomplice."

"Unless Otto, his accomplice, has killed him," chuckled Don Luis.

"What makes you say that?"

"Why, remember the prophecy made to Vorski in his youth: 'Your wife will die on the cross and you will be killed by a friend.'"

"I doubt if a prediction is enough."

"I have other proofs, though."

"What proofs?"

"They, my friends, form part of the last problem we shall have to elucidate together. For instance, what is your idea of the manner in which I substituted Elfride Vorski for Madame d'Hergemont?"

Stéphane shook his head:

"I confess that I never understood."

"And yet it's so simple! When a gentleman in a drawing-room, in a white tie and a tail-coat, performs conjuring-tricks or guesses your thoughts, you say to yourself, don't you, that there must be some artifice beneath it all, the assistance of a confederate? Well, you need seek no farther where I'm concerned."

"What, you had a confederate?"

"Yes, certainly."

"But who was he?"

"Otto."

"Otto? But you never left us! You never spoke to him, surely?"

"How could I have succeeded without his help? In reality, I had two confederates in this business, Elfride and Otto, both of whom betrayed Vorski, either out of revenge or out of greed. While you, Stéphane, were luring Vorski past the Fairies' Dolmen, I accosted Otto. We soon struck a bargain, at the cost of a few bank-notes and in return for a promise that he would come out of the adventure safe and sound. Moreover I informed him that Vorski had pouched the sisters Archignat's fifty thousand francs."

"How did you know that?" asked Stéphane.

"Through my confederate number one, through Elfride, whom I continued to question in a whisper while you were looking out for Vorski's coming and who also, in a few brief words, told me what she knew of Vorski's past."

"When all is said, you only saw Otto that once."

"Two hours later, after Elfride's death and after the fireworks in the hollow oak, we had a second interview, under the Fairies' Dolmen. Vorski was asleep, stupefied with drink, and Otto was mounting guard. You can imagine that I seized the opportunity to obtain particulars of the business and to complete my information about Vorski with the details which Otto for two years had been secretly collecting about a chief whom he detested. Then he unloaded Vorski's and Conrad's revolvers, or rather he removed the bullets, while leaving the cartridges. Then he handed me Vorski's watch and note-book, as well as an empty locket and a photograph of Vorski's mother which Otto had stolen from him some months before, things which helped me next day to play the wizard with the aforesaid Vorski in the crypt where he found me. That is how Otto and I collaborated."

"Very well," said Patrice, "but still you didn't ask him to kill Vorski?"

"Certainly not."

"In that case, how are we to know that..."

"Do you think that Vorski did not end by discovering our collaboration, which is one of the obvious causes of his defeat? And do you imagine that Master Otto did not foresee this contingency? You may be sure that there was no doubt of this: Vorski, once unfastened from his tree, would have made away with his accomplice, both from motives of revenge and in order to recover the sisters Archignat's fifty thousand francs. Otto got the start of him. Vorski was there, helpless, lifeless, an easy prey. He struck him a blow. I will go farther and say that Otto, who is a coward, did not even strike him a blow. He will simply have left Vorski on his tree. And so the punishment is complete. Are you appeased now, my friends? Is your craving for justice satisfied?"

Patrice and Stéphane were silent, impressed by the terrible vision which Don Luis was conjuring up before their eyes.

"There," he said, laughing, "I was right not to make you pronounce sentence over there, when we were standing at the foot of the oak, with the live man in front of us! I can see that my two judges might have flinched a little at that moment. And so would my third judge, eh, All's Well, you sensitive, tearful fellow? And I am like you, my friends. We are not people who condemn and execute. But, all the same, think of what Vorski was, think of his thirty murders and his refinements of cruelty and congratulate me on having, in the last resort, chosen blind destiny as his judge and the loathsome Otto as his responsible executioner. The will of the gods be done!"

The Sarek coast was making a thinner line on the horizon. It disappeared in the mist in which sea and sky were merged.

The three men were silent. All three were thinking of the isle of the dead, laid waste by one man's madness, the isle of the dead where soon some visitor would find the inexplicable traces of the tragedy, the entrances to the tunnels, the cells with their "death-chambers," the hall of the God-Stone, the mortuary crypts, Elfride's body, Conrad's body, the skeletons of the sisters Archignat and, right at the end of the island, near the Fairies' Dolmen, where the prophecy of the thirty coffins and the four crosses was written for all to read, Vorski's great body, lonely and pitiable, mangled by the ravens and owls.

Avilla near Arcachon, in the pretty village of Les Moulleaux, whose pine-trees run down to the shores of the gulf.

Véronique is sitting in the garden. A week's rest and happiness have restored the colour to her comely face and assuaged all evil memories. She is looking with a smile at her son, who, standing a little way off, is listening to and questioning Don Luis Perenna. She also looks at Stéphane; and their eyes meet gently.

It is easy to see that the affection in which they both hold the boy is a link which unites them closely and which is strengthened by their secret thoughts and their unuttered feelings. Not once has Stéphane recalled the avowals which he made in the cell, under the Black Heath; but Véronique has not forgotten them; and the profound gratitude which she feels for the man who brought up her son is mingled with a special emotion and an agitation of which she unconsciously savours the charm.

That day, Don Luis, who, on the evening when the *Crystal Stopper* brought them all to the Villa des Moulleaux, had taken the train for Paris, arrived unexpectedly at lunchtime, accompanied by Patrice Belval; and during the hour that they have been sitting in their rocking-chairs in the garden, the boy, his face all pink with excitement, has never ceased to question his rescuer:

"And what did you do next?... But how did you know?... And what put you on the track of that?"

"My darling," says Véronique, "aren't you afraid of boring Don Luis?"

"No, madame," replies Don Luis, rising, going up to Véronique and speaking in such a way that the boy cannot hear, "no, François is not boring me; and in fact I like answering his questions. But I confess that he perplexes me a little and that I am afraid of saying something awkward. Tell me, how much exactly does he know of the whole story?"

"As much as I know myself, except Vorski's name, of course."

"But does he know the part which Vorski played?"

"Yes, but with certain differences. He thinks that Vorski is an escaped prisoner who picked up the legend of Sarek and, in order to get hold of the God-Stone, proceeded to carry out the prophecy touching it. I have kept some of the lines of the prophecy from François."

"And the part played by Elfride? Her hatred for you? The threats she made you?"

"Madwoman's talk, I told François, of which I myself did not understand the meaning."

Don Luis smiled:

"The explanation is a little arbitrary; and I have a notion that François quite well understands that certain parts of the tragedy remain and must remain obscure to him. The great thing, don't you think, is that he should not know that Vorski was his father?"

"He does not know and he never will."

"And then—and this is what I was coming to—what name will he bear himself?"

"What do you mean?"

"Whose son will he believe himself to be? For you know as well as I do that the legal reality is this, that François Vorski died fifteen years ago, drowned in a shipwreck, and his grandfather with him. And Vorski died last year, stabbed by a fellow-prisoner. Neither of them is alive in the eyes of the law. So..."

Véronique nodded her head and smiled:

"So I don't know. The position seems to me, as you say, incapable of explanation. But everything will come out all right."

"Why?"

"Because you're here to do it."

It was his turn to smile:

"I can no longer take credit for the actions which I perform or the steps which I take. Everything is arranging itself *a priori*. Then why worry?"

"Am I not right to?"

"Yes," he said, gravely. "The woman who has suffered all that you have must not be subjected to the least additional annoyance. And nothing shall happen to her after this, I swear. So what I suggest to you is this: long ago, you married against your father's wish a very distant cousin, who died after leaving you a son, François. This son your father, to be revenged upon you, kidnapped and brought to Sarek. At your father's death, the name of d'Hergemont became extinct and there is nothing to recall the events of your marriage."

"But my name remains. Legally, in the official records, I am Véronique d'Hergemont."

"Your maiden name disappears under your married name."

"You mean under that of Vorski."

"No, because you did not marry that fellow Vorski, but one of your cousins called . . .."

"Called what?"

"Jean Maroux. Here is a stamped certificate of your marriage to Jean Maroux, a marriage mentioned in your official records, as this other document shows."

Véronique looked at Don Luis in amazement:

"But why? Why that name?"

"Why? So that your son may be neither d'Hergemont, which would have recalled past events, nor Vorski, which would have recalled the name of a traitor. Here is his birth certificate, as François Maroux."

She repeated, all blushing and confused:

"But why did you choose just that name?"

"It seemed easy for François. It's the name of Stéphane, with whom François will go on living for some time. We can say that Stéphane was a relation of your husband's; and this will explain the intimacy generally. That is my plan. It presents, believe me, no possible danger. When one is confronted by an inexplicable and painful position like yours, one must needs employ special means and resort to drastic and, I admit, very illegal measures. I did so without scruple, because I have the good fortune to dispose of resources which are not within everybody's reach. Do you approve of what I have done?"

Véronique bent her head:

"Yes," she said, "yes."

He half-rose from his seat:

"Besides," he added, "if there should be any drawbacks, the future will no doubt take upon itself the burden of removing them. It would be enough, for instance—there is no indiscretion, is there, in alluding to the feelings which Stéphane entertains for François' mother?—it would be enough if, one day or another, for reasons of common-sense, or reasons of gratitude, François' mother were moved to accept the homage of those feelings. How much simpler everything will be if François already bears the name of Maroux! How much more easily the past will be abolished, both for the outside world and for François, who will no longer be able to pry into the secret of bygone events which there will be nothing to recall to memory. It seemed to me that these were rather weighty arguments. I am glad to see that you share my opinion."

Don Luis bowed to Véronique and, without insisting any further, without appearing to notice her confusion, turned to François and explained:

"I'm at your orders now, young man. And, since you don't want to leave anything unexplained, let's go back to the God-Stone and the scoundrel who coveted its possession. Yes, the scoundrel," repeated Don Luis, seeing no reason not to speak of Vorski with absolute frankness, "and the most terrible scoundrel that I have ever met with, because he believed in his mission; in short, a sick-brained man, a lunatic..."

"Well, first of all," François observed, "what I don't understand is that you waited all night to capture him, when he and his accomplices were sleeping under the Fairies' Dolmen."

"Well done, youngster," said Don Luis, laughing, "you have put your finger on a weak point! If I had acted as you suggest, the tragedy would have been finished twelve or fifteen hours earlier. But think, would you have been released? Would the scoundrel have spoken and revealed your hiding-place? I don't think so. To loosen his tongue I had to keep him simmering. I had to make him dizzy, to drive him mad with apprehension and anguish and to convince him by means of a mass of proofs, that he was irretrievably defeated. Otherwise he would have held his tongue and we might perhaps not have found you... Besides, at that time, my plan was not very clear, I did not quite know how to wind up; and it was not until much later that I thought not of submitting him to violent torture — I am incapable of that — but of tying him to that tree on which he wanted to let your mother die. So that, in my perplexity and hesitation, I simply yielded, in the end, to the wish — the rather puerile wish, I blush to confess — to carry out the prophecy to the end, to see how the missionary would behave in the presence of the ancient Druid, in short to amuse myself. After all, the adventure was so dark and gloomy that a little fun seemed to me essential. And I laughed like blazes. That was wrong. I admit it and I apologize."

The boy was laughing too. Don Luis, who was holding him between his knees, kissed him and asked:

"Do you forgive me?"

"Yes, on condition that you answer two more questions. The first is not important."

"Ask away."

"It's about the ring. Where did you get that ring which you put first on mother's finger and afterwards on Elfride's?"

"I made it that same night, in a few minutes, out of an old wedding-ring and some coloured stones."

"But the scoundrel recognized it as having belonged to his mother."

"He thought he recognized it; and he thought it because the ring was like the other."

"But how did you know that? And how did you learn the story?"

"From himself."

"You don't mean that?"

"Certainly I do! From words that escaped him while he was sleeping under the Fairies' Dolmen. A drunkard's nightmare. Bit by bit he told the whole story of his mother. Elfride knew a good part of it besides. You see how simple it is and how my luck stood by me!"

"But the riddle of the God-Stone is not simple," François cried, "and you deciphered it! People have been trying for centuries and you took a few hours!"

"No, a few minutes, François. It was enough for me to read the letter which your grandfather wrote about it to Captain Belval. I sent your grandfather by post all the explanations as to the position and the marvellous nature of the God-Stone."

"Well," cried the boy, "it's those explanations that I'm asking of you, Don Luis. This is my last question, I promise you. What made people believe in the power of the God-Stone? And what did that so-called power consist of exactly?"

Stéphane and Patrice drew up their chairs. Véronique sat up and listened. They all understood that Don Luis had waited until they were together before rending the veil of the mystery before their eyes.

He began to laugh:

"You mustn't hope for anything sensational," he said. "A mystery is worth just as much as the darkness in which it is shrouded; and, as we have begun by dispelling the darkness, nothing remains but the fact itself in its naked reality. Nevertheless the facts in this case are strange and the reality is not denuded of a certain grandeur."

"It must needs be so," said Patrice Belval, "seeing that the reality left so miraculous a legend in the isle of Sarek and even all over Brittany."

"Yes," said Don Luis, "and a legend so persistent that it influences us to this day and that not one of you has escaped the obsession of the miraculous."

"What do you mean?" protested Patrice. "I don't believe in miracles."

"No more do I," said the boy.

"Yes, you do, you believe in them, you accept miracles as possible. If not, you would long ago have seen the whole truth."

"Why?"

Don Luis picked a magnificent rose from a tree by his side and asked François:

"Is it possible for me to transform this rose, whose proportions, as it is, are larger than those a rose often attains, into a flower double the size and this rose-tree into a shrub twice as tall?"

"Certainly not," said François.

"Then why did you admit, why did you all admit that Maguennoc could achieve that result, merely by digging up earth in certain parts of the island, at certain fixed hours? That was a miracle; and you accepted it without hesitation, unconsciously."

Stéphane objected:

"We accept what we saw with our eyes."

"But you accepted it as a miracle, that is to say, as a phenomenon which Maguennoc produced by special and, truth to tell, by supernatural means. Whereas I, when I read this detail in M. d'Hergemont's letter, at once—what shall I say?—caught on. I at once established the connection between those monstrous blossoms and the name borne by the Calvary of the flowers. And my conviction was immediate: 'No, Maguennoc is not a wizard. He simply cleared a piece of uncultivated land around the Calvary; and all he had to do, to produce abnormal flowers, was to bring along a layer of mould. So the God-Stone is underneath; the God-Stone which, in the middle ages, produced the same abnormal flowers; the God-Stone, which, in the days of the Druids, healed the sick and strengthened children.'"

"Therefore," said Patrice, "there is a miracle."

"There is a miracle if we accept the supernatural explanation. There is a natural phenomenon if we look for it and if we find the physical cause capable of giving rise to the apparent miracle."

"But those physical causes don't exist! They are not present."

"They exist, because you have seen monstrous flowers."

"Then there is a stone," asked Patrice, almost chaffingly, "which can naturally give health and strength? And that stone is the God-Stone?"

"There is not a particular, individual stone. But there are stones, blocks of stone, rocks, hills and mountains of rock, which contain mineral veins formed of various metals, oxides of uranium, silver, lead, copper, nickel, cobalt and so on. And among these metals are some which emit a special radiation, endowed with peculiar properties known as radioactivity. These veins are veins of pitchblende which are found hardly anywhere in Europe except in the north of Bohemia and which are worked near the little town of Joachimsthal. And those radioactive bodies are uranium, thorium, helium and chiefly, in the case which we are considering..."

"Radium," François interrupted.

"You've said it, my boy: radium. Phenomena of radioactivity occur more or less everywhere; and we may say that they are manifested throughout nature, as in the healing action of thermal springs. But plainly radioactive bodies like radium possess more definite properties. For instance, there is no doubt that the rays and the emanation of radium exercise a power over the life of plants, a power similar to that caused by the passage of an electric current. In both cases, the stimulation of the nutritive centres makes the elements required by the plant more easy to assimilate and promotes its growth. In the same way, there is no doubt that the radium rays are capable of exercising a physiological action on living tissues, by producing more or less profound modifications, destroying certain cells and contributing to develop other cells and even to control their evolution. Radiotherapy claims to have healed or improved numerous cases of rheumatism of the joints, nervous troubles, ulceration, eczema, tumours and adhesive cicatrices. In short radium is a really effective therapeutic agent."

"So," said Stéphane, "you regard the God-Stone..."

"I regard the God-Stone as a block of radiferous pitchblende originating from the Joachimsthal lodes. I have long known the Bohemian legend which speaks of a miraculous stone that was once removed from the side of a hill; and, when I was travelling in Bohemia, I saw the hole left by the stone. It corresponds pretty accurately with the dimensions of the God-Stone."

"But," Stéphane objected, "radium is contained in rocks only in the form of infinitesimal particles. Remember that, after a mass of fourteen hundred tons of rock have been duly mined and washed and treated, there remains at the end of it all only a filtrate of some fifteen grains of radium. And you attribute a miraculous power to the God-Stone, which weighs two tons at most!"

"But it evidently contains radium in appreciable quantities. Nature has not pledged herself to be always niggardly and invariably to dilute the radium. She was pleased to accumulate in the God-Stone a generous supply which enabled it to produce the apparently extraordinary phenomena which we know of... not forgetting that we have to allow for popular exaggeration."

Stéphane seemed to be yielding to conviction. Nevertheless he said:

"One last point. Apart from the God-Stone, there was the little chip of stone which Maguennoc found in the leaden sceptre, the prolonged touch of which burnt his hand. According to you, this was a particle of radium?"

"Undoubtedly. And it is this perhaps that most clearly reveals the presence and the power of radium in all this adventure. When Henri Becquerel, the great physicist, kept a tube containing a salt of radium in his waistcoat-pocket, his skin became covered in a few days with suppurating ulcers. Curie repeated the experiment, with the same result. Maguennoc's case was more serious, because he held the particle of radium in his hand. A wound formed which had a cancerous appearance. Scared by all that he knew and all that he himself had said about the miraculous stone which burns like hell-fire and 'gives life or death,' he chopped off his hand."

"Very well," said Stéphane, "but where did that particle of pure radium come from? It can't have been a chip of the God-Stone, because, once again, however rich a mineral may be, radium is incorporated in it, not in isolated grains, but in a soluble form, which has to be dissolved and afterwards collected, by a series of mechanical operations, into a solution rich enough to enable successive crystallizations and concentrations to isolate the active product which the solution contains. All this and a number of other later operations demand an enormous plant, with workshops, laboratories, expert chemists, in short, a very different state of civilization, you must admit, from the state of barbarism in which our ancestors the Celts were immersed."

Don Luis smiled and tapped the young man on the shoulder:

"Hear, hear, Stéphane! I am glad to see that François' friend and tutor has a far-seeing and logical mind. The objection is perfectly valid and suggested itself to me at once. I might reply by putting forward some quite legitimate theory, I might presume a natural means of isolating radium and imagine that, in a geological fault occurring in the granite, at the bottom of a big pocket containing radiferous ore, a fissure has opened through which the waters of the river slowly trickle, carrying with them infinitesimal quantities of radium; that the waters so charged flow for a long time in a narrow channel, combine again, become concentrated and, after centuries upon centuries, filter through in little drops, which evaporate at once, and form at the point of emergence a tiny stalactite, exceedingly rich in radium, the tip of which is broken off one day by some Gallic warrior. But is there any need to seek so far and to have recourse to hypotheses? Cannot we rely on the unaided genius and the inexhaustible resources of nature? Does it call for a more wonderful effort on her part to evolve by her own methods a particle of pure radium than to make a cherry ripen or to make this rose bloom... or to give life to our delightful All's Well? What do you say, young François? Do we agree?"

"We always agree," replied the boy.

"So you don't unduly regret the miracle of the God-Stone?"

"Why, the miracle still exists!"

"You're right, François, it still exists and a hundred times more beautiful and dazzling than before. Science does not kill miracles: it purifies them and ennobles them. What was that crafty, capricious, wicked, incomprehensible little power attached to the tip of a magic wand and acting at random, according to the ignorant fancy of a barbarian chief or Druid, what was it, I ask you, beside the beneficent, logical, reliable and quite as miraculous power which we behold today in a pinch of radium?"

Don Luis suddenly interrupted himself and began to laugh:

"Come, come, I'm allowing myself to be carried away and singing an ode to science! Forgive me, madame," he added, rising and going up to Véronique, "and tell me that I have not bored you too much with my explanations. I haven't, have I? Not too much? Besides, it's finished... or nearly finished. There is only one more point to make clear, one decision to take."

He sat down beside her:

"It's this. Now that we have won the God-Stone, in other words, an actual treasure, what are we going to do with it?"

Véronique spoke with a heartfelt impulse:

"Oh, as to that, don't let us speak of it! I don't want anything that may come from Sarek, or anything that's found in the Priory. We will work."

"Still, the Priory belongs to you."

"No, no, Véronique d'Hergemont no longer exists and the Priory no longer belongs to anyone. Let it all be put up to auction. I don't want anything of that accursed past."

"And how will you live?"

"As I used to by my work. I am sure that François approves, don't you, darling?"

And, with an instinctive movement, turning to Stéphane, as though he had a certain right to give his opinion, she added:

"You too approve, don't you, dear Stéphane?"

"Entirely," he said.

She at once went on:

"Besides, though I don't doubt my father's feelings of affection, I have no proof of his wishes towards me."

"I have the proofs," said Don Luis.

"How?"

"Patrice and I went back to Sarek. In a writing-desk in Maguennoc's room, in a secret drawer, we found a sealed, but unaddressed envelope, and opened it. It contained a bond worth ten thousand francs a year and a sheet of paper which read as follows:

"'After my death, Maguennoc will hand this bond to Stéphane Maroux, to whom I confide the charge of my grandson, François.

When François is eighteen years of age, the bond will be his to do what he likes with. I hope and trust, however, that he will seek his mother and find her and that she will pray for my soul. I bless them both.'

"Here is the bond," said Don Luis, "and here is the letter. It is dated April of this year."

Véronique was astounded. She looked at Don Luis and the thought occurred to her that all this was perhaps merely a story invented by that strange man to place her and her son beyond the reach of want. It was a passing thought. When all was considered, it was a natural consequence. Everything said, M. d'Hergemont's action was very reasonable; and, foreseeing the difficulties that would crop up after his death, it was only right that he should think of his grandson. She murmured:

"I have not the right to refuse."

"You have so much the less right," said Don Luis, "in that the transaction excludes you altogether. Your father's wishes affect François and Stéphane directly. So we are agreed. There remains the God-Stone; and I repeat my question. What are we to do with it? To whom does it belong?"

"To you," said Véronique, definitely.

"To me?"

"Yes, to you. You discovered it and you have given it a real signification."

"I must remind you," said Don Luis, "that this block of stone possesses, beyond a doubt, an incalculable value. However great the miracles wrought by nature may be, it is only through a wonderful concourse of circumstances that she was able to perform the miracle of collecting so much precious matter in so small a volume. There are treasures and treasures there."

"So much the better," said Véronique, "you will be able to make a better use of them than anyone else."

Don Luis thought for a moment and added:

"You are quite right; and I confess that I prepared for this climax. First, because my right to the God-Stone seemed to me to be proved by adequate titles of ownership; and, next, because I have need of that block of stone. Yes, upon my word, the tombstone of the Kings of Bohemia has not exhausted its magic power; there are plenty of nations left on whom that power might produce as great an effect as on our ancestors the Gauls; and, as it happens, I am tackling a formidable undertaking in which an assistance of this kind will be invaluable to me. In a few years, when my task is completed, I will bring the God-Stone back to France and present it to a national laboratory which I intend to found. In this way science will purge any evil that the God-Stone may have done and the horrible adventure of Sarek will be atoned for. Do you approve, madame?"

She gave him her hand:

"With all my heart."

There was a fairly long pause. Then Don Luis said:

"Ah, yes, a horrible adventure, too terrible for words. I have had some gruesome adventures in my life which have left painful memories behind them. But this outdoes them all. It exceeds anything that is possible in reality or human in suffering. It was so excessively logical as to become illogical; and this because it was the act of a madman... and also because it came to pass at a season of madness and bewilderment. It was the war which facilitated the safe silent committal of an obscure crime prepared and executed by a monster. In times of peace, monsters have not the time to realize their stupid dreams. Today, in that solitary island, this particular monster found special, abnormal conditions..."

"Please don't let us talk about all this," murmured Véronique, in a trembling voice.

Don Luis kissed her hand and then took All's Well and lifted him in his arms:

"You're right. Don't let's talk about it, or else tears would come and All's Well would be sad. Therefore, All's Well, my delightful All's Well, let us talk no more of the dreadful adventure. But all the same let us recall certain episodes which were beautiful and picturesque. For instance, Maguennoc's garden with the gigantic flowers; you will remember it as I shall, won't you, All's Well? And the legend of the God-Stone, the idyll of the Celtic tribes wandering with the memorial stone of their kings, the stone all vibrant with radium, emitting an incessant bombardment of vivifying and miraculous atoms; all that, All's Well, possesses a certain charm, doesn't it? Only, my most exquisite All's Well, if I were a novelist and if it were my duty to tell the story of Coffin Island, I should not trouble too much about the horrid truth and I should give you a much more important part. I should do away with the intervention of that phrase-mongering humbug of a Don Luis and you would be the fearless and silent rescuer. You would fight the abominable monster, you would thwart his machinations and, in the end, you, with your marvellous instinct, would punish vice and make virtue triumph. And it would be much better so, because none would be more capable than you, my delightful All's Well, of demonstrating by a thousand proofs, each more convincing than the other, that in this life of ours all things come right and all's well."

Yellowback range available...

1. The Old Man in the Corner by Orczy, Baroness Emma
2. The Complete Max Carrados Vol 1 by Bramah, Ernest
3. The Complete Max Carrados Vol 2 by Bramah, Ernest

THE ARSÈNE LUPIN SERIES BY LEBLANC, MAURICE:

4. Arsène Lupin 1: The Extraordinary Adventures of Arsène Lupin - Gentleman Burglar
5. Arsène Lupin 2: Arsène Lupin vs. Herlock Sholmes
6. Arsène Lupin 3: The Hollow Needle
7. Arsène Lupin 4: 813
8. Arsène Lupin 5: The Crystal Stopper
9. Arsène Lupin 6: The Confessions of Arsène Lupin
10. Arsène Lupin 7: The Teeth of the Tiger
11. Arsène Lupin 8: The Shell Shard (aka The Woman of Mystery)
12. Arsène Lupin 9: The Return of Arsène Lupin (aka The Golden Triangle)
13. Arsène Lupin 10: The secret of Sarek (aka Island of Thirty Coffins)
14. Arsène Lupin 11: The Eight Strokes of the Clock
15. Arsène Lupin 12: The Secret Tomb
16. Arsène Lupin 13: The Countess of Cagliostro (aka Memoirs of Arsène Lupin)
17. Arsène Lupin (bonus book): Arsène Lupin (novelised by Edgar Jepson from LeBlanc's original play)

18. The Complete Raffles by Hornung, E. W.
19. The Mysterious Mickey Finn by Paul, Eliott
20. You Play the Black and the Red Comes Up by Hallas, Richard
21. The Mr. Moto Omnibus Vol 1 by Marquand, John P.
22. The Mr. Moto Omnibus Vol 2 by Marquand, John P.
23. The Complete Father Brown Vol 1 (with original illustrations) by Chesterton, G. K.
24. The Complete Father Brown Vol 2 (with original illustrations) by Chesterton, G. K.
25. A Peter Wimsey omnibus: Murder Must Advertise & The Nine Tailors by Sayers, Dorothy L.
26. Was it Murder? by Hilton, James
27. The Complete Just Men Volume 1 by Wallace, Edgar
28. The Complete Just Men Volume 2 by Wallace, Edgar
29. Carnacki by Hodgson, William Hope
30. Grey Mask by Wentworth, Patricia
31. The Case With Nine Solutions by Connington, J. J.
32. Murder by Matchlight by Lorac, E. C. R.
33. The Crossword Mystery by Punshon, E. R.
34. The Cask by Crofts, Freeman Wills
35. The Bells of Old Bailey by Bowers, Dorothy
36. Crime Unlimited by Hume, David
37. The A. A. Milne Mystery Omnibus (contains: The Red house and Four days' wonder) by Milne, A. A.
38. She Faded into Air by White, Ethel Lina
39. The Wheel Spins by White, Ethel Lina
40. The Spiral Staircase by White, Ethel Lina
41. Murder of a Lady by Wynne, Anthony
42. Thirteen Guests by Farjeon, J. Jefferson
43. The Daughter of Time by Tey, Josephine
44. The Man in the Queue by Tey, Josephine
45. A Shilling for Candles by Tey, Josephine
46. The Franchise Affair by Tey, Josephine
47. Tragedy at Law by Hare, Cyril
48. The Moonstone by Collins, Wilkie
49. The Woman in White by Collins, Wilkie
50. The Circular Staircase by Rinehart, Mary Roberts
51. The Benson Murder Case by Van Dine, S. S.
52. The Philip Marlowe Omnibus by Chandler, Raymond
53. Monsieur Lecoq by Gaboriau, Emile
54. Aurora Floyd by Braddon, Mary Elizabeth
55. The Big Bow Mystery by Zangwill, Israel
56. Dossier 113 (aka The Blackmailers) by Gaboriau, Emile
57. The Mystery of a Hansom Cab by Hume, Fergus
58. The W Plan by Seton, Graham
59. Inspector French's Greatest Case by Crofts, Freeman Wills

60. Mr Bowling Buys a Newspaper by Henderson, Donald
61. A Voice Like Velvet by Henderson, Donald
62. The Deductions of Colonel Gore by Brock, Lynn
63. The Rogue's Syndicate by Froest, Frank
64. The Middle Temple Murder by Fletcher, J. S.
65. The Millionaire Mystery by Hume, Fergus
66. Below the Clock by Turner, J. V.
67. The Rouletabille Omnibus: The Mystery of the Yellow Room and The Perfume of the Lady in Black by Leroux, Gaston
68. The Complete Dupin by Poe, Edgar Allan
69. The Complete Thinking Machine Vol 1 by Futrelle, Jacques
70. The Complete Thinking Machine Vol 2 by Futrelle, Jacques
71. The Complete Thinking Machine Vol 3 by Futrelle, Jacques
72. The Complete Montague Egg by Sayers, Dorothy L.
73. The Complete J. G. Reeder by Wallace, Edgar
74. The Complete Charlie Chan Vol 1 by Biggers, Earl der
75. The Complete Charlie Chan Vol 2 by Biggers, Earl der
76. The Dr Nikola Omnibus Vol 1 by Boothby, Guy
77. The Dr Nikola Omnibus Vol 2 by Boothby, Guy
78. A Prince of Swindlers: The Simon Carne collection by Boothby, Guy
79. The Slim Callaghan Omnibus by Cheyney, Peter
80. The Fu Manchu Omnibus by Rohmer, Sax
81. The Bulldog Drummond Omnibus: The Complete Peterson Rounds by Sapper
82. The Avenging Ray by Seamark
83. The Richard Chandos Omnibus by Yates, Dornford
84. The Alan Quatermain Omnibus: King Solomon's Mines & Allan Quatermain by Haggard, H. Rider
85. The 39 steps by Buchan, John
86. At The Villa Rose by Mason, A.E.W.
87. The Eye of Osiris by Freeman, R. Austin
88. The Weapons of Mystery by Hocking, Joseph
89. The House of Dr. Edwardes by Beeding, Francis
90. The Seven Secrets by Le Queux, William
91. Call Mr Fortune by Bailey, H. C.
92. The Three Taps by Knox, Ronald
93. The Girl at Central by Bonner, Geraldine
94. The Experiences of Loveday Brooke, Lady Detective by Pirkis, Catherine Louisa
95. Mary Louise by Baum, L. Frank
96. That Affair Next Door by Green, Anna Katherine
97. Dead Letter by Regester, Seeley
98. The Tragedy of Pudd'nhead Wilson by Twain, Mark
99. The Big Clock by Fearing, Kenneth
100. The Woman in the Window by Wallis, J. H.
101. The Sexton Blake Collection Vol 1 by Hal Meredeth (or many?)
102. The Complete Simon Iff Stories by Crowley, Aleister
103. The Castle of Otranto by Walpole, Horace
104. The Adventures of the Infallible Godahl by Anderson, Frederick Irving

THE COMPLETE SHERLOCK HOLMES
105. A Study In Scarlet
106. The Sign Of Four
107. The Adventures Of Sherlock Holmes
108. The Memoirs Of Sherlock Holmes
109. The Hound Of The Baskervilles
110. The Return Of Sherlock Holmes
111. His Last Bow
112. The Valley Of Fear
113. The Case-Book Of Sherlock Holmes

114. Graustark: The Story of a Love Behind a Throne by George Barr McCutcheon
115. Beverly of Graustark by George Barr McCutcheon
116. Truxton King: A Story of Graustark by George Barr McCutcheon
117. The Prince of Graustark by George Barr McCutcheon
118. The Complete Zenda Omnibus by Anthony Hope
119. The Mad king by Burroughs, Edgar Rice
120. The Fantomas Omnibus by Souvestre, Pierre

121. The Problemist by Clinton H. Stagg
122. The Dorrington Deed-Box by Morrison, Arthur
123. The Lone Wolf by Vance, L. J.
124. The Complete Martin Hewitt Collection Vol 1: Martin Hewitt, Investigator & Chronicles of Martin Hewitt by Morrison, Arthur
125. The Complete Martin Hewitt Collection Vol 2: Adventures of Martin Hewitt & The Red Triangle: Further Chronicles of Martin Hewitt by Morrison, Arthur
126. Seven Keys to Baldpate by Earl Derr Biggers
127. No Pockets in a Shroud by McCoy, Horace
128. The John Silence Collection by Blackwood, Algernon
129. Lady Molly Of Scotland Yard by Orczy, Baroness Emma
130. Skin O' My Tooth by Orczy, Baroness Emma
131. The Wrong Box by Stevenson, R. L. and Lloyd Osbourne
132. Tutt and Mr Tutt by Train, Arthur C.
133. The Clue by Wells, Carolyn
134. The Complete Trent Case Book by Bentley, E. C.
135. The Luck of the Vails by Benson, E. F.
136. The Rome Express by Griffiths, Arthur
137. The Complete Curious Mr Tarrant by C. Daly King
138. Rope and Gaslight (2-in-1 text) by Hamilton, Patrick
139. Prince Zaleski and Cumming's King Monk by Shiel, M. P.
140. The Assassination Bureau Ltd. by London, Jack
141. Introducing Clubfoot by Williams, Valentine
142. Master of Mysteries: The complete Uncle Abner collection by Post, Melville Davisson
143. The Red Redmaynes by Phillpotts, Eden
144. Thrilling Stories of the Railway by Whitechurch, Victor L.
145. The Grey Wig: Stories and Novelettes by Zangwill, Israel
146. The Lodger by Lowndes, Marie Belloc
147. The Man from Manchester by Donovan, Dick (Joyce Emerson Preston Muddock)
148. Mr. Meeson's Will by H. Rider Haggard by Haggard, H. Rider
149. Devlin the Barber by Farjeon, B. L.
150. Checkmate by Joseph Sheridan Le Fanu
151. Recollections of a Detective Police-Officer by Waters
152. The Widow Lerouge by Gaboriau, Emile
153. The Expressman and the Detective by Pinkerton, Allan
154. Zadig and Vathek by Voltaire
155. The Stillwater Tragedy by Aldrich, Thomas Bailey
156. The Memoirs of Constantine Dix by Pain, Barry
157. Ashes to Ashes by Ostrander, Isabel
158. The Jewel of Seven Stars by Stoker, Bram
159. The Thomas Love Peacock Collection by Peacock, Thomas Love

THE COMPLETE DERLETH SOLAR PONS

160. In Re: Sherlock Holmes - The Adventures of Solar Pons
161. The Memoirs of Solar Pons
162. The Return of Solar Pons
163. The Reminiscences of Solar Pons
164. The Casebook of Solar Pons
165. The Novels of Solar Pons: Terror over London and Mr. Fairlie's Final Journey
166. The Chronicles of Solar Pons
167. The Apocrypha of Solar Pons

168. The Triumphs of Eugene Valmont
169. The Female Detective by Forrester, Andrew
170. Cain's Jawbone by Torquemada
171. The Great Impersonation by Oppenheim, E. Phillips

THE DASHIELL HAMMETT COLLECTION

172. The Complete Sam Spade
173. The Complete Thin Man
174. The Complete Continental Op Vol 1
175. The Complete Continental Op Vol 2

All books may not be available in all territories due to rights restrictions.

For more details and a full list of titles
visit https://www.hachetteindia.com/home/yellowbacks

A fan of Sherlock Holmes?
Then meet Solar Pons

The original fan fiction from the great August Derleth—the Sherlock Holmes of Praed Street.

"the best substitutes for Sherlock Holmes known."
– Vincent Starrett

"an excellent series of adventures in detection in their own right." – *The Chicago Tribune*

For more details and a full list of titles:
visit https://www.hachetteindia.com/home/yellowbacks